THE LEGEND

DYLAN ALLEN

Edited by MARLA ESPOSITO OF PROOFING STYLE

Proofread by GEMMA WOOLEY GEM PRECISE PROOFREADS

Cover Art by LORI JACKSON DESIGNS

ALLEN

PEDDLER OF PASSION

ABOUT THE AUTHOR

Rivers Wilde Series
The Legacy

Symbols of Love Series:

Rise
Remember
Release

Standalones:
Thicker Than Water
Envy

Dylan Allen is a Texas girl with a serious case of wanderlust.

A self-proclaimed happily ever junkie, she loves creating stories where her characters chase their own happy endings.

When she isn't writing or reading, eating or cooking, she and her family are planning their next adventure.

I love talking to you guys! Feel free to send me an email at dylanallenwrites@gmail.com.

Are you on Facebook? If you are, then PLEASE join my private reader group, Dylan's Day Dreamer. My Day Dreamers get exclusive giveaways, sneak peaks, glimpses into my every day, and lots of other fun bookish things! Click here to join and make sure you introduce yourself.

YOU CAN FIND ME ON ALL THE FOLLOWING SOCIAL AND BOOK RELATED PLATFORMS:

BOOK+MAIN BITES

FOR MY TINA…
THANKS FOR BELIEVING IN ME.
AND, FOR NOT BEING A VILLAIN.
LOVE YOU,
DC

... ALL THE MAGIC I HAVE KNOWN, I'VE HAD TO MAKE MYSELF."

FROM MAGIC, A POEM BY SHEL SILVERSTEIN

INTRODUCTION

Located in the dynamic city of Houston, TX, Rivers Wilde is an enclave carved into a parcel of the most valuable and coveted land in all of South East Texas.

The enclave is home to the two families that it's named after. The Rivers are old, Texas money. Sugar, oil, and natural gas are how they made their fortune. And with that bounty, they helped found the city of Houston.

The Wildes are the new money. The *bourgeoisie*. They built their wealth in restaurants, grocery stores and real estate.

And they have made a fortune that casts the old money into the shade.

In the 1980s, the oil markets were crashing and the Rivers found themselves hard up for cash. With no other viable options, they sold part of their precious land to the usurpers they'd previously refused to even acknowledge.

Seeds of resentment burrowed deep into the fertile soil of their dislike and grew tenacious roots. Thirty years later, the rivalry continues. Even though, now, no one remembers what started it and just *why* the blood between the families is so bad.

Today in Rivers Wilde, a new generation is coming to the helm of power in both families. Will they put the past behind them and usher in a new era of cooperation between the two ruling families in Houston? Or will the sins of their fathers continue to cast a shadow over them?

I hope you enjoy finding out!

Welcome to Rivers Wilde.

PROLOGUE

Present day

Rivers Wilde

1

SMOKE AND MIRRORS

REMI

"Please don't leave angry. Please." Gigi's frail voice floats behind me, chasing me like a sinister specter. I'm nearly running by the time I reach the door of her hospital room. I pull it open and look back at her. She looks harmless lying there like that, cocooned in a hospital bed, anchored in place by the network of lines that run from a bandaged spot on her arm. But harmless is the very last thing she's proven to be.

"I don't know what kind of game this is. But I don't want any part of it."

Her eyes are glassy with tears and her face is as pale as the white sheets she's lying against. "It's not a game. Ask your mother. Read that letter."

"Oh, I'll be asking her. You stay the fuck away from me." I point at her with the same hand I'm clutching the envelope she gave me. The slip of paper wrapped around a set of keys weighs nothing, yet my hand aches from holding it. I don't want to read it.

I step out of the room and stare unseeingly down the corridor. The nurse's station is a hub of activity—doctors, patients, family members dart past me. I just… stand still and try to process what Gigi Rivers has just told me.

For the first time in a long time, I don't know what I'm supposed to do next.

When my friend Hayes called and asked me to come to the hospital, I didn't ask why. I got in my car and drove as fast I could.

Our families have been on opposite sides of the most mysterious cold war for almost thirty years now. When we both became the heads of our families around the same time last year, we decided enough was enough.

Since then, he's become one of my best friends.

I spent the drive, my throat tight with anxiety, my heart hammering, preparing myself to console a him.

Instead, I walked into an ambush.

"Remi. You okay?" Suddenly, Hayes is standing beside me, his hand gripping my shoulder and his face drawn and etched with worry. I shake his hand off and turn so we're face-to-face. He's waiting for me to answer and looks as tense as a runner waiting for the crack of the referee's gun to start his race.

I stare at him; my face feels like granite and the pressure in my jaw from my clenched teeth is giving me a headache. His discomfort grows with each second that passes. I watch him squirm and then ask the question his body language has already answered.

"Did you know what she was going to say to me?"

He closes his eyes for a beat and nods. "Yeah, man. I did. I'm sorry."

"And how long have you known?" I ask him.

He grimaces in remorse. "Two weeks ago."

"You've known this shit for two weeks and you didn't think to fucking tell me, Hayes?" Surprise and a sense of being betrayed make me take a step back. I peer at him, trying to see how I missed that he'd been keeping something like this from me for so long.

His face twists up, too and he glances around. "Let's go talk somewhere else." He turns without waiting for me to respond and opens a door a few feet away. I follow him inside the room.

"She wasn't sure you didn't already know. I wasn't sure either. And the last couple of weeks have been a total nightmare."

"None of that shit can be true. How the fuck can it be true. Things like that don't happen. That would mean we are brothers, Hayes." I look at him like he's lost his mind.

He looks back at me with patient sympathy.

I shake my head in denial. "My father *died*. I have pictures from his funeral. How could they have held a funeral if he wasn't dead, man?"

Hayes doesn't respond. He just watches me, like he's waiting for me to answer my own question.

"What?" I snap.

"Have you seen his death certificate?"

"Why the hell would I have seen his death certificate. Have you seen your father's?" I challenge him.

He only shrugs.

"*I* was in the room with my father when he died. You weren't even old enough to remember what yours looked like, much less exactly when he died," he says, that patient sympathy still in place.

The knot forming in my gut intensifies, and I lean back against the door and stare at the ceiling as I think about the pictures from my father's funeral.

I was only two. I don't remember anything. But how could my mother and grandfather have told such a lie? My grandfather, before he died, had been my mentor and my best friend. We talked about my father all the time. He couldn't have looked me in the face and lied the way he did. I clutch the doorknob and my sweaty palms slip off it. My heart is racing faster than I thought possible.

What else have they lied about?

"Remi."

I open my eyes and find Hayes watching me, his lips pursed, his eyes full of sympathy. "I know. It's a total head job. I've only had a couple of weeks to process it. If this hadn't happened, I still wouldn't be speaking to Gigi. It's fucked me up. I've spent my whole life thinking my father was someone else, too. On top of that, the woman who I've thought of as my aunt is really my mother. The man who I've come to think of as one of my best friends is actually my half-brother."

Each of his statements hit me hard. I can't wrap my head around any of that. "Why should we believe them now? What if *this* is a lie?" I say and even to my own ears, it sounds like a wish, rather than an accusation.

"We both know it's not," he says, his voice grave and hushed.

I stare at him for a beat letting myself imagine that everything they're saying is *true*. I drop a wall in front of the wave of panic that is starting to build in my gut.

Not now.

"There's something wrong here." I push back.

He nods, but he doesn't back down. "There's plenty wrong. Especially on your side of things. But, it's not a lie. Go ask your mother. When you're ready to talk, I'll be here." Then, he steps around me, opens the room door and walks out.

I pull out my phone and call my assistant. "Rachel, I'm on my way to Wilde House, meet me there."

"Yes, sir. I'm on my way," she says without missing a beat.

"Before you leave, visit legal and ask them to print you a copy of my father's death certificate."

I'm met with silence.

"I know it's an odd request. But I need you to get it. Right now. Do you understand?"

"Ye-Yes, sir. I do." She sounds uncertain, but I know she'll get it the minute we hang up.

"I'll see you at the house."

"Should I let your mother know to expect us?"

"No."

"MOTHER!" MY SHOUT RICOCHETS OFF THE CEILING OF WILDE House's vaulted ceiling foyer. I fling the door closed behind me and it slams so hard that one of the geometric shaped plates of glass cracks.

"Remi, wait." Rachel comes rushing out of the sitting room on the right. She is panting, her eyes wide with panic, and her arms stretched out ahead of her reaching for me.

"Wait for what?"

I walk right past her on my way to the stairs. All I can think about is getting up to my mother's office and making her tell me the truth.

She grabs my arm to still me as I start to stride past her. "Before I tell you where she is, I need to tell you something."

I pull my arm out of her grasp and narrow my eyes at her. "What do you mean, *tell* me where she is? Where would she be but in her office?"

"I've worked for you since you a were boy. But—your mother has always been my employer. I did the job she paid me to do. But I want you to know that as much as I could, I have given you my loyalty."

My blood runs cold. "What do you mean, as much as you could? What did she pay you to do?"

She squeezes her eyes shut and pulls in a deep breath but doesn't say anything.

"Never mind. I'll make her tell me herself." I step around her and start toward the door.

"I assume, that somehow, you've learned the truth about your father." The frayed edge of panic that accompanies her explosive statement stops me dead in my tracks. I turn around slowly and look at her as if I'm seeing her for the first time. Her dark, unruly hair is caught in its normal haphazard bun. Her face is lightly made up, per usual. She's wearing one of her trademark muted gray skirt suits. Everything looks the same, but it's not. Not even a little…

"So, it's true?"

Her expression is stoic, and she squares her shoulders. "It is true."

My knees threaten to buckle. "And you've known?"

"I have helped your family keep the secret. It's what I was paid to do. That, among other things."

"Where is she?" I ask her. She squeezes her eyes shut like a child who's trying to avoid looking at something scary. Her fists are clenched at her sides and her body is rigid with tension.

"I will be tendering my resignation. I believe it's best that all of this has come to light. I know you'll never trust me again, and I don't blame you. I did as your mother asked because I needed my job. But, I do deeply regret that fact. I've known you since you were a little boy and I've loved you like—"

"Rachel, I'm not in the mood for a sentimental moment right now. Right now? I need to talk to my mother. Where the fuck *is* she?" I grit out my demand.

She gulps and steps back. "She is currently in her office attempting to shred documents."

"You told her I was coming?" I ask, unable to believe the level of betrayal. I've trusted this woman with everything.

"No. But when I requested these from Legal, *they* did. But, I have this." She holds up a black electrical cord in the air like she's holding a trophy.

"She can't shred anything. I just wanted the chance to tell you the truth before I left. I'll go now. I am so sorry."

Her eyes are sorrowful as she turns to walk away.

I let her go. And even though her betrayal hurts, there's nothing I can do about it right now. My only priority is finding my mother and getting answers.

I walk upstairs, slowly. With each step, I prepare for what lies ahead.

My entire life upended in just one hour. And now, I'm walking toward a room where my mother is attempting to destroy evidence of what I've just learned.

Our relationship is already nonexistent. I keep her far away from anything that's important to me.

She's a liar.

She has stolen so much from me.

I want to tear her limb from limb. But that would mean touching her and I'm not sure I ever want to do that again.

I push the door open and find her on her knees in front of the shredder, her hands moving frantically even as she turns to face me.

"Remi," she gasps, her face ashen. She jumps up and puts her hands out in front of her as if she's afraid. It incenses me even further.

I narrow my eyes at her, rage straining the muscles in my face as I try to keep it in check. "You act as if *I* am the violent one. As if *I'm* dangerous. Have you lied so much that you've forgotten what it is to tell the fucking truth?"

I can't begin to fathom the lengths they went to in order to keep their secrets. In all of the years that I've mourned my grandfather, I never imagined that I'd ever be glad he was gone.

I can't imagine how I would feel having this conversation with him. The thought alone is more painful than I can bear.

She shrinks, her chest caving in before she recovers, squares her jaw and holds my angry gaze with her defiant one. I see so much of myself in her right now, it frightens me. Would *I* have been capable of it?

"Remi, we wanted to protect you." She says with no remorse.

"You are a liar," I roar in her face and she leans back as if my words were hands that were shoving her away from me. We've butted heads my whole life. But she has never seen me lose my cool.

Her eyes widen, but then relax again and she swallows and composes herself. Like she's an actor who has rehearsed a scene and is now preparing to perform it for an audience. Her chin tilts up, her expression is stoic, nearly regal. "I am what life has made me. Your grandfather and I thought it best you didn't know the truth."

"People get divorced all the time. Men leave their wives *all* of the time. Why did you have to pretend he died? You held a fucking funeral." I shake my head in disbelief when she merely nods. The last vestiges of my restraint force my hands into fists at my side. I throw my head back, feel the strain of the tendons in my neck as I hold back the howl of pain clawing at the back of my throat. "Why?" I shout.

"Because everyone was told that he died. It wasn't just you—"

"Do you hear yourself? He was *my* father." I bellow at her, just completely beside myself at this point.

In the blink of an eyes, nothing is the same.

Including me. I've lived my entire adult life in service of living up to the legend they built in my father's name. It's all a fucking lie. And now, I'm done with it. I knew she was manipulative. But this…I'll never be able to understand.

"How could you do it?" Wonder seeps through the brittle cracks in my anger as I take her in. "I've spent my entire life wondering why he died so young. The night before my thirty-second birthday I was crippled with fear because I was sure it would be the year I died, too. Regan and Tyson have so many of the same fears. How could you *do* that to your children?" I ask, knowing that there's no answer that would suffice.

"Remi, your father wasn't just anybody. He was the heir to this empire we were building. His name wasn't his own. It belongs to all of us. We weren't going to let his selfishness ruin everything we'd built." She spits out.

"He left *you*. Not his family." I remind her.

Her face contorts with anger

"He didn't just *leave* me." She slaps her chest with her open palm. "He left *you* and Regan and Tyson. And his father. His entire *family*."

I can see that, even now, she feels no remorse. In the instant it takes to snuff out a candle, any lingering affection I had for her disappears.

"He betrayed us. Spectacularly, callously. He left you." She insists. A day ago, those words would have hurt, but I know they're not true.

I read his letter. I put my hand in my pocket and stroke the outline of the key inside the envelope.

"We gave him a choice. Us or her. And he chose her."

"I don't blame him. You were the alternative."

She marches up to me and slaps me. Hard enough to turn my head. But, I barely feel it. I don't feel anything but empty and rudderless.

"He loved me." Her voice wobbles and she pants, her breaths coming hard and shallow. "I was his wife. I gave him children. We had plans. Then, *she* came back." She deflates and sinks into the seat behind her. Her body droops like a broken doll.

"It happened so fast. Your grandfather warned him. Then he followed through on it. Cut him out."

"Because he loved someone else?" I shake my head in disgust.

"Because he was disloyal," her retort comes out as a growl. "A year later he left her too. Walked out and never came back. Probably fell face down in a ditch somewhere, piss drunk and never woke up."

"She thinks he's alive."

My mother blinks like I splashed water in her eyes.

"She's delusional." Her eyes widen slightly and then dart nervously to the shredder.

"What are you trying to shred?" I eye the machine and the pile of documents strewn in front of it.

She steps into my line of sight. "His death certificates. They have the real dates on there. The declaration date, seven years after he disappeared. When it was issued I ordered a copy from the county clerk. And other documents. Our divorce records. Unlike his death certificate, they were sealed, you would never have found them, but I have them here. Newspaper clippings. Things that if you ever looked, might have told you the truth."

She lists the items like they're nothing and I'm beyond incredulity at this point. "God forbid I learn the truth, right?" I say, exhaustion creeping into the bitterness edging my voice.

"Yes. God forbid. I would never have told you."

"Why is that your decision to make?"

"Because I am the one who was left to pick up the pieces, to raise you as best I could. I was twenty-three. I'd only come here from Jamaica seven years prior. I had no one but him and his family. Nothing but quick thinking and the sense the good Lord gave me. I made a decision and I would do it again." Her eyes fill with tears.

I've never seen her even come close to crying. It renders me dumb.

She looks at me with a plea in her eyes, but she's not begging me for forgiveness. She doesn't think she's done anything wrong. She wants me to understand.

I know I never will.

"I don't know how you could do this." I say quietly, a hollow numbness has started to soften my anger.

"I haven't remarried. I haven't done anything but help your grandfather grow Wilde World so you'd have something worth inheriting. Everything I've done has been for that."

"Was making sure Kal and I broke up and stayed that way *also* for me?"

Her expression goes from woeful to angry in a flash.

"I wish I'd never heard that girl's name."

"I wish you had to hear it every day." I retort.

"She would have ruined you." Her hand slices through the air in anger. "The way Georgina ruined your father. And I would *not* allow it. One day, when you have children of your own you will understand." She lifts her chin and crosses her arms over her chest.

"I *loved* her." I say, angrily.

"You loved her too much. But once she was gone, you hit your stride. You've done so much." She looks like she hopes I'll agree. I don't even hear her anymore.

"All I wanted was her."

"Look what you have achieved without her."

"Look how I've suffered *without* her," I shout back and her eyes widen and fill with tears again.

"Oh, God, Remi." Her fingers flutter to her face and press against her trembling mouth. "You can't say anything. Or do anything. This cannot become public knowledge. I don't want people to know your father sired Hayes Rivers. People can't know that he wasn't the man we've said he was. It would ruin the branding we have created for Wilde World."

"Branding? Are you serious?" Just when I thought nothing could surprise me, she proves me wrong.

"Yes. I'm serious. You *know* this." Her tears clear and her expression grows stern.

"You were *groomed* to know it. Wilde World built is bigger than all of us. It will live longer than all of us. What *we* want isn't important." She waves her arms around the room. "This family is an institution now. We built Rivers Wilde. We are one of the largest grocers in the United States. We service nearly every single prison system in the country. We run the food programs for eight countries in South America. Do you think you can just dismantle that because you didn't get to grow up with your father and his whore?" She sneers at me.

"She was his wife," I remind her, just to twist the knife in.

"*I* was his wife." She points at her chest. Then she looks at me the same way I looked at her a few minutes ago. As if the light around me had shifted and she could finally see me clearly.

"Oh, the irony." She throws her head back and laughs dryly.

"What?"

"After all of my efforts to make you a better man, you still ended up just like him. At least he knew he couldn't have both. You still think life is fair. You're such a fool." She sneers at me.

"I think I hate you."

Her face falls. The sorrow in her eyes isn't feigned. She folds her hands in front of her and nods.

"I know you do." It's the saddest thing I've ever heard. Yet, I feel nothing.

We stare at each other. Mother and son. Enemies. Broken. With nothing between us but a sea of broken glass neither of us are willing to hazard crossing.

This isn't my family. This isn't my home. I don't know who I am. Or what I am. I've lived my entire life with a lie guiding my decisions. The man I tried to be was shaped by myth. It grew roots that bound me when the woman I love slipped out of my grasp.

And it was all a fucking lie.

Including me.

An hour later, I drive away from Rivers Wilde and if I have my way, I'll never be back.

I

THE START

EIGHTEEN YEARS AGO
HOUSTON, TEXAS.

LEGENDS AND LIES

KAL

THE DOOR TO THE LIBRARY OPENS AND I STOP WRITING. MY HEART races and my hands tremble so badly that my notebook slips from my fingers and lands with a thud on the floor. Loud voices and the blare of music that flood the room disguise the noise. I pick it up and press my body close to the wall and hold my breath.

My mother will kill me if I get caught in here. We haven't even been at the party for thirty minutes. I thought I'd have at least another couple of hours before I had to go looking for her.

The sound of approaching footsteps sends my pulse into a wild gallop. My heart feels like it's attached to a boomerang inside my chest. But for those footsteps, the library is as quiet as it had been when I'd snuck in here.

The door opens again and I lift my feet off the ground and hug my knees tightly to my chest and hold my breath.

"I told you to get upstairs," a woman's voice cracks through the air like a whip even over the loud din from outside, and I nearly jump out of my skin and my eyes widen in terror. All I can see is the dark blue backing of the curtain.

"Don't just stand there, answer me." Her voice is so cold, so hard that I close my eyes again the figure forming in my mind. I imagine her to be tall, with a narrow face that's shrouded by the thousands of snakes that slither on her head where her hair should be. They hiss and bite each other constantly.

I imagine that her eyes are entirely black. But her mouth is strangely beautiful—it's heart shaped with lips that are coated with a poisonous apple-red lipstick.

"I just came to get my books." The boy's voice is frightened and sad. I wish I could give him a hug. The way he sounds is the way I feel a lot. With my eyes closed, I can just imagine him. He's small and skinny, with hair that needs cutting and shoes with that are so small, the toes are rubbed thin. The worn cuff of his two sizes too small pants stop above his bony ankles.

"Just make sure you don't linger. And don't let me catch you sneaking downstairs one more time, Remington."

"I just wanted to see the other kids."

"Why?" her voice is like the surprise of a clap of thunder when there's not a cloud in the sky. I press my lips together and bite them to stifle the whimper that's bubbling in my throat.

"You have forgotten who you are. What your responsibilities will be. You don't get to mingle. You've got to set yourself apart. And you don't do that by sneaking down to a party when you should be in your room working. Get your act together," she warns.

"Yes, ma'am," the boy says.

"Get your stuff and then get to bed. You've got school tomorrow." The door opens again, the din from outside is fleeting this time as it shuts quickly.

"I hate you," I hear the boy say in a voice that's full of anger that I know all too well. The kind that comes when you're a kid who knows your parents are missing something regular parents have. He sniffles softly. Then he does it again. This one sounds muffled like he's covering his mouth. Then another and another right after it.

I forget my notebook, and I forget that I wasn't supposed to let anyone see me and I scramble from behind the curtain to console the poor kid who's crying by himself. Just like I've always wished someone would do for me.

As soon as I step out from behind the curtain, he stands up. I stop right where I am and stare at the most beautiful boy I've ever seen.

He's not a small, skinny kid in clothes that are too small. The only thing my imagination got right is that he's a kid. And even that, just barely. He's tall, and a little lanky, but in his Houston Rockets jersey and shorts, I can see the muscles that declare him an athlete.

His shoes might be too tight, but given how brand spanking new they look, I doubt it. With his perfectly cut, close-cropped mop of dark curly hair on top of his head, he looks more like a kid in a boyband than he does a kid who would cower in front of anyone.

He's got a face that looks like it was carved out of stone, all sharp edges, and rounded curves and smooth skin that reminds me of the creamy nutty inside of an acorn shell.

But his eyes make my heart leap into my throat. They're as dark and beautiful as the starless skies Houston nights are known for and are full of hostility as he watches me.

He looks just like one of the kids who throws spit wads at me from the back of the classroom. *Just* like one of the kids who sticks his foot out when I walk by in the lunchroom and then laughs when I fall on my face with my lunch splattered all over me.

They're all perfect and tall with great clothes and great hair and teeth that are being trained into perfectly straight lines by braces.

It's me whose clothes are too small; whose shoes are too tight. Me, who needs someone to come to her rescue.

"What are you doing in here?" He jumps from the couch he'd been crying on and wipes his tears away. He sounds mad now and not scared at all.

My stomach starts to hurt. I've probably just gotten myself and Mama into big trouble. And for what?

"Who are you?" he asks, louder now.

I step backward toward my little hiding spot and wish I could click my heels and transport myself back behind the curtain.

"I'm sorry. I only came out because I heard you crying. I didn't mean—"

"I wasn't crying and you better not tell anybody I was," he says angrily.

"You were too, crying. I heard you," I argue even though I know I shouldn't.

"Then you need to get your ears cleaned." He shoots me an annoyed glance but then sits back down on the couch and stares at his hands as they rest in his lap.

I stand there, torn between wanting to help him and wanting to hide. I watch the door nervously and pray his mother doesn't come back.

"I was just trying to be nice. I'm sorry. Just pretend you never saw me," I plead with him.

He looks up from his lap and wide, dark eyes are full of suspicion, his thick slashing brows are drawn together.

"What are you doing in here?"

I don't know what to say. I don't want to get in trouble. But, I'm already caught, and he's not supposed to be in here either, so maybe he won't be rushing to rat me out. Maybe he'll just get his books and leave and I'll go back behind the curtain until Mama comes back.

"My mom brought me with her to the party. I was bored, so I came in here to wait until she's ready to go." I run a hand over my hair, my nervous tic, and have a momentary shock of not feeling my normally, thick tangle of curls. Tonight, my mother sat me down and mercilessly blow dried and then flat ironed every curl into straight submission.

He looks me over. I make myself stand still and wait for him to reply.

His gaze flits over my shoulder at the curtain. "You were hiding back there?" He tips his head at it.

I nod.

"So, you heard everything my mom said?"

So snakehead is his mother. My mother's terrible, but she never talks to me like that. I feel sorry for him again.

I nod again.

He sighs and closes his eyes.

"Where do you go to school?"

"T.H. Rogers."

"You're in middle school?" His eyebrows shoot up. He eyes me up and down, and I can see the doubt on his face. My mother has been dressing me like this and bringing me to these events with her since I turned twelve.

She tells people I'm her younger sister. I'm tall for my age and had breasts by the time I was eleven. So, throw me in a skintight black dress, paint my lips red and stuff my feet into some heels, and there are some places that won't even card me.

I shrug. "Seventh grade. What you about you?"

"Eighth, I go to Rainier." He mentions the middle school that serves Rivers Wilde.

"Oh, okay." I try to cover my surprise. He looks older, too. He's taller than any of the boys in my middle school.

"You know anyone at Rainer? I don't want it getting around there that I was crying."

"No." I don't add that I barely know anyone who goes to T.H. Rogers either. I have one friend, Nikki and even she only eats with me because her other friends have a different lunch period.

"That's good." He runs a hand over his face like he's tired. "You want to sit down?" he asks, and when I hesitate he pats the seat next to him.

I'm tempted, these shoes aren't exactly a joy to stand in. But I hesitate for a second and gauge how quickly I can be back behind that curtain if someone comes in.

"Come on. No one's coming. I promise." And there's something in his smile that tells me he takes his promises seriously.

So, I walk over to the couch and sit down next to him. He leans back like he's getting comfortable and stares up at the ceiling.

"I wasn't crying. My mom just makes me mad."

"It's okay. I hate my mom sometimes, too," I admit with a shrug.

"I don't hate her—I don't know. She just—"

"Doesn't like you very much. Is never happy with you, no matter what you do? Wants to you to be everything you're not?"

He slides his eyes over to me again and looks me up and down. I push my glasses up my nose and smile nervously. He doesn't smile back.

"How do you know that?"

"Because, mine's the same way. And… I heard what your mother said." I give him a sly smile and he smiles back.

It's such a nice smile, complete with twin dimples. I'm sad when it disappears as quickly as it was there.

"Yeah… so that's it. Basically. I'll never measure up to my dad."

"Why? Is your dad famous or something?"

"Even worse. He's dead."

"Oh, I'm sorry."

"It's okay." He shrugs like he means it. "He did all of these great things before he died. He went to business school and was a marketing whiz. He and my grandfather built Wilde World from nothing and my mom wants me to step in and do the same."

"Is that like AstroWorld, but with animals?"

He laughs and shakes his head. "No, it's the name of my family's business."

"Oh…" I glance around the library. If this is his house, his family must have some sort of huge business. This library is bigger than our entire apartment and has more books than the public library in my neighborhood.

"So, you're going to be in charge one day?" I ask him in awe.

"Yeah. I guess." He shrugs like it doesn't matter.

"You should count your blessings. I wish I had a family business or something more than my mother's pretty dresses to inherit," I tell him.

He flushes. "I know I'm lucky. I know. I just… I don't know. I want to be myself, too. They want me to be just like him. I just want to play basketball." He slumps forward and stares forlornly at the carpet.

"The best way to get people to stop telling you what to do is to show them what you can do. If you want to play. Play. Can she really stop you?"

"I like that. Your mom's advice?" he says slowly.

"Nope. *Cosmo.* If I listened to my mother, the only advice I'd be able to give you is that you could never be too rich or too pretty," I say and stare at the door, my eyes trained on the handle for signs of it moving. I really want to have time to get behind that curtain again if snakehead comes back.

"So, what have you done to disappoint your mother?" At his unexpected question, I turn and find him watching me closely. I blush and let my hair fall forward so it hides my face. I worry the tasseled edge of the huge rug with the toe of my peep-toe heels. I can't wait to take them off.

"Have you heard of The Fly Girl?"

"Yeah." A flush stains his tanned cheeks and he laughs. "Everyone knows The Fly Girl. aka, public enemy number one."

My stomach dips. A lump forms in my throat as his words hit home.

"Really? Why?" I whisper.

"Don't know why. My mom's little gossip circle calls her a home-wrecker."

"She's not," I protest and look him in the eye earnestly. My mother's a lot of things, but she's not that.

"How do you know what she is? Are you a fan?" he asks in amusement.

"She's my mother," I grit out.

"Oh, shit. I'm sorry." He winces

"It's okay. I mean, it's just what everyone else thinks." I do really hate my mom sometimes. But for some reason the idea that anyone else would makes me want to cry. It's always just been us.

"No, I'm sorry. I shouldn't have said that—it's just dumb gossip. I don't think any of them have even met her. Just seen her picture all over the place." He peers at me. "I see it, though. The resemblance."

"That's because she recreated me in her image. Take the makeup off and throw some water on my hair, I don't really look like this."

My mother's always telling me that girls like us have to use what we're born with. Except, I wasn't born with what she was. She's a bomb-shell. I'm her skinny, frizzy-headed daughter. When I'm not dressed like this and people see us together, there's always a double take when I call her "Mama."

It's not just that, without her head to toe makeovers, I look like a Fraggle. It's because she's only sixteen years older than me and we look more like sisters than mother and daughter.

She *treats* me like a sister, too. It's fun when that means we stay up late and watch *Grease* and paint our nails. But most of the time, I wish she would check my homework, tell me no, and give me a curfew. Instead, she brings me to parties like this.

Dressed like this.

His eyes widen as he puts it together.

"You kind of look like her. The hair… your eyes."

"You think so? I'm convinced she stole me from a hospital somewhere."

He bursts out laughing. It's so easy and uninhibited and I can tell he laughs a lot. Even though he's just had a fight with his mom, he seems really relaxed. *That* relaxes *me*.

"She says I look like an owl with these on," I confess sheepishly and pull my glasses off.

His laughter dies. "Then, she must never have seen an owl before. And, don't you need them to see?" He sounds offended.

"I do… it's just that she says I look better without them." I say the words like they don't matter. But they do, so very much. It hurts to know that the way I look drives my mother crazy. So much that she's always trying to change me.

"I'm not sure how you look when you're squinting like a creep 'cause you can't see, I think you're pretty right now."

I drop my face again, this time to hide my smile.

"No one's ever called me that before," I admit shyly. Even my mother only ever says, "You'd be pretty if…"

"Then everyone *else* needs glasses." He says that so easily. I turn to face him fully for the first time. He starts to say something, but then his eyes widen suddenly and he looks back at the door.

I follow his gaze and sigh in relief when the knob doesn't move. I can hear the distant noise of the party, but that's been there all night.

"What's wrong?" I ask him.

"Did you say you're the Fly Girl—I mean, your mother is here?" The alarm in his voice brings my eyes back to his.

"Yeah." I nod.

"Oh, shit. My mom's gonna flip." He's wide-eyed as he looks back toward the door.

"But, it's just a party, isn't it?" I ask in confusion. Granted, it's the nicest party she's ever taken me to, but we walked right in.

"The Listers are here."

"How do you know about them?" I ask. That lump in my throat is back and my heart's beat thumps wildly.

"The fight your mom had with his wife at the All-Star Games last year was all anyone talked about for months."

I look to the curtain and feel a sense of terrible foreboding coming over me. I heard Mama tell one of her friends that if she ever got within ten feet of him again she would "light his ass on fire."

My stomach drops and I stifle a fretful groan as I imagine what's happening outside this room. "It was nice to meet you. But maybe you should do what she said and go back upstairs. I'll just go back behind the curtain."

He ignores me and stands up and walks over to the window. "What were you doing over there?"

"I told you, I just needed a place to wait for my mom." I dart around him and get there first. I bend to pick up my notebook and clutch it to my chest.

"What's that?" He nods at it.

"Just a notebook," I say impatiently and flash the front at him.

He doesn't leave, instead, his eyes train onto my notebook. "Happily Ever After?" he reads the words I've scrawled on it.

"Yeah."

"That's like fairy tales, right?"

"If I tell you, will you leave?" I ask impatiently.

"Probably not. I like talking to you," he says with a cheeky smile. I sigh, but I can't even feign annoyance. I like talking to him, too.

I look at the curtains and then back at him.

"Fine. But let's sit back there, if your mom comes back she won't see us." I cock my head to the windows.

His smile widens, his dimples deepen and I find myself smiling too.

He walks over, holds the curtain open and says, "Come on."

I duck behind the curtain and he steps behind it to join me. I picked the window because it has a nook underneath it and it's just big enough for both of us. When we're both seated and the curtain is drawn, we're completely hidden. The light that pours in from the room through the top of the curtain makes it easy to see. He scoots close to me until our shoulders are touching. I glance over at him and he's looking at me. He flushes and looks down at the notebook in my hand.

"So tell me about your fairy tales."

"They're not fairy tales… I read a lot of missing person's mysteries and I like to imagine that they're out there living a happy life. Instead of just gone, you know? Like, if I disappeared, I would hope people would imagine me out there living my dream. So that's what I do. In here." I show him my notebook.

"Wow… That's cool. So you turn them into fairy tales?"

"No, not fairy tales. These are real people." I tap the book.

"Hmm," he says through pursed lips. I flush and imagine what he must be thinking. It's what everyone thinks.

"I know. It's weird," I say to preempt the inevitable teasing.

He frowns and shakes his head in disappointment. "Thank goodness you have other talents; 'cause mind reading isn't ever going to be a moneymaker for you."

"Whatever, it's what everyone else thinks."

"Are these the same everyone's who also need glasses? Glad I'm not one of them. It's not weird."

"Really?" My shoulders relax a little and I probe him with my eyes for traces of a burgeoning laugh… the one that usually follows when someone finds out my hobby.

He draws a cross over the center of his chest.

"Really. I used to pretend my dad had just gone missing. I would look for his face in airports. I mean, I know he's dead. It's just nice to pretend that he's not gone forever. You know?"

"Yeah. I do," I say slowly. My heartbeat has slowed a little. The instant understanding and connection I feel at hearing him say that he's… like me, it feels like a touch coaxing the tension out of me. The fear of being caught that's been clouding my vision recedes.

He may look like one of the boys I know from school, but I can see now, that he's not.

"Can I see it?" he asks, not flippantly, not easily, but like he knows he's asking for a lot.

The respect in his request is disarming, and before I process what I'm doing, I hand it over. He flips to the first page and reads the inscription there. "The Legend is a love story. But it's also a cautionary tale. It tells you to love deeply, believe in happily ever after, but don't try to live anyone's life but your own. That will be your undoing. All legends are lies. Make your own truth."

He reads the inscription that's scrawled on the front out loud.

"You wrote that?" he asks and I wish I had because he looks really impressed.

"No. It's from a book I read once, called *The Legend*. It was the opening line. I read it in one afternoon, on the floor of the library. I've never been able to find it again, but it's my favorite story. About a girl on a quest to find her father…" I trail off because he probably doesn't care.

"A missing person story, I see." He grins at me and looks back at the notebook.

"Yeah, I love them."

"So you just woke up one day and decided this was what you wanted to read and write?"

"I wouldn't say *that*. I just… I don't know… I just like it." I don't add the rest because I know it sounds crazy. I really used to think my mother stole me from my real parents. Parents who looked like me, who spent time with me, who didn't look at me and wonder where in the world I came from.

I believed it so strongly, that when I was eight, I started searching library archives for newspaper clippings about children who went missing around the time I was born. I'd sit for hours and scroll, hoping that I'd find proof that this woman who cared more about men and parties than she seemed to care about me was just an imposter.

I never found that proof. Instead, I found all these other stories about people who had just gone missing. From grocery stores, from shopping malls, their homes—never been heard from again.

As soon as I was old enough, I used the Internet at the library to really research them.

"Which one's your favorite?"

"Amelia Earhart. She was my first. And she's my muse."

"Amelia Earhart?" he asks as he scans the first page.

"Her story is the most fascinating, I think. I read everything I could find about her. And they all ended the same way—her plane malfunctioned and plunged out of the sky, sending her into a watery grave somewhere in the Pacific Ocean. I just couldn't believe such an amazing, brave woman, meeting such an ordinary, end."

"How did you imagine it ending?"

"You really want to know?" I ask.

"No. I'm only asking you to tell me because I don't want to know," he says sarcastically and I can't help my grin.

"Okay." I flip open my notebook and skim the story.

I peek over the top of the book; he's watching me closely now, his eyes scanning my face.

I flush. "She was my first. Now, I have notebooks full of happy endings for people I'll never know, but who I'll never forget."

"What's your name?" His left turn from his questions about my book surprises me, and I offer my name without thinking twice about it.

"Uh, it's Kal."

"I'm Remi." He sticks a hand out for me to shake. I stare at it for a second before I reach for it. Our palms glide together before he wraps his finger around my hand and butterfly wings tickle the inside of my chest. My breaths shorten, and I look up from our joined hands to find him looking at them, too. His eyes snap up to mine, and before I can save myself, I drown in their dark depths. I pull my hand away and he smiles.

"So, have you written a happy ending for yourself?"

It's just eight words. Just one question.

Yet, somehow, it feels like the key to something. Then, my heart does the strangest thing—it thuds hard against my chest, but not in fear.

In excitement.

"No… I've never thought of that." I admit.

"You should. Maybe write one for me, too. It could be like a roadmap, in case one of us gets lost, and we can find our way back," he says like it's actually going to happen.

"You act like we're going to be friends or something," I say, even though, that flutter in my chest has spread to my belly at the idea of being friends with him.

"Aren't we already?" he asks.

"I don't know… I'm not really a people person. I've always preferred books."

"I have a sister like that… so I'm speaking from experience when I tell you that you don't have to be a people person, just a Remi person," he volleys back, and for some reason, the butterfly wings flap and flutter deep inside me.

A Remi person…

The tingle his words cause is muted by the increasingly loud voices behind the door. A sense of doom takes over. I look over his shoulder, my eyes trained on the door handle. "Are you sure your mother's not going to come looking for you again?"

"Don't be so nervous, my mother yells a lot, but she wouldn't really—"

The door bursts open and slams against the wall behind it.

"Lee," my mother's shout ricochets off the walls of the library. I jump out of my skin and scramble out from behind the curtain. She's racing across the room like a bat out of hell.

She's carrying her shoes and speed walking. Her bleached blond hair flies behind her like a war banner, her dark green eyes, really the only thing I wished I inherited her from her, are blazing with anger.

My stomach drops and I glance back to the curtain. Remi comes out too, and he's watching her like she's some sort of mythical creature come to life.

She takes me by the arm, not even giving Remi a second glance. "Come on, Lee. We're leaving." Her voice is angry and anxious all at once, and I don't resist. I look back at Remi and he's watching us with undisguised fascination.

"I thought your name was Kal," he calls after me, and in the midst of all of this upheaval and my mother's frantic energy and my own panic and fear, I find the presence of mind to explain.

Just as she pulls me the through the door, I look over my shoulder and smile at him. Because that's how I want him to remember me.

"It's Kalilah."

He smiles back. I memorize the expression on his face. It's the friendliest one I've seen in a long time, and I hope I never forget it. And then, I turn around and struggle to keep up with my mother's hurried steps.

We step out into the huge marble-floored corridor, it's lined with torches and huge magnolia trees that are so perfect they look fake, but the sugary sweet scent from the tremendous white flowers that bloom on its branches declare them to be the work of nature. Our footsteps are muffled by the long rug that runs down the center of it and from a distance I can hear the strain of music and merrymaking voices.

I look up at my mother in bewilderment. "Mama, what's going on? Why are we leaving?" Her jaw is clenched, her eyes fixed ahead of us like she's on a march to battle. Her chest heaves, leaving her breathless as she drags me down the corridor. I try to pull my arm free and she only tightens her grip.

"Mama, there's no one chasing us, can you please slow down?" I plead with her.

"Oh, they're chasing us all right. I've just got a good head start. Keep up," she snaps.

We round a corner and the stairs I'd run up to find this library come into sight. She speeds up and then brings us to a sudden, lurching halt when we find our path blocked by a woman flanked by two men.

The woman is beautiful. Certainly, the most beautiful woman *I've* ever seen. Her cocoa skin glows like she's walking with a ray of sun over her. She's tall, dressed all in black and has a silver streak of hair that cuts through her dark tresses like a flash of lightning. Her eyes are a startlingly dark... and familiar. But in them, her beauty disappears. The anger that lurks in those eyes, the tight set of her red painted lips is scary.

"Morgan. You are not welcome here. Don't bring your trouble and mess to my doorstep."

I'd know that voice anywhere.

It's snakehead.

Remi's mother. Of course, they have the same eyes, except hers have something terrible in them. It's more than anger, there's sadness swirling there, and... something else I don't recognize, but that I know isn't good. I look away from that terrifying glare, and only then do I notice that the two men are burly, scruffy bearded giants in dark suits wearing flat, menacing expressions. They eye my mother like she's a wild animal they're trying to decide how to trap.

My heart feels like it's going to fly up my throat and out of my mouth, and I tug on my mother's arm. Not to get loose, but to try to pull her away from them. She gives my arm a sharp, impatient tug in return. I look up at her and her eyes are full of warning. I clamp my mouth shut and stare straight ahead.

"Thank you, Ms. Wilde, I'm just leaving," she says haughtily and tries to step around the trio.

"It's Mrs. Wilde. I know you've had trouble recognizing that distinction before so, I'll excuse your oversight. And yes, you are leaving," Snakehead hisses. "Scott, James, please escort them out, through the back of the house."

"We can leave on our own." Mama's voice has got a pitch of fear in it that only amplifies mine.

"I'm sure you can. I just want to make sure none of my silver leaves with you."

"As if," she gasps in affront.

"As if nothing. Everyone knows about that con man you're dating. God only knows what or who you managed to get your hands on before I saw you."

"You've got nothing I want." My mother's words are muted by the tremor in her voice.

"Good. Now, get out. Take your love child with you." Snakehead slings these malicious words with the cruel carelessness of someone who knows they've got the upper hand.

The blow they land is brutal. Each one of them changes the way I see myself, my mother, my future. She sweeps her eyes over me. If I were made of anything less than flesh and bone, her gaze would have incinerated me. I shrink underneath it and then even more when my mother's only response is to say, "With pleasure."

One of the men grabs my mother's arm. She wrenches it out of his grasp and we both stumble backward. "Don't you dare touch me," she says and then, with my arm still in her grasp, she walks down the stairs.

The long hem of her sequined green dress hisses as it drags behind us on the marble floor. When we reach the bottom of the stairs, she finally drops my arm. She runs nervous hands over her dress and looks down at me and gives me what I think is supposed to be a brave smile. But I can see the humiliation in her eyes. "We will leave through the same door we came in through," she says and then walks toward the front of the house.

"No, that door is for guests. Take them out through the back," Snakehead calls from her dais at the top of the stairs. They grab our arms. I try to shake loose and my mother grabs my hand and squeezes it.

"Let's not make a scene. They aren't worth it." She nods toward the small crowd of people who have gathered outside of the huge ballroom to our left. I nod and we allow ourselves to be turned and marched down the hall in the opposite direction.

Once we're outside and alone, I finally find the voice to speak.

"Mama, what happened?"

"They think they're better than us. That's all. Let's just go."

We're both silent on the walk down their seemingly endless driveway, back to the street back to where we parked her car. Halfway there, I look back at the house that looms over Rivers Wilde from its perch at the top of the hill. In a second-story window on the left side of the house where the library is, I see the shadow of a boy watching us leave.

Remi.

And it's only then I realize my arms are empty. I start to tell my mother I left my notebook, but I know that would only annoy her and that there would be no going back to get it. But then when I think that maybe he'll find it and keep it... a part of the knot that has made a permanent home in my gut unfurls.

Just a little.

I'm not sure I'll ever see him again, but I know I'll never forget him. And just thinking that he might have a piece of me makes me feel like someone sees me. I'll write both of our happy endings as soon as I get a new notebook. And I know he'll be in the version I write for myself.

2

BAE WATCH

REMI
Four Years Later

"REMINGTON, WAKE UP." MY MOTHER'S NOT SO GENTLE NUDGE shakes me out of a deep, dreamless sleep. I sit up slowly. "What time is it?" I grope my bedside table for my alarm clock and groan when I see the time.

"Get your brother and sister up and tell them to be downstairs in fifteen minutes. I want to have a family meeting before your grandfather wakes up." My mother draws the curtain and sunlight floods my room. She doesn't say another word as she stalks out, and she doesn't wait for me to respond. She knows there's only one answer I'd dare give.

I stumble down the hall, bleary-eyed and wake my twin sister, Regan, up first. I tell her Mom wants to see us in five minutes. Regan can't do anything in five minutes, but maybe if I tell her five, she'll actually be down there in fifteen.

I get my brother Tyson out of bed and wait until he's walking to the bathroom before I head back to my own room and get ready. I dress for the day because I know that whatever else happens, I won't be going back to bed. I have a delivery to make in an hour, anyway.

"Good, you're all here." My mother strides into the kitchen exactly fifteen minutes after she walked into my room.

"Morning," we all mutter back in unison. She doesn't say another word until she slides into her chair at the head of the table. That's my grandfather's chair. At least I know it's going to be a quick talk. He'll be down at no later than eight fifteen and he's got a thing about anyone sitting in that chair.

"We've got a situation." She takes a long sip of her coffee and then passes a sweeping, calculating gaze over me and my siblings.

Impatience makes my throat tight.

"Mom?" Regan, my twin, asks in that way she has of sounding excited when really she's just as annoyed as I am.

"A family of criminals has just moved to Rivers Wilde," she says and pauses to look at us as if for dramatic effect.

I share a glance with my brother, Tyson, and I know we're thinking the same thing. I can't believe I got out of bed for one of my mother's gossip-fueled rants. She normally saves those for dinner.

"Okay… what did they do? Wear white after Labor Day? Put their fork on the right side of their place mat?" Tyson quips. My mother rewards him with a glare so frosty he chokes on his laughter and coughs. He drops his eyes to the table to avoid my smirk.

My mother is the self-appointed leader of the Rivers Wilde Decorum and Etiquette Committee. She takes that position as seriously as she does her role as head of Wilde World's Restaurant and Dining Division.

"No, they broke the law," she says and looks at us to gauge our reactions. Our blank stares disappoint her and she sneers. "Did you hear me?"

"Yeah, I just don't know what you mean," I say.

"It means Laryce just called and told me that David Lister sold his bookstore to a woman who ruined more marriages in this community than I can count." She nods her head in the direction of the Lister Estate next door. I shake my head. Laryce Quincy is the biggest gossip on this side of the Rio Grande. She and my mother are thick as thieves.

"She's living with Lister?" Tyson asks in surprise. His wife and son died in a car accident last year and he's become something of a recluse.

"God forbid, no. She's in the little apartment above the bookstore, but they are living in our community." She says it like it's a crime.

"Rivers Wilde is everyone's community," Regan recites our pitch line sarcastically.

My mother glares at her. "That's right, Ms. Regan. And I'd like to keep it that way. We've taken painstaking care in making sure that the people who live here are going to be upstanding members of our community." She shakes her head in disgust. "She was in that foster home because her mother went to jail for identity theft and credit card fraud. Now, they're here to sully our pristine community with the scandal she's sure to bring along with her. According to Laryce, she's trying to make a *fresh start*." She puts the last two words in air quotes and makes it sound like that's a crime, too.

"What's wrong with that?" Regan asks.

My mother slams her hand down so hard that the coffee in her mug splashes onto the table. She leans forward and glares at Regan. "What's *wrong* with it is that this is supposed to a safe, family-friendly community. Not a place for criminals on the run to come. I don't know what is wrong with Lister, selling to a Greer of all people."

"I wonder why he sold it. It's been vacant since Jill died." I'm thinking aloud, but my mother is ready with an answer.

"Because she used to be the most notorious gold digger in Houston. She probably slept with him even though he's old enough to be her grandfather. Doesn't matter. Now they're both here. We all know the apple doesn't fall far from the tree. So, there goes the neighborhood."

I exchange a glance with Regan. We've both already decided that these apples have fallen very, very far from the trees we sprung from.

"How old is she?" Regan asks.

"Your age, so, eighteen or so…" My mother waves a dismissive hand in the air.

"Is she gonna go to Lamar?" Tyson sounds excited.

My mother fixes me with one of her eagle-eyed stares. "You're in charge of delivering catering orders from Eat!, right? What's on your roster for tomorrow?"

"I won't know until I go in this afternoon," I tell her.

"Laryce told me she placed a huge order for morning delivery from our bakery yesterday. Obviously, we can't refuse their business. That would be too public of a snub. I don't want people to think I'm unkind."

"Yes, it's much more your style to talk about them in back rooms than to be upfront about how you feel," Regan mutters and then grins at me. I don't grin back. I don't think it's funny. Because it's true. My mother is the queen of the whisper campaign and honestly, on the list of things that bothers me about her, it's very close to the top.

My mother glares at her until Regan's eyes drop to her coffee and her grin disappears. Then she turns to face me.

"Remington, when you make your delivery, you are not to linger. And you are in charge of making sure your brother doesn't end up over there, too."

"Why would I end up there?" Ty whines.

"Because, you're girl crazy, and everyone knows it," my mother retorts.

"True facts," Regan chimes in. Tyson throws his toast at her.

"Please don't behave like you were raised in a barn," my mother snaps. "I have to get to the office. I want you both to please heed my warning." She stands up and takes her mug over to the sink.

"You didn't give me one," Regan says dryly.

"You're not good at making friends. You'll be fine," my mother says without even looking up from where she's washing her hands.

Tyson sticks his tongue out and Regan gives him the middle finger.

"Please be productive today." My mother dries her hands and leans back against the counter to survey us. She's in one of what she calls her "nutcracker" pantsuits that she has a seemingly infinite supply of in her closet. Her hair is pulled back into a chignon, that streak of gray she refuses to color to match the raven-black curls she tames with her blow dryer and half a bottle of pomade every day. She looks like an army general and she runs this house like one.

"I know summer is just beginning and that you'll all be tempted to come home and do nothing after you get off work, but I expect that list I gave you to be complete when I get back. And, Remi, no basketball until you're done."

"You and your fucking lists, Tina," my grandfather's deep rumble voice fills the room as he ambles into the kitchen.

"Oh, Liam. Your language," she admonishes, but with an air of respect she never shows anyone but him. I used to think it was because he was our benefactor. We've lived in his home since my father died. But it's not that, at all. He and my mother have been partners in the explosive growth Wilde World has experienced over the last fifteen years.

The respect they have for each other, and what they've built together, is soul deep. And he's the only person she's always nice to. Well, as nice as she's capable of being, anyway.

"Morning, Pops," I greet him with a smile and start to stand up and help him over when Regan beats me to it.

"I don't need help," he scowls at her when she takes ahold of his arm. His sky-blue eyes, a trait none of his grandchildren share, are clear and focused this morning.

"I know, Popsy, I just want to hold your hand." She smiles sweetly at him. Regan doesn't smile sweetly at anyone. In that way, she's like my mother. But that's where the similarities end. She's got what I fondly call a Resting Fuck Off Face. Her lack of a smile is in complete contradiction to her sweet, affable nature.

My grandfather smiles warmly down at Regan, only she gets that smile from him, and lets her lead him to the chair at the head of the table. He lowers himself slowly into the chair and folds his still straight, big hands in front of him. "To what pleasure do I owe the company of all of my grandchildren this morning?"

"I suppose I should tell you, too. You're out in the garden so much these days." My mother walks back over to the table, this time sitting in her normal seat, beside him.

He had a minor stroke a month ago. His recovery has been slow, and he's turned a lot of the day-to-day running of Wilde World to his executive team. He's been outside, sitting and reading and sleeping in the chair we placed near the butterfly garden for him.

"Well, spit it out. I'm too old for suspense." He glowers at my mother from under his heavy brow.

"There's a gang of criminals living in Rivers Wilde. A bookstore owner and her eighteen-year-old girl," I say and waggle a brow at him.

"Is she robbing people in their gardens?" my grandfather says, his eyebrows raised with dry mock horror.

"It's not funny," my mother, never one to allow light to be made of anything, says. "You all have grown up in the lap of luxury. But trust me, I know what it's like when unsavory elements start moving in. It's just them now, but next thing you know their friends from Third Ward will start visiting. And there goes the neighborhood."

"Third Ward is a historically significant neighborhood and home to many of our stores," my grandfather reminds her in that stern, disapproving way that only he can.

"Isn't Beyoncé from Third Ward?" Regan asks.

"Yes, she is. And you can tell… Money doesn't buy class. Breeding is important. Remember that you are Wildes. Stay away from that girl."

"Well, this is more excitement than I can remember having in a long time. I might walk down to the town square just to catch a glimpse of our very own Thelma and Louise."

"Liam, it's not exciting, or funny, and I don't want you encouraging the kids. It's bad enough that Remi has to deliver things to that store every day," my mother says with agitation.

"Nothing encourages a kid like telling them not to do something. Sounds like you got the encouraging covered. And, Remi and Regan are both old enough to drive. They aren't kids." My grandfather's voice is stern and full of warning.

"They're my kids," she pushes back with that thread of steel she always gets when he challenges her like this.

"Funny how she remembers that, now," Regan whispers to me, and I give her a warning glance.

"What was that?" My mother's voice is cold and lets Regan know that she heard her and is daring her to repeat it.

Regan's never been good at playing chicken. "Nothing. I'm going back to bed," she says as she snags an apple from the huge bowl of fruit in the center of the too big table and shuffles out.

"That girl has the worst attitude," my mother says and shakes her head disapprovingly.

"I thought you were leaving for work," Ty says and walks over to her and puts an arm around her. She leans into him for a second and pulls out of his grasp. She's always been uncomfortable with affection. Tyson, with his endless optimism, keeps trying with her.

"I am. I just want to make sure we're all on the same page before I leave. I mean it. Keep contact to a minimum."

"REMI, I THINK THAT'S HER." MY BROTHER NODS AT THE WINDOW that overlooks the entire main street of Rivers Wilde. Our house was the very first home built in the neighborhood and my grandfather put it on one of the artificial hills they erected.

From the second-story family room that also serves as our study area, you can see straight into the square, even though it's a good quarter of a mile away. It's a perfectly designed grid, and from here, I can see how well-thought-out it is. It's small-town America in the middle of the urban sprawl of Houston. The minute you drive through the majestic iron gates that mark the entrance, it feels like a different world.

I follow Tyson's gaze over the pristine treelined street until I see what caught his eye. A young woman is making her way up the street that serves as the main artery of the town square.

Her hair is a crazy mess of curls gathered at the top of her head. She's got on a red T-shirt that says Bae Watch and some tiny denim shorts, that show off long, toned legs. She's wearing bright blue Jordan's, and her hands clutch the front straps of the backpack that's slung over her shoulders. The dozen or so silver bangles that adorn her arms glint in the sunlight. And, there's something very familiar about her.

It's been bugging me all day. When Pops and I were walking through the square this morning, she was outside the bookstore, wiping down the huge bay windows that jut out onto the sidewalk and make it look like a real small-town bookstore.

She was wearing those same sunglasses.

I started to cross the street to get a closer look when Pops announced that he was tired and wanted to head home.

She turns onto the street leading to the bookstore and we lose sight of her.

I look back at Tyson and find his narrowed eyes tracing the girl's movements and his fist caught between his lips. I snort in disgust and reach over and slap him on the back of his head.

"What the fuck was that for, Remi?" He rubs his head dramatically and turns angry eyes on me.

"Don't ogle grown women like that, it's disrespectful."

"Then why are you doing it?" He scowls at me.

"'Cause, I'm a grown-ass man." I wink at him, close the notebook I've been writing in, grab my iPod and headphones, and start toward the stairs.

"Where are you going?" he calls after me.

"To the square," I shout back

"Oooh, I'm coming too. That girl ain't no criminal. Mom is just being a snob." He slams his book shut and jumps off his chair.

"No, you're not. And don't use double negatives when you talk. You sound ridiculous."

"I'm on vacation, man." He does his best Chris Tucker imitation. "Do you even know what that word means? I'm the only sixteen-year-old on summer break who's got study hall every fucking day and gets lectures on his grammar."

"You're the only kid who's got me for a brother," I remind him.

He groans like he's in agony.

I slap the back of his head again.

"That'll give you something to really groan about. Trust me, being your big brother isn't a picnic. Now, shut up and do your homework." I close my folder and stand up.

He shoots me the finger but sits back down at the counter. I feel a rush of affection for him. He's a pain in the ass. But he's a good kid, and he doesn't push back too hard when I have to put him in line.

"I saw her first," he protests.

"Too bad you can't do anything about that." I wink at him and then head down the stairs.

I'm pulling it shut behind me when I hear him call out, "I hope Mom finds out." He tries one last-ditch attempt to stop me.

"Hope your mom finds out what?" My grandfather's rumbled question startles me. I didn't realize he was down in the living room. He's sitting in his recliner that faces the window overlooking the back garden, his copy of the *Houston Chronicle* folded on his lap and his glasses resting at the end of his narrow nose.

"Oh, nothing. I was just about to walk down to the square. Tyson's just being a shit because I won't let him come."

"Oh, good. I forgot to stop by Sugar Plum on our way back. Margie made some of those macarons I love today. The green ones? Pick me some up on your way back."

"You're not supposed to eat those."

"And you're not supposed to be going to talk to that girl. But, here we are." He raises an eyebrow at me.

"How do you know where I'm going?" I don't even bother to deny it. My grandfather has an uncanny sense about things. And, for all of the lectures he's given me about what my responsibilities are. He's acted as the counterbalance to my mother's strict, no-nonsense parenting style.

"Have a seat for a minute, Remi." He nods at the chair next to his. I almost groan because I know a lecture's coming. But whenever I feel like this, I remember the sickening dread the day of his stroke, and I sit my ass down with a smile on my face because I know that one day, I'll miss these chats.

"How you feeling, Pops?"

"I'm not dead yet, don't look at me like that. Now sit and tell me what's going on." The question is, on its face, innocuous. He's asking me something more but I'm not in the mood to give it.

"Nothing much. Practice starts next month. I'm just working." I sit back in the chair and make it clear that it's all I have to say.

"This is a big year for you, son. College, away from home, part of a team that plays for more than just glory. Keep your dick in your pants."

I laugh in surprise. "I was just going down to the square. Where'd you *think* I was going?"

"To find trouble," he says with grave certainty and my laughter fizzles.

He leans forward and pins me in place with his steely gaze. "You're behind the deli counter at Eat! tonight. Skip that bookstore until you make your delivery tomorrow. You've been careful about girls so far. I'm proud of you for that. This isn't the time to test the waters. Your mother was being a little unfair this morning. But she's not wrong. That girl has a troubled past. From what I've heard, anyway."

"I didn't know gossip was your thing."

"That doesn't make it untrue, Remi, and I like to know who's moving in here. Her mother bought that store for a pittance from Lister. Much less than it's worth. But before that, she was in jail, for embezzlement. And that girl was in a foster home. For nearly two years. Do you know what years in a place like that will do to someone?"

"No. And you don't either," I challenge him. But, I make a note of the information.

"Not firsthand. No. But I've seen it up close, and she's got baggage you can't even imagine. You should listen to your mother. And if you don't want to do that, I'm going to insist that you at least listen to me."

I owe him that, at the very least.

"Sure Pops, I promise."

3

TO BE READ

REMI

THE BOOKSTORE, TO BE READ, IS THE LAST STOP ON MY ROUTE. I've been anticipating it all morning and by the time I pull up outside, I'm practically chomping at the bit to get inside.

I peer in through the huge pane glass window covered in their red logo.

I see her, she's facing me but her face is turned downward. This small glimpse makes my pulse jump in a way that unsettles me. I pride myself on my nerves of steel. I decide to heed my grandfather's warning. In and out.

I shake it off, exhale a calming breath, and put my hand on the door to open it.

"You making a delivery or preparing for a game, Remi?" Henny Harper, shouts at me from her perch on a bench in the square.

She's one of Rivers Wilde's first residents. She's retired and notoriously nosy. But, she's got a heart of gold and a wicked sense of humor. I shoot her a deprecating smile. "Aren't you supposed to be at Sweet &

Lo's by now? The kolaches will be cold if you wait much longer to head over."

"Don't try to change the subject," she says, but stands up. "You be nice to that girl," she calls over her shoulder and then saunters up the pebbled walkway that bisects the grass-covered square.

"I'm always nice," I mutter to her retreating back before I turn and open the door. A small bell jingles and announces my presence. She doesn't look up from the box of books she's bent over.

She's got white earbuds stuck in her ears and she's singing "Don't Speak" by No Doubt at the top of her lungs. Her voice is terrible, and she's fucking up the lyrics, but damn she's into it. Her eyes are closed as she belts out the song. What she lacks in talent, she makes up for with her passion.

The late morning sun is high and it bathes her in a warm light that illuminates her face. I can only see her profile, but it's striking. She's wearing glasses, instead of sunglasses this time. The black frames rest on the sharp line of a high cheekbone that swoops and flares and reminds me of a drawing I saw of the Egyptian queen Nefertiti.

My eyes follow the outline of full lips and the small jut of her chin and move along the smooth line of her jaw and down the graceful sweep of her long neck. Her hair, a mass of thick dark curls, is caught in a huge bun at the top of her head that sways as she dances.

She's short, at least compared to me, the top of her head would hit me at shoulder height. Her slim shoulders roll and her hips, snug in a pair of tiny white shorts, sway to the beat of her music. She reaches up on her tiptoes and the muscles in her long legs flex with the motion. I forget my pledge to my grandfather and walk into the store.

I start up the aisle where she's working. She senses me, stops singing, looks up sharply, yanks the headphones out of her ears, and turns to face me fully.

All of the air steals from my lungs.

It's not just because she's the kind of pretty that makes you pay attention. Though she's certainly that. Or that behind her dark-rimmed glasses, her eyes are perfectly symmetrical almonds centered with pools of brown molasses and cinnamon. It's that, despite how different she looks now—from her hair down to her makeup-free face

—I know right away she's the girl from the library all of those years ago.

The girl who left her notebook of amazing stories behind. I should have expected that in the four years that passed that she would have had a growth spurt. But the girl I'm looking at has done much more than spurt.

She's blossomed, and I am awestruck at the barefaced beauty standing in front of me.

I've wondered about her so often since that night. That night in the library, there'd been an openness and honesty in her eyes, that even as a fourteen-year-old, I recognized as special. And, I still have her notebook. I found it on the floor of the library the day after the party and put it on my bookshelf.

But it wasn't until I was confronted with my own moment of truth that I truly understood it. My freshman year of high school, I tried out for a citywide basketball team. I've always been the best player in my school district. I didn't even need to practice before games.

But those tryouts showed me that hard work beats talent every single day.

I didn't make the cut for the team.

I'd been devastated. A few days later the coach called to say it had just been a mistake that they hadn't called me after tryouts. I was fifteen, cocky and dumb.

In the locker room before practice, I heard some of the boys talking. Turns out that just days before, my grandfather donated a brand new athletic center to the city in exchange for my place on the team.

Humiliated is an inadequate word to describe the way I felt. The coaches barely paid attention to me when I joined the team for practice. And, I didn't blame them. The day after our first game, I came home and was pulling something off my shelf when that book fell from where I'd put it. It opened to the inscription "All legends are lies. Make your own truth."

Something clicked for me then, I may not have deserved to be on that team initially, but I was going to earn my place. I wrote the words "The Legend" on the side of my basketball shoes as a reminder when I was tempted to quit. And I busted my ass to make it true.

45

I practiced as many hours as I could. I worked harder than everyone else. And the first time they put me into the game—one we were losing and only had minutes left to play—I scored twelve points in less than two minutes with back-to-back three-pointers that snatched victory from the jaws of defeat. A few performances like that and I was moved to the starting lineup.

One day, someone in the crowd called out "The Legend" after I'd scored a triple-double and the crowd joined them in a chant. The name stuck. And now, it's what everyone calls me.

The architect of that is standing right there. Close enough for me to touch. And I can't seem to find the ability to string a coherent sentence together.

"Hello?" she says and peers at me. I look up to find her standing with her arms crossed over her chest and a scowl on her face. There's no indication she remembers me from that night. That stings. But only briefly. It'll be even better to see her face when she figures out who I am.

Besides, her scowl is fucking pretty.

"Why are you staring at me like that?" She sounds so annoyed. I smile at her and it deepens, her dark, lightly arched eyebrows wing upward, and she looks like she wants to kick my ass.

Oh, yeah… really fucking pretty.

"Like what?" I feign ignorance. I know just how I was staring at her and I don't mind that she saw.

"Like you've never seen a girl before."

"Well, maybe it's because I've never seen a girl like you before." I give her my most charming smile.

She grimaces like she just took a sniff of spoiled milk. She shakes her head and laughs out loud.

"What's so funny?" I ask her. Now, I'm the one with a scowl and my arms crossed over my chest.

"*You* are funny. That line was so lame." She rolls her eyes and turns back to her books.

I stand there, thrown by her clear dismissal. And also… very, very pleased by it.

I would have been disappointed if the girl from that night in the library, the one whose stories captivated and motivated me, turned out to be just like everyone else, after all.

I take an appraising glance around the store and whistle appreciatively as I see what they've done to the place. A dozen rows of gleaming dark wood, shoulder-height bookshelves take up the entire back of the store. I can smell the citrus from the wood polish mingled with the dry scent of cardboard boxes and all that paper.

The area of the bookstore directly in front of the door looks more like a really comfortable reading nook—complete with a huge round glass-top table with a bowl of what looks like M&M's on it. I look to my left and see the small counter they've set up to sell the pastries they ordered, complete with an espresso machine.

"This looks great. You guys have really done a good job."

"The bookstore doesn't officially open until tomorrow," she announces in a faux-friendly voice, but she doesn't look back at me. She pulls more books out of the box and puts them on the shelf.

"Really? You look ready for customers right now."

"We're not," comes her less than friendly reply. Undeterred, I decide right then and there, that by the end of the week, I'll have her smiling at me when I walk in the door every morning.

"I've got something for—" I start to point to my delivery van where her order is waiting.

The slam of her book as she drops it back into the box at her feet silences me. She whirls to face me. "Listen, asshole. You're not the first boy to walk in here today."

"Asshole?" I ask in real surprise.

"Don't act innocent," she scoffs "I know your mothers have been talking shit about me and my mom all week. So, let me save you some time. No, I won't give you a blow job. Or show you my tits, or let you finger bang me if you promise to take me to the movies." She ticks them off on her fingers.

I am taken aback by her words and angered by them, too.

I know that some of the founding families, mine included, act like their shit doesn't stink. But to think that someone came in here and said things like that to her, or anyone, makes me want to find out who they are and go and straighten them out.

I'm far, far away from being able to actually lead my family's business, but I feel responsible for it already. And none of the people who do business here should have to deal with shit like that. I make a mental note to pass on to the retail property managers when I get home.

She bends over to take some more books out of the box and I can see the tremble in her hands. "Now, you can leave. And if you try to touch me, I'll kick you in the balls," she says, and that shakes me out of my stupor.

"Has someone tried to fucking touch you?" I take a step toward her, a tentative, small one because I don't want to get in her space.

"Isn't that what you boys do for fun? Fuck with girls who are just minding their own business? Just because they can." Bitterness drips from her words.

I go from cautious to offended.

"I wouldn't know what *boys* do for fun. I'm a man." She turns to face me then; her jaw is tight with anger.

"Okay, man. Why are you still here, I've made it clear I'm not in the mood for company?"

"And, not to sound like a cocky asshole—"

"Too late," she quips.

"But I haven't offered you any company. But if I did, you wouldn't be saying no."

She glances over at me, sweeps me from head to toe and quirks her lips in a dismissive smirk. "If you say so."

"I haven't had any complaints," I say and shoot her an exaggerated wink.

She frowns at me. "Listen, I know your family owns whatever business they own. And you've probably got a hot car. Or whatever. But we own this store. I want you to leave." She finally turns to look at me and there's anger in her eyes, but I see the bone-deep wariness there. The same wariness I saw the night we met.

If my grandfather and mother are right, life didn't get much better for her after that night. I wonder what she's seen in the last four years. The skittishness from that night has been replaced by cynicism. I want to tell her I'm not like them. To ask her to tell me where she's been and to tell her where I've been, too.

Our eyes hold and for a minute; I'm transported back to that night and the ways it changed my life.

"I found your notebook," I tell her.

Her expression goes from blankly enigmatic to shock and then back to enigmatic. But she doesn't say anything.

"Do you *really* not remember me?" I ask, completely nonplussed that she might not. She sighs and leans against the bookshelf. Her shoulders fall a little and some of the fire goes out of her.

"Of course, I remember you. I was kind of hoping you wouldn't remember me." She stares down at those beat-up blue Jordan's.

I want to tell her that would have been impossible. Instead, I ask her why.

"Because that night was embarrassing. My mother and I were kicked out of your house. And it was the beginning of what turned out to be a pretty terrible chapter in my life. So yeah, I was hoping you'd have forgotten it. I've tried my hardest to." She puts the books down and turns to face me. Her expression tense, like she's expecting me to laugh.

Laughing is the last thing on my mind. I'm just amazed that she's gone through so much and is standing here, same as me.

"I could never forget how interesting your stories were. And how pretty you looked." I say.

She flushes, but this time doesn't try to hide her smile. That feels like a victory to me.

"You came up with those stories when you were just thirteen years old," I say as if she doesn't know it herself.

She shrugs as if it's not a big deal and smiles deprecatingly. "Yeah. I did. I was into some crazy shit back then"

"I still read them, you know. Especially that inscription. It's in my bedroom on my shelf with the rest of my books."

Her hand covers her mouth, she pulls the earbuds out of her ears and she walks over to the counter and leans against it, her back to me.

"Wow, I can't believe it." She shakes her head at the memory.

I join her at the counter and rest my elbows on top and look over at her.

"You want it back?"

She thinks about it, cocks her head to the right and exhales loudly.

"I mean, I guess. I don't know… I haven't thought about that stuff in a long time," she says, her voice full of awe.

"So you haven't been keeping up with all the new cold cases that've cropped up since then?"

"Don't tell me you do," she says.

"No, I don't. One notebook full was enough to last me a lifetime." I don't tell her that I flip it open and read that line "All legends are lies" before I leave for a game or head out to take an exam. That through those words, she's become my de facto good luck charm.

"That feels like a lifetime ago." She sighs. "And yeah, I still keep up with cold cases, yes. Research them and try to solve them sometimes. But, I've grown up a lot since then. I don't believe in happily ever after anymore. So, I don't write them."

My brain hears those words and my competitiveness rears its head and for some reason, I take them as a challenge.

"Do you write at all?"

"Oh, yeah. But just for my school paper these days. And more investigative stuff—like where did the money the school board was supposed to spend on AV equipment disappear to? But I still love reading books about unsolved mysteries."

"Have you heard of Murder By The Book?" I ask her as an idea starts taking shape.

"Nope. What's that?"

"A bookstore my sister likes. There's a group that meets there to discuss unsolved cases."

She waves a disbelieving hand at me. "No way."

"Oh, yeah, we went in there once during one of the meetings and we stayed for it."

"What was it like?" she asks wide-eyed, her guard down, her enthusiasm is palpable.

"Fucking weird. I mean, they believe some far out shit. But we went back a few times."

"You did? So, you're like… really into it?"

"Nah, But the lady who runs it used to bring these tamales with her every week and they were good as fuck. Totally worth sitting through the meetings for."

A bark of delighted laughter is melodious and clear as a bell. It feels like a reward

"That's ridiculous," she admonishes with a playful shake of her head.

"Not as ridiculous as sitting around talking about Jon Benet Ramsey for an hour."

"Oh man, that sounds like heaven to me." She closes her eyes and moans.

"You should go."

She glances at me; her face transformed by the beaming smile on it.

"You think? I mean, I would love to. It could be research. Get some ideas for displays, you know?" She claps her hands together excitedly and then gives me a shy smile that makes me want to coax more just like that out of her. "I love bookstores. I know it's weird."

"I remember that about you from the night we met. That you loved books and thought you were weird." I take a tentative step toward her. Her dark eyes widen, her lips part a little and she takes a step toward me, too.

The air around us changes, grows heavy with impatience and I wish I had super long arms so I could reach out and pull her to me.

"I've never stopped thinking about you," I say.

Her gasp is audible and visible in the sharp rise of her shoulders. She pulls her sandy-pink bare lip between her bottom teeth and nibbles it. I'm jealous of her teeth.

She peeks up at me through her lashes. "I've thought about you, too," she confesses quietly.

"Did you write your happy ending?" I ask as she gets closer.

"I did… wrote you one, too." She smiles shyly.

An unexpected rush of warmth comes over me and I reach for her. "I want to read it—"

I've just touched her shoulder when the bell over the door jingles. A woman with dark hair caught up in a tight ponytail, dressed in bright blue hospital scrubs walks in with a handful of bags. I recognize her right away as the woman from the library.

Kal's mom. Like Kal, she looks like a totally different person now, but like Kal—she's so distinctively beautiful, I'd know her anywhere.

"Who are you?" she asks and her tone leaves no doubt that she isn't happy to find me here. I turn to face her and smile.

She frowns.

"I'm Remi. I'm making a delivery. From *Eat!*" I point at my truck.

"You are?" Kal asks in complete surprise and I look back at her.

"Yeah, I guess we got to talking and—"

Her mother snaps her fingers to get my attention. "I know your family owns this town, but you're blocking the entrance to the book-store. I have a photographer coming to take pictures of the place today, so I need you to make your delivery and get that truck out of here." She points angrily to my white delivery van on the curb.

"Shit, sorry," I say and start outside.

"And next time, use the entrance in the back," she yells after me.

"Yes, ma'am," I call back as I rush out.

When I come back in with an armload of pastry boxes, Kal walks past me on her way to the back of the store and says, "Thank you for being nice." Her fingers skim my arm and I look at her in surprise.

Her eyes hold mine. "I'll see you tomorrow," she whispers and then disappears around the corner.

4

THE LEGEND

REMI

"Delivery," I call out from the back of the bookstore, I make my way through the loading bay and into the storage room.

"Come on through," Kal shouts back. I make my way onto the sales floor of the bookstore and feel a sense of relief that her mother is nowhere to be seen. Her back is to me as she fiddles with the espresso machine and I admire the lean lines of her back and neck.

She looks over her shoulder and smiles wide when she sees me.

Her hair is down today, and it looks like nothing I've ever seen. It's wild, and long and thick and so many different kinds of curls in one. It's fucking pretty and I could stand and look at it all day. Admire the slim set of her shoulders and the way her bright orange tank top clings to her slim waist. But I don't want to linger in case her mother happens to come back. I remember how my mother treated her that night all those years ago. I wasn't surprised she wanted me out of here yesterday.

"Hey, there. Morning." Her voice is friendly today and I relax as I walk through the door.

"Morning. Do you want me to put those over there like yesterday?" I nod at the stack of boxes in my arms.

"Yes, please."

I put them down and turn to get more from the truck. I glance at the small black notebook on top and imagine her face when she finally turns around and sees it.

When I come back in, she's picked it up and is thumbing through it. She looks up as I approach and her eyes are bright with tears, she's grinning from ear to ear. My step falters. Her smile is like a punch of liquid sunshine. I want to see it again.

"Thank you so much for bringing this back to me." She presses a palm flat against it.

"You're welcome. As much as I've loved having it, it's nice to be able to return something that was clearly missed."

She closes the notebook, rests her forearms on the counter and leans forward giving me a very nice view. A small smile playing on her lips and a mischievous glint in her eye. "I heard they call you The Legend." She drawls slowly.

I lean forward too, arms resting on either side of hers. "You been asking about me?" I ask with a smile.

Once she's put some distance between us, she rolls her eyes but laughs. "You wish. I got a part-time job at Sweet & Lo's. Some girls were in there talking about you."

"You work at Sweet & Lo's, too?" I'm surprised. I go in there almost every day and haven't ever seen her.

"Just a few nights a week. You have this whole harem that come in and do nothing but talk about The Legend on the basketball court. Apparently, you practice with your shirt off." She glances at my forearms.

"A harem?" I ask like I'm considering the word.

"Well, maybe that's an exaggeration, but certainly a good group of them." Her fingers twitch and I wonder if she wants to touch me, too.

"Oh you mean Joni and her friends. Yeah they come watch me play every day." She steps back from the counter and moves her arms.

"That sounds like a total waste of time, to me." She tosses her head and stalks around the counter, her nose tipping up as she approaches me like she intends to pretend she doesn't see me standing there.

I nudge her with my shoulder when she walks past me. "Come on… you know you want me to show you. I look really good with my shirt off."

She laughs at me. "Wow… I guess you believe your own hype?"

"It's not hype. It's all true."

"Okay. Then tell me. Besides those girls, who else calls you the Legend?" She cocks her hip and crosses her arms, this time like she's prepared to wait as long as it takes for me to think of an answer.

I went through a phase where I doubted that I deserved that nickname. But I don't anymore. I've earned it with sweat, tears, time, and pain. So, I shrug.

"Everyone… I'm the baddest basketball player my school has produced in thirty years."

"I guess if you go to school around here. I mean, can't imagine the competition is that steep or anything. How do you do when you play the kids at Yates?"

She mentions the high school that was our biggest rival. "You must not follow basketball. 'Cause if you did, you would know we've beaten them every game we've played."

"I bet you kiss your biceps in the mirror, too." She quips with an amused scoff.

"You'd kiss them, too if you could see them." I flex one arm and she laughs.

She glances at the clock on the wall. "Oh, shit, look at the time, I gotta get this done. We open in an hour." She turns to the shelf, pulls a stepladder up and grabs some books.

"Here, let me." I put my hand out, and she stares at it for a second and then back at me. "What?"

"You're gonna help me?" She leans back; eyes me up and down in disbelief.

"Why not?"

"Don't you have other deliveries to make?"

I glance at the clock. I'm ahead of schedule. I was going to go by Sweet & Lo's before I went back to the store, but I'd rather stay here and talk to her.

"You're my last delivery and I have a little time."

"Well, that's nice of you. Thank you," she says and for the first time since I walked in, there's no mask. There's no smirk, there's no teasing. It's a sincere thank you and it makes me feel really fucking good.

"So, The Legend, huh? You're good at everything?"

"Pretty much." I shrug. I'm not bragging. It's true.

"What's everything? Besides basketball?" She takes the book from me and sticks it on the shelf.

"I'm a good student."

"That's it?" She frowns, unimpressed.

"What else is there?"

She groans. "What else is there? Everything, that's what," she says with an incredulous smile on her face.

"Well, ask away, and let me prove it to you."

"You a good dancer?" she asks.

"Of course." I drop down and show her my best break dance spin and hop up with a grin and wink.

She shrugs. "Basic."

I clutch my chest like she shot me through it.

She chortles with amusement. "Can you cook?"

"My mother is Jamaican, I can make curry stew in my sleep."

"What other sports do you play?"

"I'm a natural athlete. I'm good at them all. Basketball is the one I love."

"What about roller skating?"

"Roller skating?" I give her a side eye. "Come on. What are we? Six?"

"What does that mean? Roller skating is the shit, and it takes a lot of skill."

"Whatever. That doesn't count 'cause, like we established, I'm not six."

"Well, it counts to me. So how about this? We just call you The Legend of all the boring things."

"Who are you calling boring?" I ask in mock affront

"You." She raises her eyebrows in challenge.

"What do you do for fun that's so exciting?"

"I read, and write, and try to find ways to get my favorite books signed. In fact, I checked out the website for the bookstore you mentioned. Andre Dubus is coming there tonight. I want to get my copy of *House of Sand and Fog* signed and find out about the group you told me about yesterday."

"Who's that?"

"He's just my favorite author. It's his first book, and it's amazing and he's kind of my hero. Worth riding my bike all the way over there to get it signed."

She gets this dreamy look in her eyes, and I feel a pang in my chest that smacks of jealousy.

"I can take you." I find myself saying before I think better of it. I promised my grandfather this is the last thing I would do. But, that was before I knew it was the girl from the library. I've been waiting years to spend more time with her.

She blinks in surprise. "You don't have to do that. I'm fine riding my bike," she dismisses me.

But I'm nothing if not persistent. Especially when I'm right. "It's not close and you can't get there without crossing the 610. If you're going at seven, that means you'd be riding at the tail end of rush hour, it's kind of busy. I'll take you."

"You're bossy," she says grudgingly, but with a smile.

"Yeah, 'cause I'm in charge."

"Not of me, you're not" She shakes her head for emphasis.

"You live here now, and Rivers Wilde is my neighborhood. So, I am. I'm taking you."

She raises her eyebrows and I can't tell if she's surprised or annoyed.

"I mean… if you really want to, I won't say no. It'll beat getting there all sweaty. You're going to stay and drive me back?" She eyes me like she's expecting me to say no.

What kind of friends does she have that this is even a question? "Yeah. Of course."

"Thanks."

"Cool, well, sounds like a date."

"Oh, no," she stammers when I grin. "Not a *date* date. Just an appointment."

"Yeah, of course." I keep my expression light and fight the urge to pump my fist. "So, I'll see you tonight?"

"What time do we need to leave?"

"Be downstairs at six o'clock. I just have to run an errand for my mother right before that, and then I'll stop by."

Her smile falters and when she recovers, it doesn't quite reach her eyes.

"What's wrong?"

She clears her throat, and she fidgets with one of the books she's holding. "Your mother's made it *really* clear she's not happy about my hanging around you guys. I'm not trying to piss her off. Any more than I do just by existing."

My hackles rise, but not at her. My mother can be such a bully.

"How did she make it clear?"

"It's okay… It's just that I haven't had a place to call home… in a while. I like it here and I don't want to rock the boat. You're nice, but maybe not."

"What did my mother say?" I ask, this time firmly. She looks torn— her eyes dart away from me, her teeth worry her bottom lip.

"You can tell me," I prod, gently.

She sighs. "Just what every mother has said to her kids about me. If any of the kids suddenly decide to walk on the wild side, she'll know who to blame." She shrugs like it's no big deal.

Suddenly, I'm ashamed of the people I've grown up with. Their behavior is such a contradiction to the values we use to sell people on life in Rivers Wilde.

"I see," I say quietly.

"I'm happy you liked my stories. I'm glad you're not an asshole. It's nice to see you." She smiles and puts the books I just handed her onto the shelf.

I'm not letting her get away that easily. I don't know why I'm pushing. Houston's full of some of the prettiest girls I've ever seen anywhere. So, it's not that. It's that for five years, I've thought about her and that night in the library. It was just that one interaction, but it made an impression. She made an impression.

I never thought I'd see her again and now that I have, all of the pent up conversations I've been dying to have with her are on the tip of my tongue.

And all from that one night. What's it going to be like to see her every day?

I lean one shoulder against the bookshelf and cock my head to the side and watch her and try to decide what to say next.

She steps off the footstool and mimics my pose. "Why are you still here?"

"We're already friends, remember? We decided in the library."

"Yeah… okay." She shrugs as if to say, so what?

"Let me take you to the bookstore. I'm good company and a safe driver. I've never even *thought* about running a red light."

I reach over and pick up one of the thick strands of curls resting on her arm and rub the silky tresses between my fingers and then let go.

Her eyes are bright and her lips are parted just slightly. I lean forward close enough that I can smell the cinnamon on her breath. I can't wait to kiss her and see what it tastes like on her tongue.

"What do you say?" I ask when she doesn't say anything

"I want to ride with you," she says hesitantly.

"My mom's overbearing. But tonight, in the car, it'll just be us."

Her darkening cheeks and the smile she graces me with are sweeter than anything I've seen in a long time. When I walked in here yesterday, I wouldn't have guessed this girl had a smile like that in her. Knowing I helped put it there, makes me feel like, maybe, I am a fucking legend.

"I'll see you tonight. And maybe we'll live dangerously and speed through some yellow lights on the way," she calls as I head out.

"Let's not get ahead of ourselves." I wink at her and head out.

5

SQUARE

KAL

"God, I can't stand that stuck-up lady," my mom chirps at me as soon as she walks into the store. She never says hello. Never says goodbye. She never beats around the bush. She always gets straight to the point because according to her "time is money and no one has nearly enough of either."

I don't mind. I'm just always glad to see her.

I remember the day she walked into CASA to get me. She looked like a new woman. Her hair, that she'd always bleached blond and blown straight, looked more like my own dark brown curly mop again.

She came promising me a new life, one that we'd build together. Things were off to a good start until I got mixed up with Wes. The worst part of all of that was how disappointed she'd been. How afraid she was that I was going to make the same mistakes as she did.

"Don't know which stuck up lady you mean... but whoever it is, from what I hear, the whole *I can't stand that lady* feeling is entirely mutual." I give her a knowing look and then turn back to spray the last bookshelf with the wood cleaner and start wiping it.

"Fuck 'em." Her scowl disappears as she walks deeper into the store. "Oh my goodness, Lee. The store looks amazing." You didn't have to do all of this by yourself, baby. I was planning on us doing at least some of it together when I got back." She drops her bag and disappears down the aisle where we keep the old classics.

"I know… I started and then I couldn't stop. You really think it looks good?" I nibble my lip as I watch her walk up and down the aisles, inspecting.

"It's amazing. I'm so happy we were able to buy it." She beams at me.

"Me, too. It's small, but it's perfect. So many people have stopped by, peeked in. I think they're excited to have a bookstore again. And I was thinking, once we really get up and running, we can have signings here, too. Like the ones at Murder By The Book."

"Yes, that would be great…" She sighs and trails her fingers over the spines of the books, her eyes dreamy as she gazes at them. "Books are magic, aren't they?"

"The only kind I've ever known," I agree. Our eyes meet and we grin, big silly grins that we call our "bookworm grin." She twirls in the aisle; her dark hair flies out around her. I've never seen her so light.

"So, people came by? Excited people? Or people like that the Wilde lady who thinks she's Queen Elizabeth, and this is England?" She doesn't have the venom in her voice that she used to when she talked about Mrs. Wilde. I'm glad she's letting it go. I wish I could.

She flops into one of the two chairs we've put in the bay window's reading nook.

I sit down across from her, let the fading sunlight that's flooding into the window warm me.

"A little of both. But mostly excited people. You know… book people, who can't wait for us to open so they can get their fix daily."

"And what did the rest want? To warn us to keep our evil vaginas away from their husband's and sons?" This place, it could be home.

"Basically." We share a laugh and the tension that was building dissipates. She has bad memories of the time we were here. Mrs. Wilde's treatment of her was the first in a series of events that started her spiral downward and eventually put her in jail. She's trying so hard to make up for the early years of my life. I know coming to live in Rivers Wilde wasn't ever on her list of things to do, but we're making the most of it.

"I hope you're happy here, Lee..." she begins to ask me the question she always asks.

"I am happy." I give the answer the way I always do.

This time, it doesn't feel like such a burden on my lips. "I made a friend today," I add and can't stop the smile I feel when I think about the ridiculously handsome, charming boy who was as nice as I remembered.

"Oh, I'm so glad, what's her name?" She smiles lazily over at me.

"We're going to Murder by The Book together tonight," I respond and evade her question.

She sits up a little straighter and looks at me skeptically. "I hope this friend of yours has herself a car. I can't take you all the way to Rice Village tonight and you're not riding your bike either."

"I'm not riding my bike—"

"You need to buckle down and get your license, though, honey. You're the only seventeen-year-old in this entire city that doesn't drive." She wags her finger at me.

"That's not true. I am working on it. I just... don't know. I like riding my bike."

I drop my eyes to the frayed hem of my shorts so I can pretend what I'm about to say isn't a big deal. "Anyway, it's fine. My friend has a car. He's coming to get me at seven."

"Oh." She sounds surprised and curious. "And, who would *he* be?" She raises her eyebrows expectantly. I try to keep the nerves fluttering in my stomach off my face and say as casually as I can, "Um... His name is Remi. He was in here the other day making a delivery."

"Oh, Kal... please don't tell me you mean Remi Wilde," she shouts.

"Why are you yelling?" I ask, raising my own voice.

"Because he's a Wilde. Don't you remember how his mother treated us? They don't like us."

"Well, he likes me. He's nice," I say. I hear how defensive I sound, but it's because I know what's coming.

She walks over, her face pinched with worry and my stomach knots as I wait for the lecture.

"Listen to me. I know you grew up watching me do certain... things. But I don't want all of my mistakes and the way I've paid for them to have been for nothing."

"Mom, we're just going to a bookstore," I protest

She cups my face in her hands and searches it with those green eyes I used to covet. "You're a good girl. But so was I. I can tell you nothing changes that faster than men with sexy smiles and fancy cars. Women in our family, those kind of men are our downfall. It's in our DNA." She smiles wistfully and strokes my cheeks with her thumbs.

I pull out of her grasp. "It's not like that. He's not looking at me like that," I tell her.

But, I'm totally looking at him like that. I almost fainted when I saw him yesterday. Some things were the same. His hair is still beautifully curly and close cropped. His eyes are still so dark, they're fathomless eyes.

But that's where the similarities ended. He looks like some sort of god. He's an elite athlete and his body shows it, his face is saved from prettiness by a heavy brow and permanent five o'clock shadow on his taut, strong jaw. His lips... talk about a perfect bow.

"Give him a minute, Kal. He'll do something to show you what he wants and who he is."

I bristle a little and don't know why I feel compelled to defend him. Maybe it's the nostalgia from our first meeting. Maybe it's because he was really very nice.

"He's the only one who came in here today who didn't look at me like that. Or treat me like that. He just offered to give me a ride. He's leaving for college in the fall. He probably thinks I'm just some dumb kid."

"Girl, if that boy has eyes, he's not thinking of you like a kid."

She studies my face, and her expression grows even more worried. "I know you want to make friends, baby. I know it must feel really nice to have someone like him pay attention to you. But boys like that... they don't date girls like us. They will fuck us though."

"I'm not doing anything like that," I protest.

"I want you to promise me something. That you will focus on why you're here, not get distracted by a boy. Getting pregnant so young was the biggest mistake..." At my wince, she closes her eyes in regret.

"I don't mean it like that. I'm just saying... I was only able to buy this bookstore because I scraped and saved and then sold my house. I still have to go to work every day and clean out old folk's bedpans and earn a living that keeps food on our table until this store's business picks up. I wish I'd stayed in school. I wish I'd had someone step in to help me when I was your age. I want more for you than what I had."

I stare at my hands.

"I know. You don't have to say it. Don't worry. Nothing's going to happen. He's not like that." Her eyes turn sad and she gives me a pitying frown.

"You're still learning who you are. What you like. What's good for you. You finish school, and you can have anything you want."

"I plan on finishing school. I'm not going to get pre—"

"You won't find yourself dealing with the scorn of women who think they're better than you because they've never been desperate enough to do what they have to in order to keep their child in ballet shoes and karate uniforms. You won't need Daddies to make your Christmas special."

My stomach twists when I think about the parade of Daddies she brought through our lives. And how, in the end, it was her downfall. But, it also turned out to be my redemption. She was grooming me to live the same life she did. Getting arrested, being in jail all these years has helped her see the light. "Be better than me, Kal."

There's a knock on the glass-paned door and we both turn to look. It's Remi. He waves and points at his watch. I flash him a smile and put my hand to let him know I'll be right out.

"You be careful. And you better be home by nine o'clock. It may be summer, but you've got work to do."

"Okay." I smile and agree with a nod. "Do you want to meet him?"

"Already did, remember? You go ahead. I don't want you to not have any fun. Text me when you get there and when you're on your way home and if you want to come home and he won't bring you, call me."

"Okay." I smile as reassuringly as I can and then I grab her and hug her.

"I love you," I whisper in her ear.

"Not half as much as I love you." She holds me tightly then lets me go with a quick pat on my bottom.

"Be good, okay?" Her solemn tone makes me turn back and I nod and make a promise I mean.

"Promise."

I RUN OUT THE BOOKSTORE'S FRONT DOOR AND SEE THE HUGE black car idling at the curb. He hops out and walks round to open my door for me. No one's ever done that before and those butterflies I've been trying to ignore since he sauntered into the bookstore are back.

God, my mother's right. At least when it comes to *this* boy with his sexy smile and nice car.

"Hey," I call as I approach. He's all cleaned up in dark jeans and a white button down that is rolled up at the sleeves. He's wearing loafers and looks good enough to eat. I look around to see if maybe someone's lurking behind a bush with a camera, waiting to jump out and tell me this is all a joke. But there are only people milling around Rivers Wilde Main Street, like they always do.

"Hey yourself. You look great." He puts a big hand in the small of my back and leans down to press a kiss on my cheek. "And you smell great, too."

Those butterflies? I was wrong… they're birds. Big ones that just took off in a mad flock of flutters in my stomach.

Oh my.

I'm so discomfited that I just stand there.

"Uh yeah, you too." I say and look down at myself, my white t shirt and bright orange shorts, in confusion though. I've been wearing them all day.

"Hop in," he says and waits until I'm seated before he closes the door and walks round to his side. I watch him and shake my head. He's too good to be true. I'm asking for trouble letting myself get mixed up with him at all.

But…truth be told, I couldn't stop if I tried. There's something about him that just draws me in. He's handsome, but it's also that I can tell he gives a shit about the people around him. And that's rare in my world.

"We're going to be late," he says as soon as he gets into the car.

"Just a few minutes," I say trying to steady my hands enough to buckle my seat belt. I put newly discovered inner freak back in her cage and smile at him.

"A few minutes, five minutes, an hour—it doesn't really matter. Once you're late, you're late."

"Gosh, okay. I'll keep that in mind." I give him a wide eyed glance.

He smiles sheepishly. "Sorry, I'm anal about time."

"So, you're never late?"

"Nope," he says quickly.

"Not even to school?"

"Especially not to school."

"I bet you had perfect attendance, too."

"What's wrong with having perfect attendance?"

"Nothing, if you're a square," I tease him. He's fun to tease because he's so sensitive about his "coolness" and tries to pretend he's not. He takes my bait and frowns at me, taking his eyes from the road for the first time.

"I'm the least square guy I know."

"Sure." I shrug as if I don't believe him.

"Just because I don't oversleep doesn't make me a square. And I like school."

"I didn't say anything about oversleeping. I don't know... you were never sick?"

"Nope."

"Have a doctor's appointment?"

"You can schedule those around classes."

I lean back and eye him skeptically. "You never wanted to skip school so you could go to the rodeo during the week?"

"Nope. Never."

"I highly recommend it. I got caught once, but it was worth it to not have to wait in line for my smoked turkey leg."

"Yeah, that sounds like a great reason to miss class," he says irritably.

"You're just mad I called you a square." I nudge his thigh with my fingers.

"I'm not mad. Since it's completely untrue."

"It's very true. You're a hot, athletic version of Carlton from *Fresh Prince*."

He winces and puts a hand over his heart. "Damn. That hurt."

I laugh and he eyes me and shoots me a sly smile deepening the ever-present dimples in his cheeks.

"If I'm Carlton, you're Will. You know... the cousin from the hood?" He waggles his eyebrows and I know I should probably be offended, but I'm not.

"Okay, I deserve that." We laugh, our eyes hold and there's something in the way he's looking at me that sets those flutters loose inside me again.

God, he smells so good. I glance over at him and put on my best I don't care at all face, but inside the butterflies have multiplied.

He turns on the radio and I turn and pull out my notebook and open it to the spot where I stopped last night.

"I can't even read in a moving car; how can you write?" His question comes when I'm only two sentences in. I give him a sidelong glance. He's watching the road. His profile is a study in perfection and suddenly, I wish I could draw because I'd like to capture him right now when he doesn't know he's being watched and he doesn't have that cocky smirk on his face.

When I take too long to answer, he looks at me and smiles.

"Yeah, I know. I have the same problem every time I look in the mirror. It's pretty damn breathtaking."

"Ugh, okay, Carlton," I joke and when his eyes dart toward mine in surprise, I laugh out loud.

"Whatever. What are you writing, Will?"

"More happy endings."

"You started again?" He gives me a knowing smile.

"I forgot how much I enjoyed it."

"Tell me yours... the one you wrote," he says.

"No, it's silly."

"Tell me," he says softly, but his voice has a demanding edge to it. I don't know why, but it excites me.

I trail my fingers over the words I've just scribbled and can't help but smile at them. I'm not good at anything but this. Everything else, cooking, drawing, singing, talking to people, cutting out snowflakes, I just get by. But when I have a pen in my hand and a piece of paper under it, and a set of inconclusive facts to pore over, I know why I was put on this planet. I close my notebook and look at him.

"My happy ending is me living somewhere I can see the stars. I've never left the city. I've never seen a *really* starry sky?"

"Really?"

"Nope. Never."

"And what are you doing in this place where you can see the stars?"

"Playing with my kids, sitting next to my husband reading a book. I have the investigative journalist job of my dreams where I travel around trying to figure out something that no one else has been able to. I'm not afraid to answer the door or the phone for fear of debt collectors."

"That's a very specific happy ending."

"Yeah. I've always known the kind of life I wanted. Because it's the exact opposite of the life I had."

He just nods and we ride together in a comfortable silence until we pull into the bookstore's parking lot.

"So, you collect author's signatures?" he asks.

"Yeah, for my favorite books. I only have a couple. I got some from half-priced books by chance, but this is my first time meeting an author face-to-face."

"If you could have any signed book, what would you choose?"

That's such an easy question to answer.

"*The Legend by Ama Baidoo*, and *Where The Sidewalk Ends* by Shel Silverstein"

"That's the book your quote is from," he says. Even though he told me he read it, I'm startled that he remembers.

"Yeah, it's such a great story. It's old, but still so relevant."

"Why Shel Silverstein?"

"Because it's the first book I ever owned, and it made me feel like there was someone in the world as weird as I am."

"You keep saying that."

"When I compare myself to everyone else I grew up with, I have all these dreams and passions that are a little strange..."

"At least you know what they are." There's an edge in his voice that wasn't there a second ago. It's subtle, but I'm an expert people watcher and I hear it. It piques my interest. I close my notebook and turn in my seat so I'm facing him.

"What's wrong?"

"Nothing," he says cryptically and I feel my first prickle of annoyance.

"You've been asking me all sorts of questions. I've answered them."

He glances at me and gives a resigned sigh.

"I play basketball and I love it. But..."

He gives a quick side glance and the corner of his mouth lifts in a smile.

"But what?"

"It just feels so... I'm starting to realize that I played more out of defiance than I did out of passion. And now, it doesn't feel like the place I'm supposed to be. I mean, it's great to be good at it, but..."

"But that's not enough anymore?" I ask

"That's it exactly," he says with a smile. That smile makes me feel like I aced a quiz.

He sighs, deep and thoughtful and then shrugs again. "It's not that I don't like winning. In fact, I think I'm addicted to it. But, when I first started playing, I wasn't really that good. I had something to prove. I practiced like I'd never made a three-pointer. I played like I'd never lost a game. Winning felt like the only thing. It's what everyone expects. It's what I expect..."

"What would you do if you weren't afraid to fail?" I ask him.

"I would go to law school," he answers right away. Without hesitation and for the first time since I got in the car he really smiles. Not like the ones he throws because he's being flirtatious, but the ones he throws when he's happy. Every time I see it I remember my mother's warning about men who are so, so dangerous to a girl like me who's a sucker for a smile.

"If saying it makes you feel like that, you should totally do it."

He smiles wistfully "Between us, I'm really considering it. Besides my grandfather and my father, Thurgood Marshall is my hero. I read his biography in my freshman year history class and his story resonated with me in a way that felt like I was reading my future.

I get good grades, but studying doesn't come easy. I'm not the smartest kid in my class, but I've got the highest grade point average because I work twice as hard as everyone else. Just like in basketball, but this... it's all for me." A muscle in his jaw jumps, but because he's pulling the reins on his smile.

I feel chills just listening to his honest assessment of himself and his passion. I want that, just a little bit of it, for myself.

"Is it weird that part of me wanted to play just so I could have something that hadn't been his, too?"

"No. Especially if you feel like you've been chasing his shadow."

"I don't know if I've been chasing it or..."

"Running from it?" I finish his sentence for him and then apologize because I realize I have a habit of it.

"Why are you sorry? I like that you get me." His eyes linger longer this time and heat rises up the back of my neck. He looks back at the road, a satisfied smile on his face and I want to ask him to look at me again.

I bite my lip to hide my smile. "My mother has been a shadow I've been trying to climb from under forever. I love her. But being like her is the very last thing I want to be."

"I should want to be like my dad. He died so young; I pray that in that way at least, we're very different. And... this is going to sound terrible. But I don't know if I want to be the kind of man who marries a woman like my mother." Then he winces like he wishes he could take it back.

He pulls into a parking spot outside the bookstore and throws the car in park before he turns to look at me. "Let's table this for later, okay?"

"Deal." I put out my hand to shake his. He takes it and as soon as our hands touch, my whole arm starts to vibrate. Our eyes hold where they are for a few seconds, suspended in a conversation that doesn't need words. His eyes release mine, but only so that they can roam my face. I feel his gaze as it skims down my nose and when it lands on my lips, I lick them.

"That freckle, when you lick your lips, can you feel it? Or is it flat?" His voice is gruff, his eyes on my mouth and full of something that appears close to desperation.

My racing pulse pounds in my ears and I lick the spot he's talking about.

He starts to lean forward and the look in his eyes reminds me of the promise I made my mother just tonight.

I pull my hand out of his and fumble for the door handle.

"All right, Carlton, let's get in there so we're not late," I quip, open the door and hustle away as fast as I can.

6

GO AHEAD AND TOUCH

REMI
FOUR WEEKS LATER

"COME ON, REMI, HURRY. THE LINE IS ALREADY ALMOST OUT THE door," Kal yells at me through the passenger door of my black Camaro. She's leaning down and her blouse, which is already dangerously low cut, is giving me the most tempting view of her perfect tits and the lacy bra that's practically pushing them in my face.

"Eyes here, Remi." I look up into her scowling face. I'm starting to really like that scowl. A lot.

"You go ahead, I'll catch up." I smile up at her.

"Catch up? We're already late. What're you doing?" She starts to get back in.

I put a hand on her seat to stop her. "No, go ahead. Grab seats for us. I want to park somewhere else."

"I'll come with you," she says.

"No, I need privacy," I say and she stops and glares at me as she climbs back out.

73

"You want to call one of your girls before you go in? Make sure they know what time to be ready for you tonight?"

"Your jealousy is out of control. Just admit you want me." I say dryly.

"I don't want you." She laughs like she always does when I flirt with her. "Besides, don't you have enough girls in your harem?" She asks with a smirk.

"The only one I want's not in it. So, no." I don't smile this time,

She throws her head back and chortles. "Do any of these girls ever actually speak to you? Because I swear, your pickup lines are the worst, ever."

"You've got jokes today. Close the door. Now. I don't want to be later than I'm already going to be," I say sharply and her smirk disappears.

"I was just joking. Fine, bye." She scowls and then slams the door.

I pull into the alley behind the bookstore, lower my seat, and wait until she's turned the corner before I unzip my pants and start to stroke my dick.

When I got my windows tinted, it was because I loved the way it looked. Little did I know they'd come in handy when I woke up as a complete pervert two weeks ago.

I sigh in relief and ease into a stroke. I don't feel like rushing now. I don't care if I'm late.

I've lost my fucking mind. I don't even know who I am anymore. The last month of getting to know Kal has made me crazy. Between my deliveries to the store in the morning and what has turned into a standing Tuesday night visit to this bookstore, I've found myself in a real quandary.

Because, with every conversation, I like her more. I like that she pushes back on my shit. What I don't like is the way I want her. It's harder and harder to pretend it's cool just being her friend.

She likes me, but she's made it very clear she wouldn't touch me with a ten-foot pole and that my ten-inch pole will never touch *her*.

She slid into my car dressed in that red T-shirt she's always wearing stretched across her perfect breasts. And her tiny little shorts that left most of her legs bare to the world. I am a sucker for those legs and that perfectly round ass and that face. And her laugh. And her smile. And the way she talks with her hands and the way she chews her lips—those lips that are always bare and that I want to kiss—when she's writing.

And the way she fucking breathes.

We've formed a really easy friendship over the last couple of weeks. She's even made friends with Regan who's come with us to Murder By The Book a couple of times. She's smart and has an opinion on everything. So, I ask her for it—often. Even her glasses, which she only wears to read, turn me on.

She thinks I have a harem. I don't. A few of the girls in Rivers Wilde show up everywhere I am. But, I never touch them. Heir to a fortune, a basketball prodigy and political science aficionado and the picture of discipline. I don't dip my pen into just anybody's ink pot.

I've fucked before. But she was older than me and she went off to college a couple of months later. I see her when she's home, and she always teaches me something new. But, besides her, none of these girls in Rivers Wilde have made me feel like going to the trouble of dealing with dates and shit.

Until Kal. The girl who laughs in my face every time I think I'm being charming.

And fuck, I love it. She's turned me into a rutting fool. I wake up grinding my hips into my mattress because I have endless dreams about her. She's a living breathing wet dream that was custom built just for me. I can't get her out of my mind.

I speed up my hand. I close my eyes and instead of thinking of all the reasons I can't have her; I think of all the reasons I want her. I start with those thighs and that ass. And the sliver of smooth skin her shirts always manage to reveal.

She only ever wears just enough clothing to cover the essentials. So much of her smooth, caramel skin, complete with that glow is always on display. I think about fucking her in my car on our last day together and making her say sorry for teasing me all summer long.

That thought sends me over, and I throw my head back and groan and lift my shirt so my cum splatters my skin and not my clothes.

Then, I pull wet wipes out of my console. Regan opened it last week and found my stash of wet wipes and lube. She called it my Pussy Preparedness Kit and told me to throw some condoms in there.

I let her think what she wanted. But really, it was more like my Kal Gives Me a Constant Hard On kit. And I didn't need condoms because fucking is never going to happen.

Feeling satisfied and a little less tense, I push my door open and nearly have a fucking heart attack when it hits something that lets out a yelp of pain and very familiar "Fudge!"

I look up and find Kal doubled over next to my door.

"What the fuck are you doing here?" It's harsher than I meant it to be, and she glares at me.

"I could ask you the very same thing." She steps back and her face is wrought with surprise and dismay.

"I saw you walk into the building."

"I forgot something."

We speak at the same time and stare at each other. And I can see the heat in her eyes and right away I know.

"You watched me?" I ask.

Her dark eyes widen, but she doesn't look away.

"Yes." She swallows hard.

"Did you like it?" I ask her.

"Remi," she admonishes sharply, but I don't miss the way she shifts her stance. She liked it.

"I want to hear you say it." I ask again.

She nods and sucks her fat lower lip into her mouth.

I want to suck it, too.

"You know you could have gotten in and watched up close. You could have helped if you wanted."

I circle her wrists and hold her hands in front of my face.

"They're a little small, they wouldn't fit all the way 'round."

She draws in a big gulp of air and takes a step closer to me.

"Really?" she whispers her eyes flit down to my pants.

"I would have covered your hands with mine. We could have done it together."

I let go of her wrists and slide my hands up so that we're palm to palm.

Skin to skin.

It's not nearly enough.

I'm *this* close to crossing a line I shouldn't. But, when it comes to Kal, I can't seem to help myself.

"Remi... we shouldn't." Her voice is husky and her fingers flex a little against mine.

"Yeah, probably not," I agree, but I see the reflection of my own disappointment flash in her eyes and it emboldens me.

I know I should stand down. Even if it feels like it, we aren't a good idea.

But she's so tempting. And when it comes to her, I can't seem to get a grip on my control.

I link our fingers and bring her hand to my lips for a kiss. She inhales sharply and looks up at me through the inky fringe of her lashes.

Her gaze lingers longingly on my mouth and I smile.

"Oh, Kal. We have a dilemma." I drawl.

"Really? Then why do you sound amused? A dilemma isn't generally a good thing." The corners of her mouth turn up in a small smile.

"It's a very good thing... because even though you don't want to be, and I absolutely shouldn't be, we're interested in each other."

"Well, that's the perfect recipe for an unhappy ending, if I ever heard one."

But she doesn't pull away and she doesn't deny it.

So, I press my advantage.

"I'm more of an optimist than that. Let me take you out on Saturday."

She pulls her hand away. "I can't. I have plans on Saturday. And, honestly, I'm just getting settled and there's your... mom. I think we should stick to just friends. That way, we don't make things more complicated than they already are. You're going away to school, right? So... let's just have a nice summer." She squeezes my hand like she's trying not to let me down too hard.

I don't want her to feel pressure to date me. I'm not that type of guy.

Girl says no, that's it. Even if I want her more than you want your three meals.

I wink at her. "Well, at least now you have a visual to go with all of your dirty thoughts about me."

She looks up at me with wide eyes and then does the last thing I expect; she starts to laugh. "The only place I have dirty thoughts about you is in your ego drenched dreams."

If only she knew what drenched my dreams, she might turn and run.

"Ouch." I clutch my chest in mock pain. The tension between us is gone, and she rolls her eyes and runs over and opens the passenger door.

"What did you forget?"

"My notebook," she says and then stuffs that small black moleskin notebook she carries everywhere with her in her backpack.

Well, shit. If I'd known it was in the car, I would have spent my time reading it instead of jacking off.

"You gonna let me read what's in there one day?" I ask and lean over the top of the car toward her. I squint against the setting sun and grin at her.

She blanches and says, "No. And stop squinting. It'll give you wrinkles." And then she spins on her heel and walks quickly back to the building.

"Are you coming?" she calls over her shoulder.

I wink. "Already did."

"Lord, get some better lines."

7

BITTER HIGH

KAL

"Oh, God, please don't seat them in my section," I whisper to Sweet before I scurry off the chair I've been lounging in during a lull in the dinner rush.

"Don't seat who?" she calls after me. But I don't turn around or stop to answer, I fly across the floor, not even slowing to admire the huge wagon wheel chandelier that I watch with awe every time I walk underneath it. I burst through the swinging double doors that lead to the kitchen and then peek through the small circular window cut through it.

"What are you doing, Kal?" Syd, our line cook bumps me with her hip as she passes me.

"Hiding."

"Oooh, From who?" She joins me and I move over so she can see out.

"Him." I nod at Remi and his little posse of what I refer to as his harem. But tonight, there are guys with them, too. He's dressed in a white polo shirt and jeans. He doesn't look like he's lost a wink of sleep and he's laughing like he doesn't have a care in the world as he strolls with his entourage. I want to throw something at him.

"I wouldn't be hiding from any of them if they were looking for me."

"Me neither," I mutter. I am pretty sure the very last thing Remi is doing is looking for me. The day after our crazy conversation outside the bookstore, I waited for him to come to the store to make his delivery, waited for him so I could explain about Saturday.

Instead, his brother, Tyson, showed up. He hasn't made a delivery all week. It's made me crazy to think that me turning him down for a date meant he wasn't going to bother with me at all.

I hadn't wanted to turn him down. But maybe it's for the best.

It was wrong of me to watch him in his car. Clearly he drove around the corner to be alone. But...no. Turning away had been impossible.

The sight of him stroking himself riveted me. I couldn't have turned away to save my life.

Then, the way the veins in his neck had bulged and how his mouth dropped open before he lifted his shirt and came all over his ripped stomach. I almost came, too. I should have run as soon as it was over. But I couldn't move. And then suddenly his door opened and there I was.

The girls at school have always called me fast. But I'm not. I'm as pure as the day my mother pushed me into this world and I've yet to meet a boy who has made me think he'd be worth the trouble that sex always seems to bring.

But after seeing Remi... he looked so beautiful. And his dick, oh my God, my mouth waters. I swear my brain sent a message to vagina that said "soul mate".

Because it *quivered.* Lord. Maybe those girls were right and all I needed was to get my first glimpse of a dick I actually liked. Because I am feeling mighty fast.

Sweet's annoyed, determined face comes into view as she strides toward the kitchen.

"Noooo, please don't say I'm serving them," I plead as soon as she steps through the door.

"Come on, they've got a huge party, your section's empty."

"God, no. You don't understand."

She frowns at me.

"No, *you* don't understand. You don't have a choice. Serve them or go home." She crosses her arms and waits for me to concede.

I sigh and deflate in resignation.

"Fine. But I won't be responsible for anything that happens."

"Oh, yes, you will." She walks out of the kitchen and then steps back in, her pretty face full of sympathy. "Just help them with the drink orders to start. I'll see if I can get someone to switch with you."

"Okay. Thanks. You're a doll." I squeeze her.

"No, I'm a woman. And I know how it is when you want to avoid a man." She smiles knowingly and strolls out.

I follow her and walk over to the table and keep a smile on my face as I approach their table. When Remi sees me coming, he smiles and waves. I'm so surprised by it that I drop my notepad. I hear a snicker from the table and a flush creeps up my neck.

I start on the side of the table farthest away from Remi. I can feel him trying to catch my eye and I don't let myself dare look at him. When I finally get to his side of the table, the side of my face feels hot.

"Hi, Kal," Joni says sweetly and links her arm through Remi's. I force my eyes back to my pad.

"Hi. What can I get you?"

"We'll have a double root beer float," she says and gestures between her and Remi.

"We don't have those here," I say flatly.

"Oh, that's too bad. We had the best one on Tuesday night at Fuddruckers."

"That's nice, sorry I can't help you recreate the memory," I say and Remi pulls his arm free of hers and shifts in his seat.

"Can I get you anything from *our* menu?" I ask and try to blink away the mist of tears that blur my vision.

"Sure, I'll just have a diet coke. And I'll take some calamari to start."

"I'm only taking drink orders. I've got your diet coke." Then I steel myself and look at Remi.

I want to laugh at myself. There's no steeling myself when it comes to him. Every single time I see him, I get weak in the knees. Even when he's hurting me.

"What can I get you?" I say without looking up from my pad.

"Will —"

"Excuse me, but why can't you take my appetizer order?" Joni her fake sweetness from earlier has a serrated edge to it now. She puts her hand on my arm, and I turn around to face her and step out of her touch.

I point to the girl at the other end. "She's taking those. She'll be here in a minute."

"I want *you* to take it. I don't understand why you can't."

"Joni," Remi says in a low warning voice.

"No, really. I'd like to know why you can't write calamari down on your little pad and then put the order in when you get back there." She raises her voice and I feel the eyes of the rest of their party on me.

"Joni, she's only taking drinks," Remi says.

"I can speak for myself," I say quietly. It's humiliating enough without him rushing to my rescue.

I look Joni in her maliciously gleeful, dark blue eyes and wonder why she seems to dislike me so much. *She's* the one sitting next to Remi.

I'm the one serving him.

I want to shove my little pad down her throat. But, I like this job and the extra money means I can save faster.

Eyes on the prize, Kal.

"You're right. I'll put it in." I scribble it down, smile and leave without taking Remi's order.

I walk away with my back as straight as possible.

"Kal, wait," Remi calls after me. I turn around and see him striding after me, his face a mask of determination. I pick up the pace, rip the drink order off my pad and drop it on the bar as I zoom past. I'm heading for the safety of the door marked Employee Only.

I press the four-digit code and slam it shut right in his stupidly gorgeous, scarily determined face.

I sit there for five minutes, collecting my thoughts, catching my breath, and praying for the serenity not to throw her drink in her face when I deliver it to the table.

It doesn't matter if he's here with her. I told him I just wanted to be friends. Who cares if I can't remember why now? He obviously took me seriously. She's more his type, anyway.

The breakroom door opens and I jump up out of the chair and sigh in relief when it's one of the servers.

"Is there a guy waiting out there?" I ask as she walks past me.

"Nope," she says and opens her locker.

"Thanks," I say and hurry out. As soon as the door closes behind me, he steps out from the shadows. My heart leaps into my throat and I glare back at the door. "That liar."

"I paid her ten bucks," he says and shrugs unapologetically.

"She shouldn't have done that. You could have been my stalker, for all she knows," I hiss.

"We went to school together. She knows I'm harmless."

"So basically, she doesn't know you at all."

"Why are you mad at me?" he asks.

"You disappeared on me. You stopped coming to the store just because I only wanted to be friends." I step around him.

I'm already at the bar and trying to figure out which of the trays of drinks are my order when he comes to stand beside me.

He wraps one of his big, warm hands around my bicep and turns me to face him.

"Kalilah." He puts a finger under my chin and lifts my face so I have to look into those dark eyes.

"There's no fucking way that could ever be true. I wouldn't do that." His voice is low and quiet. His eyes soft, but intent on mine.

It thaws some of the cold that's gripped my heart all week.

"So where've you been?" I ask and pull out of his grasp because I can feel people looking at us.

"They changed my schedule at the store. I wake up at five in the morning and work until one. Then I've got practice from two to five every afternoon. *Then,* I have to work out. By the time I eat, shower I'm barely coherent. I've been falling asleep by nine thirty every night."

"Oh, okay." I drop my head and release a breath I feel like I've been holding for a week.

A ring of laughter that I know is Joni's washes the temporary relief his words brought.

"Glad you made time for your date."

His eyes widen and his grin is huge.

"What are you smiling at?"

"You're jealous."

"You *wish*. You should go and sit down." I snap at him.

"Only if you promise to talk to me later."

"After your date?" I say pertly and turn my back to him and pretend to start checking my order. I wait for him to walk away. He comes and stands next to me.

"How many times are you going to count those drinks."

His teasing tone is too much because I *am* jealous and I have no right to be. But I can't help it.

"You're going to get me in trouble," I complain.

He stops laughing and steps back. "Can we meet tonight?"

"I'll be asleep." I cross my arms.

"Oh, Kal, you're so stubborn." He taps the tip of my nose before he turns and walks away.

He takes a few steps and looks over his shoulder. "But, so am I."

And with a wicked grin, he turns and walks back to the table.

8

FOOL FOR YOU

KAL

I AM NO STRANGER TO DISAPPOINTMENT. I TRAINED MYSELF AT A very young age to expect it. But, somehow, this hurts in a way that feels selfish and indulgent. Remi taking Joni out isn't the worst thing that's ever happened to me. So, why am I lying on my bed sobbing my eyes out like I'm the victim of some teenage melodrama?

The sharp rap at my window startles me mid-cry and I sit up and stare at the drawn blinds. I must have imagined it. There's no way anyone's out there. I stand up though and walk over to it.

I'm just starting to pull on the cord that opens it when the knocking sounds again. I yank it open and gasp when I see Remi perched on the trellis that's under my window. His face is covered in sweat and a grimace of exertion on it that belies the idea that he's simply floating. I yank the window open.

"What are you doing?" I yell at him through the screen between us and a quick scan shows me it's held in place by screws that prevent it from being removed.

"Your mother wouldn't let me up. We need to talk."

"About what? Your date?" I frown at him.

"As glad as I am that you're jealous, I'm also not trying to die."

"Then get down. That thing is going to break." I yell.

He shakes his head, a bead of sweat runs down his forehead. "Not until you say you'll come out and talk. Otherwise, you'll have to live with the knowledge that you were responsible for the broken leg that ended my basketball career."

"You shouldn't joke like that." I glower at him.

"I'm not. This thing is flimsy." He glances down nervously.

I narrow my eyes at him. "You've got five minutes." By the time I've started to drop the blinds, he's gone.

I slip my feet into my docksiders and run down the stairs.

"He made it up, I take it?" my mom yells as I run past her office. I come to a skidding stop and walk back toward the office. I stick my head in the door. She's got her glasses in her hand, a stack of papers in front of her.

"Yeah…" I say uncertainly.

"I told him to go home. I guess he doesn't listen any better than you," she says, her voice drips with disapproval.

"You think I shouldn't go talk to him?" I ask her even though I can see the answer in her eyes.

"You *want* to talk to him?" She quirks an eyebrow.

"Yeah," I answer with no hesitation. I've been wanting to all week.

"Then it doesn't matter what I say. Just… whatever he says, Kal. Make him prove it." She looks at me meaningfully. "You're worth the work."

I run into the room, circle her desk and throw my arms around her neck and hug the woman who is responsible for all of this.

"I love you." I know she doesn't love hugs, but sometimes, I just need to give her one.

She always lets me.

And then she shrugs me off.

"Don't stay out there too long," she calls after me as I head back out of the door.

I run across the long black-and-white tiled floor. As soon as I pull the front door open, Remi's standing there. He's wearing jeans, his white T-shirt is smudged with dirt and torn on the right shoulder.

"I can't believe you climbed that thing." I shake my head at him in disbelief, but a smile has worked its way on my face and it's so wide my cheeks hurt.

"I had to get to you." He says, his smile is just as wide, but his eyes are smoldering. "Hey, Will." He says huskily.

"Hey." I'm nervous suddenly. I didn't expect him to really show up.

"Can we sit?" He nods at the swing seat where I sit to write every night.

"Sure." He grabs my hand and links our fingers. It feels so good. I fold my fingers over his hands and hold on, too.

As soon as we sit down, he lifts our joined hands to his lips and presses a kiss to mine. His touch burns in the best way; a jolt of sweet heat runs up my arm and I wish he'd do it again. He lifts his dark, normally so hard to read eyes, and he looks at me through the lush dark sweep of his lashes.

"Joni and I—"

I bristle at the mention of her name. "We're just friends, Remi. You don't have to explain."

He grabs my other hand; his expression grows intent.

"We're not just friends, Kalilah." The timbre in his voice, him using my full name, the look in his eyes, makes my heart race.

"We're not?" My voice is just above a whisper.

"No. We're not. And it's not something we can help."

I hear that. It resonates through me like the vibrations of a ringing bell.

"Yeah, it's like we just—"

"Get each other, right?" He finishes my sentence.

"We don't have to explain. We don't have to pretend. It's just... good. I like you... a lot." Those words do something to me, make cracks in the protective layer I've put around the most sensitive parts of my heart.

"I like you a lot, too," I say.

A cocky smile tips up the corners of his lips.

"I know you do… And even though I'm glad you're jealous. I shouldn't have joked about it."

"Your mom probably likes *her*," I grumble.

"But *I* don't like her. Not like that. I did take her to get a burger, but it wasn't a date. We were working on something and got hungry. Tonight, we had a founding family meeting at the club and decided to grab dinner afterward. No date. It was a group of us."

Relief softens the tension in my shoulders. "I thought…"

"Our families are old friends. I don't want her. Not at all. But I do want *you*."

My heart is pounding so loud that I'm sure he can hear it, too. I don't know what I expected him to say, but I didn't expect this. I stare at him, eyes wide, my mouth open and elation starting to brew inside of me. Is it possible, really…

"Really?"

His eyes soften even more, and he smiles.

"Yes. Really. I mean, I honestly wasn't sure what we should do. I'm going away to school in the fall, you've got another year here, but so what? It doesn't mean we can't have fun this summer."

The way my heart is pounding scares me. This can't really be happening. "Really?"

"I kind of pride myself on being in control … but I can't control the way I feel about you." He strokes the inside of my wrist and I shiver.

"You have feelings for me?" I croak, my throat is suddenly parched.

"I have since we met in the library." His voice is deep, soft and yet his words boom inside my head.

"Me, too." I say. My breaths are coming so fast that I feel dizzy.

"And all I want right now—even when I'm supposed to be apologizing and trying to do things the right way—is to know what your lips would feel like if I kissed you."

I look down at our joined hands because I don't trust my eyes not to show him how I'm feeling. I'm sure it would scare him. That blooming of happiness, the shifting of my vision from cloudy to rosy, accelerates, and I decide to take this offering and run with it. While I gather my courage, I trace the veins that crisscross the back of his large hand and count to five.

Then, I surprise myself with my own boldness. "Well, then, why don't we kiss? Get that out of the way, and then you can finish apologizing."

He smiles. His free hand slides up my arm, a trail of gooseflesh rises in its wake and by the time he reaches my shoulder, my entire body is vibrating.

"You are so beautiful, Kal. Every single part of you." His eyes never leave mine and between the spell they're casting and the heady sensation of his touch, it's a wonder I haven't melted in a puddle. He leans forward and presses his lips to my forehead.

"This mind that is so curious and full. I could talk to you forever and never get tired of it."

He kisses my cheeks.

"Those dimples that tell me when you're laughing because you think it's funny or because you don't want to hurt my feelings and tell me how lame my joke is."

I giggle at that because as much as I bust his chops, there are times when I do laugh when it's not really that funny. "You're so sensitive I don't want to hurt your feelings…" I stroke his hand.

"I'm not sensitive, but fuck if you're not so damn sweet."

"No, I'm not, Remi."

"I think you are." He leans forward and I close my eyes. He drops a kiss on my eyelids. "These eyes that see things most of us miss and are the windows to every single one of your thoughts." He presses our foreheads together. "I'm sorry I put hurt there tonight."

My heart races so hard but I can't speak, my throat is clogged with emotion. No one has ever spoken to me like this.

"And these lips, that fucking freckle. They're a work of art and I'm a little scared of what will happen when I finally kiss—"

I lean forward and press my mouth to his. His lips are beautiful, too. They've got a deep bow on the top and are full and lush on the bottom and I've been dreaming about kissing them.

He groans and cups my face with both hands, holds me there and kisses me like no one has and I suspect no one will again. I've imagined this. I've dreamed of it. I thought I knew what it would feel like. But this… Remi's kiss… It feels like coming home and going on an adventure all at once. Safe and reckless. Weightless, but so firmly rooted to this moment. And when he runs his tongue over my lips, I open for him.

"So fucking perfect," he murmurs before his warm tongue slides into my mouth. I moan and slide closer to him until I'm nearly in his lap. I clutch at the front of his shirt and hold on while his mouth shows mine what a kiss is supposed to feel like.

Behind my eyes, a million points of brilliant light explode, and I hurtle through time, space, and at the same time, I remain grounded, held in place by the gravity of his kiss. It's not my first one, but it's the first I've felt all the way to my toes. And I know, I will never forget it.

His hands grab my waist and he lifts me up and puts me down so I'm straddling him. And the kiss changes. It's feverish, my hands go from clutching to tugging, his hips ruck up into me, his erection presses against the softest, hottest part of me and I start to ache.

"Remi—" I break the kiss and try to catch my breath.

"I need more," he growls and his lips drag across my jaw, sucking and biting. I whimper, sigh, and hold on for dear life.

Suddenly the lights on the porch flash and my mother sticks her head out of the door. Remi breaks our kiss and pulls away from me abruptly.

"You're outside our place of business, Kal." My mother barks and then shuts the door. Remi grimaces as he looks around and realizes how right she is. Thank goodness, the sun has set and most people are home.

I blink to clear my eyes and struggle to catch my breath. His chest heaves, too. We gaze at each other and smile.

"That was—"

"Can I take you out this weekend?" he asks, his voice is low, urgent and his eyes are hooded with desire.

"This weekend… I can't. I—" I falter because this is the very last thing I want to talk about right now.

His eyes cool and he pulls back. "Why not?"

I take a deep breath and gather my courage. "I need to tell you something. I was going to tell you, it's just—it's embarrassing. But, I need to explain."

"What, you've got a criminal record?" he says with a boisterous laugh and my stomach drops.

When he sees my expression his smile disappears.

"Oh." He says quietly and I blanch.

"No. Not a record. But, I was arrested a few months ago."

He stares at me blankly for a minute like I spoke in a different language.

I look away and use a hand to lift the hair off my suddenly very hot neck.

"I understand if you've changed your mind."

"Tell me what happened," he says quietly.

"You probably already heard. I lived in a foster home for a couple of years," I start.

"Yeah, I heard. Did something happen there?" he asks quietly. His voice is full of concern, but I can't bring myself to look up at him.

"No. I was thirteen, so it was a group home, but it was probably the most peaceful two years of my life. Not all foster care facilities are nightmares. Mine felt a lot like home," I tell him.

"So, then, when did you get in trouble?"

"When my mom came to get me, we moved to Third Ward. I started kinda talking to this guy. He went to my high school. His father owns this restaurant over on Wheeler Avenue. He's kind of a big deal in the neighborhood. I don't know what I was thinking, really. I think I just liked the attention," I admit.

"Okay." Remi takes my hand.

"One day, he came and picked me up from school and we were on our way to get something to eat and we got pulled over. He had some weed in the trunk. A lot of it. Enough to sell, they said. I didn't even know it was in there. But they took us both in. He told them it was mine. Former foster kid, my mother just out of the state penitentiary… so basically, they believed him. He wasn't even charged. I didn't get any time. I was a minor. It was my first offense. But I have to do community service."

"That's so *fucked*-up. There is something wrong with a system that doles out justice like that." He runs a hand over his face in annoyance.

"Yeah. Well, it is what it is. And I've got to serve my sentence. And that's why my mother wanted us to move here. This is a fresh start. For both of us."

"I'm happy for you. But, what's that got to do with us going on a date?"

I drop my eyes and swallow down the ball of nerves in my throat.

"My community service. I'm doing it at my old foster home. Casa De Los Ninos De Esperanza. I go Friday and Saturday nights."

"Okay. Then I can go with you."

I give him a skeptical glance. "Um… it's not exciting or fun or anything… I just spend time with the kids. Read to them, cook them dinner, put them to bed."

"I'll go with you," he repeats.

"There's a ton of paperwork. And you have to get a TB test and have a criminal background check done."

"That's easy. I can get those to you in a day or two," he says as if it's nothing.

"Remi, it's not a joke. I take it seriously and those kids, they get my full attention. It won't be like a date."

"I'm taking it seriously. And from now on, we're always on a date." He pins me in place with his eyes and I would do anything he said right now.

"Always?" I say with a smile.

"As long as you want to be." He presses a kiss to my hand. And just like that, my butterflies are back.

"Okay, I'll call Lupe, the director, tomorrow and we can arrange for you to go by and fill out their paperwork."

"Sounds great." He leans in to kiss me again.

The door opens and my mother sticks her head out.

"Kal, come on in. Remi, you need to get on." Her frown is deep and disapproving before she goes back inside.

Remi looks at her and nods and then looks back at me. The expression in his eyes makes my entire body shudder. Oh my God. Yeah, maybe my mother is right because I am totally going to give him whatever he asks me for.

He leans in, kisses me again swift and hard before he stands up.

"Night, Will. See you tomorrow."

"You're making deliveries again?"

"No, the schedule won't change," he says and I can't help the disappointment that flares.

"Tomorrow, though, I'm going to take you out, okay?"

I stand on the porch and watch him walk down the path that leads to our gate before he's gone down the sidewalk and disappears into the dark night.

And only then do I go inside. I call a giddy good night to my mom and run up to my room. This time, there's no sadness, just excitement, lips that are burning from his touch and a heart that's so full I know that when this ends, the emptiness will be more than I can bear.

My poor heart.

He's going to break it so badly.

But, I'm going to do this anyway. He's offering me a taste of something I've never had before.

I know the magic of happy endings only exist in books and sometimes in my mind. So, when it's over, I'll remember this summer as the one that brought me close enough to touch mine.

9

CASA

KAL

"Yo, come on, we're going to be late." Remi's voice floats up the stairs to my room and I roll my eyes but pick up my pace. Not because I'm worried about keeping him waiting. But because I don't want to be late to CASA. This is Remi's last time before he has to stop for the summer. He has a trip with his grandfather next weekend and then he leaves for school a few days after he gets back.

I worked at Sweet & Lo's this afternoon and he picked me up from there and walked me home. This is what we've done all summer long. Held hands, stolen kisses and recently, a little more. But we only have the weekends. Weekdays are a wash because of his schedule. But we talk on the phone every night until we fall asleep.

Summer's almost over. And soon, he'll be gone. Maybe we'll stay in touch, but I can't imagine that once he's in college, living whatever adventure life brings him, that the summer he spent making out with me will register high in his memories.

But, for now, he's mine.

I teasingly asked him if he misses his harem and he responded by putting a hand around my waist and pulling me hard into his side and pressing a swift kiss to my lips.

"Harem of one now, and everyone's on notice." I don't know if Joni is. She's still got that smug smile on her face when I see her in the town square.

I run down the stairs and hold the rail in preparation for the moment I lay eyes on Remi. He never fails to make my knees weak. He's standing there, in jeans and a white button-down shirt with tiny red stripes on it. It should be illegal for someone to look that good in jeans.

He's frowning at his watch when he hears the creak of the stairs under my footfall. He looks up, and the smile on his face makes my steps falter. "Hey, Will," he drawls in that sexy voice of his.

"Hey, Carlton. Hope you brought a change of clothes. We're babysitting a house full of kids, that white shirt will be a casualty of dinner," I tease and wrap my arms around his trim, muscled waist.

He wraps his arms around me and hugs me back.

"I want to look good for my last night. I'm going to take some pictures and shit."

I lift up on my toes and press a kiss to his cheek.

He's so sweet. Really sweet in a way I didn't expect. Our nights here have definitely been a highlight of this summer. The kids all love Remi and he's already talking about coming to visit when he's home on break.

He's gotten particularly close to one of the kids who's been there since I was. Carlos is severely disabled—cognitively delayed, deaf, and confined to his wheelchair by a palsy that means he'll never walk. But he practically radiates with joy whenever he sees Remi.

I'll be sad for him once Remi's gone.

Sad for myself, too.

He closes the door he opened for me and walks around to the driver's side. I admire him as he goes. He's so handsome, his profile is chiseled perfection, he has cheekbones I would kill for and his skin is the nutty light brown perfection I've only ever seen on the inside of the acorns that fall from the trees in the yard of our old house.

He starts the ignition and buckles himself in before he reaches across and buckles me in, too. When he does, I slip my hand around his neck and he growls slightly before he takes my lips in a kiss that we've both been needing since he got to the house. Our lips suck and nip at each other before he pulls back, trails kisses up my cheek.

Every time we kiss, I feel weightless. Like if he wasn't holding onto me, I'd defy gravity and fly away.

"I missed you, Will," he whispers when his ear comes to rest on my ear. His hands caress my shoulder and I nestle my face into his neck and take a deep breath. He smells like soap and the cinnamon candy he's started eating, too.

"Missed you, too, baby." I kiss his throat and wrap my arms around his shoulders and hug him.

"I want to take you somewhere special tomorrow, but you need to come to my house."

"Your mother is not going to let me spend any time in your house."

"Let me worry about that." He says it so easily. I'm not convinced, but I smile because I don't want to do anything to dim the light in his eyes1

"Okay... I can't wait. Even though, really, I can because it means you're leaving."

He gives me an enigmatic smile, like he's got something to say but doesn't quite know how.

"What?"

He pulls away from the curb and we begin the scenic drive out of River's Wilde.

"You know... Georgetown has a Creative Writing program."

"That's nice..." I say not making the connection.

"Well, maybe you should apply."

"Why Georgetown? I don't know anyone in DC."

"You'd know me," he says and I do a double take.

"Remi, last I checked, UT is in Austin."

"You're correct on both points. But... I applied to Howard. I got in. I think I'm going to go."

I blink at him. I'm not surprised that he wants to go. But I'm shocked that he's actually going to do it.

"You are?"

97

"Yeah." His voice is full of so much wonder that I know he's surprised at himself, too.

"What about your mom? Your grandfather?"

He sighs deeply, his brows draw together and then, he shrugs. "This summer, I've had so many signs that this is the right thing. But volunteering here has really solidified it for me. And Lupe's told me so much… The stories of how some of the kids end up there. How some of the kids enter into the system and then for lack of a good advocate end up right back in situations they've just escaped from. Or end up aging out and having nowhere to go because no one's helped them plan. I don't know, but Kal, there's something about the idea of stepping into that breach, of doing something to change their outcomes, that strikes a chord with me. It resonates the way reading Marshall's biography did. I want to make a *real* difference. I have so much, what good am I if I don't give something back?"

I put my hand, upturned, on his thigh. His slides his hand onto it and we link fingers.

"You're wonderful." I beam up at him, and the last sliver of sun as it falls from the sky slides across his face just then. His eyes, which are normally as dark as the night sky are set ablaze by it.

In their fire, I see all of the happily ever afters I thought wouldn't be mine.

God, how I want to be *his*.

He cups my face in his strong cool hands. "You're the one who introduced me to CASA. If I'm one hundred percent honest, this started because I wanted to spend time with you."

"I knew it."

"Of course you did. You've known me from the minute we met. We're the same, you and I." My heart is racing so fast, each word bringing me closer to total annihilation. And I'm so here for it.

"And now?" I breathe up at him. My eyes firmly on his lips.

"I love their mission. When Lupe started listing all of their issues, I immediately started thinking of solutions. And one of the most important ones is strong advocacy. I could do that."

"Then you will." I'm so proud of him. He's got such a big heart.

"Because of you, I will. Thank you for this summer. I can't remember a better one." He presses a kiss to my lips then starts the car.

We don't speak much on the way. At times, the car is completely silent. But on the inside, a cacophony of sounds echo and they're all clear, melodious, and beautiful.

We're special.

Him and I.

Since the night we met in that library, we've been a part of each other. I can't believe that this man, who just a few weeks ago felt so far out of my grasp, is right here, putting himself in the palm of my hand. I hope I never have to let him go.

REMI

"So, how was it?" Liz, the house mother asks, a small smile playing on her lips as she tries not to laugh at me. I don't blame her. I look like I ran through a rainstorm of spaghetti sauce. My shirt and jeans are covered in it.

"It was fun. Carlos and I finally convinced Kal to watch *Finding Nemo* with us." She called it her favorite missing person story of all time —complete with a happy ending.

Liz smiles at me, her eyes much brighter than they had been when we first arrived. I can imagine the night of our visit does her a lot of good. There are only three children in the house at once, but it's got to be emotionally draining for her and the other "house mother".

"Remi really liked the spaghetti," Kal teases and tugs at the hem of my shirt.

"Carlos likes to throw it. I'm going to miss him," I tell them and Kal slips an arm around my waist and gives me a comforting hug.

Liz smiles sadly. "He'll miss you. He's such a sweetie. His sister is in the house a few doors down and he misses her. This house isn't licensed for anyone over the age of seven. So, we've had to separate them. I hate it. But I hope we'll find a joint placement for them soon."

I think about that little boy, he's almost completely incapable of communication. But he understands love and receives it with open arms. Then he gives it right back. This experience has been one of the highlights of my life.

"All right, you two. See you next week."

"Oh, no. I'm leaving for school, I won't be here next week."

"Yes. Of course. And Lupe told me about your donation. It was so generous."

"What donation?" Kal pipes up curiously.

That wasn't information that was meant to be shared. I smile at Liz and then turn to Kal.

She smiles at me like she just heard I cured cancer. It feels so good to have her admiration. So good, in fact, I wish I could bottle it up and find a way to tap into it all the time. I've always volunteered. But there is something about being here that makes me want to do so much more than that.

Kal used to live here. They gave her a safe place to live and the work they do here is remarkable and selfless. When I look at the kids here and reconcile that with the fact that she'd been one of them, I know that all any kid needs is a chance and a system that works for their benefit.

"It was nothing. They wanted to upgrade their computers and software, so I got a friend at HP to hook it up."

Liz scoffs.

"He's being modest. He wrote a check so that we could buy the house from the landlord we've been renting from."

Kal's jaw drops. I groan inwardly, I could have done without her knowing.

"It's ours. Free and clear and having that monthly expense gone means we can add another location. Serve more children. Bless you, Remington. And you, Kal, for bringing him to us."

"You're welcome," we say in unison and I slip an arm around her shoulder. That also happens a lot. We are so in sync. Have been since that night in my father's library. She's so easy to talk to. So open, honest, and her mind is so expansive. And she... she is fucking impressive.

We bid Liz good night and walk out into the humid, but pleasantly fragrant evening and start the walk to my car.

"You hungry? Let's head down to Twist and get something to eat."

"I could eat. And I love that place. But, first, I want us to find a place where I can thank you for doing what you did." She leans against my car and smiles up at me. I reach up to brush at the thick lock of curls that's fallen on her forehead off her face.

"It's a special place. When I wrote that check, I was a little ashamed. My car costs more than what I gave them. I can't wait until I can do more," I murmur while my fingers trace the line of her cheekbone and down to her jaw to tap on her chin.

"Me, too. I can only give my time. But if I could do anything, it would be to take care of Carlos. Make sure that even if he's never adopted, he always has a home."

I stare at her and mark this moment as one I won't forget it. This is when my feelings for her turned from mere attraction, respect, admiration, and desire to something more.

10

EVERYTHING

REMI

"I don't like that girl." My mother issues her indictment from the table where she's reading her newspaper.

"That's shocking," I return dryly without turning around.

I can't take my eyes off the vision walking toward me. She's wearing a dress, it's bright yellow with thin straps that are both sliding off her bronze shoulders as she strolls up our drive and toward the front of the house. The breeze picks up the dark cloud of curly hair and it bounces and sways with each step she takes.

Her face is half covered with huge sunglasses so I can't see her eyes. But I know they're sparkling because she's wearing a smile that outshines everything around her.

I've made a total fool of myself for her this summer—taking her flowers, waiting for her outside work, buying her bags of that cinnamon candy she loves. I even painted her toes last week.

I've loved every second of it. Even the uncertainty of what we'll do when I leave for school hasn't been able to put a damper on us.

My mother's constant complaining about me seeing Kal hasn't done it either. For once in my life, I don't care if she's happy with my choices.

I love talking to someone who doesn't think it's crazy that I want more than fame and fortune.

She's a quiet storm that rolled into my life just when I needed her. And instead of bringing destruction, she watered seeds that had been dormant inside of me for a long time

Now, my convictions about my own life are taking root... Right alongside my feelings for her.

"Remi. I'm talking to you." My mother's sharp reprimand brings me back down to earth.

I turn to face her. "What did you say?"

She huffs in disappointment and closes her paper. "You've got a semester and season ahead of you that are going to be very jealous mistresses of your time. The last thing you need is to be trying to maintain a relationship with her. And don't forget sweet Joni. She won't wait forever. I'm just grateful she can see this dalliance for what it is."

"It's not a dalliance," I say firmly.

She raises an eyebrow before she frowns.

"It *can't* be anything else, Remi. Finish sewing your wild oats, and make sure you're discreet about it. She's nothing like Joni. Or anyone I'd approve of."

"Nothing like Joni," I say and move to the door and watch her stop to talk to old Mumford, the gardener.

I want to tell my mother how "sweet" Joni's been offering her pussy to me for two years and see that knowing look on her face disintegrate. But she's easier to manage when she thinks she's right.

This issue with Joni and I, however, is a nonstarter because *we're* a nonstarter. She's a nice girl. But, I'm not interested in dating someone just because it would be good for my family.

Kal throws her head back and laughs at something Mumford says and I watch the nearly seventy-year-old man pull his cap off and hold it to his chest like he's pledging his love. She waves at him and continues down the long drive toward me.

No, she's nothing like Joni or anyone else I've met. She's got a wildness in her that's contagious. Her imagination is full of magic that's more than a cheap trick of the eye and she's got a beauty so distinctive that I know I could travel the whole world and not find anyone who reminds me of her.

I think about my grandfather's warning and I know he was right. She's a siren whose call is pitched perfectly for me.

Her face is coming into focus and I find myself eager as a puppy to get outside and get even closer.

"Remi, I mean it. Remember your goals. Don't get sidetracked."

"My goals? Or yours?" I mutter under my breath.

"Don't be cute." Her voice is cutting and sharp and she stands up from the table as if looking up at me while she scolds me takes some of the sting out of it.

In truth, there's no sting in it at all anymore. Any compliance from me is for my sake, not hers. I just let her think she can still intimidate me as a sort of indulgence.

"Be careful. Don't go catching feelings," she calls after me as I open the door and step out onto the porch.

Too late.

"I'll see you later," I call as I walk out the door.

I cross the driveway to close the distance between us. The small brown paper-wrapped parcel is tucked into the back of my jeans. I want my hands free so I can touch her.

"Hey, what's up?" I ask as soon as we're close enough to touch. I have to restrain myself. I want to slide my fingers through her hair and kiss the soft pink center of her lips.

I settle for just gazing down at her beautiful face.

I frown at her.

"You're not supposed to frown when you see me." Her lips pucker in disapproval.

I lift her sunglasses off her nose.

"Nah, not frowning at you. I just wanted to see your eyes." She smiles and bats her eyelashes, in that way she does whenever I pay her a compliment.

Her eyes are my favorite thing about her. At first glance, they're a deep dark brown. But when the sunlight catches them, they glow an amber that I swear would rival the actual gemstone. I can't resist placing a kiss right at the turned-up edge of her left one.

I know my mother's watching from the window and I don't want to give her a show.

Or ammunition.

Kal, knowing nothing of my mother's hard-eyed stare, lifts up on her toes and I feel that tingling start. Every time her lips are in proximity to mine, they wake the fuck up. She never wears any lipstick or even Chap-Stick. Her lips are always naked and they're smooth and full and so fucking beautiful they're practically begging to be kissed.

And I can't deny my lady anything. I lean down and take a taste of her bare-naked lips. They're the essence of her. Soft, strong, and they need absolutely zero enhancement to make them stand out.

I start to pull away.

"Remi."

She cups my neck and holds me in place and deepens the kiss. I could do this forever, but I can feel my mother's eyes burning into my back. I break the kiss.

"Your lips are the sweetest things I've ever tasted. I plan on kissing them as much as you'll let me until I leave for school."

"So why are you stopping now?" She pouts and pulls me back.

I pull away again. "My mother is inside watching everything we do from that window." I jerk my thumb over my shoulder.

"She is?" She stands on her tiptoes and peers in the direction I'm pointing.

"Yes."

"She knows we're dating, right?"

"Yeah, but…" I trail off and hate that this is even a conversation.

"She doesn't like me much," she says.

I feel like shit that she knows my mother's not a fan. It's so bitchy and childish of her and I'm embarrassed that she's acting this way.

"Ignore her. She's just miserable."

"She doesn't seem miserable to me. Just kinda… mean."

"She's mean, too. Come on, let's go." I pull her toward the side of the house.

"Go where?"

"We're not going over there today." I sling an arm over her shoulder and lead her away from the little gazebo on the other side of our property where we usually sit in the evenings. She slips an arm around my waist before I can stop her.

"What's this?" she asks tugging the little package out of my pants and pulling it up and holding it in her hands.

"Oh, just a little something I got you." I smile down at her. I feel pleased as a motherfucker that she's smiling like that and hasn't even opened it. I snatch it back from her and tuck it under my arm. "I want to give it to you. Later."

"Why later? What's wrong with now?" She ducks her head around me and reaches for it.

I move it out of her grasp. "Nothing, it's just that I have plans for us."

"Plans? Like what?" She stops and crosses her arms over her chest. The yellow cotton of her dress stretches tight over her very ample tits and my mouth waters.

"It's a surprise," I say and walk us around the side of the house to where my grandfather's truck is parked. Tonight the huge flatbed has got a small mattress rolled up in it and a stack of blankets along with some torches and bottles of water.

"You're full of surprises," she says happily as she surveys the stash when I drop the door of the pickup gate.

"You're the best surprise I've had all year, Kal. I know it's just been a couple of months, but it's been fucking amazing."

She slides those eyes at me and the sun hits them just right when she does. They turn into that translucent coppery color that mesmerizes me. She slips her hand into mine and squeezes it.

"It *has* been amazing. I don't know what happens next, but I'm thinking maybe, this story of ours has a happy ending."

"If it's not happy, it's not the end." I chuck her under the chin. And stroke the soft, supple skin right below her lip with my thumb. "Now, let me turn that *think* into *a know*.

I tug her around to the passenger side and open the door and give a short bow. "Your carriage."

She starts to climb in and I grasp her hand and squeeze her fingers until she looks back at me. As soon as those luminous brown eyes meet mine, I forget what I was going to say.

"You okay?" she asks in that soft voice of hers and a familiar stirring starts in my fucking pants. I don't ignore it this time. I've got plans for it. And soon.

"Yeah. I'm good. Just wanted to get one more look at the prettiest girl I ever saw."

She tucks a lock of hair behind her ear and bites her bottom lip as a smile breaks and I swear it feels like the sun is rising in them when her eyes join her lips in the act this time.

"You're the prettiest boy I ever saw." She leans forward and presses a kiss to my cheek; her lips are wet and soft and cool against my cheek. I cup the back of her neck and hold her there. Her breath hitches and when I pull away so I can see her face, her eyes are closed.

I lean back in and put my mouth to her ear. "I'm not fucking pretty."

She throws her head back and laughs in delight.

"I know, you're a badass motherfucker, too, Remi. But you're a pretty one, too. Accept it."

She winks and steps up into the truck.

When I climb in, I open my palm on the seat between us and she lays her hand on top of it. I run my fingers up her palm before I link them with hers. I press it to my lips for a kiss and as we drive off toward the lookout I found; I know this will be a night I'll never forget.

11

FIRSTS

KAL

After dinner, he drove us out of the city. To this park in Rosenberg where the lack of streetlights makes it possible to see the stars.

"You remembered," I whisper. My heart is so full it could burst.

"Yeah... I did. You wait until the sun finishes setting... it's beautiful here," he says and wraps an arm around me to pull me close. It is beautiful here. The truck is running and "Your Body is a Wonderland" by John Mayer is playing on repeat.

If I'm honest, I've never loved Houston. Rivers Wilde and all its quaint suburban perfection is the first place I've lived that I could imagine myself staying. Before we moved there, I couldn't wait until I was old enough to go live somewhere glamorous. Maybe Paris. Wherever it is, I need to be able to see the stars.

"Thank you so much. This is perfect."

"I have one more thing." He sits up and reaches behind him to pull out the brown paper-wrapped package I'd seen him slide into the truck with us.

"You've spoiled me so much." I nod at the bouquet of flowers laying by my side.

"Those are nothing." He nods at me to open the package. I sit up and unwrap it taking my time not to tear the paper. I plan on keeping it.

"Oh." My breath catches in my throat and I run unsteady fingers over the dust cover of the book. *Where the Side Walk Ends.*

"It's signed by the author," he says and I press it to my chest as if I can hold back the bursting dam of happiness inside of me. If I couldn't hear the music, and feel the breeze and see the stars, I might think I was dreaming.

"This is… oh, I'll treasure it. Thank you so much."

"You're so welcome." And then he gives me the best present of all.

The flowers were beautiful. This book is beyond precious. But nothing compares to Remi's smile. It lights up his entire face. The star of the show, wide, full, dimpled and sincere—it steals my breath. And he had the most perfect teeth I'd ever seen on a guy.

I am so smitten. This summer we've spent together has been full of firsts.

He's the first boy to hold my hand.

The first boy to give me a present just to see me smile.

He's the first boy to hold a door open for me.

He was the first boy to kiss me like my kisses were the only thing keeping him alive.

And tonight, I'll ask him to be my first lover.

If he'll have me.

I've stopped holding him at arm's length, but he's never tried to take us further than making out.

I suspect it's because his whole life is about to take off in a way that doesn't include me. The thought causes an ache in the middle of my chest, but I push it away. Not tonight on the most perfect day. With my dream man lying next to me under the sky that reminds me of his eyes.

I'm going to give him my virginity. He may go away and never think about me again, but I know he'll give me a "first time" worth remembering. With someone who looks at me like I hung the moon. Who makes me laugh. Who helps me believe that all of my secret dreams are actually possible. I'll never forget him.

I sigh into his shirt and tip my head up to look at him.

His eyes are flooded with the last light from the sun that's dropped from its high perch in the sky. It's going to start to set soon. I want to lie out here with him all night and see the sun rise again. "I want today to never end," I say wistfully.

His smiles spreads and the fingers that have been twirling in my hair move to my cheeks and start to write a word, letter by letter on it.

"It's been a pretty perfect day," he says as he strokes out a *M* on my cheek.

I giggle at the tickle and squirm against his side. But as soon as my thighs brush his, my giggle dies and my squirm becomes more languorous. His body feels so good.

"What are you writing?"

"Did you catch the first letter?" he asks instead of answering me.

"*M*." I confirm with a nod.

"Good, spell along."

"*I*."

"*N*."

"*E*."

I repeat each letter as he paints them onto my skin.

"Mine?"

"I want you to be," he says.

"Me, too," I admit and then push back the sadness I told myself I wouldn't acknowledge until after he was gone. "I know summer's going to end and you're going to leave... but maybe we can pretend?"

"I want to do more than pretend, Kal."

My heart thumps in my chest at the serious expression in his eyes and at the heat behind it.

I nod.

"Okay," I say and when he starts to lower his head to kiss me, I raise my face to meet him halfway. When our lips touch a moan passes my lips right before his tongue sweeps inside my mouth. I'll never get used to how delicious he is.

His tongue swipes against mine and I taste the apples we ate after dinner. I grasp his face in my hands and hold on for dear life while I let his kiss brand me.

He peppers kisses on my face, on the lids of my eyes, down the bridge of my nose, and then his hands slide under the straps of my dress and he yanks it down.

"Damn, Kal," he groans when he finds me bare underneath it. He rubs the firm, but soft pad of his thumbs over my nipples while he kisses me again. In a few seconds, they're as hard as thumbtacks and I'm coming out of my skin.

"Please kiss them," I pant. I've never asked a boy to do anything to me, but I've never known a boy like Remi. And since he showed me how good everything can feel, my body is so hungry I can't take it.

The urgency of the night drives our hands and mouths to seek, touch, taste. I spent most of my summer pining for him and I could kick myself for keeping my distance. Because what wouldn't I give to have had that first month full of touches like this.

His breathing is ragged and his chest heaves against mine when he breaks the kiss and flips us over on the pile of blankets he's laid in the truck's bed. He's been treating me like this since I met him. I don't even know how I'll go back to my everyday life after this.

I push these thoughts away and focus on the way his heart is thundering against mine.

And just when I think I'll die wanting his mouth, he gives me what I want. His first touch is a reverent swipe of his tongue on the edge of my breasts and I writhe, grasp his head, and try to pull him to my already pulsing nipple.

He chuckles

"Easy, beautiful. We have all night. I want this to be good for you," he says and then brushes his lips over the throbbing peak of my breast.

"Then do something," I pant.

His laugh blows hot breath on my feverish skin and I whimper when his tongue's raspy texture runs over me.

He closes his mouth over my nipple.

"Remi. Yes. Oh my," I cry as a storm starts to build fast inside me.

He sucks hard as his hand drifts down my abdomen, and he cups my pussy through my dress, but it does nothing to lessen the heat radiating from his hand.

"I want to taste you, Kal." He's out of breath and his chest heaves, and he grinds the heel of his hand right where I need him to. I reach between us and pull the skirt of my dress all the way up to my waist. He slips a hand inside my panties and his fingers slip into the slickness that's been spreading between my thighs since we got into his truck and drove out to this little lookout.

"Yeah, shit your clit is so hard." He rubs, strokes, and presses the little nub with his thumb. Little shocks of what I think might be pleasure—but what feels like something much more than that—spark all over my body. I grind my hips into his hand and when he slips a finger inside of me, I arch off the mattress.

He kisses his way down my body and then his mouth is where his hand is, and the wet of his tongue as he runs it up the seam of my pussy's lips is the strangest sensation.

"Don't ever shave this," he mutters as he nuzzles the tuft of dark hair that covers me.

"Don't ever stop doing that and I'll do whatever you say."

He laughs again and then he spreads my thighs. I close my eyes and drop my head back onto our little bed. He presses a kiss to my inner thigh and kisses his way up and up until...

I forget we're out in the open; I forget that he's leaving soon and I try to focus on his mouth.

But, I can't.

"Remi... are you sure you like it?" I breathe when his tongue probes me.

He pulls away abruptly and I look down to find his eyes intent on my face. His lips are slick with my wetness and split in a wicked grin.

"I love it. Do you not?"

"I do," I say hastily "So much. It's just... I've never... I don't know. Does it... taste okay?" I'm grateful for all this melanin and the way it hides my blushes because my face is aflame with embarrassment.

But I have to know.

"Hmmm... you taste great." He hums against me before he puts his mouth back on me. I lie there, and it's so quiet. I can only hear the harshness of my breaths as I clutch the mattress in search of purchase as Remi's mouth gives my body a lesson in pure pleasure.

Nothing could have prepared me for the feel of his tongue pushing into my body. For the feel of his lips sucking my clit the same way he sucks my nipples. I've made myself come before, but when Reml slips one finger inside of me and pulls me into his mouth on a long languid suck, I break apart in a way I know will leave me changed. My entire world flips and I cry out his name and call for him to save me all at the same time.

I can't tell the difference between the spangle of stars across the now dark sky and the ones I see when I close my eyes.

He pulls himself up so that he's on top of me. He presses his forehead to mine and catches his breath with his fingers fisted in my hair.

"Did you like that?" he pants and I can smell myself on his breath.

"So much, yes." I nod. He pulls the skirt of my dress down and pulls my top up and I stiffen.

"Aren't we going to… I mean, I thought we were going to…"

He stops fixing my dress and rolls off me.

"No, I didn't think we were… you're a virgin, right?" he asks.

"Yeah, I am."

He cups my cheeks and kisses me. "I wasn't going to ask you for that when I know I can't be here or give you anything more right now."

"But it's what I want. I mean, I have to lose it sometime and I want it to be with you. Even if we never see each other again, I would want it to be you."

"Don't say that. We'll see each other again. And if you're sure, Kal—I want you, too."

"But—" I ask when he doesn't go on and looks uncertain.

"Um, I'm big," he says quickly.

"Like, what do you mean? You mean like your dick?" I ask.

"Yeah." He nods seriously.

"I've seen it, remember?"

"No, you haven't, really. Let me show you. Not to scare you, but so you'll know why I'm going slow, okay?"

I grin excitedly.

He gets on his knees, unfastens his jeans and pulls them and his boxers down in one swift tug. His cock springs out, bounces off his flat, cut stomach and then points at me like a thick spear. My eyes nearly pop out of my head.

"Wow."

He fists himself and gives it a pull. "Yeah, that's what they say… that, and Oh my God,"

I laugh. "Lord save us all from your huge ego."

"Kinda hard to be humble with this cock, but I try," he jokes.

I find myself unable to take my eyes from it. I don't know why, but my mouth is watering. "Can I taste you, too?" I ask him.

He look startles and then, pleased. He nods.

"Yeah… but only take as much as you can, I don't want you gagging…"

"I wanna gag," I say and think about how seeing women do that in porn turns me on.

"Walk before you run. If it's too much, let me know by using your teeth, just not hard," he instructs as I get up on my knees and try to wrap my fist around the thick root. I'm so surprised by how velvety and warm the skin around it is, that I gasp.

"You okay? You don't have to."

In response, I press my lips to the dark, broad head of his dick and he groans. I slide my tongue across it and have my first taste of him. It's heady. He cups the back my head and I open my mouth so he slips inside of it. The slide of his soft warm skin against my tongue makes me moan.

"Fuck… okay… just a second to get it wet," he grunts. His hips start to thrust a little, his hands clenching in my hair and I feel powerful. I try my best to mimic the girls I've seen do this. I take as much of him in my mouth as I can, hollow my cheeks and suck.

He holds me in place while he fucks my face, two, three, four thrusts and then he pulls out.

"I'm not going to last long, I want to make this good for you." He reaches into the pocket of his jeans and pulls out a condom. "Always prepared," he quips as he tears it open and rolls it on his now huge, dark, hard as a steel pole, dick. I gulp and look down at myself. I feel a pang of worry that he won't fit.

"Don't worry, baby, I'll take my time. Take off your dress and lie back." He says like he can read my mind.

I do as he says and lie down naked, and instead of feeling vulnerable,

I feel blanketed, protected by the diamond-studded night sky. I can't take my eyes off it.

"Thank you for this." He parts my thighs and settles his hips in the cradle of them and hovers over me. His beautiful, sculpted face shadowed by the night and yet, in my mind's eye, I can see him so clearly.

His eyes shine with promises of a happy ending I'm starting to believe in again.

"Thank *you*," I whisper and snake my arm around his strong neck and reach up to kiss him.

His hand slips between us and his eyelashes flutter when he feels the wetness of my pussy. "Oh, Kal, you're so ready." He moves his hand and lines his dick up with my opening. My heart rate jumps at the same time as my lungs constrict.

He rests on one elbow and grabs my hip with his other hand and nudges forward. At first, all I feel is pressure. His eyes stay on me and even when mine fall closed, I know he's looking at me. He nudges forward again, and the pressure turns into a sharp pain and my eyes fly open. "It hurts," I gasp.

"I know, baby. Here… I can help." He slips a finger between us and rubs my clit. He pushes forward again, but this time, his thrusts are tiny.

He kisses me and my mouth opens under his and just as his tongue slides inside, he thrusts hard and seats himself to the hilt. My back arches off the mattress in pain and the most provocative fullness I've ever known pulls a moan from my core that pours out of me in a long keening sound.

"Yes, let me show you," he says softly and then he starts moving. He holds me tight, his face pressed into my neck, his lips moving as he tells me how good I feel, how he wants to stay inside of me. I pray that I can remember every detail.

I run my hands down his back and whisper in his ear, "This is the best night of my life."

"Mine, too…" He presses a kiss to my neck. "Open your eyes and look at the stars. They're shining for you. And every time you look at them from now on, you'll think of me, won't you?"

"Yes." And at his words, what is just the joining of skin and bone turns into something so much more.

I'm falling in love with him.

I want him to fall in love with me, too.

His hips jerk suddenly and he pulls off me. "I'm coming. Watch my face. See how amazing you make me feel." He grips my hips and drives into me. I watch his magnificent body, the shifting, flexing muscles in his chest, the bulge in his biceps and all of that beautiful skin as he moves above me.

"Fuck... fuck, fuck." He groans and moans and throws his head back and groans long and loud at the sky. Seeing his strong neck thrown back and vulnerable makes me feel like the queen of the world. And when my titan collapses onto me, I hold him close and savor feeling safer than I've ever imagined.

Even if we never have more than this, tonight was more than I've dreamed of. I'll never forget it.

REMI

THE RIDE HOME IS SHORT, EVERY LIGHT WE APPROACH TURNS green. Traffic is nearly nonexistent. It's like fate is rushing us apart.

I wish I could cancel this weekend. I just hope it goes by quickly and that we can figure out what's next.

I want to be with her. Beyond this summer. The timing is fucking inconvenient. And if I'm honest, so is she. She's still in fucking high school. My mother hates her, and soon we'll live in different cities. The odds are not in our favor, but I've never been more determined to defy the odds. I never want this connection to end. It feels really good to be so understood. *She* feels really good, in general.

When we pull up to the bookstore, I turn the car off and we both sit there.

"So, you're missing the big party this weekend?" she asks quietly.

"Yeah, it's not a big deal. We have it every year."

"Well, we weren't invited. Not surprised." She shrugs like she really doesn't care. But, I hate that they weren't included in our annual gala.

"I'm sorry. I wish I had some control over the guest list."

"No, it's okay. I don't care. But my mom does."

"Tell her she's not missing much, anyway. It's kind of a drag."

I cup her cheek and she turns her face so that it rests in my palm. I lean in and press a kiss to her lips and she throws her arms around my neck and kisses me back.

Her lips are salty and her mouth is sweet. I slide my tongue against hers and pull her into my lap. Her hips start bucking and I rock upward so she can feel what she's searching for. I hiss when my dick presses against the heat of her.

"I'll miss you." She presses her forehead to mine and we pant into each other's mouths. I squeeze her ass and grind my cock into her and nuzzle my way through her hair to get to her ear.

"I'll miss you, too… I'll be back on Monday."

"I know," she whispers in a tight painful voice.

"I want to make you come again before I go," I whisper.

"I want to make you come, too," she rasps back. She scoots back, so her back is pressed against the steering wheel. She peers out of the window. The main street of Rivers Wilde is dark and deserted. It's after ten p.m. and this part of the square closes up around seven.

I look up at the bookstore and all of the lights are off. And even if they weren't, with no sun, the tint on the windows is impenetrable.

The dim overhead lights of my car make it bright enough that I can see her. "Make me come another day. I want to focus on you." I grasp either side of her waist and pull her to me. I lean up and kiss her. Her soft lips part under mine and I taste her before I let her go so I can focus on what I'm dying to do.

"Pull down your dress. I want to suck your nipples." I say and then push up her skirt so I can slide my hands under the elastic of her panties.

My fingers glide through the soft thatch of her hair that I dream about nuzzling my nose against and in to her wet heat.

I skim past her clit and her head falls back. The long smooth column of her throat is exposed and I press my lips to it.

I slip a finger into her and my thumb rests on her clit. She crosses her hands in front of her and tugs the bottom of her dress and begins to pull it over her head.

She's bare before me and I don't wait for her to finish taking it off before I pull one of her dark honeyed nipples into my mouth. She cries out. Her hands dive into my hair and she rolls her hips and sets a rhythm for us.

I thrust my finger into her and circle her diamond hard clit while I make a meal of her breasts and in minutes, her pussy clamps down on my finger and shakes over me.

I lean back and watch her. Her eyes closed, her head thrown back so that her hair spills all over the steering wheel, her kiss-swollen lips form my name, even though she doesn't make a sound.

Uninhibited, beautiful, complicated, damaged, and all fucking mine. I told myself I was going to make her believe in happily ever after again, and I meant it. Once this shit weekend was over. I'm going to tell her that I'm in love with her. Then, I'll find a way to convince her that when it is time, she should join me in DC.

12

PARTY

KAL

"Surprise! We're going to a party," my mother sails into my bedroom and throws what looks like a dozen garment bags on my bed.

"What? You hate parties." I sit up slowly, push my hair out of my eyes and frown at her.

"Have you been just lying there like that all day?" She frowns at the rat's nest that's masquerading as my hair.

She looks at my shorts like they gave her the finger. "You need to throw those away."

I frown down at them. "Why? I love them." I run a reverent finger along the frayed edges of my shorts. When my fingers brush my thighs, I close my eyes and remember Remi's fingers skimming the same spot the night before.

"What if you dropped dead in that and that's how you were taken away?" she says dramatically. She flings my closet open and starts rummaging.

"Well, then the people at the morgue would know that I always saw the potential in things. Even in a pair of jeans whose knees had finally given up the ghost. They were headed for the trash and I wrote them a happy ending," I say with a smirk.

"Not everything gets one of those, Kal," she says over her shoulder as she shoves things around. Not even her dismissal can diminish my dreams. Maybe not everyone gets theirs, but at least I got to touch the outer ring of the constellation orbiting mine this summer.

I hop off the bed and wince when my sore thighs protest. I can still feel him there with every step I take toward the closet. I love it.

She's opening random shoe boxes and muttering under her breath

"What are you looking for?"

"Shoes. I got you dresses, but I didn't even know your shoe size and since you didn't answer the phone when I called you from the mall, I decided to take a chance on your closet."

"I didn't hear the phone."

Because I've spent the day with headphones on, listening to John Mayer and replaying every minute of last night with Remi over and over again.

"You've been in la-la land since you came floating in last night. I hope I didn't let you have too much—Aha!" She pulls out a pair of strappy sandals that she gave me last year. They were hers. I haven't worn them because I've never had an occasion to. The four-inch, pencil thin heel might as well be a "broken ankles guaranteed" sign.

But more than that, I thought of them as a bad luck omen. The last time she'd worn them had been to the party at The Wilde's estate. The night that our lives started to career downhill like a car whose brake wires had been cut.

"I'm not wearing those," I say and shake my head.

"Why not?" She looks at me with a dejected pout, her eyes wide with reproach. "They're beautiful. The crystals are gonna be so pretty when they catch the light." She waves them in the air to demonstrate. "And wait till you see the dresses I bought you. You're going to look like a princess."

"Where in the world are we going?" I eye the offending shoes with skepticism.

"The Rivers Wilde Gala. Our invitation arrived this morning." She clutches the shoes to her chest and gets a starry-eyed look about her.

"It's kinda last minute, don't you think?" I yawn and walk back to my bed. I'd rather stay home and read.

"I'm sure with us just getting here and the shop being unoccupied, they didn't remember until the last minute to invite us." She says it even though I know she doesn't believe that for a second.

"Right, because somehow they totally forgot we were here." I'm not convinced.

"I think it'll be nice, with you and Remi dating. If you show up and make nice with his family."

"It's too bad he's with his grandfather on that trip. But if he wasn't, he might not be there, he said it's kind of a drag."

"Well, he's going to miss seeing you dressed like the princess you are."

She walks over to my bed and sits down beside me. She lays the shoes down gingerly on the bed between us and grabs my hand and turns to face me. I do the same. Our gazes lock and in hers I see hope. She wants so badly for things to be different. She wants this community to be our home. The place where we belong. I do, too.

"I know I fucked-up the first fourteen years of your life. I was a hot mess of a mother." She presses our joined hands to my chest and holds them there. "But, there's nothing about my life that has to define yours. You've got everything I didn't. You're making the right choices. You've got a healthy fear of trouble and you're a heck of a lot smarter than I was."

"You're smart." My first instinct will always be to defend her.

She smiles sadly and her eyes roam my face. "When you were born, I was so young, so scared and very alone. Every adult in my life had encouraged me to consider putting you up for adoption."

"Really?" I ask, but I'm not surprised. I heard my grandmother say things like that all of the time before she died.

"Yeah. I was sixteen. Single. Your father... well. It doesn't matter." She closes her eyes momentarily, the way she always does when she mentions my father.

"I didn't listen. I knew you were going to be the thing that saved me.

You were born at sunrise. And I swear, Kal, a beam came right in the window and kissed your lips. You opened your little mouth like you were trying to swallow it. Remember, that you are nobody's victim. You've already survived a lot. Including having a shitty mother."

"You're not."

"I was. I've been scared straight. But if I had been smart, I would have looked at you and seen a future. Instead, I was looking over my shoulder at a past I couldn't change and making a mess of both our lives in the process."

Her eyes well with tears and her lips press together.

"It wasn't that bad… But I don't miss the way we lived. I like having a stable place that's ours."

She gives me a sad smile. "I'll make sure we never live that way again. I didn't grow up with someone who loved me more than they loved anything else. But, I hope, that no matter how misguided my decisions were, you know that I love you more than anything else."

"I know," I whisper.

"You're going to make it." Her brows knit together in a fierce scowl that makes me smile.

"Keep telling me that with that look on your face, I'll believe it. Thank you for bringing me here. It feels like a real second chance. And I know it's only been a month. But… Remi's special. He gets me. He never judges me and I'm falling for him." I sigh dreamily at the ceiling.

"He's a good kid. And tonight, you'll get to dazzle his family the way you've dazzled him." She taps my nose with our still joined fist and smiles brightly.

"Come on. We've got to do something with that hair. Let's get you ready for your coming out, sweetie. Tonight, we make our triumphant return to Wilde House as guests."

My stomach gives an odd turn. I grab her arm and pull her back to the bed. "I don't want that. Let's just go and do whatever most people do at a ball and leave out of the same door we came in. That would make it feel like a success."

"Oh, baby. It's going to be incredible. Maybe you'll meet some of the young people you'll be going to school with in the fall. Just in time for senior year." She shimmies her shoulders excitedly.

I smile and don't tell her I've met plenty of them at Sweet & Lo's and that I wouldn't mind if I never saw half of them again.

"Okay, so show me those dresses." I point at the bags at the foot of my bed and her smile gets about one hundred watts brighter.

"Thought you'd never ask."

"HAVE YOU EVER SEEN ANYTHING MORE ENCHANTING?" My mother grabs my elbow and leans into me to whisper in my ear. "I'd forgotten how beautiful this house is."

"It is." I realize I haven't seen the inside of Remi's house since that night, either. And then, I barely saw any of it.

I guess I'm not really seeing it now either, though. It's decorated with in an inch of its life. It's an enchanted garden come to life.

Walls of flowers divide the room into sections. Each one color themed, with its own bar and seating area. The huge room is lit by thousands of white fairy lights that are woven into the huge swaths of fabric that form a canopy over the dance floor.

The party's in full swing, a live band complete with three dancers belts out Prince's "Kiss" and the revelers are dancing and blowing kisses in time with the music. It has the feel of something out of a fairy tale, but I can't shake the feeling that something sinister is lurking in the darkened corners.

Maybe it's just PTSD from the last time I was in this house. Whatever it is, it makes my stomach feel like it's home to a flock of agitated birds.

"Come on, let's go find the food," she whispers and starts to lead us around the edge of the dance floor. I try to shake the feeling of foreboding and I tug us to the left, so we cut right through the mass of revelers. I feel safer lost in the crowd somehow.

"Why didn't we just go around?" she asks when we come out on the other side.

I shake my hips and wink. "Because I love that song. Seemed like a waste of a dance, to walk around," I lie.

"Ah, to be young. My feet are killing me now."

"Oh, mine too. These shoes are ridiculous." I wiggle my toes. In these strappy sandal deathtraps, there was nothing to protect my toes from being trod on a few times as we walked through the crowd of dancers.

"Thank God those shoes are pretty enough to be worth the pain."

"They are, aren't they?" I preen and lift the skirt of the pale yellow ball gown before I drop into a curtsey. "I do feel like a princess," I admit

"You look like one."

"Thank you so much for this. It's nice to mingle and feel like part of the community."

"I'm just glad we could have tonight." She squeezes my hand.

"Hello, ladies," a deep voice rumbles behind us and we spin around at the same time and both smile when we see David Lister smiling down at us.

"Hello, Lister." My mother leans in to press a kiss to his weathered cheek. Her voice is stiff. and she wraps an arm through mine and pulls me close to her.

"You're the prettiest ladies here. I hope you're enjoying yourselves." His gray, bushy eyebrows draw together in his trademark scowl, which is in fact, his smile.

He's been so nice to us. He's the only person in Rivers Wilde who really has been.

Given their acrimonious past, it's ironic that we own the bookstore that had been his wife's. She would never tell me what the spat was about. Whatever it was, they've both clearly gotten over it. He comes by the bookstore some afternoons and strolls the aisles and tells me stories about the time his wife spent there.

Business has picked up thanks to our themed nights and promotional events. We're having our first author signing there in a couple of weeks and we started a used section where we buy back and then resell books that have been lovingly used by previous owners.

"I've got to mingle, but I'll see you both later." He gives her hand a squeeze and pats my shoulder as he moves on. I want to grab his hand and ask him to stay. There's something about his presence by our side that's comforting. I watch him walk away and try to calm my nerves. Everything is fine.

"Oh, this is so nice, look at all the people." She points at the dance floor where Sweet, very heavily pregnant, and her husband, Lotanna, are cutting a rug and laughing out loud the whole time.

She's a bit of a hard-ass—but who runs a successful business without being that? I happen to know that at the center, is also plenty of soft. And she's let that soft be my cushion more times than I can count.

Rivers Wilde is a special place. I look around at the sea of happy friendly faces and think that maybe, after I'm done seeing the world, that this could be home.

"Ah, Morgan, Kalilah, welcome. We're so glad you could come," a voice dripping with false warmth says from in front of us.

"Tina, hello," my mother croons, drops her hold on me and grabs Mrs. Wilde's hand. "Thank you so much for asking us." She pumps their joined hands excitedly and Mrs. Wilde pulls hers out of the embrace and smiles coldly. I feel that cold down to my bones. I step away from them.

"I hope you're enjoying yourselves."

"Oh, we are. The flower walls are amazing," my mother gushes and I squirm.

"Kalilah, you look lovely," she says, her eyes flit over my dress and she gives me a stiff smile.

"I wonder if you wouldn't mind excusing your mother and me for a few minutes. I just have a few things to discuss with her," she says as if she doesn't really give a shit whether I mind or not.

My mother's grin falters, and she looks like she's not sure if she should be excited or scared. "You want to talk? To me? Tonight?" she stammers.

"Only for a moment. Kalilah, the young people are in the smaller ballroom. We've set up a small casino for you all and the band in there's playing music that's a little more contemporary."

"I'll send Morgan to find you when we're done."

I don't like the look in her eyes, and suddenly, I'm thinking I'd just like to go home.

"Kal, go on. Us ladies are just gonna have a quick gab and then I'll be back."

"Okay," I say and watch as Mrs. Wilde links arms with my mom and leads her out of the room into the large foyer of the house.

1 3

MIDNIGHT

KAL

"Kalilah, you're still here?" Fifteen minutes after she and my mother disappeared, Mrs. Wilde is back. And she's alone.

"I thought you were going to find the young people." Her cool silky words coil around me and my breathing constricts.

She's up to something.

"Where's my mother?" I watch the door for a glimpse of her dark head.

"She'll be along in a minute. I think she's using the powder room." She waves in the general direction of the hallway.

The unease in my stomach intensifies and I start to walk away. "I'll go find her."

"My goodness, you two are attached at the hip," she purrs as she gives me a once over.

"You *do* look lovely tonight. I see why he likes you." Her cold appraisal makes the hair on the back of my neck stand up.

"I'm going to look for my mother." I start to back away.

She grabs my arm. "Come, let me show you to the young people's room. Let your mother enjoy a night with her colleagues and neighbors."

She steers me into a long corridor and then up the stairs. She takes her hand off my back, but her presence behind me is heavy and menacing. We reach the top of the stairs and stand at the mouth of a long, wide corridor.

The light gray walls are bare save for a huge painting of a woman caught in the middle of a sweeping leap on the wall. Her body is wrapped in a white cloth, her arms are raised over her head and her eyes are closed in an expression of bliss. It's arresting and as I stare at it, I realize the beauty captured in the painting is none other than Tina Wilde.

"Oh, wow. Is that you?" I ask in wonder. I turn around to find her watching me, much the way I'd been staring at her painting.

"Yes. I used to be a dancer and my late husband had it commissioned before he died. Do you like it?" she asks conversationally.

"Very much. You were so beautiful. I mean you still are, but this could be in a museum somewhere."

"Hmm, thank you. It feels like a lifetime ago," she says absently.

"I've always wished I could paint, capture things like this. Never had the chance to take lessons."

"Maybe one day," she says in a non-committal way before her smile brightens. "Anyway, just go to the end of the hall, it's the last door on the left. Have fun." She stands there, waiting for me to go. I glance down the hall and I gather my courage.

"What are you waiting for? All of your friends are there."

"Okay. Thanks," I mumble to myself and start down the hall. I rub my bare arms as I walk. It's cool in the house but these goose bumps and the pangs of dread in my gut, I just can't shake.

I walk down the corridor and see all of the family pictures I didn't see downstairs. There are pictures of Remi with his siblings from when he was a toddler until what looks like a very recent picture. His twin sister looks nothing like him. She's just as striking as he is. With the same hazelnut skin, dark loosely curled hair and keen eyes—but their faces are completely different. Tyson and Remi look more like twins than he and Regan.

130

I keep moving, admiring the pictures and then I get to the last one before the doors to the bedroom start. It's their whole family. I gasp at the resemblance he bears to his father. He told me he was Irish. The only difference in their appearance is that Remi's skin is darker and his eyes are not that startling blue. It's like seeing what Remi will look like when he's in his thirties.

Then, I hear Remi's voice and stop cold. My heart plummets to my toes. I listen again, and I know my ears aren't playing tricks on me. It's coming from behind the door, but I would know that voice anywhere. He's laughing, it's loud and raucous.

Blood rushes in my ears and my eyes fill with tears. My whole body flashes hot and the cold. I wipe the tears that are flowing down my cheeks away and try to find something to hold on to. But I can't and I lean against the wall across from the door. Remi's voice, mingled with what sounds like dozens of others, taunts me.

I turn to look back down the long brightly lit hallway. Mrs. Wilde is still there. Smiling.

The horrible truth becomes clear.

This is why she invited us. She knows that Remi lied to me. She expects me to open the door and crumble. I look away from her. I won't give her the satisfaction of seeing me broken. I look down at my feet. These shoes are fucking back luck.

My heart throbs like it's caught in a vice. But, this is exactly what I expect from life. The only happy endings I've ever known are the imaginary ones I've written. I've always known, deep inside, that the legend I'd been spinning this summer would turn out to be the biggest lie of all. I'm going to confront him. Let him see that I know and that I don't care.

With that resolve, I march back to the door. I put my hand on the knob and suddenly the threshold feels like the cliff edge of my fate.

My heart is caving in on itself. My courage fails me.

I can't open that door. And I can live my whole life without seeing what's on the other side. Sure, my imagination will run wild, but nothing I'll imagine will be as bad as having the reality burned into my memories.

But, before I can turn and walk away, the choice is taken from me. The door flies open.

Loud music blares out into the hallway and standing at the door, dressed in a tuxedo, looking as handsome as the devil he is, is Remington Wilde. The boy who I let be my first. The boy who made me think he was falling in love with me the way I was falling in love with him. I want to punch his fucking lights out for ruining this.

He looks like he's going to throw up.

"Kal." His voice breaks at the end of my name and I want to cry.

"I'm leaving," I say stiffly. I'm fighting with everything I have not to give him one more piece of myself. My heart's not ready for this, I have no idea how to handle the waves of pain that are starting to radiate through me. I hold his eyes, the panic in them a weird sort of harness on my own. I start to back away.

"Kal, no. Please, let me explain," he begs, his arms out to grab a hold of me.

Then, the nail in our coffin appears behind him.

"Remi, you're the *worst* date ever. I'm waiti—" Joni's words and smile die simultaneously when she sees me standing there.

"Oh, it's you." She squeezes herself next to Remi in the doorway. They stand there, both looking down at me. If my chest didn't feel like someone was standing on it already, the smug satisfaction on her face hits me like a freight train.

I suck in a fortifying breath. "I'm leaving. It's okay."

"Don't leave, please—" Remi reaches for me, I lurch away from his outstretched hand. My heel catches in the loops of the edge of the rug in the center of the hall and I flail for a second before I fall and land with a painful thud on my backside.

I glare at my feet and the fucking shoes on them. I start to unstrap them from my ankles. My trembling fingers make the task difficult.

Remi crouches in front of me.

"Leave me the fuck alone, Remi," I hiss. I pull the left shoe off and then start on the strap of the right one.

"I'll wait for you inside," Joni says quietly, and her hand rests possessively on Remi's shoulder before she disappears.

Now, *I* want to throw up. I glare at him, let him see for a moment, just how badly he's hurt me.

He blinks and swallows hard. "Kal. This is *not* what it looks like.

Please, please let me explain." His hands cover mine and a wave of cold washes over me. I shudder and gasp.

"Do *not* touch me." I'm trembling, my heart thunders in my ears.

He pulls his hands away immediately.

"Kal, listen."

"No. I don't want to know. You *lied* to me. You didn't have to do that." I hate myself for the sob that ends my sentence. I want to scream and hit him. But I know the minute I do, those men in the suits will be here to carry me out. That's what she wants. I won't give it to her. Not again.

Once those cursed shoes are off, I use the wall behind me to pull myself to my feet. The door opens and chatter fills the hallway.

I look up in horror. It was bad enough already. But when I look up and see all of them, the crème de la créme of teenagers in Rivers Wilde… I stare out at the sea of mocking, smug faces. God how I wish those fucking fairy tales were true and that I could count on a fairy godmother, the click of my heels, or a white knight to come and rescue me.

What made me think I would ever fit into their world? I almost laugh when I take in their expertly made-up faces. I've got on a swipe of lip gloss I bought in the 99 cent basket at Walgreens.

They're real princesses. Tonight, I was just playing one.

"I'm leaving," I say stiffly and then, turn on the bare ball of my foot and start walking down the hall.

When I hear Remi's hurried footfalls behind me and I turn around with my arm out in front of me to stop him. The expression in his eyes breaks something inside of me and I can't hold my tears anymore. The flow freely down my cheeks

"Baby don't cry, I'm so—"

"Please don't make a scene. I don't want to give people any other reason to talk about me." I try to wipe them away.

"It doesn't matter what they say. They're not important. Let me talk to you." He steps up to me and tries to hug me.

I stiffen in horror and yank my body away.

"It matters to me." I point at my chest. "I wish you'd left for college without me finding out that all of this has been a lie."

"It wasn't a lie," he says from where he's standing. His expression is pained, and he's clutching his sides like he's got a runner's cramp.

"It doesn't matter what it *was*. It's a lie now."

"No, it's not. Can we just go somewhere and talk?" He has the nerve to look frustrated.

"Are you *kidding*?" I would laugh if I could push it past the lump in my throat. "Your mother went to a lot of trouble to set this up. I don't think she's going to sit quietly while you go anywhere with me. I just want to leave the way I came."

His eyes fill with a sadness that breaks my heart. I can see he's sorry he hurt me. He hugs me and this time, I let him because I know I'll miss these hugs. No one in my whole life has ever hugged me like this. God it hurts.

"Please. Let me go," I ask as coherently as my hurt will let me.

"Not like this." He holds me tighter. I squirm now because if I don't get away, he'll have his way. I won't let him make a fool of me again.

"Let me go. Or do you want to take what's left of my dignity, too?" I say in a scathing tone, just loud enough for him to hear.

It does the trick.

His shoulders slump a little and he loosens his hold. "I'm so sorry. I don't want that. I just—can I come see you tomorrow? Please." He sounds so defeated and so desperate. I hate myself for caring. I need to get away from him.

I nod.

But, only so he'll let me leave.

With his assurance that he won't follow me, I turn and walk back into the ballroom. The ground is cold and wet in places. But I'd walk over burning coals before I put those shoes back on.

My dress is long enough. So no one who looks at me can tell that I left my shoes and my heart on the floor at Remi's feet.

I see my mother from across the room. She's staring blankly at the dancefloor. Her arms are wrapped around her waist like she's cold. "Can we leave?" I ask her as soon as I'm standing next to her.

She turns, and her face is pale. She looks like she's seen a ghost. And when she looks at me, it's like she's looking right through me instead.

I don't even need to ask to know that Mrs. Wilde has had her way with her as well. She attempts a smile, but her lips don't quite make it. She takes my hand, presses a kiss to the back of it and says, "Yes, sweetheart. I've had enough. Let's go."

This time, when we leave the Wilde house, we walk out of the door we walked in through.

This time, I don't look back to see who's watching.

This time, it doesn't matter.

KAL

"Lee, wake up."

My eyes pop open at the sound of my mother's hushed voice. She's standing next to my bed, a sad smile on her face.

"You always were such a light sleeper. That's probably my fault, too."

She sits down next to me, her eyes roaming my face as she reaches up to brush a lock of hair off my forehead.

"Mama, what's wrong?"

"You're everything you shouldn't be. Everything, I'm not," she says absently. Her face is pale, her eyes red like she's been crying. I've been in my own fog of heartbreak for two days. I feel like someone put me through a meat grinder. I haven't left my bed, and I've put my phone in the drawer to keep myself from checking it for a missed call from Remi.

I haven't heard from him since that night. And the replay of that night is practically eating me alive. I feel a pang of guilt as I sit up and look at my mother. Something went down with her and Remi's mom, but I've been so caught up in my own upset that I've barely said two words to her.

"What happened?" I ask through a huge yawn.

"We're moving," she says in a monotone voice.

That clears the tiny vestiges of sleep from my brain and I come fully awake. "Moving where? Back to Third Ward?"

"No. To New York City. I got a job."

"Are you crazy? Why?" Alarm rings through me.

"It's a really good job. And I have family up there. I think we need that."

"What about the bookstore? What about our fresh start, here? This was supposed to be home."

She looks like she's in pain.

"Lister bought it back. He's sorry to see us go, but he gave me a great price for—"

"You *sold* the bookstore? In one day? How could you do that?" I look around my bedroom in bewilderment. Panic and confusion whirl around in my chest.

"It's a chance to make a clean break."

Her eyes dart to my window. "But Remi—"

"Kal, you've been crying over that boy for two whole days. Where's he been? He hasn't been by once. He hasn't called. Nothing. That says everything, don't you think?" Her voice is angry. She sounds defeated.

I *feel* defeated. Remi didn't come by. None of the names on my missed calls or texts, when I chanced a glance, were from him.

She comes to sit beside me in bed and takes a hold of the hands I've been resting in my lap. I can't look at her, though. I think I might cry if I do. And it's the very last thing I want to do right now. It's enough.

"I need to tell you something. I promised never to tell you, but I think it's time because I want you to understand."

My eyes are no longer reluctant and fly up to her face. She's staring distantly and looks like she's seen a ghost.

Dread pools in my gut. "Go ahead, Mama."

"Your father's not dead. He's just never wanted anyone to know you were his." She says flatly, with no emotion. But her words are like a wrecking ball slamming into what's left of my heart

"What?" I gasp and clutch my throat.

"I wasn't going to tell you because I'd hoped you'd never have to know. But... It's David Lister."

"*Lister?*" My eyes feel like they're going to pop out of my head. "He's old enough to be your father." I picture him with his head of silver hair. His visits to the bookstore.

"I know. I was young. Stupid. He was married, and I was his secret. And when I told him I was pregnant, he threw me out like yesterday's trash." Her voice is devoid of anger. There's just so much sadness.

"Oh my God." I clamp a hand over my mouth and don't say another word.

"I just made my way forward the best I knew how. I know I messed up, but we didn't need him. I didn't want you to know that your father didn't want you. I hoped you'd never find out. At the party, your boyfriend's mother tried to blackmail me with it. She threatened to tell you if we didn't pick up and leave town."

That hits me like a punch in the gut.

"Lister is my *father*?"

"No, he's the sperm donor who made *me* your mother. He only sold us that bookstore because I threatened to sue him for back pay of his child support."

"He's always known that he's my father?" I ask and think about the time he's spent with me.

She nods. "He doesn't deserve that title and you're better off. I promise."

I shake my head, dazed. "Why are you telling me this."

"I told you." She snaps.

"Mrs. Wilde?"

"Yes. She thinks you're going to ruin her son's future. After yesterday, I think it will be the other way around. Those fucking people. They have may have all of the money in the world. But they are empty vessels. I pity them," she says in a voice dripping with disdain.

I told her about my humiliation on our walk home. She hadn't said a word then, and I was glad. But, right now, I need answers. My mind is reeling. That man is my father? And he hasn't wanted to know me?

"I don't understand," I whisper numbly.

"It's simple," she snaps. "Boys like him don't ever take girls like you to parties like that. They don't marry girls like you. All of that is for girls who come from good families. With mothers who are all members of the same club."

"But… we were different. He made me promises."

"Clearly he didn't mean them. We're leaving tonight."

"Tonight? What? No," I cry, the melancholy that has gripped me for the last two days clears, and I scramble off the bed to stand in front of her.

"Yes," she says firmly.

"But… I don't understand." I look around my room and can feel all of the pieces of my life slipping from my grasp.

"I got a job in New York. My cousin Sabrina's going to put us up until I find us somewhere to live. I start work on Monday, I need to enroll you in school. We have things to do. I know it's sudden, but I also think it's divine timing. One door was closing, and another one opens," she says with manufactured enthusiasm.

"I don't know what to say. I need to talk to Remi—"

At the mention of his name, her patience seems to snap.

She grabs my arms and rattles me slightly. Her eyes burn into mine.

"Don't be a fool. His mother couldn't have done any of that if he'd told you the truth. It's better for you to have a broken heart now rather than live with a string of them your whole life. He's one boy. You'll meet others. Someone whose feet touch the ground. We can't play on their level, Kal. I put all of those fool ideas in your head, but in truth, you're no different than me. Forget this fantasy."

I start to sob and sit back on my bed.

"Now, pack." She points to the suitcases lined up at the door and walks out without saying another word.

The shock and humiliation of that evening have feasted on the sorrow that followed and now, I'm just numb.

She's right, there's nothing here for me.

So, I slide off my bed and start to pack my life up.

Again.

14

GONE

REMI

THE BOOKSTORE HAS BEEN ABANDONED.

The books are still there. They look like they're open for business, but the lights are off and the doors are locked.

I've been by every day this week and have finally accepted that they're gone. Without a trace. Without a word. Everyone is shocked. The square is ablaze with chatter about them packing up their car and leaving in the middle of the night. Lister owns the store again, according to Regan's intel.

I haven't been this close to crying since the night I met her.

I've never felt more frustration and helplessness in my life. There's an ache in my chest that has grown more and more acute every day.

I stroke the tiny box in my hand and shove it back into my pocket. I shouldn't have waited to give it to her. I had the locket made just last week. A *W* is engraved on the front. Be Legendary engraved on the back.

The morning after the party, I went to To Be Read. Her mother refused to let me in. She had cut the trellis down after the first time I climbed it and threatened to call the police when I started throwing twigs at Kal's window in hopes that she'd come talk to me.

I left. I didn't want to make an already fucked-up situation worse. Surely, she would calm down after a few days and talk to me.

How wrong I'd been.

I haven't slept well or been able to eat since that night. I'm sick with regret and now, fucking scared at the prospect of not ever seeing her again.

I'm also out of time. I'm leaving for school in a few days. and I haven't even told my family that I'm heading to Washington, DC and not Austin.

I haven't spoken to my mother since the night of the Gala. I blame myself more than anyone. *I* lied to Kal. But she orchestrated it so that she found out in the most humiliating way possible. I haven't been able to stand being in the same room with her.

But with every step I take away from the bookstore and toward my house, I start to look forward to *this* conversation.

"Two can play that game."

"What game would that be?" My grandfather steps into the foyer just as I open the door and I jump out of my skin.

"Stop sneaking up on people, Pops," I grumble.

"Well, I wouldn't need to sneak up on you if you hadn't spent the last three days avoiding everyone."

His voice is gruff from years of chain smoking and drinking whiskey. Yet even as he scolds me, there's a tenderness in his manner that softens the often stinging bite of his rebuke.

"Easy on the guilt trips, old man, they don't work anymore." I start walking toward the stairs.

"Remi. Come to my office." He's using a tone he hasn't taken with me since I was a boy. He's not taking no for an answer. I follow him into his office and sit on one of the chairs on the other side of his desk.

"Glad you're finally listening to someone."

"You're not the one I'm mad at anyway," I grumble and sit across from him. He hands me a small silver frame that's always on his desk.

"That's Tex Harrison, former coach for the Harlem Globetrotters and that's two-year-old you in his arms."

"You've only told me a million times."

He ignores my churlish words.

"Your father loved basketball. But he wasn't any good at it. But, he loved watching it. Did you know, it's how he met your mother?"

"No. I didn't know. Not sure I care." I hand him back the frame.

"She was working the concession at The Summit nights while she was in school. She was assigned to our box. He came home one night and told me he'd met a girl with a fire in her eyes and he thought she might be… something. I took one look at your mother and knew he was right. She would be something, all right. She had a bigger pair of balls and I knew she'd be the making of him. Or at least, I hoped." His voice is wistful.

"Still think you were right?" I ask.

He contemplates me, like he's sizing me up.

"Your father was in love with somebody else," he says and completely blindsides me.

My jaw drops.

"Say *what?*" I sit up straight and lean toward him. The weight that had felt like it was pressing against my chest eases as shock and curiosity replaces it. I hadn't expected that at all.

"Yes, when he first went off to college. Before UT. We didn't approve, and he got over her, Remi. Met your mother and got to work building a family. Because that's what men do. They don't lick their wounds." His eyes come to me then, full of reproach.

I flush, embarrassed that he's calling me out. "I'm not licking my wounds."

"You've had a wonderful summer. You've got an important year ahead of you. Focus on that."

"You sound like my mother."

"She just wants what's best for you," he chides.

"She wants what's best for the family."

"Those are the same thing, Remi." My grandfather's stark white brows raise in question.

"If you say so." I purse my lips.

"Remi… try to understand your mother. She's damaged. Your father, before he died…"

"What did he do before he died that you all talk about him like this?" I have never asked this question because I know that they won't answer it. But I can't take this shit right now.

He appears completely unmoved by my outburst. He gives me the once over. "He was my spitting image. You don't look like us. All that dark hair, those dark eyes—that's your mother."

He gestures to the picture of her on the small table beside his chair. "But everything else about you is just like every Wilde male that came before you. We love beautiful girls. We make fools of ourselves for them. And in some instances, we ruin ourselves for them. It's happened to every man, in every generation, and, Remi, as harmless as it may sound, it's never been anything less than devastating."

I do roll my eyes now. He's not prone to dramatics. But maybe his stroke did more damage than I thought. "*You* seem okay. Dad died young, but you can hardly blame Mom for that."

"Let me tell you how I'm okay. I married a woman I could live without." I look at him like he's crazy. "Nana must have loved knowing that."

"She didn't know. And I loved her. Just not too much. I had a vision and I knew everything would have to come second."

"I don't want that kind of relationship." I shake my head.

"What you want doesn't matter. What I want doesn't matter. Any woman you have to go after, steer clear of. That path is lined with mines that will explode without warning and cut your legs out from underneath you. Trust me. You've got a lot to lose. Don't go and blow your life up over a girl you just really like to fuck."

My cheeks flame at his crude language. "That's not all I want."

"Well, then I'm doubly glad she's gone," he snaps.

"Of course you are."

"Look at the Riverses. They're only one bad marriage away from having no more heirs. The woman Jacob married is a disaster. She's a shrew, and it's a house in constant turmoil."

I look at him askance. "How in the world do you know *that*? Did you cross the border of Rivers Wilde and actually go and see them?"

"I would set myself on fire before I ever set foot in those people's house. I regret like hell letting your father talk us into adding their name when we were naming this development. They just spat in our faces and live in that stupid mansion like they're kings and this is their fiefdom. Like we are their serfs."

The venom in his voice when he talks about the Rivers family never fails to surprise me. He's a ruthless businessman, but he's more of a float like a butterfly, sting like a bee type of man. When he talks about the Riverses, it's with pure contempt and a very aggressive anger that is so unlike him.

"Do you know that Regan is friends with one of those boys? That girl has no loyalty. His name is Stone of all things. What kind of name is that?"

"Oh, come on," I chide him. "Regan isn't friends with any of them."

He looks at me askance, but his eyes aren't focused. "One day, they will come and kneel and pay their respects. And the minute they do, I'll make sure they never get back off their knees again." He slaps the arm of his chair.

"Pops. Chill you're going to give yourself another stroke." I nod at his fist. He's clenching the newspaper so tightly that it's nearly balled up.

He relaxes his hold and brushes his still full head of white hair off his forehead. "You're right, and they are certainly not worth it. Lazy and lucky is what they are."

I change the subject because once he really gets going on the Riverses, he can talk for hours. I reach into my back pocket. Pull out the letter I've been carrying around.

"I need to show you something."

"What's that?" he asks and I hold it out to him. My heart thumps a little because I already know what he'll say.

He eyes me intently for a few seconds before he takes it from me. His fingers, gnarled by hard work and age, tremble slightly as he opens it. His eyes, rheumy yet with still nearly perfect vision scans the letter and he then he holds it out to me again.

"What does this mean?"

"I want to go."

"To do what?"

"It's a college. So clearly, to go to college."

"They're not even a division one school." He shakes his head dismissively.

"No, they're not. But they have a good basketball team. I'll play, but I'm not looking to go pro anymore."

His mouth drops open and the paper in his hand flutters to the ground. I bend to pick it up and sit back down on the chair and face him. His hand is covering his mouth and his eyes have a vacant look in them.

"You've always wanted to play. You love basketball."

"No… I don't. I'm really good at it. I win. If I practice, I'm the best player on the court, but I don't love it."

"I don't know what to say." His face is pale, and I feel a pang of worry. I reach over and touch his shoulder to reassure him.

"Pops, I still want to work for the family. I just want to do something more meaningful than make money."

"Athletes make a difference. They use their money for good. They build schools, and hospitals…" he trails off, his eyes losing focus again.

"I already have money. I can do those things without basketball. But if I play basketball, I won't get to do the one thing money can't buy. I want to practice law. I want to make a difference *that* way."

"Your mother's going to lose her mind when you tell her." I nearly sag with relief at the acquiescence in his tone.

"She doesn't have a say. I have my own money and I am not asking for permission."

"No, what you're asking for is a shit storm."

"Will you support me? If you do, she won't say no."

He looks down at the letter and then back at me. "You do something that's a credit to our name, and I will support you. That's always been the rule. If you are part of this family, then you've got to act like it. And convince your mother."

"She'll be fine," I say even though I fully expect her to lose her shit when I show her the acceptance letter.

"And so will you." He hands it over to me. "People leave. People look out for themselves. You're making a choice now, one that is all about what you want. You'll meet someone else."

"I love her," I say without hesitation.

His head jerks backward in surprise. His eyes narrow and I see a flash of anger in them.

"Don't be stupid," he barks, glaring down at me in the way that used to intimidate me when I was a boy. But, I'm not that boy anymore.

I meet his glare with one of my own. "Only stupid thing I've done is to lie to her."

He shakes his head and rests back in his seat. He looks so tired and I instantly feel bad for putting this on him.

"These youthful, passion-filled liaisons are nothing but a pathway to pain and tragedy. That's not how you live up to the things your family expects of you. Your story is already written, son. You have great things ahead of you."

"I don't know... She made me feel... feel a lightness, Pops, that I'd never felt before."

"Legends aren't born to live *light* lives." His voice is full of reproach.

"You know my nickname?" I ask in surprise.

"Just because I don't hang out on the basketball court doesn't mean I don't know what's going on. It's fitting. You are destined to be great, Remi. And you've got to accept the sacrifices that come with that. You've got so much of everything. In ways your father didn't. You've got staying power that he didn't."

I start at that. "Pops, why do you say things like that? He died. That's hardly a failure."

My grandfather shakes his head like he's trying to dislodge something.

"Before he died, he stopped trying. He stopped putting the family first. You forget that so much of our responsibility is your family, Remi. Men like us can't be focused on our own desires. You will taste the kind of success that most people can't even imagine. That isn't free. My father came here with nothing. You think you live in this house because he followed his heart or his dick?"

"It's not that—"

"You're eighteen. *Of course,* it is."

He stands up. "I'm happy to support law school because it's a noble profession. But I will not support you chasing after a girl who didn't even have the decency to say goodbye."

The truth of that stings. I clench my jaw and look away from his steely, triumphant gaze. He sighs and reaches over to put one of his huge hands on my shoulder.

"Joni's going to apply early decision to Georgetown. Pursue *that*. Someone who understands the demands, the obligations that come with a family like ours. Not everyone is cut out for it. Not everyone can do what it takes to preserve it. It takes an iron stomach and the willingness to sacrifice. You'll see, son, one day. You'll look back and know that her leaving was one of the best things to happen to you."

My insides feel like they're mangled together in my gut.

"I can't imagine a day where that will be true."

"You won't have to imagine. It will come," he says with a certainty I know he really feels.

He reaches into his pocket and pulls out a small velvet drawstring bag. He tugs it open and empties it into his upturned palm and holds it out to me.

In his palm is a gold signet ring with a horse on its face.

"This was your father's. We got it back after he died When you take the helm, it will be yours. You will wear it with pride. And you will honor your family's name."

II

THE IN BETWEEN

6 YEARS LATER
HOUSTON, TX

15

DONE

REMI

"I can't believe she's here," Joni says as I step into the open door of our hotel room. I walk over to the California King-sized bed in the middle of the huge room and fall backward onto the white comforter.

"I can't believe it either." I stare up at the ceiling and try to gather my thoughts. They've been racing at the same clip as my heart since I saw the name, Kalilah Greer, on the seating chart outside the reception room where Regan's rehearsal dinner is being held tonight.

Well, actually Joni saw it. And per usual, the minute the subject of Kal comes up, Joni lost her cool. If only she knew the half of it, she might actually lose her entire mind.

There hasn't been a single day since the last time I saw her that I haven't imagined what it would be like to see her again. Part of me had given up hope that it would ever happen.

I had no clue where she was. Besides one random picture where she was in the background that Regan found on Facebook three years ago, there's been zero proof she was even still alive. I didn't even know where to start looking.

She is, by far, the person who holds the strongest place in my memories. And not just because of the drama of that last night. From the moment I met her, she and I belonged to each other. And not knowing where she was has been a special kind of torture.

My life has taken me on a journey I never imagined and I have met all types of people. I've learned that people like Kal, interesting and introspective, brave while also being kind and generous, funny and smart, are like needles in a haystack.

I miss her the way I imagine I would miss my right arm if it was gone. I chuckle at a memory from that summer.

"Share the joke?" Joni says a moment before she lies down next to me. When she drops her head on my shoulder, I want to sit up.

"It's nothing," I say.

"Nothing. It's never nothing when it comes to her." Joni's voice is full of suspicion. It's been there since that night, early on in our relationship, when I called Kal's name when we were fucking.

I lied and said I had no idea where that came from, she'd believed me. But, she brings it up every time we argue. From the look on her face now, we're about to have a doozy of a fight.

"What is it about her?" She sits up and peers down at me and I sit up, too.

"What are you talking about?" I ask wearily.

"I mean, it's been years since you've seen her and I get the impression that for you, it feels like yesterday."

I sigh and get off the bed.

"Let's not do this right now. I've been traveling all day and had to share a car from the airport with your half-dressed, drunk for no reason colleagues. I am not in the mood, Joni."

"Sorry, my friends aren't all social justice crusaders or whatever you've become, but they're fun. And I think you could use some of that. I want you to have a good time. I swear I don't think you're happy to see me at all." Her eyes pool with tears and her lower lip trembles.

God, anything but tears. I can't fucking stand them. Not from her. Not when she's weaponized them so expertly.

I stare around the room and try to pick my words carefully. I feel guilty because I know—that in my heart—I haven't done right by her at all. But, outwardly, by action and deed, I've been nothing but the model boyfriend. "Let's not argue."

"I'm not arguing, Remington," she drawls, but there's a sharpness in her voice that makes a lie out of her words.

"Good..." I bend down to grab my bag and throw it on the bed.

She crawls over and plants a kiss on my lips.

Shit. She's not wrong. Seeing Kal's name on the board sent me back in time. Just now when she kissed me, I tasted those cinnamon candies Kal was always sucking on.

"I'm going to get dressed for dinner. Want to watch?" she asks and without waiting for me to respond, she slips out of bed and starts to strip. I lean back and watch.

And of course, as my girlfriend prances around in her lace bra and panties, my mind leaps back six years to Kal's plain white panties and bra and how much I enjoyed peeling them away from her beautiful body.

Fuck. This is going to be an interesting weekend and not in a good way. The timing of this is fucked. Our relationship is basically over. Unfortunately, I'm starting to realize that only one of us seems to see things that way.

That one of us being me.

I look at her for a moment, just to take her in. Her dark hair spills in perfectly styled waves around her heart-shaped face. Her dark eyes are round, lushly lashed and her mouth is as lush and red as a tender rosebud. She's beautiful, poised, polished, accomplished, and ambitious. She's everything I should want. And yet, being with her has always felt like settling.

It's not that I'm better than her or smarter than her, or even nicer than her.

It's just... she's kind of an asshole. A lot of people would say the same about me. Maybe it's true. But, no fucking way do I want to date myself.

And despite her vehement and frequent declarations of love, I'm not convinced.

Not that it really matters if she loves me.

I certainly don't love her.

When we got together in college. She was a completely different person. She seemed relaxed and happy, not uptight and worried about appearances. She'd even expressed her regret at how she'd treated some of the girls back in Rivers Wilde. We started hanging out and then we started dating. Our families were ecstatic, so we just fell into place. Turns out, that regret she expressed, that was just a phase.

I chose to stay in DC for law school, and she chose to come back to Houston. At first, the distance was cool.

My first year in law school was brutal. I had very little free time. And I spent all of it on planes flying to see her. Every fundraiser, every opening night, every gala, she wanted me there. It was stressful, but it was fine.

Until Joni fashioned herself the leader of a clique of former debutantes turned full-fledged divas in Houston. She sits on boards, holds fundraisers, gives speeches, volunteers at a children's hospital.

But, she loves doing it under a spotlight. Every moment is captured on social media. It was like her entire life was a show.

Every time I was in town, there was a small note about it in the *Houston Chronicle* style section. I hate it. I'm a private man. I don't live my life on the pages of the style section the way some people do. If I ever seek the spotlight, it's to use my platform to shed light on an important cause.

The public scrutiny—were we holding hands when someone snapped us walking through the Galleria?—started to wear on me. Attention, that in my youth, had been flattering, started to wear thin.

I like being able to go grocery shopping without being accosted for a selfie. I don't enjoy having my so-called love life scrutinized by a bunch of self-appointed journalists armed with iPhones and immediate access to the Internet. I didn't sign up for that.

Six months ago, things started going downhill and fast.

She started acting like we were on the verge of being engaged. She joined forces with my mother to try and pressure me into marriage. I'm only 24, that's not on the cards for a long time, if ever.

Six months ago, my mother flew to DC for work and came by my Massachusetts Avenue apartment to give me my grandmother's ring.

"Remember that this is bigger than you. Use this when you're ready," she'd said when she pressed the three-carat emerald-cut diamond into my palm.

By that, she meant right away.

This morning when I was leaving for the airport, she called to remind me to take the ring with me. I left it right where it was.

It's not that I'll never be ready, but she's not the woman I'm going to put my ring on.

No matter how badly I want to please my family—I won't be frog-marched down a wedding aisle and spend my life with a woman who is as vindictive, shallow, and dishonest as Joni.

I hope my mother will understand.

I laugh at my wishful thinking. I know better.

She won't understand.

But it doesn't matter. My life is going to be built on something more meaningful than a convenient marriage.

I want to make a difference. I take my career seriously.

It doesn't help me look like a serious attorney when *People* magazine is reporting on what it means if Joni and I aren't holding hands when we stroll through the mall.

And the truth, at this point, my career has become more important to me than she is.

I will admit that when I realized we were not going to work out, I was disappointed.

I am trying to build a serious career, I also hoped to build a serious relationship with someone who might share my views on giving back and being a voice for the voiceless.

Joni, I've realized, too late, only likes what the attention does for *her*.

Kal reappearing just as I've made that decision feels like a sign, a crossroads, telling me exactly where I need to go now. I've never stopped wanting her, even when I gave up ever having her.

I'm not one to wallow in regret. I've had plenty of disappointments and setbacks. I never see them as failures, I see them as me being given an opportunity to learn something.

But, when I think about Kal and the way things ended, I feel like a failure.

I spent a summer convincing her that she could trust me, convincing her that I trusted her. And then, in one night, I ruined it, and hurt her profoundly. All because I thought... well, I thought like an eighteen-year-old with poor judgment and not quite enough courage.

If I had explained that Joni and I had been going to this event together since we were twelve and that I hadn't even thought about it until a few weeks before the party when my mother reminded me to take my tux to the dry cleaners for a press. By then, I thought it was too late to cancel without causing a big stink and I just wanted the summer we were having to end on a happy note.

It was just one weekend. My mother told me they hadn't been invited. Nothing should have brought Kal anywhere near my house that weekend. But, my mother figured out my plan and its fatal flaw and she went in for the kill.

That lie I told is my biggest regret.

The biggest mistake I ever made. That, and not telling her that I loved her.

That summer, we found something special with each other. Something, we'd never find with anyone else again.

I was just a kid, but I knew it in my bones, then. I still know it, now.

"Remington, could you try not to look like you're waiting for the executioner to drop a guillotine blade on your neck?" Joni drones as she walks over to the full-length mirror right beside the door. Her long, thin body is draped in a skintight black sequined dress that leaves nothing to the imagination.

"How do I look?" she asks and then turns her back to me so that I have a view of her perfectly round ass.

"Good," I respond honestly, but without any real conviction. Her beautiful body isn't enough for me, not anymore and my cock doesn't stir.

"Good? That's it? Remi, what's going on? You haven't seen me in two months and you haven't even tried to touch me." She crosses her arms over her chest and pouts. The evening hasn't even started and I feel tired already.

This isn't fair to either of us. When the wedding is over, I'll talk to her. But for now, I want my sister to have the day she deserves, so I just smile apologetically and rub my temples.

"You look great. I just have a headache. Go on down, I'll join you in a few minutes."

Her eyebrows are raised in impatience. "I don't want to walk out alone. People will think we had a fight."

My hackles rise. "Why in the world would anyone think that? And why do we care what they think?" I stay planted firmly on the bed.

I don't like being told what to do. Not by her and not because she wants to impress her completely unimpressive friends.

"We care because these people will be our social cohorts once you're back in Houston." She says this like it's supposed to be enough of a reason.

I raise an eyebrow at her. "Oh, well, then of course. That sounds like a good reason to give a shit."

"Be sarcastic if you want. I know how these things work. You've been out of the loop. I'm working really hard to establish us and it would help if when you are around, you do your part to develop the right image." She acts as if I'm not around because I'm off on vacation and not because I'm busting my ass to graduate at the top of my class.

"Fine, let's go," I bite out and take her outstretched hand and leave our room to meet the rest of the party.

And when our hands touch I feel… absolutely nothing.

16

SURPRISE

REMI

"REMINGTON, can you please put that thing down for five minutes and let me introduce you?"

My finger pauses mid-press and hovers over the keyboard of my phone. I slide my eyes to Joni and am met with her disapproving frown —what's become her standard facial expression when she's talking to me.

"Right, sure." I quirk my lips in an attempt at a smile, finish scanning my email quickly, and then slip my phone into the inside pocket of my suit before I look at the man who she's been talking to while I've been checking my email obsessively to see if there's any news about my interview.

As soon as we stepped off the elevator she saw someone and rushed off in their direction. I followed absently, reading my emails as I walked. The room was packed and loud, the volume of the music warring with people shouting to be heard above it. But it was like white noise to me.

Society weddings like the one my mother was throwing for Regan were nothing but an excuse to party, get drunk and not feel like a loser in the morning. The only reason this one would be tolerable is because it's my beloved sister's party and I'd walk over burning coals for her.

Even though, I also spend a lot of time wanting to strangle her. I look around the room at the half-dozen bars where our nearly three hundred guests are drinking like fish, the ice sculptures, and huge garlands made entirely of roses and thank fuck my sister's expensive-ass taste is about to no longer be my problem. And thank fuck her husband is even richer than we are. Or else, she'd have him in the poorhouse in less than a year.

"Remi—" Joni's voice is a hiss and I finally turn my attention to her. She scowls at me and then plasters a huge smile on her face before she turns to face the man she's trying to introduce me to. "Paul, this is my boyfriend, Remi. He's a third year at Howard Law School in DC. He got into Georgetown, of course, but he's obsessed with Thurgood Marshall so that's where he went." She says it like she has to explain my attendance at Howard. It is, of course, a lie. I never even applied to Georgetown.

"Remi this is Paul." I look up with a practiced smile on my face and almost choke on my inhaled breath.

Behind the man Joni's pointing at, is a halo of dark riotous curls that I'd recognize anywhere.

"Kal?" I say her name and my throat tightens around the word. Paul's eyes widen, and he looks behind him like he forgot she was there. There's a beat of nothing, breath, movement, sound all stop. And then Kal steps out from behind him.

I have imagined this moment, and yet, nothing could prepare me for the force of the longing that slams into my chest when I actually see her again.

I see her.

I miss her.

I *want* her.

"Remi." Her voice is high pitched, breathy, and full of surprise that rings as false as that smile on her face.

I narrow my eyes at her. She was fucking hiding from me.

I clear my throat and force my expression to remain neutral. But inside, my mind is hurtling backward through time to the summer I spent with this girl. No longer a girl, not at all.

She looks… so beautiful. Her skin still glows like she's been brushed in rays of sunlight. The space below her high round cheekbones not as full as they had been. But those lips are still bare, and they still make mine pulse just to look at them. They're not in the soft set of the innocent she was that summer. They're firm, determined, experienced.

Someone else made them that way and I feel my first of, what I know will be, many pangs of envy. I drink her in, trying to see if everything is as I remember it. One thing is exactly the same. She doesn't look like anyone else here.

It's a spring wedding. Everyone is in pastels and neutrals.

In a sea of pale pinks, buttery yellows, and icy blues, Kal stands out like an orchid blooming in the desert. Her slim, but curvy body is draped in a rich, candy apple red dress that is cinched around her waist with a gold chain. The dress leaves swaths of her dark honey skin exposed—at her shoulder, and at her waist. My fingers itch to touch her.

Her deep, wide-set dark brown eyes flare when our gazes meet and I see all the questions in her eyes. But I also see the same longing I'm feeling.

Holy shit, yes. My heart is going to fucking explode and I'm not sure I would even mind.

I was so not ready… I've dreamed. I've imagined. But all of that falls short to the reality of how beautiful she is. The noise falls away as I take her in.

And memories start flooding me.

Us in my car.

Us on her porch.

Us at CASA.

Us on the phone until the sun came up.

Us saying we loved each other in every way, except for with words.

Her leaving and taking a part of me with her that I've never been able to find again.

Fuck.

And she's standing with the man Joni's been talking to. The one she's been trying to introduce me to. His arm rests casually around her waist, but there's no mistaking the possession and intimacy in that touch. I can't fucking breathe. Seeing him *touch* her makes me want to strangle him until he swears he'll never do it again. I clench my fists at my side and force myself to stand still.

"Kalilah Greer, is that you?" Joni asks in a tone that makes it clear, she's praying the answer is no.

"Yes."

"Yes."

We answer at the same time. But then, we just look at each other, again. My ability to speak seems suspended in the viscous tension that's gripped me. Joni clears her throat loudly and I shake myself out of my stupor and remember where the fuck I am and I smile apologetically at all of them.

"Sorry, it's just been a long time... I didn't expect to see you here, Kal."

Kal tucks a lock of her thick curls behind her ear and smiles at me. It doesn't reach her eyes.

"Yeah... I didn't realize who the bride was until we got here. Paul and Marcel are old friends. When we checked in and I heard the last name Wilde..." she presses her lips together like it hurts to say the name. "So, of course, I knew I'd see you." Her throat bobs with the effort that steadiness in her voice cost her.

"I had no idea that she was friends with the great Remington Wilde. How auspicious—you're quite the dark horse, aren't you?" he says to Kal in a way that feels wrong. He's smiling at her, his dark eyes twinkling, but there's a thread of something in his voice that I don't like. And it's not just that he's talking to her.

Before I can think about it much more, he turns to me. "Marcel is a good friend from business school, and your girlfriend," he nods at Joni as if he needed to clarify which of the two women he's talking about, "sits on the board of a charity with my sister. It's just a coincidence that we're all meeting at this wedding."

"Yeah, what a coincidence," I say with no humor. It's more like a big fuck you from fate.

"So, are you here for the entire weekend?" I ask him, not because I care how long he'll be here, but because I need to figure out when I can get Kal alone.

"Yes. We're heading back to New York on Monday."

I look back at Kal and she looks distinctly like a deer caught in the headlights.

"I see. Is that where you live?"

She nods and runs that nervous finger down the side of her throat. I want to trace its path with my tongue.

I have fucking missed her so much.

God. There are so many things I've questioned over the years. My choices, my purpose.

But just like the first time I saw her in that library—there's no questioning us. There's just something. An understanding, a connection that, no matter how much time has gone by, never needs refreshing. It just needs us to be in the same space. And right now, it's screaming.

Kal's expression is making me crazy because I can see she's feeling everything I am. I wish I could talk to her right now.

"So, *that's* where you've been all this time?" Joni asks and steps into my side, she intertwines our arms and grasps my hand. We never hold hands. I look sharply just in time to see the possessive glint in her eyes before she tosses her head and looks back at Kal.

Kal's eyes dart up from our joined hands, and I don't miss her scowl before she smiles stiffly at both of us.

"Yes. My mother and I moved to New York when we left Houston." Her voice is soft. Too soft, like she's having a hard time breathing.

"You okay, Kal?" I ask before I can stop myself.

Everyone looks at me and I smile.

"Do I not look okay, Remi?" she asks, her eyes stony.

"No. You look great. You've just changed… I guess." I feel like such an idiot.

"You haven't changed at all." She casts her eyes toward Joni and then downward, so I can't look into them. But, I don't miss the accusation in her voice.

She's jealous.

Even though she's looking at me like she wants to knock my lights out, I can't help but smile.

"Hey, Will." And a surprised smile turns the corners of her mouth briefly.

"Hey, Carlton." I hear that undercurrent of a laugh and fuck, it makes me happy.

"Darling, you never mentioned that you and Kal had nicknames." Joni sounds like she's three seconds from running from the room in tears.

I glance at Kal to find that she's watching me and her eyes narrow slightly before she looks back at Joni.

"I was just a blip in his life. I'm sure he just forgot." She says tightly and I want to laugh.

Fuck *yes*.

"Impossible, Lee. You're unforgettable." Paul smiles at me and there's a glint of worry in his eyes. He may have his arm around her, but he knows he doesn't have her.

"Anyway, hate to bust up your reunion," he pulls Kal closer to him.

"You're not." I say coldly.

His smile disappears. "I see someone I need to speak with. Will you walk with me?" He turns Kal and steers her away before she can respond.

I look back over my shoulder as we make our way to the bride and groom's table and find Kal also looking over hers. She doesn't look away quickly, this time. Instead, she holds my gaze and I see everything then, everything I've wondered. Hope flares. We still have a chance and I'm going to take it.

1 7

WINDFALL

KAL

My head and heart are still spinning when I see Remi and Joni walking to our table. And then, Remi's eyes find mine. It's a jolt to my heart. I swallow the lump in my throat and force myself to look at Paul instead.

Whatever cruel twist of destiny reunited us at the worst possible moment in my life can go and fuck itself.

I was finally starting to think that maybe I had everything I wanted.

I nursed a broken heart for years after we left Houston. I threw myself into school and found a home in the sociology department at Columbia.

I was able to indulge my natural curiosity about other people in a place that encouraged studying their interactions.

It was the perfect training for journalism school.

Just a year ago, I landed the job of my dreams.

I met Paul on my second day at work. I work for one of his family's magazine's and and he's the Chief Operating Officer of their publishing company.

They're a large family. He's the youngest of six. They didn't mind that I was a nobody, that my mother worked as a nurse's aide and lived in her third-floor Bronx walk up. They made me feel like part of the family and so, I snatched what he was offering me and held on.

Even though I knew, from our first kiss, that I was trading passion and love for stability and certainty.

He pursued me hard. Freshly in the grip of my determination to finally get over Remi, he had felt like a godsend.

When he told me we were coming to Houston for his friend Marcel's wedding, I hadn't even considered our paths might cross.

He lives in DC.

If I had known I was going to see him, nothing could have convinced me to come.

Just thinking about him makes my head and heart ache with the same intensity as the day he left them both bruised and battered.

He was the boy who taught me just how painful love could be. But, I've never stopped carrying a torch for him. I know that now because seeing him brought all of my feelings rushing back. Like a volcano that suddenly erupted, the wash of affection, desire, and longing took me by complete surprise.

And then, as if I jumped out of the fire into a frozen lake, it's gone. And in its place stands ice-cold jealousy.

He's standing there next to Joni. And all I can think is that she gets to fuck him. She gets to hold his hand and see him naked. All of that should have been mine.

It was a lifetime ago. He's hers now. And, I'm with Paul. But to know that's who he ended up with, seeing how right they look together, it hurts.

I turn those crazy thoughts off real quick. He's nothing to me. A summer fling in the burgeoning youth of my womanhood.

I smile up at them as they join us at the table. I can't believe these seating arrangements. I put it down to my overactive imagination that I feel sure that it was deliberate.

Joni's eyes are darting all over the room like she's taking note of who is watching her and who dares not to.

Remi's face is tense as he looks everywhere but at me.

He still looks like the quintessential college basketball player. Tall, well-muscled, and lean.

God, his light gray suit fits him like he was sewn into it and I hate that I missed the chance to watch him grow from the very fine eighteen-year-old to the drop-dead gorgeous man who looks like the tall, dark and handsome prince in every single fairy tale I've ever read. Right down to the small cleft in his chin.

And yet, inside all of that, wrapped in all of that perfection is the Remi I knew. The one who picked me flowers. The one who drove me out to the country so I could see the stars. The one who kept my journal and read the first stories I ever wrote.

The one who fucking lied to you, Kal.

"Remington, where's your drink?" Paul shouts

Remi taps his temple and smiles with all of that swagger he drips and says, "I don't need a single thing to stimulate this mind. I'm high on life, man."

"Rubbish! Come let's leave the ladies to it, walk with me," Paul declares and then lurches out of his chair. He's a terrible drunk.

Remi eyes him and then seems to decide it's not worth the trouble to argue with him. He gets up. "Excuse us, ladies."

I can't bring myself to look at him.

"Kal, so tell us about your new windfall," Joni shouts at me across the table, her smile curved vindictively.

I don't understand how in the world Remi is dating her.

"Windfall?" I ask, attempting to sound bored, but really my stomach is roiling. I don't want to be here alone with these women. I've purged my life of people like them, and I can't stomach the petty one-upmanship they seem to thrive on.

"I meant, *Paul,* Kalilah," she says caustically. "That windfall."

Her friends at the table gasp. One of them lets out a nervous giggle. Joni waves a hand at them in annoyance. "Oh, settle down. I'm not saying anything you all aren't thinking. The apple doesn't fall far from the tree, does it? I mean, you learned from the best when it comes to snaring rich men. Just congratulating you on getting a good one."

She winks. And I wish I could wipe that smug smile off her face with my hand.

She saw the way Remi looked at me. I wish I could tell her not to worry. That need in his eyes, doesn't mean anything. Because when it mattered, he still chose her over me.

I've made peace with it. I know men like him only dally with girls who aren't just like them.

Even Paul, to an extent has made it clear that I should feel lucky that he *chose* me.

I'd already earned my spot at the magazine before I met him. That hasn't stopped people from insinuating that I slept my way into that position. I hear it from his family's friends in the snide comments and sometimes even from Paul.

But, I'll be damned if I sit here with people who have had every single thing handed to them, who have no clue what it means to struggle and dignify their shit with a response. I don't even acknowledge that I heard her question. I finish my drink and stand.

"It was nice to see you all. Tell Paul I went to our room." Then I look directly at Joni.

Sure, she's beautiful, in an obvious kind of way. But, I don't understand how Remi could be with her.

"Yes. Are you going to say something or just stare?"

I shake my head in disgust.

"You are living proof, there's absolutely no cure for cunts."

She touches her cheek like I slapped it. God, how I wish I had.

I turn my back on her and walk away.

18

CHANGES

REMI

"You were right. She's here."

Lupe's text flashes on my screen. I've been dressed for hours waiting for it.

I swing my legs over the side of the bed and slip my feet into my shoes.

"Remi—it's six in the morning. Where are you going?" Joni calls from the bed.

"I have an errand to run before the wedding. Go back to sleep. I'll be back for breakfast." I grab my phone and keys and head to the door.

"Okay—bring me a Starbucks when you come back, the coffee here is awful," she calls after me.

As soon as I'm in the hallway, I break into a run. The thought that Kal could be gone by the time I get to CASA is like a whip at my back.

I sprint through the lobby not caring that I'm giving the early morning staff fodder for gossip. I self-parked last night so that I wouldn't have to wait for a valet driver to get my car, and less than seven minutes after I got Lupe's text, I'm driving down Woodway and turning left onto the 610 Freeway.

I knew she wouldn't come here without going there. I knew it would be the only time I'd find a way to talk with her without anyone around. I haven't lived in Houston for six years, but I've supported CASA financially since I started volunteering. And every time I'm home, I go visit. Lupe loved Kal. Every time I see her she asks if we're back together. So, when I asked her to help, she was happy to do me the favor.

I just need to talk to her. Need to say all of the things I didn't when I had the chance.

See if there's any hope for us. I touch the small locket dangling next to the small gold cross that hangs from a gold chain around my neck. I've worn it ever since I realized I wouldn't get to give it to her.

I pull up and see the Nissan Maxima rental in the driveway and let out a sigh of relief.

She's still here.

I race up the walkway. Lupe opens the door as I approach like she's been waiting for me.

"Hello, my love." She props up on her tiptoes and presses a kiss to my cheek. I hug her back. I've come to love Lupe. She's the perfect combination of grit, persistence, and kindness. She's kept this place running by sheer strength of her love for these children.

"She's with Carlos, in the back. I told her you were coming," she says and there's a gentle reproach in her eyes. I had asked her not to say anything.

"I didn't want her to feel trapped. And I wanted her to have a choice. I don't know what happened between you two, but I remember the way you were when you were here. So, I guessed she'd be glad you were coming. And I was right." She pats my cheek with affection and smiles softly up at me.

"You were?" I glance over her shoulder, eager to get to her.

"Let me know when you're leaving so I can lock up after you."

She pads away down the hall, and I stand there gathering my nerve. I can see the crack of light under the door to Carlos' room. We always knew he'd never be adopted. And every year, I've highlighted part of my contribution to supplement the reimbursement the state gives Lupe and CASA for his care.

I gird my loins and walk down the hall to talk to the girl I've been waiting almost a decade to talk to.

KAL

"HE'S HERE."

Lupe's text makes my heart jump. I press a kiss to Carlos' cheek and stand up. I take one last look around the room and marvel how it has all the space and light he needs.

It's all thanks to Remi's donations. Lupe took me for a tour around the house, showing me all the improvements that have been made. Over the years, she's kept me updated on Carlos, the only kid who is still here from the time I volunteered. He's aged out of the system, doesn't have to worry about being displaced. This is his home.

All because Remi loves him.

Not that I'm surprised, he's an excellent human being. Larger than life, brighter than the sun. It's why I fell so hard for him. Distance from that evening has cooled my anger about it. When I'm feeling extremely rational, I even understand why he lied. But, I hate that he felt like he had to.

It was fucked-up, but I've told myself, drilled it into my thick skull, that things have worked out as they were meant to.

So, why does thinking that feel so much like swallowing broken glass?

"Stop being dramatic, Kal." I scold myself under my breath.

I steel my shoulders and steady my breath. But nothing can calm the wild beating of my heart. I close my eyes and remind myself he doesn't hold my heart the way he used to.

I've moved on.

I'm happy.

I'm building a life.

I repeat these words to myself over and over again until I can say it without stumbling over the words. And then, I step out into the hallway.

Our eyes find each other immediately and I see the same uncertainty as I feel staring back at me. But it's different, rougher, less restrained than mine. And in his gaze is so much hunger. I feel it as though he was touching me and I have to steel myself against it.

"Will." His gruff voice is just a decibel above a whisper and he swallows hard when I brush a tear away.

"Hey, Carlton," I manage.

He walks up to me, his lips pressed together in a determined line, his eyes intent on mine. Without missing a beat he wraps his arms around me and pulls me into a hug.

I hug him back. It feels *so* good to be back in his strong arms that for minute I forget the way we left things and how much it hurt that last time I saw him.

But only for a minute.

I pull out of his hold, and he lets me go, but reluctantly. A shiver of dread and delight runs the same course as his hands slide down my arms. He grasps my hands, holds them in his and my heart beats wildly.

I see the instant the stone of the ring on my left hand presses into his palm.

His eyes never leave mine and tears well at the back of them as I see a whole rail of emotions move through his.

Surprise.

Confusion.

Disbelief.

Hurt.

"What the fuck is this?"

I force myself to smile; it feels watery and thin and brittle.

"I'm getting married," I rush out in a breath before I lose my nerve.

"To who?" he asks flatly and drops my hand.

"To Paul. I'm here with him. He knows Marcel..."

"I thought you worked for him?" He holds my hand, his eyes on the ring.

"No. I work for his family's business. He's not my boss or anything."

"Do you love him?" he asks, his tone is harsh.

I close my eyes because I can't look at him and say it.

"I'm pregnant."

The room is silent.

He doesn't say anything, but his chest heaves sharply on a silent gasp, and I can't bring myself to look at him.

"Do you want to get married?" His voice is so gentle, so tender that it makes me want to weep in his arms.

"Yes." I say even though, I want to confess that I'm not sure.

"Do you love him?" His voice is still gentler when he asks this time, but I can see the truth, the devastation in his eyes.

It makes me angry.

"You don't get to look at me like that." I spit.

"I fucking know, Kal." He says and he sounds like he's in pain. "I know that night was a shit show. But you disappeared without a trace. I had no idea where you'd gone. Why didn't you ever try to get in touch?" His question is devoid of accusation, but I can see it in his eyes and the audacity of it is shocking.

"Why would I? We didn't leave for four days after... that night. I never heard from you." I almost choke on the memory.

His eyes narrow and he clenches his jaw.

"I came by the very next day, your mother said you didn't want to see me. I came every fucking day until you I realized you were gone." He grits out angrily.

I reel backwards.

My mother lied to me. Granted, I shouldn't be surprised. It was just one in a string of lies that she told me my whole life. But when I think what might be different if I'd seen him before I left. If I'd known *he* wanted to see me... I can't bear the thought.

They played games with our lives and they won. We were kids without a say. What's done is done. I look over at Remi and he looks as despondent as I feel.

We stand there in a heavy barbed silence that makes the room feel very small.

I break the silence because I want to make sure he knows everything she did. I saw her today and I'd trembled when I remembered how she plotted to hurt me. "Your mother blackmailed my mother."

His jaw goes slack.

"What?"

"She promised to make our lives a living hell unless we got out of town."

He closes his eyes. "I knew it didn't make sense the way you disappeared." He groans like he's in pain. "God, that woman. I'm so sorry, Kal. I didn't know."

"I know." I say uselessly.

It's too late for all of this.

"I thought I was such a man. I was just a powerless, clueless *kid*. Maybe I still am." He shakes his head.

"Yeah. When my mother packed us up, I didn't think about refusing to go. I was hurt and confused and she used that to her advantage. We moved to New York and I finished high school there."

"You still live there?" he asks, but he sounds dazed.

"Yup, I went to Columbia. Got a job with an investigative journalism magazine. I live in Harlem now, but I'm moving in with Paul soon."

"Well, all you need is the book and your porch, and your happy ending is basically here," he says dully, but his words hit me like poison tipped arrows and the resentment and anger in them seep into my skin.

"It's been six years. And you've moved on, too. You're with Joni." My voice betrays how defensive I feel.

"Not for long. It's basically over." His voice is devoid of emotion, his dark brows are furrowed in a dark smile.

"Oh. I'm… sorry?" I'm not sure if he's upset or if it's a good thing.

He looks back at the window without responding.

"So, when's the wedding?" He asks quietly.

His change of subject gives me whiplash.

"Uh, soon. His family is Catholic. They want it done before I start to show." I stare at my feet and close my eyes and try to remember that this is all going to be fine. It hurts now, but it won't always.

I'm making the right choices. For myself and for my child. Remi owns my heart, but love isn't enough. I owe my child the best start I can give her.

"Congratulations." He looks so sad even though he's smiling.

I don't know why I feel like I've broken his heart.

I know that's not the case. It's my heart that's got a permanent crack in it from loving him when I shouldn't have. He never felt the same way.

He slides his hand up my arm and caresses the inside of my elbow. I close my eyes because his touch is bliss and I want to savor it.

"You know... I wanted things to be different..." His words aren't a question.

They are the final words in this chapter of our lives.

It a stab in the gut.

"I'm so fucking sorry about that weekend, Kal. So sorry I didn't just tell you about the event. Sorry I hurt you. Sorry I let you down. We were a lot of things to each other. But most of all, we'd been friends."

I nod. "I know you are. I knew it then. And yes, I miss our friendship." It's such an understatement. There is so much unspoken in his words, too. And for now, it will have to stay that way.

"You just miss me driving you around."

"Yeah, I don't miss your slow-ass driving at all."

He smiles. It's a flash of light from a shooting star across a dark moonless sky. And just like that, I don't feel so fucking shitty.

Life has gotten in the way so many times and now, it's time for us to get off this ride.

It takes effort to step away from him, away from his touch. But I do it with a smile. "So, you're about to be a Supreme Court Clerk?"

"Still asking around about me, I see..." A bark of surprised laughter escapes me.

"I guess so. Congratulations. It's a big fucking deal."

He shakes his head as if he's amazed by his own achievement. "Kal, there's a voter ID law coming up for review. I would be involved in a really historically significant moment. I mean every decision the court makes is historically significant, but it's a brand-new question and I get to be right there. If I get it."

"You'll get it. You're Remington Wilde. The Legend. You're damn good at everything," I quip, but it sounds brittle and hollow in my own ears. I just smile wider.

"I'm not good at everything, Kal. I just work harder than everyone else." I'm so proud of him and sad for us.

"You did it." I imbue my voice with that pride.

He nods and then shakes his head like he disagrees. "No, Kal. I've fucked-up so bad." He sounds despondent.

I forget the distance I tried to create and move closer to him. "What do you mean? You're a shoo-in for that job."

"No. Not that. This. Us." He reaches out and presses his palm between my breasts and at his touch, tears spring to my eyes.

The bone-deep regret in his voice scares me. I shake my head at him. "We didn't stand a chance. We had everything against us. Your mother hated me. Life…"

He moves so quickly; I don't even see it coming. His arm wraps around my waist and he pulls me up against him. And then drops us onto the low-slung couch under the window.

He holds me in his lap, his eyes hook onto mine and that wolf-like keenness he had whenever he was determined appears.

"Remi—" I start to admonish him.

His big, warm hand cups my jaw and the words die in my throat. His hand on my skin ignites every synapse of need in my body. It's like he flipped a switch.

"Yeah… I know. I feel it too," he says quietly. His hand moves up my jaw and to my hair. I close my eyes against the shiver that runs through me when the pads of his big fingers caress my scalp.

"Remi…"

"You're so beautiful," he says, and I look down at him.

"You are, too," I whisper. And he is. Inside and out.

He brings his face to mine until our foreheads touch and our noses brush each other. I rock mine back and forth over his forehead.

His eyes roam my face. "I missed that fucking freckle." He whispers and his breath dances on my lips.

So close.

So, *so* close.

A wave of longing crashes against my resolve and my breath hitches.

"Can I kiss you?" He asks, holding my gaze, piercing my very soul with it. I've never wanted anything more. I have to bite my lip to keep from begging him to *please* kiss me.

I shake my head.

He groans softly and slides his nose along mine. I exhale a shuddering breath and he inhales sharply, like he's trying capture it.

"Don't you remember how good it felt when we kissed?" He asks.

Oh, *how* I remember. How I have dreamed of it. How I've tasted it, measured everything by it.

And just like when I was a girl, I can't deny him anything. And our time apart has only amplified our feelings.

The tips of our noses rub against each other as I nod.

He cradles my head and brings my mouth to his.

The touch is electric. It sizzles. And our sharp gasps are synchronized.

My lips quiver as his brush back and forth across them and a wildfire of gooseflesh covers my entire body.

When his tongue, hot and wet and so fucking delicious, sweeps across my bottom lip I'm transported.

To a place where he and I are together. Without parents interfering, without fucked up timing. Without heartbroken nights that made me careless. Without anything but my best friend, my lover, the man I would have followed anywhere he'd asked me to.

It was one summer, but it had been the most wonderful, unexpected interlude in the shit show that had been my life.

I let my chest press against his and wrap my hand around his neck and the kiss deepens.

His tongue sweeps inside my mouth and tangles with mine. He licks and sucks and reverently, lovingly reminds me of everything I've missed. *This* is the most perfect kiss. Because this is the most perfect man. Even in the ways that we are flawed, we are each other's perfects.

His hand drifts down my shoulder and he cups my breast and his thumb sweeps my nipple. His fingers twist and fist the hair at the nape of my neck, lips skid down my throat, his teeth and tongue working in beautiful concert – nipping and then soothing.

I am *unraveling*. I'm approaching a place I shouldn't be going. The warning bells start to ring. This is wrong. And, I won't ruin my chance at having the life I always wanted.

Not when the last time I let him close enough, he decimated my heart.

There's a loud crash in the hallway and I yank my mouth off his and jump out of his lap. His fingers circle my wrist and he yanks me back.

"No. Not yet," he says and his lips press to mine again

"Remi. No. Please… let's not. I feel it, too. But… no."

I put a hand over my still flat stomach.

He lets go of my wrist. The light in his eyes cool and he drops his head, and shakes it.

When he looks up at me again his eyes are clear. Like he's dropped a mask over the raging emotions that had nearly drowned us a few minutes ago.

"I know. I'm sorry. That's not the man I was raised to be."

Hearing him say he's sorry, even though I know I should be too, stings.

"It's just seeing you… just everything makes me forget myself."

"It's okay. Nostalgia and all." I say lamely.

"And, I know how much you like kissing me." He winks and flashes me a grin. It doesn't quite reach his eyes, but I can see he's trying. So I smile back. And when I do, he nods his head as if accepting something and stands up.

"So… friends?" he asks and watches me

"We've always been. And will always be."

When I leave thirty minutes later, I feel better. I have Remi back in my life and I've made the right choice. I'm going to be somebody's mother. Someone who didn't ask to be born and I want to do right by him or her. I won't put a child through what I went through. Not even if it means having to settle for friendship with the man I love.

19

THE WEDDING

REMI

"WHAT ARE YOU TWO DOING?" MY MOTHER THUNDERS AS SHE bursts into the small vestibule where Regan and I are huddled.

I don't look at her. I've had about as much of her shit as I can take this week. And after this morning with Kal, I'm about as raw as an open wound.

"Mother—I'm just not sure." Regan pleads. I want to tell her to save her breath.

"Well, that baby in your belly says at some point you were *very* sure. You'll be sure again. You will not embarrass your family this way."

"Remi says—"

"Remi," my mother infuses my name with caustic dismissal, "doesn't know the first thing about a relationship or marriage. He's the very last person you should be taking advice from."

I'm not even mad. She's right. But I won't let her act like she knows any better.

"As opposed to you and your long, successful marriage?"

"Your father died, Remi."

"Nice of you to remember that today. Most days you act like he ran off to join the circus."

"Your disrespectful tone and subversive efforts will not be tolerated today." She glares at me and stomps over to where we're sitting and looks down her nose at Regan.

"You've got two hundred and fifty family members and friends waiting in that chapel. Marcel Landel is standing at the end of an aisle waiting to marry you. Despite your shameless antics and your hysterics two days ago, he's there. You should be on your knees thanking your lucky stars that he'll still have you. Instead, you're here with your brother hatching whatever harebrained scheme you can think of to get out of doing what is right."

"Mother, I am not. I know Marcel is a great man. I know I'm lucky. But I don't love him," Regan pleads.

My mother grabs Regan's chin and yanks her face upward.

"Do you think that matters? He's a good man. You're clearly attracted to him." She shoots a glance at the small swell of Regan's belly. "He's got money and most importantly you're carrying his child. You must not soil our name with illegitimacy. You will not. Now, get up."

She turns and walks out of the room.

Regan shoots me a helpless glance and stands. I grab her hand and pull her back down to her seat. I lean forward and hold her gaze. This is my twin, we may be as different as the sunrise and the sunset, but she's still my true other half and I want more for her than marriage for expediency.

"Reggie, you don't have to do anything. If you don't want to marry him, I will walk you out of here and I'll explain it to him. He's a reasonable man. A good man. But that doesn't mean you have to spend the rest of your life with him."

My mother spins on her heels and marches back toward where I'm sitting. She stands toe to toe with me looking upon me with the anger that so often clouds our interactions. Our relationship has deteriorated to the point that we only speak to each other when we need to. I keep the things I care about out of her reach.

"You are not the head of this family. You are not the person who will have to deal with the fallout of what you're advising. Stop being so selfish and immature and do what your father should be doing and walk your sister down the aisle."

I stand up now. Sick of her browbeating insults and her disdain.

"Or what? You don't have basketball to use as your stick anymore. You got rid of Kal, so what do you have to hold over me now?"

Her hand flies to her chest and her face is a picture of indignation. But I know my mother and indignant isn't an emotion in her tank. She's pissed and can't believe I would dare speak to her like that.

"Yes, I wanted her to know that she'd never be one of us. But how am I responsible for your little tart's disappearing act?"

"Um, well let's see. How about blackmail and extortion?"

"Remi!" Regan gasps loudly. I take in her shocked expression and immediately decide to stand down.

"I'm sorry. It's your wedding day."

"Yes, you can chase your conspiracy theories another day. And one day, you'll thank me. She wasn't suitable, and she's the reason you became obsessed with civil rights. And now instead of working for your family's corporation, you're about to become a low-level civil servant. Joni being your partner is the only reason you still have any clout in Houston. If you marry her, you can go off on your legal journey gallivanting and still have the social status to do the Wilde name credit. I won't apologize for what I did."

I stand up then, even though I don't move from my sister's side.

"Of course not. That would require you to actually care about how I feel."

She sneers and steps toward me. "The girl you love is marrying someone else because she didn't love you enough to come after you, Remi. She chose that. I didn't do that. You can't blame me for all of your troubles—"

"Please stop," Regan stands up and shouts. "Please don't fight. Don't say such ugly things to each other. Please. Not today." She looks between us and her eyes are full of a begging plea.

The fight in me dissipates. It's not about me today. My grandfather asked me to walk Regan down the aisle and I've seen it as a solemn and sacred responsibility.

"I'm sorry, Reg. You're right. But you have to decide because it's not fair to keep him waiting. Do you want to go or should we walk down that aisle?"

She looks down at her hand and twists the large solitary-stone engagement ring around on her finger. Her fiancé Marcel is twenty years her senior. He's the owner of the multinational media company that owns the television station Regan works for. And he got her pregnant. When she told me I hadn't taken it well.

"I want to do it." Regan's quiet statement jolts me back to the present.

"Of course you do. You're not a fool." My mother casts her eyes on me so that it's clear what she was leaving unsaid.

"Come on. I'll let them know you had a snafu with your dress and are on your way out."

"Oh, and Remi... you should use the ring I gave you soon."

"Oh, Mother. I've decided I'd rather pluck my eyes out with hot pokers than marry Joni. So, I'll be giving it back to you. Maybe give it to Tyson. He'll need it before I ever do."

"You are such a disappointment." She casts those words over her shoulder as she walks out and I look at Regan in shock.

"Remi. It's okay." My sister tucks her arms through mine and pats my hand reassuringly. "We'll get through this together. Like we have everything else. I'm just glad you're here and able to give me away."

"I am, too. Come on. Let's go get married."

20

TRY

KAL

I DON'T KNOW WHY I CAME. I DIDN'T DECIDE UNTIL AN HOUR AGO. When I got back from CASA, I told Paul I was sick. He believed me. For once, he relented and would have let me stay where I was if I'd insisted.

But, the truth is, I couldn't bear the thought of not seeing Remi again. I couldn't stop thinking about our conversation at CASA, and the way he'd looked when I said I was pregnant. The way it felt to hear he didn't get my letters. There is so much unsaid between us. So many moments deferred by life.

I have managed to convince myself that everything is as it should be. We're both where life intended us to be. And every time I think about my baby, I feel so much love that I know it alone can sustain me. I've got my dream job. I'm living the happily ever after I never thought I'd have. So, why does it feel so hollow?

When the church doors open and Remi and Regan stepped onto that carpet, I had known for a fact that this had been a mistake. I should have stayed at the hotel. Being here with Paul only exacerbated the feeling of "wrong" that has settled on my shoulders like a cape. I don't love Paul. I don't think I ever could – at least not the way I think. Because that belongs to someone else.

Now, the party is in full swing. Paul and I are seated at the table farthest away from the bride, groom, and bridal family. I've watched Remi lead his sister in the traditional father-daughter dance. All of that young charm has morphed into a mature charisma that makes everyone smile as he walks by. He's the most handsome man in the room. His hair is closely cropped, the strength of his jaw is magnified by his short, immaculately groomed beard.

I wish he was mine.

"You want another Shirley Temple?" Paul asks and I give him a wan smile and nod. "And a glass of water, too, please."

"Be right back. There's an open bar, so I'm going to get another one of these." He jiggles his empty lowball glass. I bite my tongue against the warning that he's drinking too much because the last thing I want is to have a fight with him.

"Hey, friend. Can I have this dance?"

I freeze in my seat. It's Remi.

I turn and take him in. He looks like a tall glass of ice water in the middle of a sandstorm. His tuxedo is cut to fit, and fit, it does. So very, very well.

"Uh… hey, sure" I say and find my words are more of a sigh than anything else because I'm struggling to breathe. My heart is hammering in my chest.

"You look incredible in that dress," he says and looks me up and down. I flush and run a self-conscious hand over my hair which I had blown out and flat ironed for today. October is the one month a girl with a head full of natural curls can get away with a style like this in Houston, so I went down to the hotel's salon on a whim.

"Let's dance. Come on."

He sticks his hand out and I take it.

"Okay."

We're on the dance floor in a few steps. Remi's arm goes around my waist and he draws me into him in one fluid motion. I swear, my insides are melting.

"Kal," he whispers my name in my ear and there's an urgency in his voice.

"Mm-hmm." Because my tongue is tied.

"I'm drunk," he confesses.

"You don't drink," I chide him.

"It's the only way I would have survived Regan's pre-divorce party," he whispers and I giggle.

"Don't say that."

"Just telling it like it is. And I don't want to talk about her."

"Okay." I let him twirl us around. Then I lean back and look him in the eye.

"You having a good time?"

"Fuck no."

"Why? You have a headache from the drinks already?"

"Nope. The only thing that hurts is this." He takes my hand and lays it on his chest. I can feel the beat of his heart against my palm and gasp.

"Remi." I pull my hand away.

"Doesn't yours? I could have sworn you loved me, too."

My heart stops.

"You loved me?"

"*Love.* Present tense."

I shake my head in denial.

"I should have told you then." He pulls me to him and presses his lips to my ear. On the crowded dance floor, it feels like we're alone.

"You were everything I wanted before I even knew I wanted it, Kal. You made me wonder and think and you changed my life in ways I can't quantify."

My heart thuds against his chest and I can feel the vibration of it throughout my whole body.

"Do you ever wonder what if?" he whispers and my heart starts to crack.

"Every day," I admit, on a whisper.

"Do you know I think about you when I'm with her. When I kiss her, sometimes I taste you."

My heart cracks in a way I feel to my bones.

"Me, too," I admit.

"Is this okay? For us to feel this way and let each other go?" he asks the question I think I'll ask myself for the rest of my life. I can only do what I think, at this moment, is right.

"Hmm," he hums. I tremble from the wave of pure, unadulterated lust that slams into me, from just the way his breath brushes against my skin. Then, I feel the insistent press of his hard cock in my stomach. I can't stop myself from pressing closer.

"I want to put that inside of you. I miss your pussy, Kal. We were only kids… and it's still the best pussy I've ever had. And I could take such good care of it now. I know things." His hands slide down my back and stop short of grabbing my ass. I clench my thighs in a failed effort to quiet the throb his touch is creating between them. I am so turned on and yet so sad at the same time.

"We can't be friends," he whispers in my ear, his lips skimming the sensitive shell of my ear before he drops his forehead onto my shoulder. And my heart hurts so profoundly because I know he's right.

I know when he comes to his senses, sobers up, or whatever, that he'll regret this and will never do it again.

"I know," I whisper.

"*Fuuuuuuck.* I don't want to let you go. Not again. Not after all this time. Leave him, Kal." He grates, his lips lingers on the side of my face.

I've never been more tempted in my life. The crush of bodies on the dance floor makes a nice camouflage, but we're being very reckless… holding each other this close in public. Neither one of us can afford to be seen. Neither of us seems to care.

This time his lips dust the fine hairs at my temple. "What if we're supposed to be together? What if it was my baby you had growing inside of you? It's my last name you should have been getting ready to take. My house, you come home to. Me, you're going home with. My dick you're riding until you come all over it." He growls, hot and angry in my ear. I want to respond by shouting "yes." After each sentence. I am completely undone and I feel the loss of him and our chance so keenly.

"Remi… please don't." I hug him and want so badly to cry. And then, he goes and guarantees that I will leave there knowing exactly what I've missed.

"I'm so in love with you. So, so, in love."

My heart constricts and then starts to race.

He presses his nose into my hair and wraps me tightly in his arms.

"I'll miss you, Will." He says like he's about to let me go and I start to panic.

I want to stay like this. In his arms. The rebel in me hopes that Paul sees us.

But, the girl who grew up with her chaotic mother showing her just what life as a single parent looked like wins.

I've made my choice.

I pull out of his embrace and shake my head.

"Remi, I'm sorry."

I can't read his eyes, but I can feel his disappointment and his anger. It permeates the space between us and mingles with mine. He leans forward and down so that his lips are at my ear.

"For me, it's always been you." My heart aches and I bite back a whimper. He skims his fingers down my arms. "If you change your mind... you want to run away from it all, now, later, ever—say the word. I'll be waiting." And then he presses a kiss to my cheek, lets me go and walks away.

21

ECLIPSE

REMI

THE MORNING AFTER THE WEDDING HAS BEEN A BLEAK ONE. THE guests are gone. Kal is gone. I'm on autopilot now. If I stop to think about yesterday, I'll lose my shit. I have never felt so sick to my stomach as I did when Kal said she was pregnant.

She was right that I'd moved on, too. But, I didn't realize until yesterday, when it was too late, that I'd been carrying an ember of hope inside me that somehow, one day, we'd get it right.

But just like I had when I was a boy, I overestimated how much control I'd have over what happened between us.

Yesterday, if she'd said yes when I asked her to leave him, I would have walked out of there with her and not given a damn about what came next.

And now I understand my grandfather's advice. I would have thrown away everything for her. And if he'd turned his back on me for it, I would have lived with it. For her, I would have done anything.

So maybe it is for the best. I'm cleaning my slate and focusing on the things I can control.

Breaking up with Joni has been on my to-do list for months. After this fucking disaster of a weekend, I've decided it's time.

She may be right on paper, but I'd rather have nothing than settle.

So, as we're eating breakfast on the balcony of our hotel room, I tell her it's over. She eyes me stonily while she finishes chewing her bagel and wipes her mouth.

"This is because of *her*." She says icily.

"It's been a long time coming." I feel like shit because I know that's what it looks like. But I need to do this before I leave.

She raises a skeptical eyebrow and purses her lips. "So, it's just a *coincidence* that the day after you saw your little secret girlfriend from high school, you're breaking up with me?"

"She wasn't my secret girlfriend. And no. It's not a coincidence." I'm honest because whatever else I may be, a hypocrite isn't one of them.

"She's not good enough for you," she says through taut lips.

"You don't know anything about her *or* what's good for me, Joni." I say in a warning voice. I'm mad at Kal, but fuck if anyone can talk about her like that.

"Isn't she getting married?" She looks at me like I'm the most pathetic asshole she's ever seen.

She's not wrong.

"So?" I shrug, the weight of resentment and disappointment has left me numb.

"So, are you running off together? She's leaving her meal ticket? I guess it makes sense, you've definitely got deeper pockets." Her sarcasm is ugly and dry and I'm an idiot for feeling like Kal is still mine to defend. But I do. I always will.

"You're the one who cares about how deep my pockets are. And no, she's not leaving him. I just don't want *this* anymore." I point between us. She curls her lip in disgust.

"So, after you spent the weekend humiliating me by mooning after her and practically making out with her on the dancefloor, you're breaking up with *me*?" She laughs humorlessly.

"I'm sorry." I say with as much contrition as I can muster.

"No, *I'm* sorry. That I didn't dump you first." She throws her napkin down.

I blow out a breath, "Me, too."

We stare at each other. She's beautiful. It would have been a lot more convenient if I'd fallen in love with her.

"I won't take you back," she says after eyeing me. Her is voice even. She's not threatening me. This is the truth.

I nod in agreement. "You shouldn't. You deserve a man who can love you. That's not me."

She sits down across from me, crosses her legs and assesses me coolly. "I'm not looking for love. I don't believe in it the way you do."

"The way *I* do?" I lean back and look at her like she's grown horns.

"Yes. I've been very surprised at how sensitive you are, Remington."

"I am *not* sensitive," I growl. That gets under my skin. Because after this weekend, I feel raw.

"It's not an insult, it's just an observation," she says evenly.

"I'm not insulted. It's just not true. And if you don't want love, why do you want to get married so badly?"

"I want power and freedom."

"You're already powerful, Joni. And I don't see any shackles around your wrists."

"Just because you can't see them, doesn't mean they're not there. And the only power I have is because my *father* is powerful. I'm just his daughter. I have ambitions greater than that. And there are some doors that will only open to me if I have a powerful, wealthy man beside me."

"Well, shit if that's all you want, there are about a hundred men in this hotel who fit that description."

She scoffs. "Ninety-nine percent of them are either, too old, gay, or psychotic. It's hard to find a good-looking, wealthy, young, straight man. If I'm going to let someone lock me up in the proverbial tower, I would at least like to enjoy the view."

She looks me up and down like I'm a horse she's considering buying. And I feel like I'm seeing her, really seeing her, for the first time.

"You're cold, Joni."

"As a brick of ice." She clears her throat, but otherwise, she appears completely unfazed.

"So, you don't *really* care that we're breaking up?" I ask surprised.

She gathers her purse and phone from the table and stands.

"Like you said, there are a hundred men in this hotel who will do the job. I'll miss the view but I've got my pride, Remington. And I won't miss the constant reminders that you were settling for me."

She looks me up and down and shakes her head. "What a waste." She says before she walks out of our hotel room and out of my life.

AS I BOARD MY FLIGHT BACK TO WASHINGTON, I FEEL LIKE I'M living in a whole new world. The hope-fueled torch I've carried for Kal has been snuffed out.

We're not getting our happy ending.

I fucked-up.

She's moved on.

Somewhere between those two facts is our full story.

A story held together by a mortar made up of my mother's manipulations and her mother's fuckups, my idiocy and the unpredictable twists of fate.

Look at what love does to people. Look what it did to me. I don't care what Joni thinks, it's the last thing I want to fuck with again.

I'm in the middle of a crucial, final year in law school. I'm competing for a federal clerkship that would put me on the path to US Attorney or Assistant Attorney General.

I've busted my ass in law school and not only am I number one in my class, but I've already established myself as one hell of a litigator in training during our moot court hearings.

People thought basketball was my gift.

I used to think so, too.

But, how good I am on the basketball court is a mere trifle compared to how good I am in a courtroom.

Advocacy is my gift and deciding to follow my convictions and go to law school was the best thing I ever did.

And now, it's the only thing I've got. I feel sick as I think about Kal being with someone else. It's not the future I imagined. But, I'll make it be enough.

III

AGAIN

Present Day

CONCRETE JUNGLE

KAL

New York City
Eight years later.

"Dammit, ouch!" I reach out to grab the yelping, stumbling woman I just plowed head first into, while I grab my throbbing fore-head. "Oh my God, are you okay? I'm so sorry, I snagged my hose on something and I was looking—"

"Look where you're going," she yells, the red of her wool knit cap seemed like the perfect accessory for her ruddy face, which is pinched in pain. She pulls out of my grasp and stalks away, with an angry glare over her shoulder.

"I'm sorry," I say to her retreating back and then step out of the flow of pedestrian traffic on East Twenty-Eighth Street and duck into the drugstore.

I dig in my coat pocket for the pack of tissues that's taken up perma-nent residence there this winter. My nose has been running pretty much nonstop for two months and I haven't been able to find the time to go see a doctor about it.

"Welcome to Duane Reed," a young girl behind the counter calls without looking up from her phone.

"Where are your pantyhose?" I ask.

"They're in the same aisle as the travel-sized stuff." She points in the general direction of the back of the store.

Without looking up from her phone.

I want to tell her that when I was her age, I would have killed to have a job at a nice drugstore in Manhattan.

But today, my own life is such a mess that I can't scold anyone.

For anything.

My phone rings as I stalk down the aisles looking at the hanging signs above them for a clue about where pantyhose might be. I yank it out of my purse and feel a jolt of panic when I see my lawyer's name flashing on the screen.

"Hey, Fallon. I'm sorry I haven't paid your invoice—"

"Yeah, me too. Too bad sorry doesn't pay my kid's tuition."

Mine's either.

"If you don't pay me by the end of the month, at least half what you owe me, I'll have to turn your account over to a debt collector. I can't have this sitting on my books."

I knew this was coming. She's one of the Peters I robbed to pay Paul last month.

"Okay. I understand. I'll get paid by then, I'll just shuffle some other stuff—"

"I like you, Kal. I do. But we all have bills."

"I know, I appreciate you letting me pay monthly in the first place."

"I want to help you, kid. But that ex of yours is a special kind of asshole. It was time-consuming to answer all of his fucking motions. Next time you get married, get to know him a little better before you sign your life away."

"Oh, Fallon. I can't even imagine a next time." I sigh into the phone.

"That's what they all say. But most people are a sucker for a good old romantic heartbreak. Not complaining— keeps me in business. Let me know what you want to do."

She hangs up without saying goodbye.

I trudge up to the counter and hand the girl, who has still yet to grace me with the gift of a single glance, my box of tights and my credit card.

I pull up my phone while I wait for her to complete the sale and try to find Fallon's last invoice.

"It was declined. You have another one?" She hands the card back to me. She's finally looking at me. Her expression is impatient and annoyed.

"Try it again," I say, but without any real confidence because it's quite possible that I don't have enough money in my account to cover the thirteen-dollar price tag of pantyhose I'm trying to buy.

"Okay." She shrugs and swipes it. I watch the machine and when it gives that single beep I gulp back a ball of humiliation and stick my hand out for my card.

"Don't know what's wrong. My bank must have made a mistake." I sound so lame and she quirks her lips in a "yeah right" and then looks past me.

"Next," she calls to the customer waiting behind me. This is a new low for me—buying pantyhose from a drug store. That appears to be the theme of my life right now, new lows are all the new year has brought me.

I gather my purse and the shattered fragments of my pride and walk out of the store. I duck into the McDonald's next door and hurry into the bathroom. I take the pantyhose off and stuff them into my purse. I tell myself that it's fine to go without pantyhose in early February in New York City. But the sharp bite of winter wind against my bare legs as I walk to work, tells me very differently.

It's not fine.

Nothing is.

I'm officially a disaster. And by the time I get to the Fifth Avenue office building I'm freezing, despondent, and on the edge of a panic attack.

How am I even going to eat tonight? I hope I have enough money on my fare card for the train ride back home. Bianca's supposed to be with me tonight and I was planning on grocery shopping.

Shit. How in the world is this even my life?

I blow my nose before I get onto the elevator and ride up to the twentieth floor with a knot in my stomach. Thank God for this job. The pay is shit, but it's better than nothing and it's just a stepping stone for me. I'm up for a producer's position that's being vacated and if I can get that job, it will relieve some of the financial pressure of starting over the way I've had to since Paul and I got divorced. But it's also a huge opportunity career-wise.

It's a viral new show on HBO where the hosts travel the country investigating unsolved mysteries and disappearances. It's like it was written for me and I have a chance to become a producer and curate content. I'm breathless thinking about being back in my field after so many years away.

"Hey… you're late. And where the hell are your tights?" my office mate and my best friend, Kelli, greets me as soon as I walk through the door.

I pat my purse. "In here."

"Glad they're nice and warm while your legs are freezing."

"I snagged them on something on my way up the stairs from the train. Couldn't get a new pair but couldn't walk in here looking like I'd slept in the park so, I took them off."

"How bad could the hole have been? You can't be outside like that. You'll catch your death."

"Bad. If I'd walked in here like that Jules would have sent me home."

"I'll run to Macy's at lunch and grab you a pair to put on," she says.

"Thank you so much, Kelli." I run over to hug her. Kelli's such a mother hen. I love it. My mother remarried last year and moved to Atlantic City. It's nice to have someone who cares enough to fuss.

"Don't thank me so fast. Jules has been in here twice looking for you."

"She has?" That can't be good. Jules is our editor in chief and she detests anyone being late. "I wonder if they've made a decision." I give her an anxious smile and shed my navy blue pea coat, drop my purse and riffle through for my things.

"Maybe, I saw Slugman come out of there just before she came here to find you."

I hold up my crossed fingers and she returns the gesture with a smile. "You better get up there before she has to come back."

I grab my notebook and pen and hustle out of the door.

"You wanted to see me?" I ask as I poke my head in Jules' office.

"Yes, come in. I've never come to look for you in the morning. Are you always late?" She folds her arms across her chest and doesn't hide the fact that she's completely unimpressed with me. Her sharp gray eyes are like chips of steel and feel just as sharp as she trains them on me and waits for me to answer.

"No. Never. Today has been extraordinary in lots of ways. I'm sorry." I hope my apology sounds sincere because it's really not. In reality, I'm less than ten minutes "late." Every other day, I'm in the office by 7:30 a.m.

Of course, the only day it actually matters, I'm late.

"The rest of the hiring committee wants to hire Jon Slugman instead of you." She cuts straight to the chase.

My stomach falls like an elevator car cut loose from its cables. I clutch the notepad to steady my hands and fight the tears that sting the back of my eyes.

"Oh." My voice is trapped in the panic clogging my throat. I clear it and try to look her in the eye.

"Can you tell me why?"

"Because he's a man. This business is a boy's club." She says dispassionately.

"I see," I whisper to my hands. That feels worse than knowing that I fell short somehow.

"Thank God money is mightier than sexism. And my husband has more of it than almost anyone. I write the checks around here. So, it's *my* vote that counts," she says in her cool silky way.

My head snaps up. I'm afraid to hope, but I clutch at the tiny ember of it she just threw my way. "And how are you voting?"

"He's good." She says and shrugs. My shoulders fall.

"I think you're better."

That ember roars to life.

"You do?" I gasp.

She nods.

"I detest tears," she hands me a tissue and I dab at the tears I didn't quite manage to stem.

"I'm sticking my neck out here, Kal. You need to show the rest of the editorial board that you're the best person for the job."

"How? If I haven't managed to do that already—"

"You've written some great pieces. But you're holding back. Dig deeper into the stories, find the human aspect. Give your audience some hope while you deliver the gloom of the story. You need to be twice as good as him. Bring your A-game."

I thought I had been. But clearly not. I swallow a ball of disappointment.

"I'll try harder."

"You fucking better. I'm throwing you a big bone." She steeples her hands under her chin and nods at my notebook.

I open it.

"I got a lead today and I think you're the perfect person to pursue it. If you can bring it home, it would be the making of you."

"Wow. Thank you. Your faith in me is—"

"Please, don't prove it misguided," she says with no warmth at all. "I've been waiting for a woman I could champion. You're it. Do not let me down."

"Okay."

"If you don't come back with this story, not only will you not get the producer's position. You're also not going to have this job anymore. We're making cuts to junior staff and your current role is on the chopping block."

"Tell me about the lead," I say, getting straight to business. Getting fired isn't an option. I need this job. If I lose it right now, I won't be able to sell my place fast enough to keep us from losing everything. No, nothing will stop me.

"You're from Houston, right?"

Surprise straightens my spine. "Yes. I mean… I haven't lived there in over fifteen years, but yes."

"Wonderful. There was this weird little news story out of there a couple months ago. A shooting. Gigi Rivers, oldest daughter of Houston's founding family. She was the family's black sheep. She's lived in

Italy for thirty years. Suddenly, she's back in Houston and she wasn't there very long before she was shot right outside the Riverses company headquarters."

"Someone *shot* her?" I gasp. I remember that family. Remi told me their families were rivals.

"Yes." She raises a scandalized eyebrow. "Word is, the bullet was meant for Hayes Rivers. The official story was that it was a disgruntled former employee looking for revenge. It could be, right? I mean it's Texas, they love guns, *right?*" Her wide eyed stare is expectant, so I nod.

"But, what if it's more than some whacko who got fired? His aunt made a full recovery but instead of scurrying back to the safety of her Tuscan villa, where not even the police have guns, she's still in Houston."

"And?" I ask impatiently. I've got so many ideas for the part of the series I'd be producing called "Bad at Love" looking at cold cases where crimes of passion had been suspected.

This story sounds a little *Lifestyles of the Rich and Famous* to me. I know that right now, beggars can't be choosers but I'm confused by the assignment.

"Jules, this sounds intriguing, but it also sounds like gossip. I want to investigate things that matter. I'm not a gossip columnist. We're not a gossip magazine. We report on real people and when they go missing it rips a hole in the lives of the people left behind."

She purses her lips in disappointment.

"They are one of the most powerful and influential families in America. Their influence is vast and people care about them. We need viewers, or we can't sell advertising. And if we can't sell advertising, none of us will have a job. So I'm sending you after a story that to you feels fluffy but is exactly what our viewership wants. You know how much interest there is in this family."

"Yes, and between E! Television and People Magazine, they get all the information they need."

She leans back in her chair and raises a haughty eyebrow at me.

"Please don't do me the insult of thinking that I would be suggesting we report this like it's salacious gossip. I've got another interesting tidbit from my source, and that's what I'm sending you to Houston for.

According to a credible source, there was a DNA test ordered for Hayes Rivers last fall."

I gawk at her. You don't have to live in Houston to have heard of the return of The Rivers King, as they call Hayes Rivers, from Italy. It was big news everywhere. They are one of the last remaining true family dynastyies in the United States. And the fact that they all look like movie stars, only makes them the subject of intense interest.

There were dozens of interest pieces detailing his background, really casting this aura of mystery onto his return. We ran a documentary that to date has one of the highest number of views of anything we've done.

"And if Hayes Rivers is *not* the heir, then who is? *That's* going to be one of the most talked about missing person's story of the year if we can get it. These are the kind of dramas that get made into movies. Your familiarity with the neighborhood and the city make you the perfect person to lift the veil."

Excitement wells in my gut. This is my chance. I've fucked up every-thing else, but if I can get my career right, maybe I can start to get back on my feet. "Yes. I agree. I can do that."

"Of course, you can. You're pretty, you're curious—almost too curious for your own good—and you're hungry, but not in a 'I'll do anything to win kind of way,' like Slugman is. I look at you and I see myself. You're what? Twenty-nine?"

I cringe. "Thirty one."

"You're in competition with a twenty-two-year-old college graduate. You reek of single mother starting over and I want you to win because I think you deserve it. So go and get this story."

I think about Bianca and what it means if I go to Houston for work that could take weeks or months to complete. But if I get it, I can pay Fallon back for my shit show of a divorce and finally get back on my feet.

I look down at my bare legs. Think about my empty fridge and empty bank account. I can't say no. I'll ask Kelli for air miles to get Bianca a ticket down to spend a weekend with me. It'll be fine.

And Houston means Remi.

I push that thought away. That's really the last thing that should be on my mind. But it is increasingly so, since my divorce.

I'm single. And he is, too. I haven't seen him in eight years. And that last time had been so painful, I'm not sure he'll be happy to see me.

It may not be a good idea to poke at old wounds. I'm just asking for more heartbreak. But the truth is, even after all of these years, my heart is still his to break. Even now, just at the thought of seeing him, the foolish thing is beating wildly.

23

MISSING

KAL

"I'm meeting Kalilah Greer," I hear a voice behind me speak softly to the maître d'.

"Regan?" I call to her back and she turns around and gapes at me.

"Kal. Is that *you?*"

I let her stare. I look nothing like she remembers.

To be fair, she looks nothing like she used to, either. At her wedding, the gawky, skinny girl with terrible acne and braces was already long gone. But even then, in her couture wedding gown, she'd still had an air of insecurity around her. Today, Regan Wilde-Landel stands in front of me in all of her glory.

She looks perfect. Her hair is a sleek sea of chocolate silk whipped into beautiful waves that hover at her shoulders. I only see hair that perfect in magazines. No one looks like that in real life.

Well no one, but Regan.

Her tanned, honey skin is polished and glows, against the white of her body-hugging blouse. Her makeup so expertly applied that I wonder if maybe she doesn't have it tattooed into place. Her body, even after three children, is ridiculously toned.

She's dressed head to toe in Carolina Herrera couture. Black pencil skirt, white blouse with flounces at the sleeves. A sexy, but simple pair of black patent leather Louboutin's adorn her small, perfectly lovely feet. Small gold hoops dangle from her ears. A simple gold band on her finger where most wealthy women wear their huge diamonds.

She doesn't need diamonds to declare that she has a right to be here. She *is* a diamond. Of the first water. And she's come fully into her own.

I'm envious of that. I'm still sifting through the rubble of my life to figure out who I am. Today I'm dressed like the journalist I wish I was. In clothes I can no longer afford to buy. My once unfettered dark curls have been blown straight, highlighted with gold and restrained in the confines of my signature ponytail. I've got a face full of makeup, that's both heavier and a lot less subtle than Regan's.

Her eyes roam over my well-tailored dark black pants, a creamy cashmere sweater that wraps around my body with a belt of gold silk, my kid leather ankle boots, and my Kate Spade handbag which all look perfectly chic and respectable.

There's not a hint of the refusal to conform that used to be the calling card of my style. But this is what eight years as a "Stepford Wife" has made me. I don't remember the last time I left my house with no makeup on.

Suddenly, it feels heavy, when I speak, I can feel it moving in the small lines around my mouth and eyes. I can't wait to wash it off.

"Kal, thank you for meeting me. You look wonderful." She leans in to kiss me on the cheek and embraces me.

"Raul, we're ready to be seated." She graces the man with a warm smile before tucking her arm through mine and leading us through the restaurant. "Come on. We have a lot to talk about. I booked us a private room for lunch. This is where the boozy bored housewives come to hang out. I only come when I need to go somewhere no one will notice me. I'm one of them now. Minus the boozy part," she says and I am a little caught off guard by how candid she's just been with me.

I only called her because I couldn't reach Remi. We barely know each other. I wasn't even sure she would know who I was when I called.

When I asked her if she had a good number for Remi, she said, "I have no idea where he is. We haven't heard from him in months." Then she burst into tears and my heart stopped.

Remi missing? It sounded… impossible. It was like saying the moon fell out of the sky. When she asked me to meet her for lunch, I'd come right away.

As soon as Raul shuts the door of our little dark wood-walled dining room, she leans in and grabs my hands.

"I'm sorry I fell apart like that on the phone." She looks like she might cry again.

"Tell me what happened." I squeeze her hand reassuringly.

"I don't know. He's gone."

"So, no one knows where he is?"

"*Someone* knows. His fucking partners at the firm. They said they're not able to divulge it. His best friend's wife works for him, and they don't know where he is either. I was hoping you might."

"Me?" I lean away, completely taken aback.

She fiddles with the edge of her napkin, and looks away from me.

"Why would you think that?"

"Look, I know you were married and you guys didn't stay in touch. But, I heard you and Paul split, kind of around the same time he went missing. I thought maybe, the two of you had finally gone for it. He's never gotten over you."

I'm stunned. "Really?"

She doesn't appear to hear me. She's staring at her napkin and tugging at it like she's trying to tear it.

"His car's GPS system was turned off. He hasn't made a phone call. He hasn't sent an email."

"Why haven't you called the police?"

"I told you, because his partners at the law firm know where he is. He's not missing. Just not talking to his family."

"But, why would he do that?"

"I don't know." She practically growls in frustration. "No one does."

"How is that possible? When's the last time you saw him?"

"The last time anyone saw him was the day he went to the hospital to see Gigi Rivers."

An alarm bell rings in my head. I lean forward, and even though I know we're alone, I still look around the room, just to make sure.

"Why would he go and see Gigi Rivers?"

"He and Hayes are best friends. They have been since Hayes moved back."

"I thought your families were feuding?" I ask and take a sip of my water to quench my parched throat.

"Well, it's never been our generation. That's something our parents know about, but never told us more than that the Wilde's weren't one of us. But, they… they're just really close." Her voice cracks.

She closes her eyes and battles back tears. "Hayes just got married. I was sure he'd come back for that. But, he didn't. And—it's my daughter's birthday today. That's why I'm so distraught. He would never ever miss this. I think something's happened to him. Those men at the office don't care as long as they're making money. Remi's out there somewhere, alone."

"Oh my God…" My mind is whirling, and my heart thuds as I try to parse and separate what she's saying about Remi from my questions about Gigi Rivers.

"Kal, Remi is intensely private. He's always been, but in the last few years, as his career took off, he's become like a different person. He's a complete workaholic, a taskmaster, perfectionist, and really kind of closed off to any real affection. He moved back here when my grandfather died. He's been really focused on building Wilde Law. He goes off sometimes, but he's never just disappeared. I'm afraid he's not coming back."

My stomach forms a knot. The thought of Remi somewhere hurt or stranded and alone sends chills through my body.

Regan doesn't seem to notice my stillness or feel my panic.

"I'm still trying to protect his privacy. He wouldn't want this to be news. Whatever is going on with him is obviously serious. His assistant quit right when he left, and I know he wouldn't trust anyone else, I've been managing his calendar. But, I fucked-up. I forget to cancel one of his appearances. He was the keynote speaker. Now, there's gossip that he's missing." Her face is pinched.

"Oh, wow…" I shake my head in bewilderment, trying to put together the meager facts she's just given me.

"So he didn't get in touch with you at all?"

Her question lurches me out of the daze that the rest of her words put me in. "I've heard nothing. But… I think I'm the last person he'd call."

"Kal, you're probably the *only* person he'd call. He talks about you all the time. Those Christmas cards Paul sends Marcel every year? He's confiscated every single one. His refrigerator is covered with them. I just assumed… I thought he would come to you…" She covers her face in despair.

"No, he didn't come to me," I say slowly.

"Oh God. I don't know what to do. Gigi Rivers won't talk to any of us." She wails.

"Why? Because of the feud?"

"I guess." She clears her throat and composes herself. "My mother's tried. She said she won't see us. I don't understand. I'm friends with Stone Rivers, but he's off in Medellín or some shit and otherwise, I have no contact with the rest of them. I don't know what to do."

"Are you kidding? Your brother is missing. And you haven't talked to the last people who saw him?" She leans away from the judgement in my voice.

"I told you, my mother tried, they won't talk to us." She insists.

"And you believe your mother?" I am incredulous. I know firsthand that the woman is a devious, shameless liar.

She frowns. "Why wouldn't I?"

I cock my head at her. She was at the party, she may not have seen it go down, but she must have heard.

Her wide eyes fill with regret as she remembers and she flattens her lips in regret.

"I know what she did to you. It was *so* wrong. But this is different. She wants to find Remi desperately. She's out of her mind with worry."

She can't possibly be that naïve about her mother. If she wants something, she gets it. If she hasn't found Remi, it's because she hasn't tried to.

But, I hold my tongue because I can see in her earnest eyes that she believes what she's saying.

I don't believe it's possible that Tina's not involved somehow, but it won't help me to distance Regan by insulting her now.

"Do you know how I can reach Gigi Rivers?"

"She's in Rivers Wilde. She bought a place. But, she's got security…"

"I'm not going to break in. I'll just go over, tell her I'm looking for Remi. If she's hostile or won't talk, then at least we'll know that something went down in that hospital room and we can start looking for answers about what."

Regan's eyes widen. "Oh, Kal. Thank you so much."

She smiles for the first time and the hope in it makes me anxious.

"Don't thank me yet. Even if I do get in to see her, I don't know how much she'll tell me."

"It'll be better than nothing. When will you go?" She takes a huge swig of water.

I glance at my watch. This detour is going to throw a wrench in my plans, but if something has happened to Remi, I have to help.

"I need to go back to my hotel and make some calls and send some emails, but I'll go today."

She clamps a hand over her mouth. "Oh, Kal, I'm so self-absorbed. I've hijacked your trip with this drama about Remi. I'm so sorry." She covers my hand with hers. "Tell me why you're in town."

My mind is so focused on unpacking everything she's told me, that I draw a blank for a second.

"Are you okay?" Her pretty brow furrows in worry.

I shake myself and hope my benign smile is convincing.

"I'm in town doing research on a story I'm writing and just thought I'd look up an old friend."

Her confused sadness clears and in its place is the other thing she and Remi share—keen, knowing gazes.

"Why didn't you just call Remi's office? Why call me? We're not friends," she says and I get my own guard right back up.

She may be nice, but she was never stupid. Her tears made me forget that I'm on an assignment. One that requires me to lie to her.

"I did call his office. No one answered. So, I called yours next."

She nods slowly as if she's processing what I've said and is deciding whether she believes it.

"What story are you working on?" she asks finally.

"It's an investigation. I can't talk about it, I signed an NDA. You understand," I say with a small, not particularly friendly smile.

She holds my gaze for a few minutes and then smiles apologetically.

"I'm sorry. I don't trust anyone right now. We've had some local press sniffing around since he missed that event and I'm just so on edge. Here you are about to do me a huge favor and I'm giving you the ninth degree."

I squeeze her hand reassuringly. "You've had a hard day. It's okay."

"Thank you, Kal. I know you always cared so much about Remi."

I smile and look down at my hands because I can't keep looking her in the eye and pretend that I'm being purely altruistic.

I am worried about Remi and want to find him, too. But, I didn't come down here expecting to find that there might be connection between Gigi Rivers getting shot and the Wildes. It seems like a long shot, but Remi up and disappearing after visiting her in the hospital feels like something…

"I'll talk to Gigi. And let you know what I find." I tell her.

"Thank you so much You have no idea how grateful I am."

"It'll be a good place to start. Maybe she can tell us if he seemed upset about something when she saw him. And if that doesn't work, I'll talk to some of the hospital staff and see if anyone saw or heard anything." I tell her.

"I should have thought of that. But, my little not so secret poison pen article hasn't exactly honed my skills as a journalist." She smiles self-deprecatingly.

"Poison pen?"

"It's just a gossip column I write under a pen name. It's an open secret that it's me. But, I haven't worked properly since I married Marcel."

"Do you want to work?" I ask. She smiles blandly and then proceeds to act like she didn't hear me.

"So, how long are you here?"

I'm very good at staying in my lane, so I let it go.

"I'll go back when I have the story. I'm thinking no more than a couple of weeks."

"You must love the freedom of being divorced. If I even mentioned going away indefinitely, my husband and children would band together and hogtie me." She laughs, but it's tinny and flat. Her eyes glisten with tears.

"Are you okay, Regan?"

She blinks back her tears and smiles. "I just want my brother home. I need him."

24

FOUND

KAL

"Miss Rivers. Thank you for speaking with me." I stand up as Gigi Rivers is wheeled into the sitting room. She looks younger than I imagined and very much like Hayes Rivers.

She lifts an eyebrow at me and doesn't smile. "Well, you say you're a friend of Remi's. And you left your phone with my security guard, so I hope that means I can speak without worrying you're recording it."

I can't imagine living like you think everyone is looking to betray you.

Her nurse helps her out of the chair and settles her on the cushions she's arranged on the couch.

"Thank you, Enid. You can leave us," she says with a tired smile to her nurse.

The young woman turns to me and sets her dark green, serious eyes on me with a warning glare. "Please remember that she is recovering. Nothing too difficult and I'll be back in twenty minutes to check on her."

What does she think I'm going to do?

"I just want to chat. I'll make sure to pay attention to signs that she's getting tired."

"Stop talking about me like I'm a deaf invalid. Enid, I said you can leave us. And Kalilah, if I'm tired you won't have to look for signs, I'll tell you. Now, sit. Let's get to talking."

"Of course, Gigi," Enid says in a cajoling voice. She gives me an almost comical warning frown on her way out.

"I've wondered when someone was going to call me. I've given up on that woman calling me back, but I'm thrilled someone actually gives a shit enough to come and talk to me." Her voice drips with disgust.

"I'm confused. I was told that you refused to speak to The Wildes. That Mrs. Wilde had reached out to you and had her efforts rebuffed."

"That's a lie. But considering the source, I'm not surprised. I've called her every day since I got home." She pulls her phone out and scrolls through it.

Then, she hands it to me. "Here, look. I'm not tech savvy enough to know how to fake that." I take the phone from her. Sure enough, her outgoing calls are interspersed with several listed to a T Wilde.

I shake my head, my mind boggled. Why would Tina pretend Gigi had refused to talk to them?

She laughs dryly. I look up and she's watching me with beautiful hazel eyes that, in contrast to the small smile she's wearing, are very sad.

"You must not know her."

"Oh, I know her. But it's been a long time," I confess.

"She's done so much lying over the last few years, she's forgotten how to tell the truth. Trust me. It takes someone who has done the very same thing to recognize it. She doesn't know what's false and what's true anymore."

I look at her with a knowing understanding.

"So, Remington's skipped out on his family, huh? The girl who comes in to do my hair told me she'd heard gossip that he'd gone walkies," she muses but doesn't offer anything else. I smile and try to appear patient.

"I understand you're the last person to see him before he left."

"Was I? I hadn't heard that. I have no idea what was going on because no one in that family will talk to me."

I swallow back a frustrated growl and smile. "Will you tell me what happened with Remington when you saw him?"

"I could. But then, I'd be telling a story that's not mine to tell. My nephew, Hayes, and Remington—they are the ones who will have to tell you the story."

My gut twists when I realize that Remi, somehow, is mixed up in whatever is happening with the Rivers family.

"Do you think Hayes will speak with me?" I ask, hopefully.

"Why don't you just ask Remi?" she asks in a voice now full of skepticism.

"Because no one knows where he is," I remind her.

She angles away from me, her arms folded tightly across her chest, and narrows her eyes at me. "How did you say you knew him?"

I sit up straighter. Give her what I hope is a convincing smile.

"We were friends when I was in high school. Good friends. We've lost touch over the years. But now that I've heard that he's missing, I want to try to find him."

She gives an assessing glance and then pulls out her phone. "You are a terrible liar."

"I'm not lying. I am really just trying to find Remi."

"Enid, I'm ready to go. Please come down."

"Please."

"No. *Please* leave. I don't know what you really want. But, I can't help you."

"You naughty girl. I can't believe you have the nerve to show your face in here after the way you disappeared." Sweet's loud voice envelops me in an embrace nearly as warm as the one she's giving me with her arms.

"I'm sorry, Sweet. It wasn't up to me."

"That mother of yours," she says without a hint of acrimony as she lets me go.

We sit down at a corner table and hold hands across it. She scans my face and then sits back.

"You look... different," she says and even though I know she's not judging me, I still run a hand over my hair.

"It's been eight years, Sweet. I've had a kid, I was bound to change."

She frowns, unimpressed.

"No, it's not that. Like... maybe you wouldn't call Joni West a cunt if she tried to push you around today."

Sweet had laughed so hard when I told her that story.

"Back for less than a day and her name crops up. Should I be worried that she's going to stroll in any minute?"

"Thank goodness, no. She's that lout of a husband's problem now."

"She got married?" I can't disguise my surprise and she laughs.

"Oh, yeah, except I doubt Remi even noticed. Now, she's making everyone in Greatwood miserable."

"Greatwood?"

"Her husband bought the golf course and they live there now. She used to come by whenever she had a new car to show off. But she stopped doing that when she realized no one cared."

I know she and Remi broke up, I saw it all over the news, but after carrying a torch for him for most of her life, I imagined that she'd never move on. But I guess that was silly considering that even though I loved him, I married someone else, too.

"Now, tell me why you're in town." She smiles sweetly.

"I'm working on a story. Can't really talk about it, but my lead is here in Houston. So I'm chasing it."

I don't add that I'm failing so far and the only lead I'm chasing is Remi. After being very unceremoniously asked to leave Gigi's house, my stomach is in knots. Something is weird is going on. I need to find him.

"So, you know Remi's not around. I mean, no one's saying anything, but he's been gone for months," she informs me with a conspiratorial glance around the restaurant. It's like she read my thoughts.

"So people are talking?" I ask.

"Not yet. His people have covered for him good, but I've noticed. And you've been in town for less than a day and you have, too. It's only a matter of time before everyone does."

"Regan told me. I promised her I'd try to find him, but the only person who knows anything just threw me out of her house."

"I don't even want to know. You know how I hate gossip." And she does. Her husband, Lo lives for it, though.

"But, she might know something." She nods at a dark-haired woman, holding a steaming mug of coffee and staring blankly out of a window.

I look back at Sweet in surprise.

"Who in the world is that?"

"She was Remi's personal assistant for years."

Ah, the one who quit. I eye her. She looks more like a low-maintenance yoga enthusiast than she does the former personal assistant to one of the wealthiest men in the state.

"Are you sure that's her?"

"Oh, yeah. She's been spending a lot of time in here. Doing nothing. But she worked for him a long time. *She* might talk to you."

ARMED WITH AN ADDRESS AND RACHEL'S COMMAND THAT I BRING Remi home, I pull just out onto Wildeway Parkway and start making my way north. I'm fiddling with my GPS when my phone rings. My daughter's face lights up my screen and I press the green circle to accept it.

"My sweets. Hi, baby," I sing at her.

"Hi, Mom. Where are you?" she asks; my heart flutters as her sweet voice fills my car.

"I'm in Texas. For work. Like I was yesterday," I remind her.

"*Still?*"

"Yes, honey. Still. And don't whine."

"But, I miss you." She moans and ugh… it feels so damn good to know someone does.

"You just miss my mac and cheese," I tease her.

My heart aches, though. I wish I could be with her. She's young, but she's great company and in some ways, I'm getting to live my childhood through her. She makes all the shit I've had to wade through worth it.

Making sure she gets everything I missed out on is what gets me out of bed every morning. I would suffer everything all over again if it meant I could have her.

"I miss you more. But guess what? I'm buying you a ticket to come and see me in two weeks. You and I are going to spend a whole weekend just hanging out."

"Really?" she squeals and I'm glad she's still so easy to please.

"Yes. I promise."

"I can't—" Her voice muffles and I hear her speaking to someone.

"Bianca?" I shout, I didn't even ask where she was when she called. She's almost eight, and she has playdates now. Paul lets her walk to her friend's house by herself. I know it's fine, and I did it at her age. But my neighborhood in Houston wasn't anything like the huge city blocks of Manhattan where my child is growing up.

"Kalilah." Paul's voice comes through clear, full of reproach and loud.

"Hello, Paul."

"It's not an authorized phone call day for you. Please stick to the schedule."

"I'm sorry, I'm not going to decline a call from my daughter because it goes against your ridiculous rules."

"Those rules are in the best interest of my new family dynamic. On the days she speaks with you, Donna is upset. It causes a heightened level of tension in our home that I would like to minimize. It would be best, actually, if these protracted visits could be kept to a minimum in general."

My anger surges. At his parent's urging, he fought me for full custody. I went broke to make sure that my daughter stayed with me. Now, Paul treats being a parent like it's an inconvenience.

"She's going to grow up one day, Paul, and she'll wonder why you didn't spend more time with her. She'll be leaving in a week, please do your best to make her feel at home until then." It's a warning and not a request.

"Maybe you should be here instead of gallivanting all over the country in the name of a career. You made your choices, now we all have to live with them." And then he hangs up.

He has never laid a hand on me, but I used to flinch every time he started to talk. Because his words were his weapon. He berated me constantly. Ruined my career and then the minute I rebelled, he divorced me and took up with his secretary. He's the one who had an affair, but somehow, the breakdown of our marriage was my fault.

I've never wanted her to feel like a piece of rope in a tug-of-war. She hated that we split. She loves us both.

"Choose better next time, Kal." I hear Fallon's voice in my ear.

Armed with that and an address that Rachel, Remi's assistant very willingly provided, I enter the onramp and make my way toward College Station to find Remi.

25

BURNING

REMI

THE CRUNCH OF GRAVEL UNDER TIRES DOESN'T SURPRISE ME. Nancy started barking three minutes ago. She always does when someone comes up this way. She spots them a few miles away, and she comes running, barking her head off. She's calmed down a lot since I found her, but she's still wary of everyone who comes here.

Mrs. Jameson comes up every Tuesday from the small restaurant that's attached to the convenience store she and her husband own in town. Nancy barks at her so hard, she refuses to get out of her car.

But today's not Tuesday. And I haven't invited anyone to visit.

For a split second, I wonder if Regan finally pulled her head out of her ass and came to find me. Or if my mother has sent some sort of special forces team to make sure I don't talk. As if I ever would. I wish I didn't know what I knew. Why in the world would I want to broadcast it?

When the squeak of brakes tells me the car's in front of my house, I stand up. I head toward the front of the house and pick up my shotgun, it's resting in a corner nook built into the wall. I pick up my pace when I hear the car door close, and I put the butt on my shoulder and open the door slowly.

I drop the gun, and it lands with a thud at my feet. I stand there with my heart racing like it hasn't in years. Kal is standing at the end of my walkway and it's like someone put an electric paddle on my chest and hit the power button.

"Oh my God in Heaven," Kal screams and throws her hands up in front of her and crouches behind the open door of her car.

I shut the door behind me when I hear the scramble of Nancy's claws across the floor as the strange voice brings her running to investigate.

Kal's lips are moving but I can't hear what she's saying over the roar of blood in my ears.

Is it possible I'm dreaming, hallucinating? Kal, can't *possibly* be here.

I stand, barefoot on the front porch of the house and stare down the long stone gravel path at the very last person I expected to see. And perhaps the only person in the world, who right now, I'm happy to see.

Her skin is still that smooth, creamy caramel that I swear I can taste in the back of my throat just looking at her.

It's like she's stopped aging since the last time I saw her, almost eight years ago. Or maybe, I've died and I'm in heaven. This is exactly what my heaven would be – somewhere quiet with Kal.

But in my dreams, she looks… different. I cock my head and take her in.

Her hair is very straight, streaked with golden highlights and scraped back off her face. Her face is made up. She's wearing lipstick. It's a neutral color, but still not close to the peachy perfection of her own lips. I sweep her from head to toe. She's dressed like she lives in a J. Crew catalog. I go from being shocked to see her to being worried.

"Will?" I say her name and she peeks out from behind her hands.

Her large, brown eyes land on me and the twin beauties stir a place deep inside of me that has been asleep for a long time.

"Remi… hi." Her smooth, deep voice is the most soothing thing I've heard in in a long time. It makes me think about things I miss—home, most of all. Because, every time I've been with Kal, no matter where we've been, I've always felt at home.

I walk toward her, barely noticing the bite of the gravel under my bare feet and completely ignore Mrs. Jameson's repeated warnings about snakes.

But, her being here makes no sense. Something must be wrong. "Why are you here?" It sounds harsh and unwelcoming even to my own ears, and she flinches.

"Um. I came for you… to see you. To check on you. I—" She blows out a nervous breath and looks around the property.

"The house is so beautiful. I don't know why I imagined I'd find you living in some burned-out, abandoned house."

I sway and take a step closer to her. Her eyes widen a fraction, but then she takes a step toward me, too

"How'd you find me?" We're only ten feet apart now and my arms are starting to ache.

For her.

She swallows and the flash of her soft pink tongue as it darts over her tender, plump bottom lip draws my eyes back to her lips. I want to wipe that fucking lipstick off with my tongue.

"Uh, I met Rachel. She told me you might be here."

My eyes follow the bob of her throat, visible even trapped behind the neck of her wool, navy blue turtleneck.

I peruse the rest of her and miss the pop of color that has always been her trademark.

My eyes snap back to hers. "Are you okay?"

She laughs. Fuck, I've missed her laugh so much. "You've been gone without a word to anyone for months. Are *you* okay?"

No one's asked me that question in a while. And it loosens something in me. And I tell her what I haven't even admitted to myself. "No, I'm not okay."

Her smiles vanishes, and I'm caught in this weird limbo of wanting to put it back and being glad that someone is looking at me like they give a shit.

At the same time, it's torture that she's not mine. That I can't just walk up to her, kiss her and fuck her until I feel better.

"Why are you here?" I ask again. Because, I don't understand at all. "Don't you live in New York City? With your husband and your daughter? Why are you in Texas? At this house, you shouldn't have been able to find?"

Her smile is a weird, glitchy, indecisive thing.

I don't smile back.

She clears her throat and her smile falters. "We have a lot of catching up to do. I am really just here to check on you. I promise. We can go inside or talk out here. Either's fine with me, but I'd rather do it sitting down." She nods at her feet and lifts one of her legs up to indicate the heel on the boot she's wearing.

"Oh shit." I shake my head. It's Kal, not the fucking FBI. If she's here, there's a reason. I'm treating her like she's a hostile enemy.

I've been out here alone with my anger for too long.

"I'm sorry. Sorry. Come in." I wave her to follow me and I head back to the house. Nancy's tongue is pressed to the glass of the door and I can see the eagerness in her eyes.

"I've got a dog, though. She's skittish. I rescued her, and she's got some kind of PTSD. Instead of running from people she tries to attack them."

I turn just as she's making her way up the stairs and I hold out a hand to her. She doesn't hesitate to slip hers into mine.

I wish she had.

That touch, the slide of her soft palm against mine is like dropping a goldfish into the mouth of a starving shark – hardly enough.

I'm trying to think, figure out how I'm going to handle sitting next to her when I want to pull her into me and hold her there. But she's someone else's wife. I let go of her.

"Oh." She looks in surprise at her companionless hand and then, back at me. I smile stiffly.

"I'll go in first and hold her back. Once she sees us being friendly for a few minutes, she'll be cool."

She eyes the dog wearily but gives me a genuinely happy smile. "I don't have pets, but I've always wanted one. You rescue her from a shelter around here?"

"Nope. Someone chopped her tail off and threw her in a ditch to bleed to death. I found her on one of my runs and brought her home. She just took to me."

"Another *Remi* person, I see." she says a wry smile tugging the corner of her pretty mouth. It's enchanting.

I look away from her, open the door and grab Nancy's collar just as she lunges for Kal.

Kal shrieks and steps backward. "Oh my God, you weren't kidding. Has she bitten you?"

"No. And she won't bite you, either. She's just trying to scare you because she doesn't know you're not here to hurt her."

I scratch her chin and smile down at her

"Do you, girl? She won't hurt you." I slide a glance at Kal and wink. "She only breaks human hearts."

She flushes.

"Come in. Rub her head once, she'll be good. She'll slink off and won't come out until she's hungry."

Kal looks between me and the dog like she's not sure she believes either one of us.

Then, she drops to her knees and brings herself almost eye level with Nancy. "Hey," she says softly in return to Nancy's growl. She puts a hand on her head. "I understand, baby. I wouldn't like people either. I'm Kalilah. I'm nice, like he said. And don't mind his talk about hearts. I've never been the one to do the breaking." She looks up and smiles in that sweet way she has and I have to look away again. She is so beautiful it steals my breath.

"What kind of dog is she?"

"I don't know. The vet said she's a mutt. But that black coat and her height say she's at least part mastiff of some sort. We just don't know."

Nancy huffs contentedly and turns her nose until it's in Kal's palm. I blink down at her. "Well, that's a record. Takes her a few visits to give that to anyone."

"Hmm, maybe she can smell the little girl in me who always pined for a friend just like her," she says.

At the mention of that little girl, I remember that Kal shouldn't be here.

"Are you going to tell me why you're here?" I ask, pulling Nancy back.

She looks up sharply and stands. "I was in Houston for work. I called your office—thought we could catch up over lunch or something. When I couldn't get a hold of you there, I called Regan."

"Regan doesn't know where I am."

"No, but Rachel does. She gave me the address."

"Rachel did? She's still in Rivers Wilde?"

"Yeah, she asked me not to tell anyone. So I didn't. I just got in my rental and drove out here."

"Why?"

"Your sister is worried sick. I wanted to make sure you're okay. You've gone off the grid completely." She looks around again.

"I'm perfectly happy out here. I have clients. They pay me in cash, food, cleaning services, and yard work. I don't have to worry that I'm living in a nest of vipers like I do with my own family." I realize my voice has gone from even to loud and she takes a step toward me. Her eyes are wide with alarm.

"Remi, what's happened? Who hurt you?" she asks and my soul takes a deep sigh. The ten-pound weight that's been pressed against my heart lightens because my person is here. She'll understand. Because she always does.

Yet even in my state of I don't give a fuck, I'm not devoid of common sense. I know Kal is my friend, but she's also a journalist. "I'll tell you, but what I tell you stays here."

26

CATCHING UP

REMI

SHE'S SPRAWLED ON TOP OF ME, HER HEAD RESTING ON MY shoulder, her eyes closed. Our chests rise and fall in almost perfect unison and we lie there in silence, trying to catch our breaths and gather our thoughts.

That was unexpected. I lost my mind for a second. I break the silence with my confession.

"I want to say I'm sorry because I kind of just attacked you. But Kal, I've been waiting for you to be free for me to do that for what feels like nearly half my life."

She slides her pretty brown eyes over to me and lifts the corner of her mouth in a satisfied smile. "I know. I've been waiting, too."

Surprise has me sitting up, thinking I missed something.

"Really? I thought... you know, you were building a life. I thought you were happy."

"Happy?" She looks away, her expression thoughtful. She sighs and shakes her head. "No, but she didn't ask to be born, I chose to have her.

225

And I wanted Bianca to have a stability I didn't. In hindsight, it was completely misguided. Her life has been in constant upheaval for the last couple of years. I'm just finding my feet."

Her smile is tight and forced. And just like when we were kids, I feel compelled to make it reach her eyes.

I shake my head at her. "Well, shit. I take my first vacation in nearly ten years and the world stopped turning. You motherfuckers can't survive without me."

She throws her head back and chuckles. "Thank the Lord your ego is still intact."

I nudge her shoulder. "I mean, it. You being happily married was something I'd come to accept as fact." I nod to my fridge. "It's the only thing that kept me from coming to you. That you looked happy in those pictures."

"Really? Well, the only person in that room who was truly happy was the photographer we paid to take our picture. For real."

We both get lost in our thoughts for a minute. I break the silence with another confession.

"Want me to tell you something?"

"Yeah, of course."

"You know, everyone thinks I'm married to my career. That I've chosen it over having a family."

"Are they wrong?" she asks.

"Very. I didn't move on because there was no one I wanted to move on with. I'm not the settling type, so I decided that I'd be alone."

"Are you serious? You were going to be a bachelor forever?" she squawks.

"Why not? I have a satisfying career. My sister's kids are like my own and I get a lot out of being their uncle. I serve my community and I date some fantastic women. Just none that gave me the urge that you did."

I trail my fingers through her hair.

"Urge?" she drawls and leans into my touch.

"Yes… to dig deeper, to ask questions, to welcome discomfort as a sign of growth. To stop believing in someone else's version of my story and write it myself. You taught me all that. From the first time we met until just a few minutes ago, when you told me you left your husband to

226

live more honestly. You've always been so honorable. Done the right thing. Been brave."

"Really?" She shakes her head dubiously. "I haven't felt brave in a long time. I certainly wasn't brave enough to walk away until I was sort of forced to. The day he told me about his affair, I'd been terrified." She grimaces.

"God, I'm sorry. Did things just get bad all of a sudden?"

"No." She skims her bottom lip with the edge of her top teeth, biting down when she gets to the very center of it.

"It wasn't sudden. Or honestly, even all that surprising."

I trail a hand over her back and press a kiss to her shoulder. I can't believe she's here. I sink my teeth in her shoulder and she yelps.

"Why are you biting me?" She pulls away from me and rubs her shoulder to soothe it.

"Just making sure I wasn't dreaming."

"Uh, I'm pretty sure you're supposed to pinch yourself to figure that out," she rubs her neck, but a smile tugs at her lips.

"Come here, let me soothe it." She leans back in and I suck the spot tenderly.

"If you promise to always do that afterward, you can bite me any time." She sighs and relaxes.

"So, what happened? With you and Paul?"

"Are you sure you want to talk about my marriage?" A skeptical frown mars her face.

"You've heard mine. Tell me yours." I nudge her.

Her body relaxes on top of mine, and she blows out a long breath. "When I had Bianca, I took maternity leave. I loved being home with her, but I was ready to get back to work at the end of the three months. Paul was very unhappy at the prospect. He was raised so differently than me. He's Catholic. Or at least he pretends to be when it's convenient. He wanted me to stay home. I didn't. There's nothing wrong with being a full-time mother, it just wasn't what I wanted. I had dreams beyond that. I also really resented the way being married changed my freedom of movement."

"What do you mean by that?" I ask.

"I mean, when I met Paul, I had just started getting a taste of living the life I wanted. I was done with school, I had a job, was earning good money, had roommates, went out. Had sex, dated, whatever. I was free. Sure, it had been a hard road to get there, but I was free. And then, I fell into a trap."

"He trapped you?" My body tenses at the idea.

"I trapped myself. I was careless about something I'd spent my whole life afraid of."

"What getting pregnant?"

"No of being a cliché: young, single, pregnant. But, I don't regret my daughter. I just wish I hadn't married her father. It bound me to him in a way that made it very hard to extricate myself. I'm not sure I'd ever want to get married again."

Surprise forces me to sitting. "Huh?"

"No, I mean, really. Our divorce was traumatic. We had a horrendous custody battle that I'm still paying off." I can hear how weary she is just talking about it. I hadn't really thought about marriage, but only because, for me, it's a given.

"Why did you marry *him*, then?"

"Because I didn't want to end up like my mother. Back then, single motherhood was akin to death."

Her laugh is humorless.

"Being a stay at home mom felt like a small sacrifice to make for peace at home. When she started school and was gone all day, I started putting feelers out about jobs at the publishing houses."

"Did you find something?"

"Yes, Paul, made such a stink. I turned it down."

"Even with her in school? What did he expect you to do all day?"

"Things other media tycoons wives do, I guess. Go to lunches, fundraisers, cut ribbons at the openings of new hospital wings. Look pretty. Hair straight. Makeup flawless. That's what he cared about. Don't stand out. Be a picture-perfect wife. Suddenly my clothes were too revealing, too risqué. My hair looked unprofessional. I changed all of those things to try to make him happy."

"I see," is all I say. But now, I understand the slightly "Stepford Wives" vibe Kal gives off.

"Last year, my old boss called me up and asked me to come back.

Said he'd bring me back in at the same level and title and everything. Bianca was almost eight. And I said yes. Paul said he was onboard. I was traveling a lot again."

I pull away a little and eye her with surprise. "Did you like being on the road?"

"There's no position in the field of investigative journalism that doesn't require travel. I can't exactly do an online search for the questions I'm trying to answer." She huffs.

"Of course."

"But while I was gone, he met someone and fell in love, filed for divorce and now he's married to her." She says it with admirable equilibrium.

I'm fucking glad that shit is out of the way but *fuck* him for throwing away such a treasure.

"He's a spineless shit."

"He is. He fought me for custody. I won, but it was brutal financially. Then, as soon as his new wife discovered that Bianca wasn't going to call her Mommy, her weekends with him became few and far in between. I had to beg him to take her while I was here."

Fuck him again.

"What about your mom?"

She sighs deeply, her absent stare is wistful. "I spent my whole life following her from disaster to disaster. From apartment to apartment. Her endless stream of boyfriends, the parties, even the arrest and foster care. I even forgave her for hiding my father's identity."

"I thought he was dead." I ask about her last sentence.

"Nope. He's alive and kicking. It's David Lister."

If she had touched me with just the tip of her finger right now, I would fall over.

"You're kidding? Lister is your father?"

"No. He's just the man who got my mother pregnant. I don't even think about him, honestly. And I don't want to talk about him now." She says firmly, so I let it go because I don't know what to make of it anyway.

"You and your mom seemed so tight."

"We were. Like sisters... I didn't know until after I had Bianca...

that mothers aren't supposed to be like sisters. She never *really* fought for me. She didn't give up anything for me."

"Not like you did for your daughter?" I finish her sentence and it coaxes her frown a little.

She nods sadly. "It's what every mother should do. Even yours did."

"Oh, mine… I don't want to talk about her." I dismiss her comment.

"She didn't think I was what you needed. She fought for you. Even when she knew you'd hate her for it. Mine just dragged me behind her as she ran from her mistakes."

"The grass is always greener, huh?"

"Sometimes, especially when you've got no grass at all." she says quietly. She looks so tired. I hate that she's had a rough time and that I've been sitting here twiddling my thumbs thinking she was happy.

"Anyway, Mom remarried. Lives in Atlantic City and we go visit a couple of times a year. Bianca looks a lot like her." She smiles dreamily at the mention of her daughter.

"What's she like, even though I feel like I already know her. All of those Christmas cards." I nod over to the fridge again.

"And of course, she's got a marvel for a mother."

"I'm no marvel, Remi. I'm just determined."

"Yes. You are. And you've never turned your back on anyone you love. If she's learned that from you, then she's incredible."

"I think so. But I just love her and protect her. Who she is… is who she is. I'm so tired."

"Where do you want to sleep? I have a spare bedroom. Or you can sleep with me." I try to keep the desperation out of my voice. But I know I failed when her eyes dart away uncomfortably.

"I think the spare bedroom is best. I'm not sure…"

"Listen, there's no pressure. Not from me. Really. That you're here is enough. When you're sure—say the word."

She nods, but narrows her eyes, her gaze thoughtful and probing.

"Are *you* sure? I mean, it's been a long time. I've changed—" I stop her with a finger pressed to her lips. She kisses it and her eyes flutter closed.

"See? Time's has just gone by. But we're still the same."

"Yes," her agreement is little more than a sigh. I pull her to me, wrap my arms around her. Her arms go around my waist and she rests her head on my chest.

There's no space between us, and I could stay right here forever.

"We still feel each other. Want each other." I press a kiss to the side of her neck before I run my nose along it.

She sighs, burrows deeper into me.

"When's the last time you had a conversation like that? When's the last time you didn't have a single blip of anxiety?"

"I don't remember."

"Me neither. So, I'm sure. And when you are, Kal. Just say the word. But you have to know… that this time, I'm playing for keeps."

27

I REMEMBER

KAL

SHIT. FUCK. WHY DID HE HAVE TO SAY *THAT*?

When Remi stepped out with that gun, I almost pissed on myself. But then he looked at me like he'd been hunting and finally had his prey in his sights. I felt every single place his eyes landed on me as surely as he had touched me with those big strong hands of his.

I'd forgotten what a thrill it always was just to be in his presence. Like dancing on the edge of a fire, the flames licking the tips of my toes, but not feeling any fear, because he'd never let me hurt myself. Safe. Cherished, seen. Remi had made me feel all of those things.

It had been so long since I'd felt any of them.

I was so desperate to touch him, I ached. He looks impossibly hand-some. His cheeks covered in a dark beard that my fingers itch to touch. His hair has grown, too. He's always worn it close to his head, but today, it's long enough to get lost in.

His dark ringlets cover his head like a crown. He's leaner, but more muscular. Every bit as tall and strong as I remember him.

Oh, God.

I want to climb him like a tree.

I deflected earlier by gushing about the scenery and trying to get us out of the pocket of tension we'd stepped into the minute we saw each other.

I've been taking huge imaginary gulps of air. It hasn't helped the feeling of light headedness that's come over me.

Being forced to think before I speak feels like a huge task. But, I have to remember why I'm here in the first place. My job.

"Kal. Did you hear me? Are you okay?" Remi peers at me.

"I'm fine. It's just a shock to see you and of course, what you tell me, stays here." I *think* I can make that promise in good faith. Whatever is going on with him, can't possibly be about the Rivers woman. "I'm listening, go ahead." I nudge.

HE TAKES A DEEP BREATH. "MY FATHER DIDN'T DIE WHEN I WAS two."

Those are the very last words I expected to hear. "Come again?"

"He left when I was two,"

"*Left*? I don't understand."

"He divorced my mother. Remarried, had another kid."

I process that quickly. "Okay, so everyone just *thought* he was dead?"

"No, they—my grandfather and mother—knew he wasn't. They let us think he was dead because that was easier in their minds than us and the public knowing that he walked away."

My eyes bug out of my head. "But, that's... crazy. Do people actually do things like that?"

"Apparently, my people do. The kicker? Gigi Rivers was the woman he left her for."

A feather could knock me over right now. My mind is racing. I make a mental list about everything that I know about Gigi Rivers. Other than she's Hayes Rivers' aunt and that she lives in Italy, and that she was estranged from her family for years, there's not much information about her. And the word is that she and the family reconciled when her brother died. She raised Hayes in Italy from his teens until he came back last year. Something clicks, the way it does when I finally find the last piece of a puzzle.

I remember the paternity test Jules mentioned.

Oh my God. It *can't* be.

"You said they had a kid. You have a half sibling? Do you know where they are?" I ask in a neutral, but hopeful voice. I need him to dismiss that impossible thought.

"Yeah, I know." He looks at me, his eyes glinting and his lips set in a thin hard line.

"You do?" My eyes nearly bug out of my head.

"But, it's not for me to tell you. That is not my secret."

But with those words, he gives it away. It must be Hayes. It makes so much sense. He's just unwittingly given me the answer to the scoop I came down here to chase. This story would be explosive. Except, of course now, I can't write it. I just promised Remi and I would never ever violate his privacy like that.

Now, I just have to make sure no one else finds out, I'll tell Jules there's no story. Go back to New York and hunt down something else to help me clinch that job. I fall backwards in my seat.

"I know, it's totally crazy, right?"

"Yeah. Totally..." I trail off as another question hits me. "So where's your dad? Is he still with Gigi? Did he move to Italy with her?"

"No, he didn't. But I don't know where he is. Gigi says he left the house to head to town for work, but he never showed up there and he never came home. She was pregnant with... their kid. She had the baby, went to Italy and planned on taking this secret with her to the grave."

"Holy shit," I exclaim louder than I intended and give him an apologetic wince.

"Sorry, I don't mean to sound excited. It's just crazy."

"Yeah, it's crazy. So crazy that I've decided I don't want anything to do with any of them."

"So, that's why you went to see her in the hospital?"

"No. I went because Hayes is my friend. She got shot, almost died. Then he led me into a room and left me there so she could tell me something he'd known for weeks." He grinds his fist into his palm. "Just thinking about that day makes my blood pressure spike. I'm so fucking pissed at everyone, Kal."

"I can't even imagine," I say; I feel totally helpless.

"My whole life is a fucking lie. My mother robbed me of really knowing who my father is. My grandfather, who I thought was my best friend, let me believe my father was dead while he played the grieving father. If he wasn't already dead, I'd fucking kill him."

I put a hand on his chest to stop him from talking. "Wait. So, are you saying your father's not dead?"

"No. I'm not saying that. But, I have no proof that he is either. I've been here for months now. No one remembers him or Gigi. Ms. Jameson, who cooks for me *thinks* she remembers Gigi, but not him. I came out here expecting to find answers easily and there's just nothing."

"Why didn't you call me? I'm like the missing person specialist. I know we haven't spoken in eight years—"

"Eight years, six months and twenty-one days, but who's counting?" he adds with a dry chuckle. "And the last time I saw you, I told you I couldn't have anything to do with you."

"Um, these are sort of extenuating circumstances, don't you think?" I chide him.

He looks at me hard and long, his expression stony. "Honestly, Kal. I just wanted to be alone. Wanted to not be Remington Wilde. To see who I was if I wasn't Lucas' son. They built this legend around him and then pushed me to live up to it. It wasn't even real. I threw myself into my work to build something worthy of the name I was given. And now, it's like it all means nothing. So, I came here hoping to just have some fucking peace of mind."

He closes his eyes and I feel a huge wave of sympathy for him. But I know if I express it, it'll just annoy him.

"So, did you find it? Your peace of mind?" I ask after a few minutes.

"No. But it's been good to cut off the world and just… be."

I look around the rustic but chicly decorated cottage. It's got every modern convenience, but it's furnished to be comfortable rather than stylish. Two huge brown leather couches make a corner around a fireplace that stands in the middle of the room.

"So, this was their house?"

"Yeah. They bought it and the farm when they walked away from their families in Houston. Gigi pays the taxes on it every year. Has it renovated regularly. She said she'd planned on telling me one day. And that almost dying made her realize it was time."

He pulls a piece of paper out of his pocket and smooths his fingers over the worn edges of it. He's got the nicest hands. Long, broad fingers, square, wide fingernails, and intricately veined. Strong, sure hands that seemed to know things about my body that no one else does.

"This is the letter. He planned on finding a way to see us again. He said my mother and my grandfather wouldn't agree to let him see us."

"Can I read it?" I ask and he hands it over without looking up.

I unfold it carefully, it's worn and even though he's folded it nicely, I can tell it's been balled up more than once.

Dear Remi,

One day I hope you'll understand that your freedom is worth more than anything.

I didn't choose her.

I chose that. And I will never love anyone as much as I love you. I will find a way back to you.

Love,

Dad

"Oh, Remi, I'm so sorry." My words feel so utterly inadequate, but they're all I've got.

"Me, too. Clearly he was a piece of shit for leaving his family, but I wish I'd had the chance to get to know the real man behind all of the bullshit my mother's taught me about him instead."

He drops his head into his hands and groans.

"I'm so sorry, Remi." I touch his shoulder and he stiffens and sits up straight. My hand slides off his shoulder.

"Where's your family?" His sudden change of subject catches me completely off guard. I stare at him blankly for a minute and he laughs. "You know... Paul, Bianca?"

I glance at the hands in my lap then back at him. His smile disappears when he sees my face.

"I knew it. Something's wrong. What happened?"

"Nothing is wrong. Paul and I got a divorce. Bianca's staying with him while I'm here. I'm bringing her down for a visit the week after next. If I'm still here."

My answer is met with silence.

His eyes lose their slightly faraway look and focus intently on me.

His posture changes – he straightens and sits up.

The hunger that was there before is back and this time he's not looking away. My throat is dry, and there's a thrumming in my core that's vibrant and strong.

I haven't felt that sensation in years.

And oh, how I've missed it. But, I need to tamp it down. I'm not here for this. There's so much to talk about.

"Remi, we shou—"

"You're single?" he asks, his voice a low growl.

"Uh - yes," I say, and my breath catches in my throat at the way he's looking at me. He looks hungry. And like he wants to fuck me. My pussy clenches, and his eyes take a quick scan of me, he shifts closer.

"Do you still burn for me the way I burn for you, baby?" he asks.

A wave of lust hits me hard at the desperate catch in his gruff voice.

I nod, fast and hard.

He lunges across the couch and without preamble, or question, cups the back of my neck with one hand, cups my ass with the other and crashes his mouth down on mine. He presses his body flush to mine and the insistent press of his erection against my thigh is the most erotic thing I've felt in my entire life. Delicious, toe curling tension coils deep inside of me.

"Then, let's do this before we say another word and ruin it." He breathes into my mouth.

He's panting like he's just sprinted to catch me. He nibbles at my lips with his feverishly hot mouth; he bites his way down my neck and I arch my back so that my throat presses into his teeth.

I want to feel the bite of it.

I am burning. Around me, everything else catches fire, too.

I've forgotten why I'm here.

I don't remember anything but how much I need him.

My lips go on their own exploration, I suck and lick his scruffy jaw and down the column of his neck, rubbing my nose in his hair, letting my senses learn him, absorb him again.

Enjoy him again. "You smell so good."

He tugs at the hem of my turtleneck and I lift my arms over my head so he can yank it off. He cups one of my breasts through my tank top and squeezes before he lowers his head and sucks my throbbing, aching nipple into the hot pleasure palace of his mouth. I shout his name and reach down with desperate, grasping fingers to tug his shirt off, too.

I grip the hem of it and I pull, my fingernails scraping him at times until his shirt is over his head. The press of his warm, firm skin against my own now topless body is akin to relief. I run my hands greedily over his smooth skin.

"God, I've missed you." He groans into my neck. He unbuttons my jeans, shoves them down my hips. I shove his sweatpants down and reach between us to wrap my hand around his thick cock. My fingers can't close around it completely and I pulse in anticipation of having him inside me again. He slips his hand into my panties and cups my pussy. I grind against his palm and moan at how dizzying the pleasure is.

The voice of reason is telling me that I'm making a mistake. That this is the last thing I need to do given what he's just told me. It's nearly drowned out by my rebel heart's shout of joy at how wonderful it feels to be in his arms.

Nearly…

"Wait," I breathe.

"Shit, you're so fucking wet," he whispers against my ear.

"Remi, wait." I let go of his cock and shift so his hand slides out from my panties.

He stiffens and pulls off me immediately and hovers over me. "What's wrong?"

A bead of sweat falls from one of the curls that's hanging on his forehead. It lands on my cheek. He leans down, his heat and breath as heady as the weight of him on me. He glides the tip of his tongue over the spot on my cheek where his sweat fell.

"Remi, this isn't what I came for. I'm not ready," I pant and press a hand to his chest. His hot eyes bore holes into me. He swoops down and gives me the most perfect kiss.

Not as perfect as the sweet friction of him sliding into my body would have been. But, it wouldn't just be sex. Not to me. My feelings for him are right below the surface. I can't afford to let them spill over.

So I sit up and pull my clothes on. "Let's talk first."

28

COMPLICATIONS

KAL

MY STOMACH DROPS WHEN I SEE THE NAME ON THE SCREEN OF MY ringing phone. I nearly decline the call, but I know that will only make things worse.

"Morning, Jules." I grimace at the effort it takes to keep my voice natural, but I'm sweating bullets because I have already fucked-up my assignment.

I got here and forgot, immediately, why I was here in the first place. I actually got in to see Gigi Rivers, and I didn't ask her a single fucking question except "Where can I find Remington?" Because apparently, my very neglected vagina usurped my brain the minute I thought we might be breathing the same air.

I stand up and head to the small front foyer of the house.

"Any updates?"

A door opens on the left side of the house. Remi must finally be awake. I step out into the already very warm morning. I make sure the door is shut and sit on the top step of the porch. I pray splinters don't find a home in my bare thighs.

"None yet."

"You've been there for two days." She says sharply.

"Technically one." I wince at how lame I sound.

"If you're already speaking in technicalities, that means you've already made a mistake," she accuses

"I haven't made a mistake," I lie through my teeth. Well, it's not technically a lie. It's so much more than a mistake.

"Kal, I'm not calling to argue with you." She snaps.

"Jule—"

"Do you know Regan Landel née Wilde?"

Her question and the mention of Regan's name completely startle me. "Yes. Well, kind of…"

"She's a rich, bored housewife who is also a failed journalist and is a sometimes gossip columnist," she says without any judgment, like she's reading from a list. She's putting Regan into a context she can understand. Underestimating her in a way that I think a lot of people do. I feel like I should defend her, but that would only make things worse.

"Okay, so why are we talking about her, then?"

"Apparently, Regan was overheard telling someone that Remington Wilde is missing."

"I don't understand," I mumble dumbly.

My plan from earlier goes up in a fiery blaze. How the hell did anyone overhear us?

"Neither do I, but you're going to go and find out if the two are related. And if they are, you're going to write a story about it."

Surprise explodes inside of me and panic starts to build.

"Woah. No… That's not the story I'm here to pursue. Wh — why would they be related?" My brain is moving at a thousand miles an hour as I try to figure how in the world she could have found out.

"Last time he was seen, he was leaving the hospital in the wee hours of the morning the day after Gigi Rivers was shot, but no one knows who he was there to visit. He was supposed to be the keynote speaker of an event the ACLU was holding and he didn't show up. His family has declined to comment, but I have this bead on Regan. Find out everything you can about him."

"What about the Rivers' story?" My voice comes out in a squeak, and I clear my throat. Holy Shit. This is a cluster.

"They're related. I just *know* it. My inner bloodhound is on fire."

She sounds more animated than I've ever heard her. My stomach sinks.

"If you can get this story, Kal, the job will be yours. People would die for a peek behind the curtain one of the country's biggest families has draped themselves in. It's catnip for our audience." She is practically crowing.

"Okay. I'll work on it today." The contrasting lack of conviction in my voice is startling.

"Kal." Jules' voice takes on an uncharacteristic softness that's as jarring as someone's shout would be.

"Yes, Jules?" I ask tentatively when she doesn't speak.

"I want you to do well. Right now though, I feel like I'm doing your job for you. I know you're probably trying to find your feet and that you've got stuff going on at home. So, I'll cut you some slack. But, just today." Her voice loses the warmth that tinged it.

"Thank you," I say quietly. I hate that I'm letting her down. She stuck her neck out for me. I know her credibility is on the line.

"I've just given you a substantial lead. I want the next one to come from you." She pauses and waits for me to agree.

"Okay." I know I sound lame, but right now, I don't know what else to say that wouldn't be a lie. I need to come clean.

"Get your head in the game. Slugman's just as hungry as you are."

"I know." I feel like a thousand-pound weight has been strapped to my shoulders. "I'll call you when I have something to tell you," I promise and hang up before she can ask me another question.

I'm going to be sick. Why is this happening? This job was my chance. I glance back at the house. But, so was this…

What the fuck am I going to do? Is there a way to write this story without including Remi? Not only did I promise him not to share anything he told me about himself, I know he would never ever agree to letting me write it. He would be livid if he even thought I'd tricked the story out of him.

I need to shut it down. I just don't know how. Especially now, when Jules has him so firmly in her sights.

I click my heels and wish I could turn back time.

The front door opens and Remi says, "You done with your call?"

I turn slowly to face him. "Yeah, it was just my edit—"

My eyes nearly fall out of my head.

He's smiling, leaning in the doorway without a stitch of clothing on. I've seen it all before. I almost had it at all last night. But, Remi naked in broad daylight is just like looking at a rare statue. His body is perfect. His muscular chest is covered in a light dusting of the same dark hair that's on his head. It swirls down his body and narrows to a trail that leads to the happiest of sights—his thick, long, left-leaning dick. It twitches and I take a step toward him. I step on a leaf that's fallen from one of the potted plants on the porch and the crunch of it reminds me that we're outside.

I rush back to the porch and try to push him back into the house. "You can't come outside naked!" He doesn't move. Instead, his arms wrap around me and pull me in for a hug. "Good morning, Will. Nice to see your face first thing."

I tilt my head back and smile up at him. "Nice to see yours, too." I cup his firm bare ass and squeeze it. "Can we go inside now, though?"

"I don't have a neighbor for two miles." He tilts his hips so his stiffening dick presses into me.

"Someone could drive up any minute," I protest, but don't let go.

"Nah. Nancy starts barking when they're a mile away." He pulls me to the wicker loveseat, drops down, and pulls me onto his lap.

"Don't you feel weird being naked outside?" I squirm.

"No. Why should I?" He spreads his thighs and leans back with me against his chest.

"I think most people do."

"Most people aren't worth knowing, much less emulating. I could live like this forever." His voice is gruff, like he's trying to convince himself, as well as me. I disentangle myself and stand up to face him.

"Remi, I know you're upset. But, what about your work? Your practice? Your friends?"

"Wilde Law is in good hands. Maybe even better than it was with me. And my friends aren't going anywhere. In fact, one of them even came all the way here to find me." He smiles with a carelessness I'm not sure he really feels.

"I don't think anyone feels like things are better with you gone. Regan is worried."

"Fine, I'll call Regan and Tyson. But what I've got to say needs to be said in person."

"Great, then let's head back to Houston, get you back in the saddle."

He stands up without any warning. "Come on." He claps his hands together and heads toward the door.

I watch the spectacular sight of his retreating back, admiring the way his muscles ripple with each step for a minute before I follow him inside.

"Where are we going?" When I get to the bedroom, I find him slipping into a pair of briefs.

"For a run. It'll be great, I'll show you the property and take you around town."

"I thought you said town was three miles away."

"It is." He pulls on a T-shirt and opens the drawer of his dresser and pulls out a pair of sweats.

"I can't run six miles, Remi." Each step of two miles I do each day feels like torture.

"Of course you can. You never know what you're capable of until you try. Get dressed."

"I'll just wait for you to come back," I say and flop onto the bed.

"Oh, no you won't." He grabs me by the arms and pulls me up to standing.

"Yes. I will. I'll die before we get there." I flail dramatically and he laughs.

"It'll feel great and if you get tired, I promise I'll carry you back home via piggyback." He reaches into my luggage and rummages around until he finds my sneakers. He peeks inside. "Still a size seven," he says before he hands them to me.

"How do you remember my shoe size?" I ask and take them grudgingly from him.

"You left those shoes in the hallway of my parent's house thirteen years ago."

I cover my mouth with my hand and stare at him wide-eyed. "Has it really been that long?"

"Yeah. It has. And I'll never ever be able to say sorry in a way that truly conveys just how shitty I feel about that night." His eyes are soft, full of regret and they search mine as if he's expecting to see the same thing reflected in them.

But it's not. Not even a little.

"Remi, that night was humiliating, hurtful, and I wish it had never happened. I know if you had to do it again, you would do things differently. But I stopped asking *what if* a long time ago. Everything happens for a reason. We might not be here, now, if it hadn't." I grab hold of his hands.

"I guess." He sounds unconvinced and he breaks eyes contact.

I drop his hands so I can cup his precious face and he looks at me again.

"Bianca is reason enough for me to know why I went through that. She's a special kid. I was meant to be her mom. Paul was meant to be her dad." I gentle my voice when I say those words, but he flinches anyway.

"She helped me find the courage to live a life that wasn't a lie. And that's what, in the end, brought us back together. Like you said, we had to walk that walk, right?"

"I guess. And you're right about asking what if, I just hate that I hurt you, Kal. You. Of all people. I'm not sure that I'll ever forgive myself." The pain in his voice tears at me and I wish I could take it away.

"All's well that ends well. I have a feeling that we're going to end well..." I press a kiss to his mouth and he grips my side and dips his tongue between my lips.

"I love that little freckle on the top, it kills me." He flicks my lip with his tongue and presses soft, small kisses to it.

His touch, light and fleeting as it is, makes me giddy. I rise up on my toes and slip my arms around his neck. "Well, why don't we skip that run and kiss the calories away?"

He pulls my arms down and grins. "I'd almost forgotten. Thanks for the reminder."

"Me and my big mouth," I grumble.

He frowns at me in exaggerated reproach. "Hey, I happen to like that mouth, watch how you talk about it." He slaps my ass before he strolls out of the room and calls over his shoulder.

"Hurry up, we'll need to stretch and warm up before we head out."

29

TIME

REMI

"You okay?"

My question is met with a wheezing sound that sounds like a groan, but I think is actually a "fuck you."

Kal's been cursing me out for the last mile and a half. The return trip has really highlighted the slopes in the terrain, we've run uphill for most of the journey that leads to the house.

"Want me to carry you?"

She comes to a dead stop and bends over, hands on her knees and squints up at me. Her face is red and her hair, soaked with sweat, sticks to her face. She pants as she peers up at me, and she looks pissed.

"Is that a yes?"

She stands, hands at her waist and grimaces. "That's an it's about fucking time you asked, you sadist," she says and I let out a loud bark of laughter.

"You could have told me to pick you up any time."

"You should have offered the first time I said I thought I was going to throw up."

"You don't ask, you don't get. Hop on." I turn around so my back is facing her and bend my knees.

She puts her hands on my shoulder, and I hook my arms around her thighs and hoist her up.

She lets her entire weight rest on me, her head lolls on my shoulder. "Thank God you're built like a gladiator, I don't think I could have made it ten more steps."

"Good thing you're not built like a gladiator or you would have had to lie there until you caught your second wind."

"Mmmm… whatever. I'm going to take a nap." She drapes her arms around my neck and sighs. I savor her weight. The sweet smell of her sweat, the thud of her heart against my back, the heat of her pussy pressed to my back.

"So, this job, it's as an investigative journalist?" She stiffens, lifts her head slightly. And then, she relaxes again and lays it back down.

"Yeah, it's actually a television show. I'm sort of auditioning for a job. When I'm done with the assignment, I'll know whether I get the permanent role that there's only one of."

"So you're in a competition with someone else for it?"

"Yeah. His name is Slugman."

"That's his real name?" I chuckle.

"Yeah. Honestly, he's not so bad. I just hate him because he's ten years younger than me, probably smarter and more tech-savvy than I am."

"So, you think the youngin's got the leg up?"

"He might… but our editor, who would be our boss, likes me best."

"So if you don't get it then what?"

"Not getting it would be disastrous. I was out of work for so long. I tried to find a job in a male-dominated business obsessed with youth. That I even have a shot at this is a miracle."

"What will you do if you don't get it? Because that's a possibility, right?"

"Bite your tongue and take that back." She stiffens.

"I'm not saying you won't. I believe in you. I'm sure you'll bring back the makings for a great story and get the job. But I'm not making the decision and neither are you. So, we can't be sure how it'll go. You need to think about what you'll do."

She's silent for a few minutes and then she says, "I don't know, Remi."

"Dig deep, Will. Rewrite your happy ending. One that doesn't include this job."

She's quiet. But it's not an uncomfortable silence. I can practically hear the slightly rusty wheels of her imagination turning.

"I'd get a regular, non-journalist job and spend my nights writing my book."

"You want to write a book?"

"Yeah, I do. My book of Legends… I want to try and get it published."

"Do you still have it?" I ask, a fond smile on my face as I remember the notebook that brought us together.

"Of course, I do. It's in New York."

"Good. So you have a good start. You have your book, next worst-case scenario."

"Why can't we do best-case scenarios instead?"

"Because you already know what that looks like. Best-case scenarios are always what we hope for or secretly expect. When we plan we need to think about—"

"What could go wrong." She finishes for me. Just like old times.

"Exactly. So… what would you do if no one buys it?"

"Keep working my regular job and write for pleasure."

"You give up easy, Kal."

"No, I don't. But I have bills to pay. I need that nine-to-five," she protests.

"But why couldn't writing pay the bills, too?"

"Because that's not up to me. If I don't have a publisher, I don't have a way to get it out there."

"So you give up?"

"How about you stop acting like I'm some sort of quitter."

"Why are you irritated with me? How about you stop treating your dream like it's up to someone else to make it come true? If you want it, take it."

"That's not true, Remi," she protests.

"Why isn't it true?" I push back.

"Because," she says like she can't believe she has to explain it to me.

"Because what? Tell me, in your own words, why you can't do it," I challenge.

"Don't say it like I gave up on it." She sounds defensive.

"If you didn't, who did?"

I hoist her higher and turn up the last curve to the house.

"You can't let one setback stop you."

"Oh, you mean like you're doing?" she mutters.

It's my turn to stiffen. I stop walking and slide her off my back. I turn around to face her.

"What? You don't like the taste of your own medicine?" she asks, a smug smile on her face.

"They're not the same thing," I say slowly. I'm annoyed at the comparison she just made.

"How are they different? You're out here hiding. I'm working a job I don't love but need."

"You're fucking talented. If you didn't find a publisher who was interested. That would be a setback. Meaning, it's one closed door. Others will open."

"If you believe that, then why are you out here, hiding?"

That comment slides right under my skin and I bristle.

"I'm not fucking hiding. And unlike you, I didn't suffer "a setback". My entire life shifted, fundamentally. Everything I thought about myself, my life, my family—very little of it is true."

Regret mars her pretty face and she walks toward me.

"Oh, babe. I'm so sorry. I know." She wraps an arm around my waist. I relax as soon as her body touches mine, and I hug her back.

"I have to reconcile that I lived with people who lied to me constantly and profoundly and that I never even had a clue. I feel like an idiot. Because now, when I think back on it, I would never have guessed any of this. Even when I think about all of the signs."

"Signs? Like what?" She leans back and eyes me skeptically.

"My mother… I have these two versions of my father that are at war with each other in the part of my mind where I keep him."

"What do you mean?"

"I mean, in public, she talked about him like he was a god. A bright light that had been snuffed out much too soon. But privately, the way she spoke of him was lukewarm at best. And when she let the curtain slip, and her grief was on full display, I thought she really hated him."

"Really?"

"Oh, yeah. It was usually around his birthday or their anniversary. It was like a cloud descended over our house. And we all lived with the weight of what felt more like rage than grief. She would drink and then cry hysterically, sometimes all night long. She would look at me—the darker skinned, darker-haired version of him—and sneer when she told me, I was just like him. She'd never say how, but I knew it wasn't anything good. I think she hates me, too." My laugh is brittle and devoid of humor.

"Oh, Remi. She couldn't." I hate the pity in her eyes. Loathe it. But, it's just nice that she gives a shit.

I loop an arm around her neck and bend down to kiss her.

"So yeah, I'm Remington Wilde. The Legend. But can a man just fucking wallow?" I stare down at her, my eyes serious as I let her absorb the weight of everything I just laid on her.

She smiles up at me, that soft understanding tempered with some regret.

"If you're happy here. You should stay as long as you need to."

"I'm fucking happy. And now, you're here." I bump the end of her nose with mine.

"I can't stay," she says quietly.

I knew it was coming, I had hoped to have more than a couple of days. I contemplate what's waiting for me in Houston and my gut clenches.

"I'm sorry, Remi. So sorry. But, my job. I need to get back to Houston so I can figure out my story." She looks up at me appealingly and I make up my mind.

I cup her cheek, kiss her quickly and then I pull back. "Okay. But before we go back, I want to cook you dinner."

She wrinkles her nose. "You're going to cook?"

"Why not? I'm—"

She squeaks and grips my forearms. "Wait! Did you say *we'll* go back?"

"Yeah. We'll go back. I'm not letting you out of my sight again." The knot in my stomach doesn't fist so tight when I add that.

She grins and then launches herself into my arms. "Oh my God. Are you sure?"

I laugh and set her back down with a nod. "I'm sure. I need to go and talk to my siblings anyway."

"Remi, I don't want you to leave before you're ready. This morning you loved it here." She frowns slightly.

"I do. But I've hit nothing but dead ends. Besides, I can't have that young buck Rivers getting comfortable with the biggest lion in the jungle."

"Well, good." She claps. "We should drive through town tomorrow. One more time, just to make sure. I mean, I'm a trained investigator. I could ask questions."

"I know I don't have your training, but I've talked to everyone."

"Let's stop anyway. On our way back to Houston. With a pro at your side?"

I've forgotten what it's like to have someone offer to do anything for me.

I'm not alone anymore.

She's back. "Okay. If it'll make you feel better. Even though, I could probably teach you a thing or two about investigations."

"Good lord, you are incorrigible."

I wink and turn around. I jerk a thumb at my back. "Climb on."

She hops on; I hitch her up higher and start running.

"Remi, come on don't try to show off and end up collapsing before we get home," she yells into the wind, and I pick up my pace.

"I see you've got jokes. Hold on. I've been running this hill every day and I can do it four times at top speed without breaking a sweat. I'm in the best shape of my life. You just hang on and keep those tits and that hot pussy pressed to my back and I'll get us home."

She tightens her grip, laughs and says, "Giddyup, stud. Take me home."

30

GROWN

REMI

"That was delicious," Kal says and snuggles against my shoulder. We took a blanket out to my truck and ate in the flatbed. I wanted to give her one more night under the stars before we head back to Houston.

"I'm glad I was able to use up most of the food in the house." I shift the small basket to my left hand and take a hold of her hand.

"Are you sure you're ready to go back? I'll come back next weekend if you want to stay." She links our fingers and steps into my side. I wish I could bottle the contentment I'm feeling right now and take a sip whenever I needed it.

"Yeah, I'm sure." I press a kiss to her mouth, we get up to the porch, I put the basket down and sit us down in the chair I keep there.

I tug on the slick straight fall of hair hanging from her ponytail. "I like your hair."

"I like yours." She reaches out to run her fingers through it.

"I'll need to cut it when I get back to town."

"Why? It's not too long. I like it."

"I'm glad you like it, but it's got to go."

"Why?"

I contemplate her question for a minute. "When I came out here, I wanted to see what it felt like to not be Remington Wilde."

"Okay... how's the experiment going? I mean, besides achieving the werewolf look, what are your other major takeaways?"

"You're such a shit talker, Kal. And my takeaways are that despite the obvious downsides—being related to my mother being the greatest of these—I like being Remington Wilde very much. He's a good man. He does important work. He loves his family, and he's only an asshole to people who deserve it."

"Don't forget best lover in the world," she says as she holds my hand tracing a pattern over it.

"That goes without saying." I shoot her a quick eye roll before I look back to the road.

My father spent his last days here. I've felt a sense of peace in the last few months that I'm not sure I've ever known. I feel the tug of regret as I think how much I'll miss it here. But this isn't my place either. Just like basketball wasn't my place. I know where I belong, and that's in that shark tank, leading and making a fucking difference.

I look at our hands and she's still tracing the pattern. I pause and pay attention and realize she's spelling something.

"What are you spelling?"

"Pay attention."

T

   H

   E

   W

   O

   R

   D

I stop at the last letter, and my heart gives one long, hard pump before it starts to race. I reach behind me to flip the switch on the porch light so I can see her eyes. Her pupils shrink and she squints, but she's got a very pleased smile on her face.

"Don't play with me. If you're not ready, I can wait."

"I ache… on the inside… for you," she says with her sweet, closed-mouth smile that gives her lips a beautiful heart shape.

"You shouldn't say shit like that. Not when I can't put my dick where it needs to be."

"Remi!" she exclaims and turns in my lap.

"What? You never heard the word dick before?" I raise an amused eyebrow at her.

"I've never heard you talk like that before… Well, except for at the wedding when you were drunk."

"I wasn't that drunk."

She slaps my shoulder. "What? You were talking all of that… you were touching me…"

"I only said that because I was fucking miserable and I needed to hold you and say those things to you without you slapping me."

"You are so crazy." She giggles.

"About you, yes. And I have been since the day I saw you in that bookstore, Kal. I've been waiting a long fucking time. I'm an honorable man. I would have never done anything to disrupt your marriage. But I won't lie, I prayed like hell you would."

"I'm sorry," she whispers.

I run a slow hand down her back "No, *I* am. When I think about the havoc my dad's decision wreaked, I feel like an ass for the way I behaved last time I saw you. I was asking you to do what he did. I wouldn't wish that on anyone's child."

"You were upset that night. You didn't mean it." She tries to console me. But I don't want it.

"I did mean it. You just loved your daughter enough to say no. My father…"

Her previously relaxed brow wrinkles, and her mouth contracts like she's had an unexpected bite of something sour.

"That's not fair, Remi. He didn't know he'd never see you again."

"He did. My mother told him. My grandfather cut him off."

"Your father came from a world where anything he wanted, he got.

Where no one dared to say no. And he thought that when he left your mother, she'd calm down and you all would find a way to coexist."

"Well, he was wrong."

"We all think that sort of thing only happens to other people. I mean, do you think I imagined that my mother would go to jail, and I'd be in foster care? She was a shitty role model, but I lived a normal life. I went to school. Lamented my looks and had crushes on boys who weren't always nice to me."

"*You* told me no," I point out.

Her eyes turn sad. "Yes. Because that kind of surety was stolen from me a long time ago. I know how easily everything can change. I know that children deserve the best we can give them. They are so innocent, and I wanted to make sure my child had the best possible chance at a normal life."

"She's lucky you're her mother," I tell her.

"I'm lucky to *be* her mother. But, that doesn't mean that I don't regret saying no to you. I regret it every day." Her quiet confession is the last thing I expected to hear.

"Really?"

"I was so worried about depriving her of things I thought she needed to be happy. But I never imagined how much I'd be depriving myself of, in the process."

I cup her face, cradle it in the palm of my hand and stare into those pools of breathtaking brown that are always a reflection of what is really in her heart.

Right now, all I can see is love. Shaped, molded, transformed and bolstered by time and distance. But at its core, it's the same love we found that summer.

"Losing you fucking hurt, Kal… but I don't think I would trade this journey for anything."

She shakes her head and smiles wistfully, but with joy, too. "Me neither."

"When I left for Howard, I was nursing the biggest heartache of my life. And I got through and was driven by my need to cling to and honor my time with you by doing something that spoke to my heart."

"So, I helped you embrace your sensitive side?" she quips.

"I'm not sensitive," I growl.

"Oh, baby… you so are." She smiles, gently.

I ignore her, pointedly. "I said all of that to say… I loved you then, but I wasn't ready."

"Well, how introspective of you," she says and I press my lips to hers and savor how they yield so easily to me.

Our kisses have mellowed since she got here… they feel more urgent than desperate.

We pull apart and I say, "I want to meet your daughter."

Her eyes dance and she claps her hands together excitedly. "I told her about you."

"Did you tell her how good-looking I am?"

She rolls her eyes. "You're unbearably cocky."

"Nah. I'm a humble motherfucker. And I have to say, it's nice to finally have a mother to fuck."

She groans and covers her face.

"Remi, you're still dropping those lame-ass pickup lines."

"How about this for a pickup line, instead?" I grab her hand and press it to my cock. Her fingers grip it immediately and fuck me, it feels so fucking good.

"I like this line a lot. I'm responding very well to it," she whispers and we stroke my cock together through my pants and when I start to get hard, I pull her hand away.

She pouts. "You tease."

"Never." I fist my hand in her hair and tug her head back so her throat is exposed. "Let me show you all of the things I've learned since you've been gone."

FIND ME

KAL

"Let's play a game. One where you hide and I look until I find you." Remi's voice is dark and deep, and wickedly sensual.

A shiver runs through me and my nipples tingle at the promise in his voice.

"Okay, like hide-and-go-seek?" I ask.

"Yes. Just like that." He's got the most wicked grin on his face. He cups my head and starts to massage my neck, I let my head fall and groan when his fingers press against a tense spot.

"Why do you want to play a game? Let's just do this," I croon.

His fingers fist in my hair, but he pulls my head forward gently until his lips tickle my ear. "Because I want to hunt for you and catch you. And when I do, I want you to do whatever I say until you can't take anymore," he murmurs and then sucks my earlobe into the wet heat of his mouth.

"You can do that without hide-and-go-seek." I press lingering kisses on the side of his face.

He pulls away, his dark eyes intense and hooded with desire and so much need that my breath quickens.

"I like the thrill of the hunt. I'm going to have you the way I've imagined having you since the last time we were together."

He runs his teeth down the column of my throat and I shudder.

"I was just a boy then. And I didn't have years of being without you to make up for."

I lean away, clutch my proverbial pearls and ask with a mock tremble in my voice, "Is this grown up Remi going to scare me and make me want to run?"

"No, he's going to make you want to come," he drawls and pulls me onto his lap again, his hard dick feels huge against my thigh.

Oh my...

I run my nose along his neck and breathe in his cool, clean scent. He stays there, pressed against me for a beat longer than necessary and then takes a hold of my lower lip with his teeth and one of my nipples between his fingers.

He bites down at the same time as his fingers squeeze and pull the pulsing peak of my breast. Then he lets me go. "Now, get inside and hide."

"Oh, shit." I scurry off his lap and he hands me a set of keys.

"You'll need these to get in. I'll give you a two-minute head start."

"What about your dog?"

"She's in her crate tonight." He sounds like he's breathing hard.

"Okay." My voice is high and breathy, my heart is pounding in my ears. Remi is about to turn me out.

Holy shit, I can't remember the last time I've been so turned on.

I fumble with the lock and get the door open. I hit the switch next to the wall and all the lights come on. I slip my shoes off and drop my purse and keys on the small table by the door.

I hear the creak of the porch chair and I know he's coming. Anticipation moves through me in the giddiest ripples of lust. I'm going to make myself very easy to find.

I giggle and slip my shirt over my head and drop it where I stand and then run in the direction of the guest bedroom. I take my jeans off there and then dash to the hall. I hear the front door close just as I'm dropping my bra over the door handle of his bedroom

I slip out of my panties and walk to the huge armoire that takes up almost an entire wall. I slip the string of my G-string onto the small handle that opens it and start to climb inside.

Just as I'm tucking myself inside, the entire house is plunged into darkness. I quiver with delight when I hear the squeak of the bedroom door's hinges and footsteps moving across the floor toward me.

I hold my breath.

I mean, I know he's there. He knows I'm there. But with every step he takes my heart rate ticks up a notch.

"Kal. You broke the rules." I yelp. He's standing right outside the armoire.

"You were supposed to run, hide and let me find you. By leaving a trail—thank you for the panties by the way, your cunt smells delicious—you've deprived me of my chase." His voice is so deep, it resonates through and gooseflesh spreads all over my body.

"Oh, I'm so, so, sorry, Remi," I purr.

"Good." The door opens, and he's standing there, naked, except for a tie draped over his shoulders and his thick, already rock-hard cock in his hand. His fist moves up and down, in a lazy stroke that immediately captivates me. The moonbeams cut in through the window and illuminate the head of it.

Oh, this has to be some sort of sin.

Nothing so tempting that it makes me forget my name can actually be good for me. My fingers are brushing the warm skin of his chest before I even realize I've lifted my hand. He steps back.

"Get down here and show me just how sorry you are."

3 2

YOURS

KAL

I TAKE HIS PROFFERED HAND AND CLIMB DOWN FROM THE CLOSET. I need the support because my thighs are quivering.

He turns away and walks to the bed. His naked ass is a beautiful thing. And I'm almost drooling by the time he turns around to face me. He sits down at the edge of the bed and spreads his thighs and continues stroking his thick dick. I take a step toward him.

He pulls the tie from around his neck and snaps it. "Offer yourself to me," he says and this time the command in voice is different. It's darker, but sensual and I would do anything he says.

I kneel first, cup my breasts drop my head down to swipe my tongue across my nipple.

"Fuck, Kal. Come and let's suck them together."

Gingerly, I place my hands on the cool wood floor and lift my head so our eyes are locked while I prowl, slowly toward him. His dark eyes are like a line that casts hooks into mine. Each move forward is driven by the pull of that tether.

"Is your sweet cunt wet?" His husky voice is so deep it's nearly a growl.

"So wet, it's dripping down my thighs." He moves his hand faster.

"I'm going to lick it off and then suck more of it out of you," he promises and his hand speeds up. His eyes close briefly and I speed up my movement.

"I want to suck you, too. Will you come in my mouth?"

"Repeatedly, baby. But when you get here, I want you on your knees in front of me and I want you to tell me how badly you want me to fuck you. Tell me you'll never let anyone else in that body."

I reach him in a dozen paces and place my hands on his knees and start to slide my fingers toward the center of his thighs. His free hand grabs one wrist then the other.

"Not until I tell you, greedy." He smirks and gives his drool worthy dick one more stroke before he lets go. It bobs right in front of my mouth. My tongue darts out, but I only manage a small swipe of his salty head before he moves away.

He wraps his tie around my wrists and I gasp.

"Do you trust me?"

"Yes."

He ties a tight knot and binds my hands together.

I lean forward to try and take his cock between my lips, again. He moves away.

"No. Not yet."

He rests my hands on the bed in between his spread thighs. Just out of reach of him. Then he grips my chin and forces my eyes up to his. They're so very dark, and yet I can see the hunger, the heat, the love burning bright in them.

"I've spent my whole life without you. Knowing that another man has been eating and fucking what's mine."

I try to pull my face away but he drags my eyes back to him.

"Do you know what that feels like?" he asks.

"Like something tearing at your insides," I tell him.

He presses his thumb into my mouth and I suck it.

"Tonight... you're mine."

266

I swallow and a tremor moves through me at the dark promise in his voice.

"I've always been yours," I whisper and his expression sharpens, turns primal and his need is a visceral, palpable force wrapping itself around me.

"That's fucking right," he growls before he crushes his mouth to mine and kisses me with an almost savage fervor that I return eagerly. While our tongues duel and dart in a wet, open-mouthed dance, my bound hands itch for freedom especially when he twines my pony tail around his fist.

"Your hair is always pulled back," he mutters against my mouth.

"It's easy this way."

"Easy…" He rolls the word around like he's testing it and tugs the elastic holding it together until my hair spills like a veil around my shoulders. "I want to fuck *easy* up." He gathers bunches of it in his hands. "I want to fuck *you* up. And then put you back together like only I can."

"You still talk so much," I tease.

He presses his thumb into my chin and holds my mouth open. "How about we both stop talking?" he drawls. And then he slides forward and the salty, taut, hot tip of his dick glides against the inside of my bottom lip. I dart my tongue out to lick it and he surges forward, slipping into my mouth while he cups the back of my head.

"Suck my dick like you've fucking missed it." His voice is ragged with need and I move my head up and down, the slide of his silken cock against my wet tongue is making me crazy. His broad head presses against the back of my throat and I gag. But I don't stop.

I wrap both hands around the base his thick long, beautiful cock and wrap my lips around it and hollow my cheeks. I experiment with my pace until his moans tell me what he likes. His grip on my hair has turned painful. His free hand roams my back and shoulders—my pussy, my nipples, my ass, my thighs, everything pulses with jealousy.

They all want what my mouth has. And when I feel the rush of his cum on my tongue, I don't waste a minute getting off my knees and climbing on top of him.

He moans low, loud and when I drape my arms over his shoulder and press my chest to his, it reverberates between us.

"Get on," he growls and I lower myself onto his still spurting cock. I slip down so easily, the slide of friction so delicious that our eyes widen at the same time.

"Best. Cunt. In. The. World," he says and fucks me in time to his praise.

"Yours," I purr, my head falls back, my hair brushes the small of my back and all of the sensations assailing me are making my body go wild.

"You're never going to forget that again."

His gaze turns determined, and he stands up. I hook my still bound hands around his neck and wrap my legs around his waist.

He stands like that for a minute, kissing me, holding me in his strong arms like I weigh nothing.

I *feel* weightless, like if he let me go, I would defy gravity and float away. I drape my arms over his shoulders and pull myself up and slam back down.

"Oh, shit, Kal," he groans my name and I feel a surge of power. I press my forehead against his. Our kiss is a teasing one, we nip each other's lips, our tongues twine and our breaths intermingle.

Then, he lifts me off his dick and lets me fall back on the bed. He reaches to the lamp on the bedside table and the dark room floods with soft, hazy light.

I've never felt comfortable being naked with the lights on. Even before I had Bianca, but especially not since. My body bears the marks of carrying and nursing my daughter.

But Remi's gaze is nothing short of adoring as his eyes burn a path up my body. I feel… nothing but beautiful.

Right now, there's nothing I wouldn't do to feel him inside of me. To have his mouth on me. His tongue in my pussy. His dick in my ass, his cum all over me.

"Please… do something."

"Tsk, tsk, tsk… no pleases here. You don't ask for what is yours." He drops to his knees in front of me. He big hands cup my thighs and he pushes them open.

"You haven't shaved." He sounds so pleased; his breath blows hot over me.

"Not since I got divorced."

His expression darkens. "All of this is mine." He drops kisses and drags licks on the inside of my thighs in between his words.

"Yes. Yours."

Like he wants to reward me, he pulls my clit between those soft, sweet lips and he starts to suck me just the way I like it. He slips his thumb, just the tip of it, into my ass and I gasp at the surprise burn.

"Does that feel good?" he asks, and I'm so distracted by the scrape of his stubble against the inside of my thigh, that all I can do is moan and roll my hips and fuck myself on his hand. Just when I feel the first flutter of my orgasm, he pulls out.

His hips fill the cradle of mine and he holds me still while his thick dick becomes my master. I open my legs as wide as I can and wrap them around him.

He presses a kiss to my neck and then takes my lips in the most delicious kiss while he slides inside my pulsing sex. The sweet sting that accompanies his first stroke is prelude to my pleasure and I welcome it.

My body arches off the mattress, a slow, reach upward for something… and when his dick hits the top of my pussy, I wrap my arms around his neck to keep myself attached to him.

"Yeah, baby, hold on. I'm about to fuck you like the blessing you are."

His muscular body quivers above me. My knees grip his waist and the ripple of muscle combined with each of his thrusts is almost as potent as his cock is in sending a fire burning through me. His mouth is pressed against my neck and the pace of his hot, heavy breaths match the pace of his hips between mine.

He tugs the tie from my wrists and growls, "touch me," before my cocky, sweet, sexy, gentleman unleashes, lets go and fucks me like the beast only I turn him into.

My fingers celebrate their emancipation by running in hungry fascination over the grooves of his muscles and pinching my nipples until I start to come.

"Remington…" His name is a moan that curls up from deep inside of me and falls from my parted lips like a hosanna.

"Kalilah…" his reply is a promise.

And then, he lets out the most exquisite, rumbly groan I swear I've ever heard and comes so hard inside of me that I feel it at the very center of me. I follow him over the edge of my orgasm where I float, suspended on a cloud of fulfillment and pleasure so raw, tears spill from the corners of my eyes.

I wrap my arms around him, hold him close to me and savor being in his arms and knowing that, at least for now, I can stay here.

"Fucking delicious," he whispers before he pulls me into him.

As his body relaxes into sleep next to mine, I think about my future.

I've come full circle. To the place where I first felt like a woman, in the arms of the man I belong to. I've imagined all of the worst-case scenarios and the only one I know I can't live with is doing something that would drive us apart. Not when we're both finally free.

It took fourteen years, but fate appears to finally be on our side.

I choose him.

This time, I'm going to outdraw love.

I won't lose this again.

33

SURPRISE

KAL

I SIT DOWN WITH MY CUP OF COFFEE AND WINCE WHEN MY ASS touches the wooden seat of the dining room chair. The apex of my thighs aches from Remi being between them for most of the night. I sip my coffee and moan at the slide of hot liquid down my throat combined with the memory of the way he used me.

All of my me. My mouth, my pussy, my ass.

God, I'd forgotten what it felt like to be thoroughly and completely fucked. His dedicated runs and work outs have left him in great shape and his stamina outpaced mine. He had to carry me to the shower when we were done in bed. I'm surprised I'm walking steadily this morning. I'm not looking forward to the long drive back to Houston.

"You have everything?" Remi walks out of the bedroom and shoves his phone into his pocket.

"Mm-hmm," I mumble around a mouthful of Cheerios. Remi leans against the counter and his pocket starts vibrating.

I raise my eyebrows. "You turned it on."

His dark eyebrows furrow in annoyance. "I'm ignoring it."

I shovel the last bite of cereal into my mouth and stand to take my bowl to the sink. "Great. I'm ready to go. I need to stop for gas, but I'll just follow you to town."

"We can leave your car here and come back for it later." He grabs my arm as I pass him and pulls me to him.

"I need my car for work in Houston. I'll be right behind you." I place the bowl on the counter and press my body flush to his.

"I'd rather you were right beside me." His warm breath bathes the side of neck.

I roll my hips against his. "I'd rather be right on top of you."

"You're insatiable." His grin is huge and proud.

"How could I not be?" I let him have that because I *love* that smile. He deserves to smile like that. I want to make sure he always does.

He hoods his eyelids and his lips, unobscured by the beard he'd shaved off this morning, curve into a sultry smile.

He lifts my sweater. "I'd like to be inside that spectacular ass of yours again."

He bends his head and pulls my tight, already throbbing nipple into his mouth and sucks hard. His teeth circle the sensitive tip and he tugs.

"Oh, Remi." I sigh. He lets go of my breast and drags his lips up my chest, up my neck and finally arrives at my mouth. But he doesn't kiss me.

"We don't have that kind of time. But... we could—"

Someone pounds on the front door and we freeze. We both turn to look at the door and see the silhouette of someone out there, but it's so frosted I can't even tell if it's a man or woman.

"You expecting someone?"

"No, and Nancy didn't bark. She's outside." He eyes the door and then heads toward it. He touches a panel in the wall that pops open and he pulls his shotgun out. The person pounds again. This time, they call out, "Hello?"

I follow him and by the time he's pulling the door open, I'm standing behind him.

An old man, with a long white, unkempt beard covering half his face, a dirty, faded, worn light blue baseball cap pulled down so low his eyes are hard to see stands before us.

But there's a friendly smile on his face. Remi's dog is sitting docilely by his side.

"Hello there, sir. Sorry to knock like this."

He pulls off his baseball cap and I gasp. He looks so much like... no. I shake the thought out of my head.

Until I see Remi's face. Then, I know I'm not wrong. He's thunderstruck and is just gaping at the man. The man's eyes dart left to right nervously. He reaches down to scratch Nancy's head, and she preens into his touch.

"I've been looking for her for almost a year."

"Well, damn," Remi says and the hollow shock in his voice makes me wince.

Oh, God.

"She been with you all this time?" The man drops down on one knee and looks his dog in the eyes. "Missed you, baby, did those boys hurt you?" He runs a hand down her sleek black coat and caresses the stump where her tail had been.

Remi puts his gun down.

"She's yours?"

"Yeah, some kids led her away while I was asleep almost a year ago. I sleep down by the underpass in—"

"They cut off her tail and left her for dead in a ditch."

The man's face crumples in anguish and drops his head into his hands. And then he sobs hysterically. Nancy nuzzles him with her nose and after a few seconds his sobs subside.

I rush up to stand next to him and put my hands on the man's shoulders. They are bone thin and shaking from his sobs. But what strikes me is how thin the fabric of his shirt is. Then he coughs, a rattling, wet, unproductive sound that I can tell isn't a normal cough.

I look at Remi, and his expression has morphed. From shock to anger.

"Remi, we need to bring him inside. He's not well."

"Who are you?" Remi barks down, his voice is brittle with anger.

The man's sobs grow loud again. The dog whines and rubs her head on his shoulder.

"Remi!" I chide him and stand in front of the man and put what I hope is a reassuring hand on his chest. His heart thunders under my palm. His eyes are narrowed and menacing, his square chin wobbles as he struggles to maintain his composure.

"I know you're scared. I'm scared, too. But we've got to bring him inside. Something is wrong with him." He just stares straight ahead at the sobbing man.

"Please," I add softly. He looks down at me, and the anguish in his eyes makes my knees weak.

"Kal, what the fuck is going on?" He grabs my arms; his eyes darken to that unreadable black that they were when I met him.

"I don't know. But we'll figure it out, okay?"

I turn back to the crying man and drop to my knee so we're face-to-face.

"What's your name?" I ask him gently.

"They call me John." He darts a nervous glance at Remi, his eyes widen at whatever he sees there and then he looks back at me.

"I didn't do anything wrong."

"We don't think you did. I'm Kal. This is Remington." I say Remi's full name because I want to see if there's a spark of recognition. There isn't.

"Well, from the looks of that fella, I'm not so sure about that."

"He's just surprised to see someone come looking for the dog. He's had her a while."

"Oh, yeah. Thank you for that. She's been with me since she was a pup."

His face is dirty, his beard is knotted, and hanging in straggly strands almost to his chest. But there's no mistaking that he looks just like Remi's grandfather. His nose, the color of his hair. But it's his eyes, that blue that rivals the cloudless sky behind us, that seals the deal.

"Sir. Will you let us bring you inside?"

"Why?" he stands back up. He adjusts his posture and I can see the same pride that runs through Remi straighten his shoulders.

"How did you find her?" Remi asks. His voice isn't angry, but its tone is taut and clipped.

The man takes a step back and shrugs slowly. "She must have seen me—she always had the keenest way of knowing when someone was coming. I was walking up that way from town"—he points in the direction of Fredericksburg— "and she just ran up beside me and then turned and came up this way."

"I see." Remi's response is distracted, his voice hollow.

He eyes the house and nods his head. "This place still looks good."

"You know this house?" I ask and Remi and I share a surprised glance.

"Oh, yeah, I've walked this way once a year for decades. Back to the place I was found."

"Where's that?"

He slips his baseball cap back on and his eyes disappear from view again. "A ditch near San Antonio," he says and then starts to cough again. I put an arm around him and have to stifle a gasp when I feel how prominent his bones are.

"Sir, come in. Let me get you something hot to drink for your cough. I just made some turkey sandwiches. Think you'd like one?"

His eyes light up. "Oh, that sounds nice. I can eat out here though. Being in that house. It gives me a headache."

"You've been *inside*?" I wince at how harsh Remi's voice is.

"Well, whoever owns it, is always having work done to it. You know renovating. The contractors pick up day workers from outside the Home Depot in Fredericksburg. I always jump on those crews. But I stopped working here about ten years ago. I would get these headaches, so bad they'd end up sending me home, and once, they wouldn't even pay me for my time."

"Headaches?"

He reaches to touch the base of his skull. "Bad ones, right here—"

"Tell us about the ditch," Remi interjects

The man's eyes widen at the impatience in his voice. I shoot Remi a disapproving look. But inside my heart is racing and impatience is making my pulse race, too. I want to know, too, but I know that the fastest way to get it isn't to demand it from him like that.

"Take your time, tell us what you can."

He glances wearily at Remi and then at me.

"Well, that's why I started crying just then. Just the thought that my girl suffered the same fate as me."

"What do you mean?" I ask, foreboding crawling up my arms.

Remi hand closes over mine and he squeezes it hard.

"When they found me, I had parts cut off, too." He holds up his left hand his ring and pinkie finger are gone. Right down to the root.

I gasp in horror.

"What happened?"

"I don't know. Don't remember. Never have. They call me John and it suits me just fine. My first memories are waking up. Calling for help. Help coming. No one knows how I got there. No one's ever come looking for a fella who looked like me."

I'm speechless and can't fathom what he's been through.

"John, let me get that food. And of course, we can sit out here while you eat."

"Sure. That would be very nice, indeed."

"Okay, we'll leave you and Nancy to get reacquainted."

"Her name's Gigi." He pets the top of the dog's head.

"Of course, it is." I smile at him.

I grab Remi's hand and we go inside. "We'll be right back and then we'll talk."

3 4

JOHN DOE

REMI

MY HEART IS BEATING SO FAST MY WHOLE BODY IS VIBRATING FROM the speed of the blood rushing through it. I'm trying to think, but in my ears, there's this loud whooshing sound that I can't get rid of.

The way it was when I saw Kal standing on my doorstep a few days ago.

Times ten.

I let Kal lead me back inside and push me down into a chair at the table. She sits down next to me and grabs my hands and starts to rub them as if she's trying to warm me up.

"Is that my father?" I ask the most improbable question. I feel like someone dropped an anvil on my head.

"He looks just like your grandfather." She shakes her head and covers her mouth like she can't believe she said it. Then she drops her hand and leans forward, her eyes wide with shock. "I mean, they could be twins. His eyes." With every word she speaks something I can't define but know I won't be able to contain grows inside of me.

"Kal—"

"Remi. He woke up in a ditch. With his fingers cut off."

"I know," I roar. My hand slaps the table, and the salt and pepper shakers in the middle rattle with the force of it.

Kal's eyes bulge and she slaps both hands over her mouth.

"I know," I say more quietly and then I drop my head into my hands.

"Oh, Remi. I'm here." She jumps up and puts an arm around me.

She presses her body into mine and strokes my neck. She feels so real, so warm, so here...

But all I can think is that this won't last either. That something will come along and destroy it. My heart constricts with each glide of her fingers across the tense muscles in my neck.

I can feel his presence outside the door, innocuous and yet goading me at the same time. I glance back at the door.

"Let's go talk to him," I say after a minute. I'm terrified of what he's going to say. But, I'm more terrified that he's going to leave and I'll never know.

She slides off my lap, and hurries over to the small coolers she packed this morning. "Let me get him his food."

A startling thought comes to me and I grab her hand as she's walking past me.

"Let's take him to Houston with us."

She puts the sandwiches on the table and places both hands on my shoulders. I look up at her and her eyes soften with sympathy. Normally, I hate that look, but right now it's very welcome.

"Let's see what he has to say first, Remi. See if he's even willing to come to Houston," she says gently.

"Oh, he's fucking coming to Houston. If I have to tie him up, throw him in the truck and drive with him kicking and screaming the whole way."

I stand up and take a steadying breath and then walk outside. She puts a hand on the door handle as I start to turn it.

"Remi, I want you to take it easy. He's sick. If we take him to Houston, we've got to get him to a doctor before we do anything else. I think he's dehydrated, and that cough doesn't sound good."

"Those are the least of his troubles." I open the door and squint against the morning sun. We're going to be late getting back to Houston, but it doesn't matter. He's sitting on the porch steps with his back to the door and I recognize the set of his broad, but very frail shoulders. It's just like mine. And Hayes'.

"John," I call his name and he turns around and smiles. It strikes me as so sad that this man, who had such a promising start to his life, has ended up here. And that he's sitting on the porch of a house he lived in but doesn't recognize. And is talking to a man he sired but doesn't know.

"Thank you, kindly. Both of you." He nods and smiles a closed-mouth, grateful smile at Kal and takes the sandwich from me. His hands are a mess. Dirty, with fingers that look like they've all been broken with what looks like decades of dirt under his fingernails.

"John, you have no idea where you came from?"

"Nope. I have some snatches of memories. I dream. But nothing I can remember. The first thing I remember is the lady who found me."

He takes a bite of the sandwich and Kal hands him the Thermos cup she's filled with hot coffee.

"She stayed until the hospital let me go. Then, she took me to an apartment in San Antonio. Said it was mine."

"She took you to her apartment?" Kal's expression is as bewildered as mine.

"Yeah. Said it was mine. I stayed there with her for a few days, but then…" He shakes his head. "It didn't feel right. So I left one night when she was sleeping. I started walking… right back to that ditch."

"Is that where you live?"

"No. I don't live anywhere. I move around. I get by with odd jobs. Sleep outside and try to remember. But I don't."

"Do you remember the lady? The one who took you from the hospital?"

"Oh, yeah. Of course. My memories from the hospital and everything after that are clear."

"What did she look like?"

"She was pretty. A black lady. Long dark hair with a streak of white down the middle of it."

35

BROTHERS

REMI
THREE DAYS LATER

"THANK YOU FOR SEEING ME." I sit down across the desk from Hayes Rivers. I study his face. I've seen it countless times in the last year, but now, I can see my father's features stamped all over it.

It's in the broad tip of his nose, that deep bow on his upper lip. His dark wavy hair, his hazel eyes and his olive coloring, he must have gotten from his mother's side.

But everything else, his height, his build, his confidence, all of that are from the part of him that is a Wilde.

"Fuck you for missing my wedding," Hayes says and I grimace apologetically.

"I didn't know there was a wedding..." I say vaguely. When he cocks his eyebrow at me, I shift a little uncomfortably. "And, I'm sorry I missed it."

He eyes me, and he smiles. "I held your spot." He picks up a picture that's facing him and hands it to me.

He and his wife, Confidence, stand in the center of the picture, kissing while their wedding party flanks them on either side. Next to his brothers, and in between another man I don't recognize is a space where I guess I was supposed to be standing. I feel a pang of real regret as I look at what I missed.

"You look great. I mean your jacket is about half an inch shorter than it should be, but other than that," I say without looking up.

"Ah, shut up, Remi. There's not a damn thing wrong with my jacket."

I huff a small laugh and hand it back to him. "Confidence looks beautiful, as always. When is the baby due?"

He picks up his phone and pulls open an app. It has a countdown clock.

"Eight weeks, three days and fourteen hours left to go."

I nod approvingly. "Congratulations, kid. You did good."

He puts the picture down, his smile falling and his eyes growing serious.

"We have a lot to talk about, Remi."

"I know. I'm sorry I ghosted on you like that. I know you were probably reeling, too."

He sighs, and steeples his fingers under his chin. "I was. But… I'd known for a couple weeks by the time she told you. I'm sorry for that. She wasn't sure that you didn't know. She said she'd come to your family to tell them she was pregnant with me and that your dad was missing and they turned her away."

He drops this last bit of news and it lands like a two-ton bomb.

"You didn't know that?" he deduces from my silence and expression.

"Clearly, I don't really know *anything*. They told us that our father died in a boating accident when I was two. That's all. I was too young to remember anything. They had a memorial service for him and everything. I've seen the pictures. What a crock of shit," I spit.

"Why is a memorial service a crock of shit? They thought he was dead, right? I mean Gigi did. She said he wouldn't have left her and not come back if he could have."

"He left us, anything was possible," I say woodenly, a hollow spot in my chest opening wider as I come to terms with that again.

"I know. I'm sorry," Hayes says.

"You have nothing to be sorry for. Our parents are fuckups. And we're left holding all of the rubble from their mess."

His shoulders fall a little and he sighs. "Thank fuck you feel that way, Remi."

"Thank fuck you do, too," I say sincerely. "We're going to need to keep our wits about us." I take a breath and tell him the rest. "Gigi didn't just give me a letter in the hospital room. She gave me keys to the house where she and my -- *our* dad lived. She said she had papers drawn up a long time ago, deeding it to me and Regan and Tyson. That she thought it's what he would have wanted."

"So that's where you've been? I have to say, your organization is a well-oiled machine. They ran seamlessly without you for months before the first real snafu happened."

"My business manager is an expert in crisis management. And I've got ironclad NDAs for every single member of my staff. And, they're loyal. We forgot that one event. If not, no one would have noticed."

Hayes leans back in his chair. "Well, if your shit is so tight, why are you back?"

"A couple of reasons. First one's a woman," I say simply

"You look like the cat who caught the canary. Is she the one who got away?"

I give him a sideways glance. "Man, shut up. I have never mentioned anybody getting away."

"You told me once, I should make up with Confidence before she got a taste of the world without me. I got the distinct impression you were speaking from experience."

"That's some damn good advice," I say.

"Just fucking tell me, Remi."

"Yes. She's the one. She got away once, but I'll be damned if she does again."

"Do I know her?"

"She grew up in Houston, but she left the same year I went to college, so I doubt it. She lives in New York. She's got a kid."

His eyebrows shoot up. "So, the motherfucker got his MILF."

I'm annoyed that he delivered that line better than I did. "Shut up, man. And as much as I'd love to talk about her all night, she's not why I'm here."

"Tell me, then."

"When I went out to the house, I had hoped I would get some answers. Find out what happened to him."

"Did you?" He leans forward, drums his fingers along the edge of his desk.

I don't pull any punches. "I found Lucas Wilde. He's very much alive. But only because the person who tried to kill him failed."

He leans forward in his leather chair and stares at me like I've just told him I saw the Loch Ness Monster.

"Remi. Listen, my brother Beau… he spends a few months in the desert doing some very weird shit and he's had hallucinations, too. Were you eating the cactus out there?"

"Hayes, shut the fuck up, please. I have never taken a drug in my life." I lean forward and press my hands to his desk. "I *found* him. I brought him back with me. He's been in the hospital. He was severely dehydrated. He has pneumonia, a slew of infections and he had to have almost all of his teeth extracted. He's a mess. And he doesn't know who he is. He only has memories after what happened to land him in a ditch."

His expression flattens. His face pales.

"You're serious?" His voice is gruff and thick with surprise.

"Very. And that's not all."

"What the fuck else could there be?" He huffs.

"I think my mother's known where he's been all the time. And that she knows exactly how he got in that ditch. He doesn't remember anything. But get this. I found a dog, wrapped in some wire, tail cut off, lying in a ditch. I rescued her, and she was with me for the last six months. She's kind of a guard dog."

"That's nice, Remi. But random."

I spear him a with withering glare. "She was his dog. *His.* Of all of the stray dogs in Texas' Hill Country, I found his."

"No fucking way? What are the fucking chances of *that*?" He shakes his head incredulously.

"I would think next to none, but that's how we found him. And guess what he named her?"

"Tina?" He laughs.

"Might have been more fitting. But, no. Gigi."

"No shit." Hayes slaps the table and laughs. "She'll get a kick out of that," he says.

"He has no memory of her."

His smile sobers and his eyes get sad. "She has very vivid ones of him. The way her eyes light up when she talks about him."

"Yeah, I figure there's something strong there if he gave his dog that same weird-ass name."

"Hey, don't talk shit about Gigi."

"Look, kid. I know she's your mom or whatever. But she's the reason my dad left us. And I don't understand how she could live with herself."

He drums his fingers on his desk and eyes me skeptically.

"Let me ask you something—about this woman. You telling me that if you loved her and she was with someone else, you wouldn't have tried to win her back."

"She was with someone else." I hate saying those words. They offend me and stir memories that never sit well with me. "For almost ten fucking years. I kept my distance and respected her marriage."

"You sure she's the one? Confidence couldn't be married to anyone else and me not at least try."

"I respect marriage, Hayes. That doesn't mean..." The memory of Regan's wedding to Marcel pops up. I meant it when I asked her to leave him. If she'd said yes, I would have walked out of there with her in my arms and not given a damn what happened.

"I did ask her to leave him. She said no. She has a kid. She didn't want to break up her home."

"What changed?"

"She's divorced."

I've been thinking about Kal's daughter a lot. She supposed to be coming for a visit and I'm nervous as fuck because I know Kal wants to live close to where she is. I don't know what that means, but if I have to move Wilde Law to New York, I'll do it.

The very thought sends a river of unease up my spine. I'm the head of our family. I run Wilde Law, but I own forty percent of Wilde World's stock. I am still the face of the family's philanthropic efforts. Moving would be... I push the thought away. Cross that bridge when I get to it. Right now, I've got a huge fish to fry.

"So, my mother's been in DC all week meeting with our lobbyists and having meetings with some suppliers. She's back tomorrow and I've invited her to dinner. I want you to come. I want Gigi to come. I want everyone in that room when I tell them I found him."

"I had no idea you were so fucking dramatic, Remi. You know that's going to be a spectacle of epic proportions."

"I don't care about optics. It's the most efficient way to find out what happened."

"So, you're going to have him walk in and see who starts confessing or tries to run for the hills?"

"Of course not. We've got a lot of he said, she said going on right now. Lots of hiding and lies. Lots of untruths. I want to know who tried to hurt him. And I want to see their faces when they realize it's not a secret anymore."

"Holyyy shit." He whistles long and low.

"To say the least. I'll send you the details."

"Can I meet him? Ahead of time, I mean?"

"You want to? I didn't think you would." I'm surprised. He was very close to the man who raised him.

"Yeah, of course. I mean, biologically, at least he's my father. I can't think of him like that, but I want to meet him. And since I'm clearly not a suspect in his disappearance..."

"Yeah, man. Of course. I'm sorry I didn't come sooner. It's been a busy week."

"Oh, I understand. You've had all that fucking to do."

I laugh. "When you meet her, you'll understand."

"No doubt."

I stand to leave and Hayes calls my name. "Wait. So... how do you feel about the fact that we're brothers?"

"Elated. I love Tyson, but if I could have picked a man to be my brother, it would have been you," I answer honestly.

"Me too. The coolest motherfucker, I know. I'm just sorry it went down the way it did." He pats my shoulder.

"Me, too. But I'm fucking glad it went down."

THREE CONVERSATIONS AND A FUCK UP

KAL

"I swear, you're the best cook in this entire city." Remi rubs his hands together gleefully as Sweet drops off two plates of steaming garden omelets.

She puts a hand on her ample hip and glares down at him, her pretty face pinched in annoyance. "That sweet talk may work on your gal here, but it doesn't work on me, Remington."

"You wound me. I'm being sincere. I've been in here every day since I got back. That's got to count for something." He gives her a charming flash of his smile and she rolls her eyes.

"You're nothing but a flirt. Thank goodness you got your girl back. Be good to see you settle down."

His girl, that sends flutters through me.

"I'm trying to convince her to stay." He grabs my hand and squeezes it. I squeeze it back.

"She doesn't look like she's going to need much convincing. I can practically see the stars in her eyes." She nods at me.

"Stop talking about me like I'm not here."

"Maybe you should try having breakfast in bed one morning instead of rolling in here every day," she says eyebrows raised knowingly before she pats Remi on the shoulder and strolls off.

"I love it here." I smile after her.

"I'm glad. I do, too. So, what do you think? Breakfast tomorrow, my place?"

"Are you asking me over to your house, Mr. Wilde?" I bat my lashes at him and drawl my words.

"I am. And not just tomorrow. When all this shit with my dad is over, I want us to talk about how we're going to close the distance between us."

"You're getting ahead of yourself." I say and try to laugh around the bundle of nerves in my gut. We've got a lot to figure out.

"Nope. Just finally catching up actually." He wolfs down the last bite of egg and stands up.

"Where are you going?"

"I have a meeting in fifteen minutes. I'll see you tonight."

"So, you'll be there by six?" I ask Remi.

"Yeah, but you and Lucas don't have to get there earlier than eight. The fireworks won't start until after seven."

"You're awfully glib for someone who's planning to try and catch a potential murderer tonight. Sure this is how you want to do it?"

"Absolutely. It's the only way. The element of surprise will be like a truth serum."

"I think everyone's going to be surprised. I doubt that will tell you who actually hurt him. Unless you get someone to confess, you'll need proof."

"You're right, I guess. But at least when we're all in one room, there can't be any he said, she said. Everyone will be shocked. Everyone except you, me, Hayes, and probably Confidence since I know his pussy-whipped ass tells her everything."

"What if you're wrong?"

"Ah, my little pessimist. But, I'm not." He taps me on the nose with a wink.

"Look who's talking, Mr. Worst-Case Scenario. I'm just asking what yours is."

"Worst-case scenario is that neither of them did it, but at least we'll know the role they played. Between the two of them, we'll find out everything we need to know."

"Yeah, we'll definitely know more than we do now." I close my laptop and reach for his hand. I wince at the way the muscles in my neck protest. I reach over to rub the points of tension that have made a permanent home in the muscles of my neck.

His fingers brush mine out of the way. "Let me do that."

"Oh, that feels so good, never stop." My head lolls forward and I groan in relief as his strong fingers work a knot that's been bothering me since I woke up.

"God, your neck is tight."

"This week has been intense. I'm actually pretty tired." I close my eyes and he digs deeper and the tension starts to dissipate. If only he could make the rest of my problems go away as easily.

He sighs. "I'm sorry. This thing with my dad has stolen all of the oxygen in the room. I haven't even asked you about your story. Did you get everything you needed?"

At the mention of the story my stomach gives a small flip. Thank God he can't see my face, because I'm sure it's turned green.

"Today's a big day for you. Let's just focus on that. We'll have plenty of time to talk about my story later."

He stops rubbing my neck and tilts my chin up with his finger. His eyes move across my face like they're taking an inventory.

"Are you okay?"

"I'm okay. This week has been intense, my story is a cluster and I miss my daughter."

"She'll be here on Friday?"

"Yeah, I can't wait for you to meet her. She's a character." I smile fondly as I think of my daughter's antics.

"I can't wait either. Things will be calmer by then. We can spend time getting to know each other and figure out how we close this gap."

My heart leaps at his words. We have a future. Our paths are clear.

"I can't either."

He glances at his watch. "Sorry I've really got to go. You good to walk back to the hotel by yourself?"

"Yeah, I know this neighborhood like the back of my hand still. I'll be fine."

CONVERSATION ONE

I'M JUST WALKING BACK INTO MY HOTEL WHEN MY PHONE RINGS.

"Give me an update. I've only got six minutes before my next call." Jules's abrasive voice snaps in my ear.

"Morning. Uh, well—I had a meeting with Gigi Rivers—" I stammer.

"That's fucking fantastic. Did she tell you anything about Remington Wilde, if he came to see her that day in the hospital?"

I clear my throat and rack my brain for a lie that will tide her over. Just until I can decide if there's a story in there somewhere.

"Yes. She said he came to see her. He and Hayes are friends, you see. Good friends, and it was just a friendly get well visit."

"That's bullshit, though, right? I mean, we see him storming out of the hospital, squealing out the garage and then he hasn't really been seen since."

"Well, I don't know what's going on with him and Regan. But no one else here seems to think he's missing. I talked to a source at his office, she said he sent out a company-wide email this week, saying he was back from his break and that he can't wait to share all of the exciting ideas he had while he was away. So, it appears he was just on vacation. So, I think we can scrap that part of the—"

"I'm sorry, are you high? Who goes on vacation for months? Nobody," she yells.

The flips my stomach has been doing intensify.

"I haven't heard a single rumor about him being an alcoholic or on drugs. Honestly, I think there's a real story in whatever is happening with The Rivers Family and their resurgence—"

"Kalilah. No one gives a shit about their resurgence if they don't know the details. If you're not up to it, come home, pack up your office, and find a job at The Huffington Post." And then, she hangs up.

I drop my phone like it's on fire and fall backwards on my bed. I can't afford not to have a job. Tomorrow is pay day, but by the time the sun sets, most of it will be gone. Fear makes my throat constrict and I force myself to face the worst case scenarios.

If I don't write the story, at the very worst, I lose my job. But I'd have at least one more paycheck and I own my place outright. Taxes aren't due for months. I may not be able to find a job as a journalist, but I could keep food on the table while I sold my place. And with the money left over, I'd have a nice nest egg until the I could figure things out…

If do I write my report, at the very worst, Remi wouldn't forgive me. But I'd have a job, it might even be the promising beginning of a career I've always dreamed of. But all of that would probably mean causing real harm to the fragile peace Remi and I have forged.

I don't even have to think about it to know which one of those poisoned pills I'd rather swallow.

I just need to think about what comes next. I decide to go for a walk to clear my head.

CONVERSATION TWO

I LEAVE MY HOTEL WITH NO PARTICULAR DESTINATION IN MIND. So, when I find myself standing in front of To Be Read a few minutes later, I'm surprised.

I planned to never come here again. I have so many painful memories about our time here; I thought being back would send those old feelings, that I avoid like the plague, flooding back. But my feet guided me, anyway. As I stand here, the only thing flooding me is love.

I had *loved* it here.

It had been the best summer of my life.

I love living in New York, but this feels like home. And now that Remi and I are both be ready to give us a go, it also feels like a solution.

It's still vacant, just as we left it.

I wonder why Lister never sold it or found someone to re-open it.

I also wonder why he never wanted to know his daughter. I can't imagine what makes a man do that. Paul may not win any awards for father of the year, but he at least made time for Bianca.

My feet, guided by my heart, lead me through the huge grassy square that's the heart of Rivers Wilde.

I can see Bianca running across it, flying her kite. We have a great park in our neighborhood in New York, but nothing like this.

I pass the massive arcade of food stalls called The Market that would put an international festival to shame. Bianca has always been fascinated by other people's backgrounds. She has a more adventurous palate at nine years old than I do at thirty-one.

Oh, she would be in heaven.

This could be a real fresh start. Not one made borne out of a moment of crisis, but a decision made in a moment of clarity.

And that's why, a few minutes later, I find myself standing at the other place I never thought I'd go. In front of David Lister's house. It is in spite of my nerves that I find the courage to take a deep breath and ring the doorbell.

He answers the door himself and if it wasn't for that trademark scowling smile, I wouldn't know it was him. The words I'd rehearsed die on my tongue as my alarm at his appearance rises. He's stooped, and pale, his cheeks nearly hollow. His pajamas, a dignified navy blue ensemble, look like they're draped on a clothes hanger instead of a human body. His dark eyes are watery and red rimmed as he takes me in.

"You look just like your mother."

"I do?" I'm surprised at the tenderness in his voice.

"You better come in. Standing up for too long is tiring." He shuffles away, leaving the door open and I follow him in.

"I hope you don't mind that I'm not dressed. Just doesn't seem like it's worth all the effort on the days I'm not going out." He says wearily over his shoulder.

"I don't mind at all." I look around the room, trying to see every picture. See if I can see glimpses of myself in him when he was younger. I see nothing but strangers faces staring back at me.

"Have a seat." He points to the small loveseat across from his reclining chair.

I hesitate for a second, not sure that this was a good idea after all.

"Go on. You came all this way, don't chicken out now." His eyes twinkle with humor as he lowers himself back into his chair.

"I'm not chickening out of anything." I sound defensive, but I don't care. My nerves are flying around like bats in my stomach and sit I down because I'm afraid my legs might give out on me.

"You've got more courage than me. I've never been able to work up the nerve to come and see you. Even though there were so many times I wanted to."

"You did?" I clutch the bag in my lap to my chest, I didn't expect that.

"Of course. I owe you an apology. It's too little, too late. But I do."

His admission surprises me. I, of course, can list my grievances against this man in my sleep. But I've never imagined he would feel any remorse.

So, I ask the one question I promised I wouldn't.

"Why didn't you want to know who I was?"

He doesn't even blink.

"I cared very much about your mother. I met her when I was going through a very difficult time. She was far too young, and I was far too old, you see. I could have gone to jail. I had a business, a family. I just couldn't risk everything for a lapse in judgment." He doesn't even sound sorry. He's just telling me the facts.

"So you abandoned her. And me." My tone is biting, and he casts his eyes to his lap.

"Yes. I did," he admits and somehow, it doesn't hurt as much to hear it as I had imagined.

"I see."

"You have to understand. My wife and son both died in a horrific car crash about a year before your mother came to see me about you—after you got in all that trouble. I wanted to help, so I gave her the bookstore. But I couldn't do more than that, Kalilah. When I looked at her, all I saw was my karma. I had convinced myself I lost them because I betrayed my wife. It was irrational, but I was grieving. So, I kept my distance. But every time she's asked me for it, I've helped her. But, I've had my own struggles."

He sounds like he expects me to feel sorry for him. And I guess on a basic human level, I do.

I glance around the room and imagine how different my life would have been if I had grown up in this house.

I may have had a nicer roof over my head, but this man wouldn't ever have been the father I needed. His explanation sounds more like excuses and they leave me cold.

They're also not what I want from him.

"Mr. Lister, I came here today because I want the bookstore. And I want you to give it to me."

CONVERSATION THREE

"Kal, this is some shit," Kelli says, her tone thoroughly scandalized by what I've just told her.

"Trust me, I know. I am ankle deep in it and sinking further every day."

"Oooh wheeee, honey. You know how to fuck up, right! You go big or go home." She chortles.

"You're not helping, Kelli." I moan miserably. I have a low-level thrumming of panic inside of my head. I called her because she knows what's at stake, in a way that no one else does.

"I'm sorry. Let me just make sure I've got this completely straight, okay?" she says soberly.

"Okay."

"So, you didn't know he was the story when you went to see him, right?"

"Right."

"Now you're lying to Jules to buy time to find an angle that doesn't include him because she stuck her neck out for you. But also, you're moving back to Houston to run a bookstore some dude just gave you."

"Right."

"So, what about this story? Is it not newsworthy?" she asks.

"Of course it is. But I can't be the one to tell it."

"So, you're going to let someone else get this huge scoop on the man you love and write it instead?"

"I don't know if anyone else will get the scoop."

"If Jules sent you down to Houston to chase this story, then trust me, it's a big enough scoop that you're not the only one with it in your sights. Someone will write it. But that someone won't be you."

The thought unnerves me.

"Kal. Tell him about the assignment. Ask him if he'll consider giving you the story. This could be his chance to get ahead of a story you can't bury."

"Yes! Oh my God, Kelli. You're right. I mean, he's very private, but if he could have some assurances about the story and maybe…"

"You need to tell everyone the truth," Kelli says as if it's that simple.

"I know," I say.

"Then why haven't you?" she asks.

"My life feels like it's all balanced on a less than firm foundation. I don't want to lose it all again." I admit my deepest fear.

"Kal." Her voice is gentle. "I only say this with love. You can't begin your relationship on the back of a lie. And honestly, if you tell him, he might help you. Give you the story."

"Oh, God. He's going to hit the roof."

"That's not the end of the world. He'll be mad, but then he'll get over it. Don't let your fear lead you down a path of bad decisions. You've got a second chance. Do it right."

Her words make perfect sense. I know it's the right thing to do.

"I'll tell Remi first. If he doesn't want me to write it, I won't. And then I'll call Jules and tell her what I've decided."

"Kal… I've known you a long time. And as talented as you are and as much as I want you to succeed in this career, I am so glad you're choosing love."

I laugh nervously. "Well, let's hope love chooses me back,"

"If he has any brains, he'll never let you out of his sight again."

"He's already threatened that."

"I'm glad he loves you that much. You deserve that. I know you're afraid, but I promise, it's not going to be as scary as you think."

My heart swells with love for her. She's such a good friend.

I just hope I'm making the right decisions.

THE FUCK UP

WHEN I HANG UP WITH KELLI, I OPEN MY LAPTOP AND START writing. It's just an outline, but I think Remi might like the direction I want to take. I'll show this to him and explain everything. As I write, I see how, with the right angle, the seemingly sordid chronology of events, really just paints a picture of the typical American family. Sure, they have more money, but these aren't rich people-problems. This could be a chance to lift the veil. Show the human side of a family that only ever shows the public a perfect face.

Worst-case scenario he says no. I would lose my job, and probably never work as a journalist again. But, after my conversation with Lister, I have a plan. I'll be okay. I love Rivers Wilde. I love Remi.

I walk to the window and look out over the square. It's got a lot more stores than it did when I lived here. There are more cars, more people, but it still looks like the idyllic slice of suburbia that I've never seen anywhere else.

Bianca would thrive here. It would mean amending our custody agreement, but I could make a convincing argument.

By the time I'm done writing. I'm excited.

After we get past this evening, I'll show him and we can plan the future we've always dreamed of.

37

THE TRUTH

REMI

"You have a beautiful home, Remington. Thank you for inviting us." Gigi smiles nervously, but genuinely as they walk into the front hall of my house.

"Yes, thank you for coming back from your months long sulk just in time to host a dinner party weeks before my baby is due," Hayes says irritably.

"I'll try to time my life crisis better next time, Rivers."

"This would be a good time to tell Gigi who else is here," Hayes says, none of the lightheartedness in his companion's tone is present in his. I'm not surprised or unprepared.

He made me promise to name my firstborn son after him before he agreed to bring Gigi today. I know that this is going to be a fucked-up day. But, there's no hiding from it anymore.

And whatever Gigi suffers today will be tempered by seeing Lucas again.

I walk to stand in front of Gigi, her smile has gone from hesitant to nonexistent in the space of a moment.

"Who's here, Remington?" Her voice is cool and even, but her eyes are wide with trepidation.

"My family is in the sitting room."

She turns to look at Hayes. He turns his unsettled gaze on me.

"Remi, maybe we should rethink this."

"Maybe you should help me keep things moving exactly as we planned," I say in a stony, unforgiving voice. There's no turning back.

"She's terrified." Hayes walks over to Gigi.

"There's nothing to be terrified of, Gigi," I promise her. "Tonight is going to be a difficult one, but I think you're the person who it will be least difficult for. I know there is no love lost between you and my mother."

"That's an understatement if there ever was one. And it's not just your mother. It's your grandfather, too."

"Yes. I know. Well, my grandfather is dead. So, it's just her you're going to see. Well, Regan and Tyson are here, too. They're expecting you. My mother is not. She wouldn't have come or stayed if she knew she had to see you," I say with blunt honesty.

"What in the world is going on?" She raises her voice and takes one stiff, deliberate step back from me.

"Hayes is the only person I've fully briefed on everything."

"What is everything?" she cries loudly, panicked. She looks to Hayes, her expression alarmed. "What is going on here? What have you been keeping from me?"

"Come to the sitting room. I'll tell all of you together." I don't wait for her to agree, I just continue walking and know that Hayes will bring her along.

As soon as I open the wide, wooden double doors that lead to my formal sitting room, my mother jumps out of her seat and strides toward me. "What is going on? Who was at the door and why in the world—"

Her words die in her throat at the same time the sounds of their footsteps tell me that the Riverses are in the room now, too.

"What are they doing here? What is this?" She turns those dark, enraged onyx eyes on me and if looks could kill, I would be halfway to dead just from that first glance.

My heart pounds in my chest. A hard drumming that steadies me as adrenaline rushes in and keeps me from running out of the room. I've never been more afraid of anything in my life as I am of the conversation we're about to have.

I inhale sharply through my nostrils and tell her. I'm not drawing things out tonight. Time is of the essence.

"They're here because—"

"It doesn't matter why they are here," she shrieks and spins on her heel and walks back toward her seat. "I am leaving. I will not breathe the same air as this vile woman." She snatches up her purse and walks back toward me.

I step into her path. "You are not going anywhere," I say sternly.

I look over my shoulder at the Riverses. Gigi's eyes are glassy and she's clutching Hayes' arm like her life depends on it. I gotta hurry this up.

I look back to my mother and say sternly, "No one's leaving until we're all done."

She eyes me like I'm an offending stain on her pristine white blouse. Her nostrils flare as if a malodorous wind just blew through.

"This had better be good," she says and then stalks back to her seat.

"Will you please have a seat?" I say to the Riverses.

They walk over to the chairs I've set up next to my family.

Regan and Tyson watch me with wide-eyed awe.

"You guys okay?" I ask them before I get things started. Regan nods yes, Tyson just looks down at his lap. He's taken the news terribly.

I never realized how much he missed my father, too. He was just a baby when he left. But he's refused to see him. Until tonight. I haven't pushed because I've thought it might be for the best.

My father's been extremely cooperative. I think he's just happy to have a clean bed and all his meals. Being here for the last week hasn't done anything to jog his memory. Rivers Wilde was only in the early stages of development when he left. Nothing here would look familiar. Certainly not his children. We've already had two sessions with a psychiatrist. After all of this time without any medical care, it's been an essen tial piece in trying to help him get the tools he needs to rebuild his life.

We've told him his real name. Told him he's from here. Yet, I haven't found the courage to say the words "I'm your son." And maybe that's because it doesn't feel like an honest thing to say.

I'm not his son. Not really. I'm the son of the Legend of Lucas Wilde. But he's not real.

I've grappled with that all week. Does that mean I'm not real either? Kal shot that question down vehemently and convincingly.

Of course, I am someone. I'm the man I've made myself. Just because I spent my life chasing what turned out to be something contrived, doesn't mean I'm contrived. I've made choices, followed my convictions and I've built a good life.

All of that is true. But it's going to take more than her sweet assur-ances to make me believe it completely. When this is all over, I'm getting back to my day-to-day as quickly as I can. I'm going back to the office on Monday. Making my appearance official and then figuring out how to get Kal to stay in Houston.

I clap my hands together in anticipation and turn to face my guests.

"Thank you for coming. I asked you all here today because while I was gone, I found out what happened to Lucas Wilde." I rip the Band-Aid off fast and without any warning. And I watch their faces.

My mother rolls her eyes.

Gigi's eyes fall shut and she grips Hayes' hand tightly.

"Remi, this is ridiculous. We already know what happened," my mother scoffs.

"We know what you *say* happened," I respond.

"He walked away from his life for love, Remi. It cost him everything. Cost us all everything." The vitriol in her voice is diminished by the extreme sadness in her eyes.

"I'm sorry, Tina." Gigi's head has been bowed all this time, but she looks up at my mother now. Her hazel eyes are bloodshot and wet. "I know Lucas and I hurt you in ways we couldn't begin to imagine. The decision we made wasn't a flippant, easy one."

"Really?" My mother's disbelieving voice is laced with relief. This is, clearly, a very long overdue conversation. My heart, so long cold to her, constricts as I watch a sadness I've never seen come over her face. It ages her instantly.

"Yes. We chose differently the first time. You didn't know that we met in college—"

"Of course I know that." My mother's voice cracks with indignation. "Lucas told me all about you when we got married. Called you a phase. Said he knew nothing lasting could be built on something that floated so far off the ground," she says spitefully.

Gigi nods and her smile is wistful and fleeting, her eyes a little lost. "Yes, that's what we told each other when we broke up. It felt like an awful lot of trouble to go to for something as unknown as love. His family hated me. Mine hated him. And we both, especially him, didn't want to make life harder than it had to be. So we went our separate ways. I stayed away. But, I've never regretted anything more. Life had a shadow over it for years." Her voice has dropped to a just above a hush.

"And then you came sailing back to town," my mother singsongs her derision.

Gigi sighs impatiently. It's the first sign of impatience or annoyance she's shown all evening. "Yes. I came back. For a love I'd held so fleetingly I wasn't sure if I had imagined it. For a love, it turns out, that was worth all the trouble."

My mother scoffs and actually rolls her eyes.

"Remi," Gigi turns her urgent, pleading hazel gaze toward me, "I know your life was disrupted in ways no apology will ever make up for. But one day, when love calls you, you will understand why we did what we did. What we had was so rare. We knew it. Please try to understand."

I watch her closely and process everything she just said. Her decisions proved disastrous for me. The revelations that are going to come to light here today will likely change the course of all our lives. The ripple effect of their decisions will probably continue to be felt.

But it wasn't her fault that my father didn't love my mother. Not her fault my mother loved my father in a way that wouldn't allow her to move on.

I understand Gigi just fine. It's the same kind of love and my refusal to be parted from mine again that brought me back.

She watches the thoughts move across my face, sees the moment I soften, and smiles.

"What utter garbage," my mother shouts. Disgust narrows her eyes and curls

her lips. She stands up and walks toward Gigi. "You are selfish, entitled, and fragile."

Her words are a sequence of poison-tipped arrows that she flings with breathtaking speed. Gigi flinches like she's being pierced by them. My mother comes to stand directly in front of her. She glowers, her body is rigid and her hands are planted firmly on her hips.

"You think getting to fuck the man you love is more important than my children knowing their father?"

Gigi blanches, but recovers and rises to her feet. She's a tall woman, my mother is not, and she uses her height to her advantage. She looks down her nose at my mother, her expression glacial.

"I do not think that. But clearly *you* do."

It's my mother's turn to blanch. She takes a step back. Gigi presses on. She points a finger accusingly at my mother. "You are the one who decided that if he wasn't sleeping next to you, that your children wouldn't see him. You are the one who told them he was dead and threatened him with persecution if he didn't go along with it. You are the one who is selfish, entitled and fragile," she spits back at my mother.

My mother laughs. It's loud, brash, and false. She spins around to face me. "Do you see why I was so dead set against Kal? She would have ruined your life. And thought somehow she was in the right. You would have ended up in a ditch somewhere and I wouldn't have been there to save you." Her eyes widen in horror as she realizes what she just said.

"Mom," I call her name quietly. "What happened the day you tried to kill him?"

Regan gasps and looks at me with shocked eyes. I don't know why. I told her I was going to ask.

"Stop saying that," she says and her chin, for the first time I can ever remember, trembles.

I feel a pang of guilt but press on. I knew tonight was going to be uncomfortable for everyone. I didn't exclude myself from that expectation. There's no stopping this train. We'll all leave here different people than we were when we arrived. But it's time to end all of the secrets and lies that have held sway over our lives for so long. I cross my arms over my chest and look my mother squarely in her eyes. The exact same as mine and I drop my bomb.

"This is my house. Here, we tell the truth. When I first discovered the true circumstances of his leaving, you told me you and Pops had decided to tell us that because you were trying to spare us the knowledge that he left us. But why didn't you tell me six months ago that you found him alive and took him to a hospital?"

Gigi's moan is tortured, and she covers her mouth to muffle it.

My mother's eyes widen in shock. But she recovers and her mask of indifference is back.

"So, you know," she says as if she's the one who has to accept an ugly truth.

"Yes. Now I know for sure."

"That's unfortunate," she says stiffly.

"You knew he was out there, and you never thought that maybe you should bring him home?" I ask incredulously.

"So he could go back to her?" she yells and points at Gigi.

I slam my fist down on the table with such force that everything on it rattles.

"What about his kids? She remarried, moved to Italy. She hasn't lived here in almost thirty years. We were here. We needed him."

Her eyes sweep across me and my siblings. "You were the most ungrateful children. You wanted him. Him. Who was not worthy of the title of your father. Who didn't give enough of a shit about his children to stay with them." She's raging.

"You hate him. You kept him away. Tell us what you did to him. Did you try to kill him and get cold feet?"

"I saved him." Her voice crackles with anger. "He was lying in that ditch and I dragged him out. Me." She pounds her chest and turns her eyes, burning hot with accusation at Gigi.

"She sat in her house for days before she even went to look for him."

"I didn't... I looked for him," Gigi yells back. I look at Hayes and he's staring blankly at my mother.

"How did you know he was in that ditch?" I ask.

"Because she put him there," Gigi shouts.

"I did not," my mother hollers.

Gigi is undeterred. She stands, stalks across the room, her finger pointing angrily. "I've always known it. You hated him for leaving you. You think I didn't know you were talking to him? You think I didn't know he was still seeing you? I knew, but I also knew how desperate he was to keep contact with his children. You and that devil he called a father wouldn't let him."

My mother's on her feet again, too. Her eyes blazing, the heat of her anger has dried her tears and the two women meet in the middle of the room.

We all watch in fascination as the two normally dignified, stoic women practically bump chests.

"You shut your ignorant, thieving mouth," my mother seethes. "You don't know anything. He loved me. Until you came to town with all of your bullshit about chasing your happiness and you stole him. I didn't kill him. I should have though. Should have left his faithless ass to rot in that gutter. But I knew he was still alive and the colossal fool that I am, I still love him. So I saved him. And then, I tried to hide him. Because if the person who tried to kill him found out he was still alive, he'd try again. What did you do? Give up your baby, marry another man and then move to Italy."

Gigi's hand flies toward her, palm open.

My mother catches it.

"You don't have the *right*," she hisses. "I wish it had been *you* in that ditch. *You* deserved to be there." She drops Gigi's wrist like it's filth she's holding and marches back to her chair.

Gigi stands there, her shoulders drooping, her eyes forlorn. Hayes walks over, drops a kiss on her forehead, shoots me a warning look that says "move this shit show along," and takes her back to her seat.

"So, what happened?" I ask my mother.

"I got him a place to live. But he left and I had no idea where he'd gone. I hired a man a few years ago and found him. The guy told me he got a dog and named it Gigi."

Gigi gasps.

"Even when he can't remember his own children. He remembered her," she spits at Gigi.

Then turns accusing eyes at me and my siblings. "And even though he left you, you still love him more than you'll ever love me. Me, who has given everything to keep you safe. I wanted to tell you the truth so many times. So you would know who he really was... is."

She sighs heavily, covers her face with her hands and bends at the waist. I watch her and wait. I want to comfort her. But I know she won't want it.

"I found him in that ditch by chance. We were supposed to meet that day, and he was late. Lucas was never late. I went as close to their house as I dared and parked and walked around a little. That ditch runs behind their house. I found him about half a mile away. And took him to the hospital."

"Why didn't you call me?" Gigi asks.

My mother scoffs. "I wasn't sure you hadn't put him there. I thought maybe he'd reverted to type and was cheating on you, too," she says snidely. The blood drains from her face.

"He would never—"

"Wait. What did you tell Pops?" I interrupt Gigi and turn to my mother.

And for the first time since this conversation started, I see real, unadulterated panic in her eyes.

"He was away when I got back from San Antonio. I went to his office to look for something and found your father's rings. The rings that had been on the fingers that had been cut off his hand."

The world stops spinning. I stare down at my hand in horror, at the ring on my own finger. The one my grandfather gave me right before he died. I tug it off and drop it on to the table.

I look between her and it. "You're lying."

"I'm not," she says so simply, with so much defeat. "I logged into his computer. He didn't even have it password protected. He couldn't imagine that anyone would dare look through his things. I found the emails—he never even bothered to delete them between him and the man he hired to kill your father. He was to bring those rings back as proof."

"Why would he do that? That makes no sense. He was his heir."

"No, Remi. He hated Lucas. He was an utter disappointment."

"So he disinherited him. Why in the world would he want to kill him?"

"Because Lucas wasn't going to go quietly into the night. Not without what was his."

"He wanted money?" I ask incredulously.

"He wanted *you*. All three of you," she says slowly, her gaze sweeping over me and my siblings.

"He did?" This question comes from Tyson.

She turns to look at him. She just nods.

My heart thuds.

Once.

Twice.

Then it starts sprinting at a breakneck pace.

I didn't realize how badly I'd needed to hear those words until she said them. Since I discovered he'd left, I've woken up every day wondering how my father could walk away from his children. It's been the thing that has kept me from being able to feel any joy in finding him.

"Your grandfather was not going to let him have you. He had poured all of his hopes into you, Remi. So, I tried to mold you in his image because I didn't want him to think you were a disappointment, too. I'd seen what he'd done to his other disappointment."

"You're saying he would have killed me?"

"I don't know. But I didn't want to take the chance. And you are so much like Lucas. This hard exterior you've developed to protect your soft inside. I knew you'd fuck up and then, he'd decide to clear the way for Tyson." She sounds sad, but not apologetic at all.

"Good God." I run a hand over my face and try to let that settle.

"I never told him what I found. Keep your enemies close—as I've always told you. In this case, I moved in with mine. But it was what I thought was best," she says.

"Best? For us to live with the man who tried to kill your husband?"

"I always did what I thought was best." She repeats.

"And you just let him get away with the attempted murder of his son?" Regan shouts and stands up. Tyson is glaring at her, his dark eyes full of malice.

"Yes." She nods as if to reaffirm how obvious the answer should be. "Everything has a price. For your lives, nothing was too much to pay. And he was good to you. You've achieved so much. All of you."

"We're all miserable," Tyson says quietly. "We are all miserable and our lives are a fucking lie. But look how much we achieved." He stands up on that last word, his voice gets louder. "Why are none of you losing your shit?" he asks the room collectively. His eyes wide with disbelief.

"I lost my shit, Tyson. I've had six months to process it," I remind him, trying to keep my voice gentle.

"But you just found out, right now that Pops tried to kill our father. His son. Pops." He shakes his hands like he's trying to rearrange the air around us. Create a whole new reality.

"Tyson—" Regan tries to calm him but he cuts her off flinging an arm in her direction.

"And she's been calm about everything. You've had months to let it all sink in, but she found out when I did. And she's sitting there like she's watching a fucking play."

"Who says I'm not losing my shit?" she asks, her voice rich with her grievance at his statement. She stands up and faces him. "Just because I'm not screaming like the rest of you?" She flings her arms wide. "I'm thinking about my own fucking children, Tyson. Something you don't have to consider."

I step in between them. "Hey. We should not be fighting with each other," I say gently and try to appear calm, although it is the very last thing I am.

"Guess what, Legend, you are the only people I want to fight with right now. I'm done with this little circus you put on tonight." His gaze sweeps the room once before he turns and stalks out. I don't try to stop him. I know how he's feeling and I know it will take time to process and come to terms with all of this.

Everything slows and I sit down heavily in the chair across from them. My mind is reeling and I just want this night to end, but I have a feeling the nightmare is just beginning. I stare between the two of them.

"I found him," I add, and Gigi's eyes fly open, her hand covering her mouth as she watches me wide-eyed.

"You didn't," my mother says.

"He's here." I watch her face.

"He's *dead*," she shouts almost as if she says it loudly enough it will be true.

"He's not." My mother's face pales as she takes in my expression. She knows I'm serious. She drops down in her chair. Regan, takes her hand. She snatches it back.

Gigi breaks the stillness in the room and rises slowly from her seat. "Remington, you know where he is? Right now?"

I nod.

"Oh my God," she cries and starts toward the door. Hayes is out of his seat and after her in a flash.

"Gigi, if you just—"

"Where is he?" Her voice is thin and ragged, her eyes move in wild swings around the room and she turns in an almost full circle.

Hayes wraps an arm around her shoulders and leads her back to her chair. "G, let's go sit down. I know you want to see him, but we have to talk first. And then, I promise I will take you to see him myself."

She looks up at Hayes, her expression dazed as she searches his face.

"Come on, darlin'. Come sit down."

"Sit down?" She pushes out of his arms and looks at him like he's got three heads. "I'm not going to sit down. Are you insane?" She spins to face me. "Where is he? I want to see him right now." She doesn't raise her voice, but I know it's time.

I nod in acquiescence and pull out my phone.

"Who are you calling?" my mother asks as my fingers start to fly across the screen. Her voice is anxious and sharp.

I glance at her. "Kal. He's with her."

"Kalilah? She's here? Where?"

"Upstairs. With Lucas. I just texted her to bring him down."

"I'm not sitting here for this." She stands and starts to stride from the room.

"You're not going anywhere." I stand in her way. She looks up at me and for the first time in my entire life I see the heartbreak, free of anger and resentment, in her eyes.

"I am not going to sit here and watch their reunion, Remington." She's speaking in a whisper, but her eyes are yelling at me.

"He doesn't remember her," I tell her.

"He will," she says quietly, assuredly, brokenly.

"He won't." I insist.

"Please. I know I don't deserve any kindness or any care. But *please* do not make me watch this. It's more than I think I can bear." She's naked, but for her pain, right now.

And I hate it.

All of it.

She didn't choose this. She married the love her life only to discover she would never be his.

I swallow down a lump in my throat as I remember how I felt when Kal told me she was getting married. It had been a knife to my gut. I can't imagine if she had been my *wife* first. I step out of her way.

"I'm going to call you when we're done and we're going to talk."

She nods and starts out of the room.

"I'll take you home, Mama." Regan, who hasn't looked up from her hands since Tyson left, stands up.

"You will?" My mother pauses and looks doubtfully at her daughter.

"Of course." Regan links an arm through hers. She gives me a wan smile, and they walk out together.

I walk over to where Gigi is sitting, clutching Hayes' hand and staring tearfully at the door. "You okay?"

She doesn't say anything. She watches the door until, nearly ten minutes later, it opens and my father walks in.

38

CERTAIN

KAL

My eyes open when the sheets of the bed are pulled back and Remi slips into bed beside me. I roll over and sit up.

"Wait, I want to see your face." I reach over him to turn on the bedside lamp and he presses a kiss to my shoulder and then wraps an arm around my waist and pulls me over until I'm straddling him. He presses his cheek to my chest and hugs me to him.

My heart aches for him. It's been a hellish twenty-four hours. After everyone left, Gigi and Lucas were left in the library talking.

Seeing her didn't bring back his memories.

Well, except for one.

When he saw Gigi, his eyes filled with tears. He stared at her and said, "I know you."

She nodded, tears running down her cheeks.

He said, "Can you tell me how? I'd really like to know."

She'd looked at Hayes and then at Remi who nodded at her before she said, "I'd really like to tell you."

We left them alone when it became clear, that for them, there was no one else in the room anyway.

Remi went back to his office with Hayes. I hadn't heard from him since. I finally decided to go to bed at midnight. I didn't expect that sunrise would bring an easier day with it, so I wanted to try and get some rest because I knew that there were still a lot of questions to be answered and I needed to tell him about the article.

"I'm so fucking glad I have you to come to home to tonight, Kal," he whispers against my breast.

"I'm glad, too. Are you okay?" I hug him and stroke his head trying to soothe him. He's radiating with energy, his skin on the edge of being hot and he's tense.

"I don't know. Everything that was certain is gone. Everything I thought I'd lost has found its way back to me. I'm so relieved, and so fucking drained." And then as if to make his point, he sways a bit, and lets some of his weight rest on me.

"Oh, baby. I know. You should get some sleep." I hold him and rock him.

"I love you, Kal. I'm scared to even imagine what you must think of me. I mean, my mother was so awful to you when we were kids. If I had a kid and someone treated her the way my mother treated you, I'd probably want to kill her."

I can't help but stiffen with surprise. I thought for sure he was going to talk about his parents. "Oh, yeah... your mother and I, we have a long way to go, I think. But, I've always been willing to try. Now that she might be, too, maybe it will be okay?" I actually want to cunt punch his mom, but I keep that to myself. Right now, I feel like I just need to make sure Remi knows that everything's going to be okay.

"How are you feeling about your parents? Are you okay? I've been so worried about you."

"I mean, honestly, I've been more worried about you," he says surprising me again.

"Really? I'm not the one who had a bomb dropped on her life in the last two days." That's not exactly true, but this doesn't seem like the time to bring up my custody woes.

"But..." He pulls back and looks at me. "I mean, he's not your father. But he is mine. And we're… us. So… it happened to you, too. I want to be here for you. You must have feelings about it too, right?"

"Right," I say and my heart softens. Remi always finds a way to take something terrible and reshape it into something beautiful.

Like he did the night I met him.

And the summer I fell in love with him.

And over the lifetime I spent away from him.

"I'm okay. If you are. I just—love you so much. I always have. It was this dizzy love that made me want to change my entire life for you."

His rumbling laugh is full of nostalgia. "But even a love like that has limits, right?"

I nod, sadly. I'm anxious about the conversation I know we're going to have soon. But right now, I just want him to get a good night's sleep.

"I just want to hold on to you. Unless you want to talk?"

He rubs his big hands in circles on my back. "I don't want to talk. I want to make love to my woman and then fall asleep with her in my arms and be certain of one fucking thing," he says and then pulls me down deeper into his lap and presses me against his rock-hard erection.

"Yeah, baby, we can do that," I whisper and press a kiss to his neck and then another. His hands grab a hold of the huge T-shirt I'm wearing and pull it up and over my head. I'm completely naked and when he pulls the sheet off him, I find that he is, too.

His cock slides between the swollen lips of my pussy right away and he cups my neck and takes my lips in a kiss. His tongue teases my lips before it slips inside my mouth and kisses me deep and slow.

I rock back and forth on his cock, each time getting closer to my opening until I finally lower myself onto him.

This, the first breach, is always such an experience. A masterclass in the worthiness of a little pain. The pleasure I know is coming is like nothing I've ever known. He grabs my hip and pulls me down all the way and pulls us chest to chest.

I roll my hips, seat myself at just the right angle and then burrow into him. He cups my head and brings his lips to my ear. The soft hair on his chest rubs my nipples, his cock feels like it's swelling inside of me and his tongue traces the shell of my ear in a slow back-and-forth sweep.

A rash of gooseflesh breaks out over my skin and I shiver.

"I love you," I tell him in a husky voice and roll my hips again.

"Fuck, I needed to hear that. I love you so fucking much," he says and thrusts up deep, but gentle.

Our love is expanding, gaining dimension, changing color. Becoming clearer every day.

"Your happy ending is with me." I lift myself up and fall back down.

"Of course it is. Tell me who you are," he asks.

So I tell him with each up and down of my hips that I hated my life without him in it.

I fuck him and tell him that I love him without limit.

When I come on his cock and with his name pouring from my throat, I tell him that I love him because he never stopped loving me.

When he comes inside of me, with his eyes holding mine, I know he never will.

39

ALL LEGENDS ARE LIES

REMI

WE'VE BEEN CURLED UP IN BED BINGE WATCHING *GAME OF Thrones* on her laptop all day. I've dozed off a dozen times and wake up when Kal shakes me awake. She's lying on her side, cradling her head in her hand, her small naked body stretched out like a meal next to mine.

"Are you okay?" She stretches, the tips of her breasts get caught in the beam of sunlight that's cutting through the window and my mouth waters.

"I'm okay," I say and reach down and take her nipple in between my fingers. She winces and I let go. She grasps my retreating fingers.

"You sucked them raw last night." She puts my open palm over her breast and I see the bruises my finger left last night.

"Shit, I'm sorry. I was too rough—" She presses a finger to my lips and shakes her head at me.

"Shhh. My body is yours. However you need it. But, I want to take a shower and eat. I'm starving."

"Yeah, and we should probably go to the grocery store. I want you and Bianca to stay here at my house when she comes, but I have no food."

Her smile falters. "Let's talk about it, later. Okay?" She swings her legs over the side of the bed and is closing the bathroom door before I can respond.

"Okay," I say to the back of the door as it closes. The water starts running and I sit back against the headboard. That was strange.

I minimize the screen on her computer and open her browser to check my email. Just as the browser opens, a document titled *RWilde* on her desktop catches my eye.

I close the browser and only hesitate for a second before I open the document.

It's an essay of some sort, the bold title is underlined, The Legend and The Lie. By Kalilah Greer.

Remington Wilde is an enigma.

He's made an art of being elusive. Who is the man behind The Legend? To know that, we must know the truth.

This is a journey into the amazing life story that's bigger than one man... and that proves that all Legends are really just built on lies...

What follows is my life story, laid out in some sort of chronological outline. Written by Kal.

At first I'm confused. And then I replay the last ten days and it call comes clear.

She's been skittish and anxious. I thought it had to do with her daughter's upcoming visit. I haven't had a minute to talk to her because I was dealing with work and my dad. We had only come together when I would collapse in bed with her every night. I assumed she'd been working during the day like me. I hadn't asked her a single question that wasn't related to my dad.

The shower stops and I close the document and open the browser. Maybe I'm wrong. She wouldn't do this without telling me.

My pulse thuds in my ears, and cold dread settles in my gut. I drop my head into my hands. I get dressed, and then sit and wait for the woman who has stolen my heart, who owns its every beat, who my soul has fallen in love with, to come out of the bathroom and tell me that she's been lying to me the entire time.

The bathroom door opens, floral scented steams filters out and she steps through it like the siren she is. "Hey, baby, I was thinking we could just order something in, I need to talk—"

She stops talking when she sees my expression. Her eyes widen with alarm and she rushes toward me.

"Remi, what's wrong?" She bends over and cups my face; her worried eyes search mine.

"Are you writing an article about me?" I ask and she recoils, agony rushes into her eyes and a groan escapes her lips.

She drops her hands from my face like it's a red hot piece of coal. She kneels in front of me and looks up at me.

Her eyes fill with tears. "I was going to tell you, Remi. I swear."

My stomach drops to my toes.

Shit.

It's true.

Fuck.

Fuck.

Damn every fucking thing to hell.

This is the woman my heart was made to worship. I love her so damn much.

Somehow though, we keep fucking it up.

I am sick to death of lies. I would rather die than to listen to another single one.

And I think one more lie from her lips might actually kill me. After yesterday, I feel as raw as I've ever felt. The one thing I thought was real has just proven to be more myth than fact.

I place a hand on her head, run it around the delicate curve of her skull, sift my fingers through her thick, damp hair. I drag them across her chest skimming the edge of the towel she's wrapped herself in and stop when I get to her heart.

"Do you know how much I love you?"

She looks up at me and nods, her lips are trembling, her eyes leaking the evidence of her distress.

"I was going to tell you." Those words, the admission of her deceit, the sorrow in her eyes, the damage she's done, what it means for us all come rushing at me and I know I need to get away from her before I say something I don't mean. Something I can't take back.

I stand up and step around her. She scrambles to her feet and grabs my arm.

"Please don't go. Please let me explain."

I turn to face her and avert my gaze, because I'm not sure I can take that look in her eyes right now.

"Are you going to tell me that you're not here to write a story about me and my family?"

"No, but—"

"I would like you to go."

Her face crumbles. "Remi, you don't mean that. I know this sounds bad, but—"

"Yeah, Kal, it sounds bad," I say and I walk over to the door and open it.

"Leave, please." I am struggling to keep my temper in check.

"If you want me to leave this bedroom, you will have to carry me out of here." She tilts her chin at me, daring me to do it. Oh.

"I've treated you with the gentlest of kid gloves. But don't forget who I am." In the storm of my hurt and anger, I do the stupidest things I've ever done in my entire life.

I throw her over my shoulder and start toward the door.

"Remi, what are you doing?" she shrieks as I throw her over my shoulder. "You cannot put me out. Not without hearing me out."

"I can. And I fucking will," I grate out and open the door and set her on her feet in the hallway. And then, I see that she's wet, barefoot, and in her towel. Her eyes are wide with terror. Her lips are trembling.

And I'm slammed backward in time to the night of the Annual Gala.

She had that same look on her face. I remember her dignity, and things that once said and done, can never be taken back.

Oh my God. My anger comes crashing down.

I made her look like that. Again. God, this is a nightmare.

40

NOT ENOUGH

KAL

I watch as Remi comes to his senses. He steps aside and I walk past him stonily. I throw my towel on the bed and rush around the room throwing things haphazardly into my suitcase.

I tense, pause for a minute, but don't look up when he comes to stand next to me. My heart is racing, my pulse beating at a million miles an hour. I'm so angry I can't speak. I can't believe what he just did.

"Will... shit. What are you doing?" His voice is a low groan. I can feel his eyes on my body, and I'm glad I didn't cover myself. Let him look.

"I'm leaving. Like you asked," I say through gritted teeth. I walk back to the small dresser where I'd put my underwear and pull things out.

He's watching me silently. "I was angry. Hurt. I'm sorry." His voice is gruff, but I can hear the contrition in it. I toss my underwear into my bag and turn to face him. And when I see his face, the completely exhausted eyes, the brackets of worry around his mouth and the way his shoulders are drooped in defeat, I sigh.

My anger loses its fervor. Right now, he's the boy I met in the library and just like then, he's in desperate need of a hug. I can't imagine how much turmoil he's in. My heart breaks watching him standing alone.

I put my feelings aside and put my arms around him.

His wrap around me immediately. He lifts me off my feet and squeezes me so tight that I wince. But I don't let go. We stand there, and in each other's arms, everything is suspended. I let him take some of my strength for himself. I know he needs it. I can show him the grace he denied me because I know he's in pain.

"I love you, Kal."

"Show me," I whisper into this neck and he shudders. He lifts my thigh up to his waist and he presses against me.

"I don't fucking deserve you," he whispers into my neck before he takes my mouth in a kiss. It's not a tender kiss, it's hard, demanding, his tongue doesn't dance with mine. He plunders my mouth, searching, and I let him get lost at the same time that I lose myself.

I'm not aware of us moving until he breaks our kiss and throws me onto the bed and crawls between my thighs.

"I want to eat this pussy so bad." He plants his big hands on my inner thighs and spreads me open.

"Stay like that." He lets go, slides one hand under my ass and parts the lips of my pussy with the other.

Then he lowers his head and licks me from my clit to my asshole. He dips his tongue inside and I gasp and tense.

"Shhh." His lips brush my taint and his breath tickles me, but I relax. His mouth moves up and I grab his head and wind my hips, pressing myself into his mouth.

His thumb presses against my tight pucker and I bear down. He slips it inside of me just as he starts to suck my clit, hard. I scream and in what feels like seconds, I'm coming.

He slides up my body. "I fucking love your sweet little nipples, Kal," he breathes before he licks one and then the next. I wrap my legs around him and reach between us.

We don't speak. He's silent when he thrusts into me. The only sound he makes is a loud hissing exhale before he starts to fuck me.

It's fast, it's hard, and I savor every single pulse, tremor, and moan he coaxes out of me. As good as it feels, I don't come again. I'm just lost in watching him. He's drenched in sweat, his expression is the picture of the kind of bliss that you can only find in really fucking amazing sex.

When he finishes and catches his breath, he takes me to the bathroom, kneels between my thighs and wipes away the smear of his cum from them.

Then, he stands up, places a hand on either side of me and pins me in place with his penetrating gaze.

"That article is not your story to tell, I won't let you publish it."

DECIDE

DECIDE

REMI

KAL'S BACK STRAIGHTENS. HER EYES REGISTER SURPRISE, disappointment and then nothing before she drops them from mine.

"Please move your arms." She looks down at the hands I've cupped on the swirling marble counter.

"Not until you promise me that you won't," I say. I know I'm pressing my luck and being heavy-handed. But there's no way in hell she can do it.

Her eyes fly to mine, the brown is flecked with gold and she's furious. If looks could strike a man down, I'd be flat on my back.

"I've already promised you everything I owe you, Remi." She delivers these words as a cryptic warning.

"What the fuck does that mean?" I step away from the sink and she hops down.

"You don't get to forbid me from doing anything. Loving me, being my man, doesn't mean you own me."

Her voice is matter of fact. She grabs a towel from the warming rack on the wall and wraps it around her naked body.

"I know I don't own you. But I own that story." I follow her out of the bathroom and lean back on the dresser as she starts to get dressed.

"You don't own that either, Remi," she says, her raised voice ratchets up the challenge in her words.

"The hell I don't. I told you half of that in confidence," I push back.

She sighs deeply, and I can see how exhausted she is. "I would never have published it without your permission. But you have to understand that you don't own it. None of us do. And even if I don't, *someone* is going to tell it."

"Why didn't you tell me about it before?"

"When did I have time? When we were falling back in love and I didn't even remember my own name? Or when your dad showed up? Or when we came back to Houston and you were busy trying to decode your family's rendition of *Hamlet*? Or when you found out before I could tell you and wouldn't let me explain?" she says in a furious whisper.

"Yes, Kal. *Any* of those times."

"That's easy for you to say now. I *was* going to tell you. You weren't exactly in a great state of mind when I got to your cottage and honestly, neither was I. And I was trying to kill it." She snaps the front closure of her bra and then pulls a long-sleeved white T-shirt out of her bag and slips it on.

"You were going to kill it? You fucking wrote it," I bite back.

"To *show* you. To maybe convince you that I should tell it. That maybe it would be good for you." She shakes her head in exasperation and digs around in her bag.

"The way you found it, I understand how angry you are. But you can't not let me explain, Remi. And you can't ever handle me like that again. Ever." She points a finger back at me and then sits down to slip her jeans on.

"Where are you going?"

"The last ten days have been intense. I don't think we should be making decisions when we're both so emotional."

Alarm pings from my head to my chest and back again. I drop down on my haunches so that our eyes are level. Hers are shuttered, and even though she's sitting right in front of me, she's never felt farther away.

"What decisions?"

"Any decisions, Remi. Except for the ones that have been made for us, I mean." She looks so tired. Her eyes are distant and I can feel her slipping away.

"Fine, maybe get some rest and we'll talk later," I say cautiously, not sure I want to know where her train of thought is headed.

"I can't focus on us right now. My daughter is coming and I don't want any drama around her. She's had enough of it and I want her to like it here. And I've got to figure things out with work. I've just got stuff to do. I'm going back to the hotel." She says stiffly.

Disappointment is a cold knife to my heart. "So... you don't want me to meet Bianca?" I ask even though I know the answer.

"I don't know if it's a good idea. I just need to think." She avoids my eyes and let her because the distance in them is almost more than I can fucking stand.

The tangle of emotions that are running riot through her have tentacles and they reach out and wrap themselves around me. I feel her regret most keenly, but I also feel her anger.

She's seething. I glance at her. She's wrapped her arms around herself and she's staring straight ahead.

"What can I do?" I ask, and hear the desperation in my voice.

She shakes her head slowly, her shoulder slump.

"Remi. You don't trust me. There's a part of me that understands. But, we have to work on that and I think maybe some space will be good for both of us. We've been in this pressure cooker for the last two weeks, and I'm fried. Maybe we'll be fine. Or maybe we'll realize that this was all too much, too soon. Either way, I think we should take a break."

42

WHITE KNIGHT

REMI

"I don't understand how a man like you can be so totally clueless when it comes to women." Regan shakes her head at me in disgust. We're lying in a double float in her pool. It's a warm night and the cicadas are singing for us.

Her huge magnolia trees dangle over the pool and the lights at the bottom of it make me feel like I'm somewhere far away.

I wish I could get far away from how shitty I feel. I don't know what to do about Kal. She asked for her break, and I'm giving it to her. But, it feels wrong. We've spent enough time apart.

I came to stay with Regan for the weekend so I could avoid being out and about in Rivers Wilde. I don't want to risk running into her.

She left my house and hasn't been in touch since. I spent all day moping around, and after Regan put her kids to bed at their ridiculously early bedtime, she dragged me outside and into the pool and coaxed the story out of me. I told her everything.

"How is this me being clueless? We were at an impasse. She wanted to write a story about me. I couldn't let her do that."

"Why the fuck not? You think you're The Prince of Persia?" she laughs derisively.

"No, Reg, I don't want the whole world to know how fucked-up our family is." I shoot back, annoyed at her nonchalance.

"Remi, there's nothing to be ashamed of. People are going to figure out that Dad is back. He and Gigi will come up for air and someone will see him. And there's going to be reporters flocking. Someone will write that story. Why not let someone you trust, someone who loves you, write it?"

"Why didn't she tell me? I hate that she kept something from me."

"Oh, for God's sake. Grow up." She scoops a handful of water and splashes me with it.

"Fuck you, Reg."

"People lie. *You* lie. That woman loves you, dummy. She wouldn't have hurt you or done anything to betray you. I know Mom fucked us up, but you're lucky. If a woman is brave enough to love you again after you broke her heart, I promise she's the one. Give her the benefit of the doubt."

I groan, my stomach feels like someone dropped a ten-pound weight in it. "Oh, shit. I fucked-up, didn't I, Reggie?"

"Big time. But now you have a chance to make it up to her."

"How?"

She kisses her teeth. "You're lucky you're pretty, 'cause you've got like zero game."

"Shut up and tell me."

She flips a lock of hair off her shoulder and turns on her side to face me. "The way I see it, that girl has saved you more than once. You told me you wanted to make her believe in happy endings? Then take a page out of a fairy tale and be the white knight she needs right now. Go give her that story. Tell her you want her to write it. Save her job, make her career. Be her hero."

When she says it, it all sounds so obvious.

Her phone rings. She looks at it and curls her lip.

"Work?" I ask.

"No, Marcel. It's about time for his usual check in," she says irritably.

"Trouble in paradise?"

"I have never lived in paradise, so I wouldn't know. But trouble, in general, yes." She flips onto her back and pulls her hat over her face.

I wish I'd been around more in the last year. She's been lurching from one mini crisis to the next. Work, her husband, her kids, everything is sort of haywire in her life at the moment.

"You want to talk?" I ask after a few moments of silence.

She pulls her hat off her head and looks at me askance. "I can't believe you're still here. You should be running over to Kal's place and practicing your grovel." She shoos me away with her fingers and covers her face again.

"Are you sure?"

"Remi, I'm floating in a pool on Friday night with my three beautiful children sleeping inside. I'm grand. You go."

"When I get back, we're going to spend some time together, sis. We need to talk." I slip off the raft and wade toward the stairs.

"It's about time you remembered you have a little sister, Remi." Her tone is light, but I know I've neglected her. Everyone, in the last few months.

"I'm sorry. I know. I love you." I squeeze her hand.

"I love you, too. Don't come home until she says yes. I'm ready to see you happy again."

43

CHARMED

KAL

"Bianca, don't answer that. I'll be right there," I call from the storeroom. First thing I did was to install a doorbell so that we could keep the door locked without missing deliveries.

But Bianca's opened the door twice when she wasn't supposed to and even though I scolded her firmly the last time, I know she'll do it again.

I wipe my hands clean of the dust that settled on them like thin white gloves and rush out. I can't help but close my eyes and smile as I step into the store. The smell of citrus wood cleaner assails me and I'm more sure than I've ever been about anything in my life that I'm exactly where I'm supposed to be.

"Mommy's in the back," Bianca says just as the small bell over the door jingles.

"Bian—" I stop dead in my tracks when I see Remi stepping through the doors, dressed in a white T-shirt and swim trunks that look like they're actually wet. He's wearing running shoes and sweating. In his hand is a wilted bouquet of bluebonnet flowers with clumps of dirt hanging from their still attached roots.

"Hey, Will."

"Uh, hi." I untie my apron and run a self-conscious hand over my disheveled hair. "I wasn't expecting you. How did you know we were here?"

"Henny told me. I was headed to the hotel and I ran into her. So, you're buying the bookstore?" He rocks back on his heels and looks around.

"Yeah, I went to see Lister." I say vaguely and hope he gets the hint. I'm not keen on having this conversation in front of Bianca.

"I hope you don't mind me stopping by," he says smiling down at Bianca, too.

"Nope, we don't mind. We're just cleaning up." She smiles up at him.

A clump of earth falls from the flowers and lands on my newly polished wood floors.

"Oh, these are for you." Remi walks over to me, arm extended.

"Thank you." I take them gingerly inspect the dangling root. "But, I'm not sure the Rivers Wilde landscapers will happy to see you went shopping in their flowerbeds." I smile grimly at the slightly pathetic, but very pretty bouquet of bluebonnets.

"It was for a good cause." He sounds nervous and I almost do a double take. I've never seen him anything less than very sure.

I'm glad to see him. I was so angry with him just a day ago, but this morning I woke up wishing I hadn't asked for space. I'm glad one of us has some sense.

I lean forward, my eyebrows raised in mock surprise and whisper so that Bianca can't hear. "Why, Remi. Have you come to grovel?"

"Absolutely," he says, his expression completely serious.

I bite my lip to stop my grin and keep my eyes serious. "Stolen weeds are a dubious start..."

"I know. I just wanted to get over here... Will, I'm sorry." He steps forward and puts a hand to my waist.

I shake my head quickly and step back. "Let me introduce you to my daughter, Bianca." I nod over his shoulder at her.

He mouths, "Sorry" before he turns around.

Bianca stands all shy with her head of dark brown curls and the glasses she started wearing this year. She looks just like I did at her age. And she's just as skeptical. She sticks her hand out for Remi.

"Nice to meet you, Mommy's friend."

"Bianca, it's a pleasure to make your acquaintance, finally." Remi takes her hand and bows over it like he's meeting the queen.

She giggles.

My little girl is so like me at that age and never, ever giggles.

But then, she's never met Remi and *he* could charm a giggle out of Medusa.

"Nice to meet you, too. Mommy showed me your picture. Said you're her best friend."

"Bianca, it's not nice to repeat private conversations," I reprimand her.

"I already knew that. And she's mine." Remi runs a hand over my daughter's head and my heart quickens.

"We just had dinner, but there's some leftover, if you're hungry," she says, batting her lashes at him. *Oh boy.*

My daughter is a firm believer that the path to everyone's heart is through their stomach.

"I ate already, but maybe we can have breakfast tomorrow? Sweet & Lo's makes a mean omelet."

"Can we, Mommy, please?" she asks and I smile stiffly at Remi.

"Of course we can. Now, run upstairs and get me a vase for these flowers."

She grins at both of us and then darts through to the back. As soon as I hear her feet thundering up the stairs that lead to our living quarters, I speak.

"Way to put me on the spot." I cross my arms over my chest in disapproval.

"I wasn't. She invited me to dinner and I didn't want to completely disappoint her. But, I do want to talk to you."

He steps toward me and I take a step back and glance over my shoulder to make sure Bianca's gone.

"Come back later. After she's asleep, we can talk then."

"Okay. What's her bedtime? Ten?" he asks.

"Eight thirty. She's only nine." I remind him teasingly.

"Oh, yeah. Of course." He *is* nervous and it's cute.

"Okay. I'll see you later." I say when he just stands there.

"Okay." He nods tersely.

"And, uh…I put the trellis back up. Step up your groveling game. Right now, it's a little lame," I joke.

Then reach up on my toes to press a kiss to his lips.

"I love you."

"I love you, too. I'll see you tonight."

44
_____

LOVE ME LIKE THAT

REMI

"THE THINGS WE DO FOR LOVE," I MUTTER TO MYSELF BEFORE I stick the stem of the rose I bought between my teeth and start to climb the trellis. I'm sure this window was lower to the ground all of those years ago. Thank fuck I work out.

I rap on the window twice before her light comes on and the curtains rustle.

She pulls them back and opens the window. Her smile is wide. And on the other side of that fucking screen.

"Oh, God, Remi. I was just kidding. Why did you climb up here? I can't open the screen, remember?"

A deafening rumble of thunder is followed by a clap of lightning that illuminates the sky and nearly gives me a stroke. I can't speak around the rose I have gripped between my teeth.

Regan's right. My game is *so* weak.

"I'll meet you downstairs," she says loudly, enunciating her words so her lips move in a comically exaggerated way. I laugh and the rose falls from my mouth.

I let go of the trellis with one hand to try to catch it and lose my footing. The last thing I see are her wide, horrified eyes before I go tumbling to the ground.

I land flat on my back; the wind knocked out of me and I feel a fat drop of rain fall right in the corner of my eye. In what feels like a split second that one raindrop multiplies and with another crack of thunder, turns into a deluge.

The lights come on in the back windows of the bookstore and I plant my hands on the ground to find that it's already muddy. It's raining so hard that I don't see Kal until she's ten feet in front of me. She's in tiny boy shorts and a tank top, and she's not wearing any shoes.

Her mouth is moving as she runs frantically toward me. But, the rain muffles her voice and I yell for her to stop.

"Kal, slow down, it's muddy." She keeps running and promptly slips and slides into me with enough force to push me backward into the soggy pit of dirt.

"Remi, oh my God, are you okay?" She straddles me, rain pouring down her face, mud is smeared on her shirt which is plastered to her body.

The peaks of her breasts are hard under her tank top, her boy shorts are thin and I can feel the heat of her cunt on my stomach. She run her hands all over my body, like she's checking for broken bones and my dick starts getting hard.

I wrap an arm around her and pull her close. "Will, I'm fine. But you're making my dick hard being out here half-naked."

She throws her arms around my neck and hugs me.

"You nearly gave me a fucking heart attack, you crazy man." She peppers kisses all over my face.

"I'm the fucking Legend, you think a twenty-foot drop could take me out?"

"Yes, I do. I know you forget this sometimes, but you're actually made of flesh and bones."

"Speaking of bones." I push up into her and she grinds down onto me and presses a kiss to my mouth.

Well, all right now.

"Come on. Let's get clean."

"How about we finish being dirty, first?" I nudge against the opening of her pussy and even through my jeans and her shorts, I can feel how hot she is.

She rolls her hips one more time before she jumps off me, extends a hand out to help me up and leads me back inside.

KAL

Remi walks around my room, drying his hair, a towel tied around his waist. His ridiculously sexy body, so powerful and muscular, still damp from his shower, immediately distracts me from everything I planned to say while I waited for him to finish.

"Here we are... back where we started," he says, peering at the pictures I stuck on the corkboard last night.

They're all of me and Bianca.

All but one. It's a selfie he took while we were at Gigi's house. I'm laughing, but Remi's looking at me with an awed expression that stole my breath the first time I saw it.

It's my favorite picture of us. It's everything we are.

Or could be.

If we take the time to do it right, this time.

"You want to get dressed?"

"No. Do I need to?"

"Yeah. You do. We need to talk and if you're naked, I'll want to be naked too and then we won't talk at all."

He drops his towel, and my mouth waters at the sight of his magnificent body and the glorious cock hanging between his legs.

"Get naked," he growls and palms himself.

"I mean it. Get dressed." I pick up his T-shirt, it's still warm from my dryer and hand it to him with a stern shake.

He curls his lip and takes the shirt from me, slips it and the briefs I also dried on, while I sit on the bed and wait.

"You're killing my buzz," he grumbles as he slips on his jeans.

"Mine died when I thought you plunged to your death thirty minutes ago, so at least now we're on the same page."

"We were on the same page when we were outside and you were straddling me."

He flops on the bed next to me and turns on his side.

I mimic his position so we're lying to face-to-face.

I drink him in. There's still so much of the boy I met in the library there. The kind, sure, funny boy who made me reach for more.

He runs a finger down the slope of my nose and over my lips, his eyes following the path and landing on my lips.

"Bianca has that freckle, too," he observes.

"Yeah. She does. I joke that it's the only thing she got from me." I start to laugh but it dies when I see how serious his expression is.

"What?"

"I want you to write the article." His declaration catches me completely off guard.

"Really?" I lean away from him in surprise.

"Yeah." He nods.

"That's not what you said two days ago."

"Two days ago, I was raw and angry, Kal. The timing of all of that wasn't ideal. And you didn't exactly give me a heads-up." His tone isn't reproachful, but I still hate that he found out before I could tell him myself.

"I'm sorry about that."

He takes my hands in his, strokes my palms with his thumbs and looks deeply into my eyes.

"I know I am the last person on earth who should be allowed to say this to you. But I'm going to say it anyway." His expression is so grave, that in the space between his words, my imagination goes wild with worry.

"Just say it."

"It's just that… we can't keep things from each other, Kal. Not anymore. If this is going to work, then we've got to be able to talk to each other. Because when we don't, we fall apart. The truth, no matter how scary, is always much easier to handle than the fallout of a lie."

"I know."

"And I want to stop the lies we've been telling about my family. I can't tell Gigi and Lucas' story. But I want to tell my own. I want you to write it. I'll even sit and let you interview me if that would be better."

I eye him skeptically. "Are you sure, Remi?"

"Yes. Very. I know there's intense interest about my family, and the Riverses right now. It's time to pull back the curtain. My dad's reappearance won't stay a secret. He and Gigi have already established a connection. The truth is going to come out, and I'd like it to come from me. Whoever gets the story, gets an exclusive and will make a name for themselves, right?"

"Yeah. It was certainly enough that it would have gotten me that job."

"Well, then I want you to write it. If I'm going to make someone's career, I want it to be yours."

I sit up and contemplate what he's saying and what it will mean.

"Remi… Lister gave me the bookstore. I want to move back here with Bianca and run it. If I write this story, there won't be any turning back. I'll get job offers. Dream ones. That will require me to travel and I'll have to work a lot."

"Will you be happy? Isn't that what you want? That career?" His voice is so calm compared to mine.

"Yes…"

His eyes narrow, focusing like he's just seen something he missed.

"What's the but, Kal?"

"But, I don't want you to have to let me write that story to make my career. I can figure things out. I don't want to be the damsel in distress anymore. I feel like I've been one my whole life."

He cups my chin and turns my face toward him.

"A damsel in distress is the last thing you've ever been. You've come to my rescue more times than I deserve."

"I have not." I dismiss his statement.

"When I was fourteen, you helped me find the courage to demand more from myself. When I was eighteen, you helped me find my purpose. Two weeks ago, you found me when I was lost. That's what we do for people we love, Kal. We help them when they need it."

"I'm scared," I admit and his eyes soften.

"Of what? Surely, not of us?"

"A little… The first time, your mother got in our way. The second time, well, that was all timing. I'm afraid that the third time—"

"The third time will be a charm. And if it's not, we'll try again." He finishes for me.

My heart is racing, a tear splashes on my hand before I realize that I'm crying.

"You mean it, don't you? We're really doing this." I didn't realize until then that I'd been worried that we'd find a way to screw up this chance, too.

"I've *always* been doing this. I was just waiting for you to catch up." His smile is contagious, and my whole spirit responds.

"You're the love of my life," I tell him.

"You are the love of mine. That deserves at least a million chances, don't you think?"

I nod vigorously.

"I'm here. I'm ready. I'm yours."

A smile breaks on his face, broad and proud, like he just reached the summit of a mountain he's been scaling. I feel it all the way in the center of my heart.

"Then, let's start right now." He pulls me into his arms for a hug and I let myself lean on him. I nestle against the soft cotton of his shirt and just savor the feeling of being safe and loved.

"I have to go back to New York." I break the silence.

"I know you do."

"I have to sell my place. Bianca needs to finish out the school year…" I look up at his face to see if he looks as worried as I feel about a potentially prolonged separation.

His expression is completely relaxed. His eyes, with their thick fringe of lashes are smiling into mine. "Don't worry, Kal. We've got this."

"I know. I just don't know when I'll be able to get back to Houston."

He shakes his head. "I have some business to take care of here. I might need a week or so. But until you're able to move, I'll be wherever you are."

Surprise rises in happy effervescent bubbles in my chest. "Really?"

"Yes. I can work from anywhere. I don't have any court appearances on my schedule and if I do, I've got a plane that can take me to Houston and back in a day. I'm not prepared to spend that kind of time apart again."

"But... my place, it's so small and Bianca—" I stammer as I race through the logistics of his plans.

"I've got a suite at the Baccarat. It's going to be fine." He strokes my arms reassuringly.

"I'm so excited. Oh, Remi. Thank you." I reach up to stroke the strong, sharp line of his jaw. He drops his head and presses a kiss to my mouth.

It's amazing, that in the gamut of extreme emotions I've run the last two days, that in the sanctuary of his arms, all I feel is peace.

"It'll give us the chance to do what we've never really done before."

"What's that?"

"Date. I want to take you to dinner. Go see a show. Walk you home and kiss you good night on your doorstep. Send flowers to your office. All of the things I thought I'd spend my twenties doing."

I'm overcome with happiness, I cover my mouth and squeal behind it.

"I'll take that to mean you like the sound of that?"

I nod. "I *love* the sound of it."

The way my heart flutters in my chest almost tickles, and I laugh as happiness bubbles inside of me.

"Okay. I'm going home," he says abruptly

"Wait. What?" I rise up on my knees and grab his arm to stop him from putting on his socks.

"I want to do this right. Your daughter is here. I'd rather see her again for the first time when I'm coming to take her and her mother to breakfast. I want to win her over, too. Show her what it looks like when a man loves a woman. So, yeah. I'm going home."

He leans down to kiss me. I clutch his waist and say a silent prayer of thanks.

"So, we're good?" he asks when he breaks the kiss.

"Yes. I love you. Like my life depends on it. With no limits. But, you have to bear with me. I was married for all of those years, but I've never really had a partner. I've always been by myself."

"Not anymore. And as long as I'm alive, you won't be again."

Be still my beating heart. This magnificent man is *mine*.

He always has been.

I see us in his eyes, taking shape, growing, cracking, frayed around the edges even, but holding together because we're writing our own story now, and in both versions, it ends with us.

45

EPILOGUE

THE LEGEND OF REMINGTON WILDE

REMI

"Are you sure? Once I hit send, it's out of our hands," Kal asks me for the hundredth time and I finally take the mouse from her and hit send myself.

"It's done. Out of our hands. Let the chips fall where they may." I press a kiss to her lips and slam her laptop closed. I lean down, scoop her out of the chair and walk us back to our bedroom.

"You're awfully relaxed for a man who just sent his entire life story to a tv news magazine." She says skeptically.

I set her down on the edge of the bed and sit next to her.

"It was written by someone I trust completely. I'm not worried at all. Besides, you titled it *The Legend of Remington Wilde*. Soon, it won't just be a nickname, it'll be a motherfucking title."

"Oh, God, you're going to be impossible after this, aren't you?"

"If impossible and glorified are the same thing, then absofucking-lutely. Now, let's fuck." I waggle my eyebrows.

"It's about damn time," she grumbles, and starts unbuttoning my shirt while we walk. I'm just pulling her skirt up when she stops walking and steps away from me.

"Wait, our flight leaves in two hours, do we have that kind of time? We still need to get B—" She glances at her watch and I cover it with my hand.

"Bianca can have a few more minutes with her dad. The plane will wait. But I can't. Not another fucking minute." I lie back and hook an arm around her waist to take her with me.

She squeals in surprise but grabs my ass and pulls me into her.

"You feel that? That's six weeks' worth of hard fucking you've missed."

She grins like the little rogue she is. "*That* was all your bright idea. I've been ready—"

I cover her lips with mine and drink the rest of her words.

Her mouth opens beneath mine and her tongue slides home.

I planned on taking my time, feasting on her body and making up for everything I've missed for the last six weeks.

But the minute I taste her, that goes out of the window because there's no way I can take my time.

"I want to feel your skin." She pants against my mouth, writhing like she's as desperate as I am.

I push up and rest on my knees between her legs and pull the shirt over my head and her eyes light up.

"You're so fucking sexy, Remi." She shimmies out of her T-shirt and unfastens her bra.

My eyes nearly roll out of my head when I lay my eyes on perfect, plump and peaked nutmeg colored nipples. I lean down to take one in my mouth, and fuck if I don't nearly come from just that one taste.

Her hands are everywhere and while I'm feasting, she frees my dick and her warm, soft palm covers it and starts to stroke.

My back arches and I thrust up into her fist. Her thumb swipes my head and spreads the small bead of precum around and I groan.

"Fuck, you're killing me."

I pull away from her, tug her skirt down to find that she's completely bare underneath.

"You're not wearing any fucking panties?" I slide my fingers into the sweet slit between her thighs to see if she's ready and then nearly black out when I feel how soaking wet she is.

"I need to eat this pussy, Kal." I bring my fingers to my mouth and suck her sweetness off my fingers.

"After you fuck me. Please." Her eyes are squeezed shut and I gaze down at this goddess who rules my life.

The gold locket is around her neck where it belongs, and right underneath her left breast the word "Legendary" is scrawled in a tattoo that matches the one over my heart.

I push into her fucking magical cunt and fill her to the hilt with one stroke. The bed's headboard slams against the wall and our cries mingle as I start to fuck her.

It's hard, fast fucking. We're not making love, but there's love in every single thrust. She grips me, holds on to me and everything around us falls away.

All that's left is us, the love that's been shaped by the journey we've gone on and two bodies that have always been each other's homes.

Those legends about happy endings are full of lies. It's not a destination, it's our fucking every day.

This love of ours has been true since I was fourteen years old and it'll be true until I take my last breath.

WE'VE BEEN AT THE RANCH HOUSE ALL WEEK. I BOUGHT IT FROM Gigi and we come out here almost every weekend so my girl can see the stars. It's twilight. She's sitting by my side on our porch swing. Bianca's in the yard throwing a frisbee with the dog we got her as a housewarming gift when they moved in with me. Kal's reading and I'm just soaking it all in.

Life isn't perfect, but it's pretty damn close.

My phone rings and I pluck it from the table where it's resting.

It's Regan calling.

"Hey, 'sup?" I ask in a cheerful greeting.

Her sobs fill my ear. "Remi… oh my God, please don't read your email."

"Why? What happened? Hold on." My fingers are clumsy because I am fucking nervous. Regan's tears are not a common sight.

I switch her to speakerphone so I can open my email. Her sobs fill the air and Kal sits up and closes her book. Both she and Bianca are watching me through eyes wide with alarm.

"Don't look. Marcel sent it to everyone." She cries.

"Sent what?" And then I see it.

The email's subject line reads, "Now the whole world knows that my wife is a whore."

I take her off speakerphone and put the phone back to my ear.

"Regan, what's in that email." Her sobs just get louder.

"He threw me out. In front of the kids. Remi, where are you?" She cries.

"He did what? What did you say?" I demand loudly and glance at Kal. She's looking at her phone in horror.

I nudge her. She looks up and her eyes are full of tears. Oh shit.

"What?" I mouth to her.

She hands it to me, her eyes like a deer's in the headlights.

"He threw me *out,* Remi." Regan repeats.

But I don't respond. Because on my screen is a picture of Regan. Her back is to the camera, but no other human being on this planet has that hair *and* that tattoo that says "Jezebel" right in the center of her back. She's naked but for a scrap of fabric covering part of her ass.

The part of her ass not covered by the fabric is cupped by the very big hand of a man I'm pretty sure is *not* Marcel.

I can't see his face because his head is bent to kiss her. The picture is embedded in an article from a French magazine I've never heard of. The headline screams, "La femme de Landel montre au monde qui elle est: La Jézabel" *The wife of Landel shows the world who she is: Jezebel*

"Regan, what the fuck is this?"

"I fucked up, Remi. Really bad. Please come home. I need you."

Add The Jezebel to your TBR: Coming late 2019.

ACKNOWLEDGMENTS

ACKNOWLDGEMENTS

This small note cannot possibly convey the depth of my gratitude, it is fathomless.

To my betas readers, Chele Walker, Serena McDonald, Andrea LaBeau, Weronika Puchala (AKA Kal) and Leslie Taylor Middleton, thank you for making my words shine.

To Kennedy, we have so many hashtags, but the one that is most true for me is #MyFavor. Thank you for believing in me enough for both of us. Love you, Turkey Leg.

Chele Walker - where would I be without you? My day 1, my constant friend and the source of so many smiles....I love you!

To my author sisterhood - KK, Ilsa, Willow, Tia, Maria, Lucy, Autumn, RC, Claudia, AL, Rebecca, Jami, Sandy and Penny I love you guys, thank you for pushing, loving and never letting me quit.

To all of my colleagues who walk this very unique path along side me, I'm glad to have you in my life and am grateful for your constant support.

To Tracey Suppo you are the sister of my heart, I love you and am so grateful for every conversation we have. Thank you for being so real, honest and loving.

To Jenn Watson and Sarah Ferguson at Social Butterfly PR, you are magicians. Thank you for picking me up when I was at my lowest and deciding that I was worth saving. Your hard work and dedication to your clients is unparalleled and I am SO lucky that you're on my team. It's a pleasure to work with you both, thank you for everything.

To Serena McDonald…Thank you for everything, I'm so glad I have you!

To my Day Dreamers and my DREAM TEAM I LOVE you guys! You make my day, every single day! You inspire me to keep writing and I am so thankful for the parts of your day that you spend with me.

To all of the blogs who have tirelessly and graciously read and then promoted my work— you are my heroes. I couldn't do this without you.

To the readers who buy my books, who email, message and tweet me! Thank you SO much for everything. You're amazing and I write with your wind at my back every day!

To my family—my parents, my sisters, my brothers-in-law and my cousins—you are my TRIBE! Thank you for being wonderful and loving.

And to my husband and my children. You are the heartbeats of my life. Thank you for inspiring me, loving me and supporting me. I love you all more than anything else in the universe!

Love,
Me.

ABOUT THE AUTHOR

Dylan Allen is a Texas girl with a serious case of wanderlust.

A self-proclaimed happily ever junkie, she loves creating stories where her characters chase their own happy endings.

When she isn't writing or reading, eating or cooking, she and her family are planning their next adventure.

I love talking to you guys! Feel free to send me an email at dylanallenwrites@gmail.com.

Are you on Facebook? If you are, then PLEASE join my private reader group, Dylan's Day Dreamer. It's where I spends most of my time online. It's fantastic and I my favorite place on the internet. Click here to join and make sure you introduce yourself.

YOU CAN FIND ME ON ALL THE FOLLOWING SOCIAL AND BOOK RELATED PLATFORMS:

BOOK+MAIN BITES

ALSO BY DYLAN ALLEN

Did you enjoy that story?

Want to read more by me?

Rivers Wilde

The Legacy

Meet the daughters Mary Hassan talked to Confidence about:

Symbols of Love Series:

Rise

Remember

Release

Standalones:

Thicker Than Water

Envy

Made in the USA
Middletown, DE
13 May 2020